Fortune's Whelp

Fortune's Whelp

A Novel

by

Benerson Little

www.penmorepress.com

Fortune's Whelp by Benerson Little

Copyright © 2015 Benerson Little

ISBN-13: 978-1-942756-60-6(Paperback)
ISBN :978-1-942756-61-3 (e-book)

BISAC Subject Headings:
FIC014000FICTION / Historical
FIC002000FICTION /Action Adventure
FIC031020FICTION / Thrillers / Historical

Editing: Chris Wozney, Danielle Boschert
Cover Illustration by Christine Horner

Address all correspondence to:

Penmore Press LLC
920 N Javelina Pl
Tucson AZ 85748

Dedication

For Bree, Courtney, Margaret, and the Wee One;
And for Mary, my wife and co-adventurer.

Chapter 1

A Numerous Issue passes in the World for a Blessing;
this Consideration made a Fox cast it in the Teeth
of a Lyoness, that she brought forth but one Whelp at a time.
Very right, says the other, but then that one is a Lyon.
—The Fables of Aesop, 1724

The rencontre took place early in the evening under a storm-darkening sky, with just enough daylight remaining to preclude the accidents that plague swordplay at dusk and in darkness. The wind had risen, bringing with it the chill of river and sea; this, along with the approaching sunset, and the location on the outskirts of the city, kept witnesses where they belonged, that is to say, away.

What had come close to being a very public affray had become instead a quietly and hastily arranged duel, thanks entirely to those more mindful of the hangman than was the brandy-fired instigator.

The offense had been anything but subtle.

The bully-fool had sought to insert himself, drink in hand, at a table where two men were talking quietly. It was one of those small tables, suitable for backgammon, cards, or intimate discussions. The adventurer had remonstrated, saying that he would be happy to drink with the fool some other day, although he did not address the fool as such.

"Damn'd pirate!" the bully-fool shouted, for all in the room to hear.

Thus began what now would be settled with naked steel.

In fact, there was truth to what the fool had said, for not two years past the Scottish gentleman-adventurer had indeed been tried for piracy. He had not vehemently denied the accusation but had rationalized his plundering as justified under the circumstances, arguing that his actions were entirely within the spirit of the law, if not within its strict black letters. He had been acquitted by London jurors who would not convict a man merely for plundering a Spanish *guardacosta* with a valuable cargo in its hold. The fact that the *guardacosta*—nothing more than a Spanish pirate with a lawful commission—had fired first with the intention of plundering the gentleman-adventurer's own privateer and claiming its cargo as *frutas de las Indias*, only added to the jury's indignation at Spanish arrogance. Naturally, the jury conveniently forgot, or more likely forgave, previous English piracies that had instigated Spanish reprisals.

Even so, Edward MacNaughton had been placed under a travel embargo in order to balance accounts with the Spanish ambassador. England and Spain were not only at peace, they were allied against France, and this accused pirate had a history of depredations against Spain, some lawful, some perhaps not quite so. He must therefore wait a few more months before returning to America.

Put plainly, the gentleman-adventurer wished to avoid affairs and affrays that might get him in more trouble with the law and thereby upend his present plans, in particular his intention to sail for Ireland on the following day. All this the threatening, inebriated fool knew, and therefore he assumed he could insult Edward at will.

"Damn'd pirate!" roared the fool again after tossing back a dram of brandy. His was a physiognomy of portly muscularity, dramatic movement, and uncurbed tongue attached to a florid, sweaty visage, a combination that denotes blustering temper, loud intimidation, and occasional backstabbing.

"True enough," said Edward, first with a sigh, then a smile. "Or so some Spaniards believe. Even so, you must excuse me, for I've private matters to discuss with an old friend."

"So, you won't answer me!"

"I have answered you," Edward replied calmly. He took a sip from his bumper of sweet Malaga and turned his attention back to Jonathan Graham, his companion at the table.

The fool, John Lynch by name, screwed up his face. As many did, he found Edward MacNaughton annoyingly inscrutable. The self-sufficient manner bordering on arrogance, the commanding voice, the martial accents of his Spanish-French style of dress, and the sturdy, Spanish-hilted smallsword all served to warn off the intrusive.

But Lynch, arrogant and commanding in his own way, was hell-bent on a mission.

"You damn'd pushing master!" he shouted, trying a new tactic now that insults of piracy had not stuck. "Don't think you can ignore me because a fencing master can refuse challenges! Wearing a plastron and pushing your foil onto the breasts of spindly, cowardly scholars—and into whores, too—doesn't make you a sword-man."

Lynch's companion grasped him by the elbow and whispered in his ear, but the bully shoved him off.

"That's true enough, too," replied Edward calmly. "If you like, I'll teach you something of pushing when I return from Ireland, although not of pushing into whores. I hear you're already well-acquainted with Bristol bawds and the burnt buttered buns of their buttocks and don't need my instruction."

A nearby wit sniggered at the knowing alliteration. Bawds were madams, buttocks those they employed.

"Damn you, sir, do you mean to insult *me*?"

"No, sir, it is you who mean to insult me, yet you are too *mean* to do so, and anyway I'm too busy to mind your *meanness*."

The wit sniggered again, adding to Lynch's brandy-stoked fury. Edward was gambling that a public mocking might best settle the issue.

"By God, then, I'll call you this: whoremaster! You seduced then abandoned that long-shanked Lydia Upcott!"

Edward suppressed a laugh and shook his head.

"All becomes clear. She's put you up to this misadventure, perhaps to challenge me in revenge for some perceived slight. And you probably hope I won't fight, given my current circumstances, thus you can safely earn her favor. Take my advice, Don Borracho: she'll nae reward you for your pains, and certainly not in her bed. Neither of us are wealthy enough to keep her happy. Now begone, sir."

Lynch stood for a moment with an expression of vacuous perplexity as only the half-inebriated can wear. He took a deep breath; his face flushed red around an already ruddy nose.

"Then here's a word you can't ignore: Jacobite! You damned Jacobite, everyone knows you're a plotting traitor!"

The atmosphere in the tavern, already hushed as patrons strained to catch the exchange of words, became tense and silent.

Edward stood. Jonathan shook his head in warning and tugged gently at Edward's sleeve.

To be fair, there had always been more than a hint of suspicion that Edward MacNaughton was inclined toward the Jacobite cause. He had been charged with manslaughter for killing a man in a duel associated with the first accusation of piracy. By good fortune, James Stuart, more formally King James II, had pardoned him prior to conviction; but James was soon afterward deposed, and now reigned only as a prince plotting in exile on a pretended throne under the protection of Louis XIV of France, who presently waged war on nearly all of Europe.

Feeling obligated to King James, as well as to kith and kin, and notwithstanding his political agnosticism and bemused contempt of monarchy, Edward had joined the Highland clans at Killiecrankie soon after James lost his throne, proof to some that he must therefore be a Jacobite, a supporter of the Stuart king in exile. That he later served honorably in King William's cause had not quieted the rumors.

Yet even were the accusation true, Edward could not let it lie. He intended to serve England again as a privateer, impossible with a cloud of treason hanging over him.

With a smile, he gracefully flung his Malaga into Lynch's face.

"Damn you, bilbo's the word!" the fool shouted as he tried to draw his sword after a moment of shock at the liquid assault. "Have at thee, damn!" he continued in the same comically dramatic vein, using language he had doubtless heard in the theater.

Several patrons pinned Lynch's arms to his side so that he could not draw his sword and attempt murder.

"As I said, I'll give you a lesson when I return from Ireland," Edward replied phlegmatically.

"By God, I'll lesson *you* today!"

"I have affairs to attend, including travel tomorrow, wind and wave permitting. Were I unfortunate enough to find myself attacked by a Jacobite who falsely accuses me of the same, I'd have no choice but to grant him a lesson; however, I don't recommend one today, for you are too far into your cups and I'm soon in a hurry."

Edward picked up his sword and scabbard and slid them

into the carriage on his narrow sword belt, over which was tied a Highland plaid sash.

"I say it again! Jacobite! Jacobite and coward!"

"Ignore him, Ned," Jonathan said, pulling again at Edward's elbow. "He's drunk, and no one doubts your courage. No need to fight today when a month from now will do—if this loudmouth is even so foolish as to meet you sword-in-hand today or any day."

"I will have satisfaction!" Lynch shouted.

Damned drunk, Edward thought, *and worse, challenging me over a lie told by a woman.*

He was no misogynist, this adventurer: he had too much respect for the courage, cunning, and fortitude of women, in many ways a match for his own, and superior more often than he liked to admit. But too many times had women served as Fortune's minions bearing ill tidings, and so had he sworn to have no close association with them until he had made his own fortune. Best, therefore, as Jonathan advised, to ignore the challenge. His left hand strayed to his sword belt, beneath which a wallet containing two secret letters lay, reminding him that his missions in Ireland were far too important to jeopardize by engaging a jealous fool.

"Let it lie until I return, Lynch," Edward said coldly, then relaxed a bit. "Lydia Upcott will make fools of both of us if we let her. Come, let's drink and pretend we're friends. Your quarrel with me can wait."

"The hell it can!" Lynch sputtered loudly. "I know you for a damned Jacobite who intends to sell his ship and soul to Prince James! I'll name you a Jacobite to the authorities!"

"Ned...." Jonathan warned, but Edward ignored him.

He had no choice now but to answer the insistent accusation, his plans be damned. As the Spanish would put it, he was "*entre la espada y la pared*"—between the sword and the wall. To fight a duel might see him arrested and spoil his plans, but to depart with the accusation unresolved would mean that would race in Bristol from tavern to coffeehouse to Tolzey, no matter what Jonathan, his friend and business partner, said or did.

Edward smiled coldly, leaned forward, and whispered into Lynch's ear: "If you won't drink friends with me here, perhaps on the Hill?"

Lynch, perhaps fearing that his ardor, brandy-fortified courage at best, might diminish significantly with waiting, answered in a coarse whisper: "As soon as possible! No longer than it takes to walk there!"

Separately they hastened casually away, Edward and Jonathan first, then Lynch and his drinking companion in the opposite direction in a form of misdirection.

"Maybe he's just a blustering bully-rock, a pretend bravo, Ned, and won't show," Jonathan said, as they walked nonchalantly down the quiet lanes between the orchards north of the city, in order to attract as little attention as possible. "He'll pretend he left his fighting sword at home, or that he lies under a cloud from a previous killing, or that his arm is still sore from his last rencontre. The fool probably intended no real offense, he's just drunk and quarrelsome, trying to incite you by whatever means he could, and all over a woman."

"Whatever his reasons, I can't ignore such an accusation made among so many ears," Edward said, to which Jonathan shrugged his agreement. "Come, let's walk faster."

"You'll be winded, Ned."

"The hell I will. Soon enough some turd of a gossip will snitch to the watchmen, and if we're caught swords-in-hand, or worse, if one of us is killed, there'll be hell's own jailors, judges, and juries to pay—and perhaps a hangman, too."

Chapter 2

'Tis safest making Peace, they say, with Sword in Hand.
—George Farquhar, *Love and a Bottle*, 1698

Within an hour the four men approached each other on Nine Tree Hill, a mile north of Bristol proper, beyond the ominous gallows where the Welsh road forked to Henbury.

"I'm here for my lesson," Lynch called as he paced the dueling ground, furtively sucking at a small flask of brandy. Edward noted that the heat was gone from Lynch's tone.

"I'm here to give it to you," Edward replied casually.

"He doesn't look drunk anymore," Jonathan whispered.

"Then maybe he won't fight. And if he does, at least he won't do anything completely unexpected. I'd always rather fight a sober swordsman than a drunk of any sort. You can never tell what a drunk will do, nor when he'll do it."

The four went over the ground to make certain there was nothing that might give one of the swordsman an accidental or incidental advantage, although in fact it was impossible to keep chance entirely out of these encounters. Fortune herself seemed devoted, not only to watching duels, in that peculiar, invidious way in which some women are drawn to dangerous competition between men, but also to subtly intervening in them, as if she had already chosen sides. Or perhaps the fickle goddess simply enjoyed the thrill of changing sides with the changing turns of skill and accident in combat.

"We fight with our coats on, agreed?" Lynch hissed. "Quicker to escape this way if we're discovered, and no evidence left behind."

"And easier to hide tricks of foul play," Edward replied matter-of-factly.

"I need no tricks to prick a Jacobite pirate."

"That remains to be seen."

"Enough words! Let's settle this before the watchmen discover us!"

"Not yet!" Edward commanded, holding up a hand as Lynch's companion, Richard Hardwood, nervously began to draw his sword too soon. "Only you and I will fight."

"It's customary for seconds to fight!" Lynch swore, his tone more angry than perplexed.

"Not today. We'll let them keep watch for witnesses and bailiffs, not to mention that four of us fighting are more likely to draw attention than two." Edward nodded to Jonathan, who removed a brace of turn-off pistols from his coat pockets and cocked them. "And Mr. Graham will ensure there's no skullduggery."

Lynch glared, his nostrils flaring. He sucked again at his flask; then, in a curiously sympathetic gesture, offered to toss it to Edward to finish.

"We're drinking friends, then?" Edward asked with a grin.

"Only in hell."

With a polite nod Edward declined.

"You really should search each other, Ned," Jonathan warned. "Him especially."

"What? I have no pistols on me," Lynch spat as he drew on a pair of heavy leather gloves.

"Let's hope not," Edward replied grimly, "for should you try to snap one at me in desperation, my friend Mr. Graham will pistol both you and your second."

Hardwood's eyes grew and he stepped back several paces, but Lynch merely exhaled dismissively. Edward looked Lynch in the eye and drew a glove onto his left hand, with which he might oppose or parry. He kept his right bare for a more sensitive grip on his sword.

"Will you at least measure swords, Ned?" demanded Jonathan.

"Nae, no time to fetch a matching blade."

"To business, then!" said Lynch boldly and drew his sword. Its blade was broad at the forte and three square, or hollow, as three-cornered blades were known. It was two or three inches longer than common, lightly sharpened on the two natural edges, and bent slightly down near the tip: a bully's blade. Put plainly, Lynch had less faith in his swordplay than he professed.

"As you please," Edward replied, prepared for treachery overt or subtle. He would keep an eye on Lynch, Jonathan on Hardwood. "Are we ready, then?"

"Are you for life or death?"

"Either, as pleases you. In other words, I'm for however this affair turns out. Myself, I'll try to avoid killing you, so that your death won't get in my way. As I said, I've affairs to attend. Nonetheless, I'll kill you if no lesser opportunity presents."

Edward grasped his sword hilt, slipping his forefinger Spanish-style into the large outside ring of the hilt, drew his colichemarde and came on guard, taking two steps backward as he did. A surprise assault as swords were drawn was a cheap trick of some duelists.

Lynch grinned. "Retiring already? And you a master-at-arms? Is it then true what they say, that he who knows nothing becomes a teacher?"

Edward touched the brim of his hat with his left hand, and with a small flourish of his sword made an informal salute, although such ceremony was usually dispensed with in duels and affrays.

"Guard yourself, sir," he said.

"And you," Lynch replied, with just a nod of his blade. "I killed a master once," he added.

Edward smiled grimly, amused at Lynch's constant stage villain manner. "I almost killed one myself when I was little more than an ignorant. The master was overconfident. Soon after, a true ignorant nearly killed me. I've never forgotten the lesson. You've clearly yet to learn it."

Lynch scowled and advanced. Edward, his arm not quite fully extended, his weight evenly divided between his legs after the fashion recommended by some Scottish masters, retreated, then suddenly pressed forward with a simple false half-thrust, quick but shallow, to judge his adversary's response.

Lynch parried. The blades rang lightly on the air, a sound that would surely bring witnesses sooner or later. Edward recovered quickly and added a small retreat. As he did, he parried Lynch's shallow riposte but made no counter-riposte, considering it unlikely to land given the distance and Lynch's quick recovery.

Lynch traversed a step to Edward's right, then quickly thrust to the outside. Edward was unimpressed: he simply shifted slightly to the right and parried easily. In these two brief engagements he had already learned that Lynch was, thankfully, not the worst sort of swordsman, the rash fool who wants to run his adversary through even if it means he himself is "pinked." Lynch, who clearly wanted to sleep in a whole skin, was but a middling swordsman, one who had mediocre technique and no real strategy, one who hoped for opportunity: he was neither an ignorant nor an expert. The former could be deadly by virtue of ignorance and impetuosity, the latter by virtue of skill. Lynch would be deadly only by virtue of Edward's mistake or ill-Fortune.

As Lynch traversed back to the left, Edward attacked quickly to his arm with a disengage. Lynch parried, barely catching the blade in time, and riposted deeply, but Edward recovered quickly, battering Lynch's blade away. Lynch smirked arrogantly, thinking that although his adversary might parry well, he lacked the guts to riposte forcefully. All he need do was be patient and renew his attack when the opportunity was right.

Edward ignored his adversary's expression and noted to himself that Jonathan was correct: Lynch was not drunk at all. A ruse, then, his apparent inebriation, that performance with the flask?

'Tis no matter now, he thought, *I have his time and measure.*

Edward shifted tactics and began to advance and retreat in small steps in a broken, varying, unpredictable rhythm, his blade moving similarly: sinuously engaging, disengaging, circling, pressing, feinting, beating, binding, gliding, and parrying, all entirely independent of his footwork—yet both blade and foot were clearly interdependent.

Lynch, recognizing his adversary's technical superiority and icy *sang froid*, retreated and nervously licked his lips. He cast his eyes behind Edward, but the fencing master smiled coldly as he looked, not behind, but briefly into Lynch's worried eyes. Lynch retreated another step to gain time to reflect and catch his breath.

But Edward would not let his adversary lie idle. He advanced aggressively and struck Lynch's blade with a powerful beat. Lynch retreated again, dropping his blade into a low guard. The Scotsman, suspecting a trick, pressed Lynch with quick attempts to gather his blade and force it back to the high line, distracting him. Suddenly, as Lynch slipped one of the attempts, Edward unconventionally flicked his own blade sharply at his enemy's sword-hand.

Lynch leaped back. Edward had drawn his blade clean through the glove's leather. Yet there was no blood, only the dull gleam of very fine mail.

"I knew you must be a liar and cheat," the Scotsman said grimly, "and you prove it. I've a mind to kill you for this, yet I'm impressed by the depth of your treachery and troubled that your death, however much you deserve it, might inconvenience me. My father told me of this very old Italian trick, but I've never seen it until now."

"Ned, lad, he probably wears a mail shirt as well—" Jonathan warned, striding toward the combatants, one pistol raised as if to clap it to Lynch's head and blow his brains out, the other warning Lynch's second away. Edward waved him off with his sword, for a pistol shot would surely draw inquiry and authority. Edward's Scots temper grew: its cold-blooded anger would sharpen his focus and swordplay, not to mention keep his fear under control, unlike the hot-blooded fury that often led a swordsman to rashly impale himself by accident.

Lynch looked briefly confused and worried, perhaps that Jonathan might actually pistol him; then, seeing him back off and realizing that powder and ball would be used only as a last resort, bit his lip and attacked hard. Edward easily parried the attack and riposted without lunging, pressing his adversary back but doing him no harm. If there were one technique of sword Lynch excelled at, it was his quick recovery after a failed attack. His corpulence did not make him a slow swordsman. Too many novices learned too late that such men can often move very fast, at least until they were winded.

Lynch's second suddenly took to his heels, no longer wanting any part in this dark comedy, not to mention any part of any prosecution. His flight did not seem to affect Lynch, who now believed he was immune to pistoling or backstabbing, no matter what he did to deserve them.

The duel had gone on too long, mostly due to Edward's caution, a product of wanting to end the fight with the least possible harm to either man. Most duels were settled in two or three passes in no more than a minute or two.

Lynch's breaths came quickly. Sweat ran from his temples down his cheeks. He stepped back again.

"A breath, shall we have a breath?" he asked, panting.

"I've a rule never to stop a man from wasting his wind. Keep your guard up, for I won't help the man who wants to kill me."

"It's not an honorable fight if you won't let me have a breath, damn you! A fight should prove the best sword-man, not the man who has the best wind!"

"You're a damned hypocrite, Lynch, your ilk always are. You deserve to have your throat cut, but I'll do my best to let you off with a hole or two that won't kill you. On your guard!"

Edward attacked hard and fast with simple actions, hoping to tire his adversary further and push him into greater disorder. Lynch retreated almost at a backward run, nearly tripping over his own feet. Edward strode toward him, unsure if he might be ready to surrender. Lynch's left hand slipped under his coat. Immediately Edward attacked with a powerful beat to his blade, so swift and sharp that sparks flew, and thrust deeply to the throat. Lynch leaped back and, fumbling, dropped a dagger as he did. The Scotsman smiled coldly.

Lynch grimaced, shrugged, stepped forward as if to pick up the dagger, his eye on Edward, who had no intention of letting him double-arm himself. The Scotsman stepped within range, well on guard: without warning Lynch lunged instead of reaching for the dagger on the ground. Expecting this, Edward simultaneously parried and leaped an inch or two out of range, then riposted without lunging. Lynch counter-parried Edward to the outside in tierce; Edward retreated, disengaging as he did, his sword arm still extended. Lynch, lured by the opportunity to redouble his attack, recovered forward and seized his adversary's blade with his own in carte, then pressed his blade down in a *flanconnade*—but too late!

Like lightning Edward yielded to Lynch's blade and parried him. As Lynch drew back, his arm extended, Edward seized his blade in turn with a *flanconnade* so fast and tight that Lynch could neither disengage nor try to hit with an angulation. Even if he could have managed either, Edward's left hand pressed against his blade, preventing him.

Lynch, realizing his peril, squealed as he made a quarter turn and tried to counter, to no avail. Worse, Lynch's *inquartata* carried his unarmed hand so far out of line that he could not use it even in a last ditch effort to grab Edward's blade. The Scotsman's blade pierced him right in the buttock.

Edward leaped back, jerking his blade free and battering Lynch's to prevent a hit on his recovery. Lynch, in pain, unsteady on his feet, and showing signs of incipient panic, disengaged and thrust high. Edward parried and bound Lynch's blade, simultaneously closed swiftly with a pass, grasping Lynch's shell with his left hand as he did, and put the sharp point of his *colichemarde* to Lynch's throat.

The bully-fool struggled, but Edward's grasp was tight as a tourniquet and his sword point sharp.

"Choose now, Lynch! Yield and live or resist and die, the consequences to me be damned. The embarrassment of explaining why you now have two holes in your ass is less distressing than the grave. Yield, or I shove my blade through your gullet, for I intend to sleep tonight and every night in a whole skin."

Lynch released his sword. Edward, keeping his blade at

Lynch's throat, drew the sword knot over Lynch's hand, tossed the sword to the side, and stepped back.

"Go, now. Make no further accusation against me, and know that if you slander me again as a Jacobite I *will* kill you."

"My sword—"

"Belongs to me. I'll have your scabbard, too, if you please. And your cheating gauntlets! And don't think to turn that pistol, the one ye surely keep in your pocket, on me. Mr. Graham will address you with both of mine until you're away."

Lynch, blood darkly staining the seat of his breeches and his right stocking as it drained into his shoe, flung scabbard and gauntlets to the ground and limped hastily away, one hand clutching his wounded buttock. Jonathan sheathed Lynch's sword and collected the gauntlets and dagger.

"Let's get going too, I hear voices nearby," Edward said quietly, his heart still beating hard. Quickly he cleaned his blade with a handkerchief, then cast the cloth aside. Jonathan kicked some dirt over it and gave Edward a look as if to say, "Just in case."

"Lynch will trouble you no more, I am thinking," Jonathan said as they stretched their legs into the coming darkness, "but what about that high-born wench? She must hate you to have set him against you like that. I suppose he was in his cups when she baited him."

"The devil with her!" Edward laughed coldly, releasing some of the tension left over from the fight.

"Still, isn't curious that a bully blade accuses you of being a Jacobite on the eve of your trip to Ireland? Don't you find this suspicious, especially given the letters you're carrying?"

Edward's hand rested for a moment against the secret correspondence beneath his sword belt. "I hope it's only coincidence. The simplest explanation is that Lynch hoped both to bed the wench and further his own intrigues. Two birds with one stone. I have to admit he's a good pretend drunk; he probably thought it would give him an advantage, along with his gauntlets, dagger, and such. Who even makes such gauntlets anymore? The Italians?"

"They're well-made," Jonathan said, inspecting the gloves, "lined inside with fine mail; a ruffian could easily grasp his victim's blade without harm."

"Keep them, then, in case you ever need a new trade," Edward said with a smile. "And the sword too, if you like."

"You keep the sword, Ned. Hang it with the rest in your school, or better yet, sell it to one of your students. It costs much to outfit a private man-of-war."

Edward grinned. "Far more than a thousand blades like his would bring."

"To Ireland, then! And may Fortune serve us there, even better than she did here today, playing the coquette and scaring the hell out of me. But have a care, Ned: I still think there's more to this affray than roaring bullies and wayward wenches," Jonathan said as they strode, swiftly at first, then casually, back to the Black Swan coffeehouse near Tower Lane where Edward lived.

Perhaps it was a good omen, this duel, thought Edward as they walked, now led by a linkboy they had hired to light their way. A message from Fortune, as it were, pointing out that he should not take her lightly if he wished for her favor; now, message delivered, she would incline events his way, or at least leave him to his own devices. He had great confidence in himself and felt certain he would prevail, no matter the circumstances.

A small ship awaited him on the morn at a quay on the Severn, and aboard it passage to Ireland, and there the means once more to his destiny.

Chapter 3

Sick Ireland is with a strange war possest
Like to an ague; now raging, now at rest...
—John Donne, "Loves Warre", circa 1596

Some fifty leagues southwest as a ship might make her course, an Irish renegade rode the black swells of the fitful sea. He listened to the waves ahead as they spent themselves on rocks and sand invisible in the night and became for a moment a hoarse whisper as they slipped back into the ocean to be enveloped, enfolded, and reborn again and again.

There!

The light winked deliberately again. Or did it? Was it instead the flash of a candle or small fire in a hut or home, briefly revealed by the rise and fall of the swell? Or was it indeed the signal he sought?

"Give way!" he shouted to the four seamen at the oars. "Put your backs into it!"

On such a night he had no need to keep his voice down, not while amidst angry wind and wave. His gang began to row again, slowly, then faster and harder, toward the dangers of sea upon shore and of armed men who might wait beyond. Ahead the Irishman saw the frothy caps of breaking waves, glimmers of whiteness in a dark night. Only the occasional light from a waxing half-moon slipping through wind-rent clouds on the western horizon permitted him to see the shore—and the rocks between.

"Hold water!" he shouted thrice to get the attention of the seamen at the oars of the jolly-boat. They paused that he might feel the swells passing beneath, to find their rhythm, to choose the moment to race ashore betwixt rock and wave.

His heart pounded, his body shivered. He swore this was due only to tired muscles and sodden clothing, and truly, he feared little except death by hanging. *Born to be hanged, thus the sea will never take him*, many had said of him so often that he had come to believe it as an unalterable truth.

He looked up, waiting to see the signal again. His muscles itched to work. He wished he were at the oars and not at the tiller.

Several waves, larger than most that had passed, crested beneath the small boat and broke just beyond. And there it was, a flash of light again.

"Give way starboard!" he ordered.

"Backwater!" he shouted when he sensed they were drifting too close to the surf. Then, "Hold water!"

He waited to time the waves.

"Give way!" he shouted.

Quickly the seamen pulled hard at the oars, trusting the Irishman's judgment. For a moment he thought that he cared not if the timing were right, cared not whether they thrust the boat into the momentary lull following the melding of two great waves, or thrust it instead into a set of plunging breakers that would shatter boat and bodies.

Then the sea behind them was scarcely distinguishable from the dark heaven. Instinctively he turned his head to look astern and saw a great wave looming over them. Like the ticking movement of the hand of a clock it grew, pausing slightly, then rising a notch higher, then pausing and rising again.

A trick of my tired eyes? he wondered. The wave now seemed over his head! Surely it would break and plunge into his boat any moment!

"Give way, you buggers!" he bellowed.

But the seamen paused instead, fearfully fascinated by the looming dark waters.

"Don't look up, you fools! Give way, damn you!" the Irishman shouted, and in that brief moment he suddenly doubted his invulnerability upon the sea.

The dark mountain broke, reaching after the frail vessel yet failing, barely, to crash upon it. Instead, the great crest transformed into a steep, dirty white slope roaring beneath the hull. Water exploded over the transom, filling the boat even as the sea flung it forward into a valley of turbulent froth and foam.

Boat and crew were past the danger of the breaking waves, speeding into the narrow cove and washing close to shore. Out the crew leaped, one with bowline in hand, and all tried to haul the small but heavy boat free of the grasp of the broken wave as it pulled seaward. Failing, they let the next incoming surge shove the boat broadside and cast it almost lightly upon the shore.

Quickly, one seaman wedged the boat's grapnel among some rocks, while the rest, with help from a surge that lifted the starboard side, capsized the boat to drain the seawater that had almost filled it to the gunwales. The Irishman ordered his crew to wait with the boat and keep watch; then he drew his cutlass and ran toward the rocks and cliff ahead, his cold, wet clothing clutching at his legs and arms. In a small cleft at the base of the cliff he sat down to listen and look.

Out of the wind he grew warm, although still he shivered, his woolen clothing retaining body heat in spite of being soaked. He heard nothing but wind and wave, saw nothing but shades of darkness. For several minutes he did not move, reveling in the relative comfort of his position and happy to have escaped Poseidon's brazen-hoofed sea steeds. He shifted his position, and once again his clothing grasped his limbs like the cold tentacles of an ancient sea monster, reminding him that he must never for a moment grow comfortable.

The Irishman grew impatient with waiting for moonlight to see by, and bothered by thoughts of his woman back in Ireland. He started to stand, then stopped. He'd heard a sound, and it was neither wind nor wave, nor of his own making. It did not belong to the rhythm of the stormy night.

Above? Above.

Several pebbles fell upon his head, and the Irishman pressed against the cliff face and stared upward. A familiar sound came and went.

And soon again the same, but this time not from above. It came from nearby, perhaps only a few feet away. Next he heard a stumble, a fall, a scrape of metal on rock, and a quiet curse, all carried quickly away by the wind. Then nothing more. Even the sounds from above ceased. The moon peered through a break in the clouds.

Two, the Irishman thought, *I might have two enemies here to greet me tonight.*

Holding his cutlass at his side, he moved slowly and quietly in the direction of the sounds he had heard nearest to him. A few yards ahead he discerned a dark, squatting form, a pair of dark lanterns at its feet. It stared upward, this shape, trying, perhaps, as the Irishman had, to discover the source of the sounds above.

The Irishman flung himself upon the form, knocking it to the ground while bringing his cutlass to bear and covering its mouth with his left hand. A wide-eyed man, for it was indeed flesh and blood, stared up at him but did not move.

No one else came forth, and the Irishman sensed no one else nearby, except perhaps above. He inspected the man's face in the darkness, grinned, removed cutlass and knee from throat and chest, and crouched down beside him.

"Damn you, O'Neal!" the man, his accent that of a Cornish gentleman, whispered hoarsely, "You might've killed me!"

"Who's above?" the Irishman asked quietly.

"Damn you!" the man repeated with a cough, his hand at his throat. He sat up as the Irishman sheathed his cutlass. "The 'good men' of Padstow. What other fools would be here on a night like this?"

The Irishman grunted. A few of the gentry and merchants of the nearby Cornish town, then, most of them fat and well-armed gentlemen and merchants, each with armed servants in tow and some of them members of the local trainband—the local militia—whose members in general were often referred to as "cuckolds all in a row." They probably watched for French invaders or smugglers, or at least made a pretense of doing so, and wished they were at home bedding their maids or mistresses instead.

"Then why did you signal me ashore?" the Irishman demanded quietly.

"I didn't!"

"Then it was their lantern I saw, as I thought it might be."

"And still you came, you damned bog-trotting cully."

The Irishman replied, his cold words contrasting oddly with his grin. "I've gutted men for less than that."

A lull came in the wind, and now both men heard voices from above.

"Wait here," the Irishman ordered.

He climbed two dozen yards up a nearby cleft to listen.

"French invaders! Irish assassins! Smugglers and pirates!

Cud Zookes, boy! There's naught here—"

"The old woman—"

"Damn the old witch! There's naught here but a mad woman's nightmares. No one has answered our false fire. If a smuggler were in the offing she'd have signaled back. Time to be home and away."

"But the old woman says she sees them every month at this time of the moon, and maybe we didn't use the correct signal—"

"A pox on her tales! And what's she doing out here at night at the same moon every month? Use your head, boy."

"And the broken oar I discovered on the shore last month, the day after this same moon?"

"Egad boy, there's flotsam and jetsam all over this Cornish coast, at least until the wreck-mongers get to it. It's the Cornishman's grace of God, a wreck is. Let's go then, it's charity we do by leaving any wreck goods on the shore. Better a roaring fire, some brandy, and a wench's plump tits and buttocks than this wind and rain."

"But sir—"

"What's wrong with you, boy? Damn your listening at keyholes and damn those gossips who claim a French pirate used to visit your aunt up the Helford—my own dear sister, God save her, and Goddamn that poxy fool I married her to. I tell you, if there's anything out there it's our tin boats and our tall-hatted fishermen, for only a fool would try to come ashore on a night like this. A few hours in a scold's bridle might teach that witch to hold her tongue, and so keep good men out of this weather. No more of this nonsense from you, boy; we're going home to warm ourselves with a fire and some good cool-Nantz that found its way here by accident from the Loire. Are you coming with us?"

And the voices were no more, either because the wind had grown great again, bringing with it the gusting rain, or because the men had gone, and the Irishman was left to wonder cynically if the speaker himself were not involved in local smuggling, including the Irishman's own cargo.

"They're gone?" whispered the Cornishman when the Irishman returned.

Annoyed, the Irishman answered distractedly, wondering about how many men might be visiting his own woman in his absence. It angered him that he could not keep her stowed away in his mind while he tended to this business of smuggling and other intrigue. Something had set her loose between decks tonight.

"I think so. Wait here and keep watch. Are your men and ponies safe?"

"Hidden nearby. Far easier for someone to find us than them," replied the Cornishman, who was a smuggler for profit as well as a Jacobite agent serving the exiled James.

"I'm going to climb all the way up this time and make sure the coast is clear, I'll make my signal if it is."

The Irishman picked up one of the dark lanterns and climbed slowly back up the sharp cleft, the wind and light rain masking the sounds of his climb. He gained the flat ground at the top of the cliff, peered across it, and saw nothing. The men of the trainband were gone, back to their wives and mistresses. Yet, as he was about to climb back down, the Irishman heard, in a brief respite from the wind, a soft snort only a horse could have made.

Minutes passed. The Irishman breathed slowly in spite of his pounding heart. He looked not at the night, but through it, knowing that sooner or later a shape would resolve from the darkness and present itself.

Then he saw the vague form, less distinct than the Cornishman had been below, but still clear enough to identify: a man leading a horse. The twain were making their way slowly along the cliff wall.

Is this the youth who had spoken earlier? the Irishman wondered. *An enthusiastic lad disregarding the cynicism and negligence of his elders? Or an older man, a retired soldier or the muster master of the trainband, who waits to see what crawls from its hole after the dogs have gone?*

No matter. I'll kill him when he comes.

He silently drew his cutlass with his right hand and his skean—an Irish dagger with a blade more than a foot long—with his left, and waited for man and horse to come blindly within range of cut and thrust.

He has no weapon at the ready, the Irishman thought, *so he'll die quickly. I can cut his throat, push steel through his belly, or just heave him over the cliff. The horse? I'll run it over the cliff to prevent it from returning without a rider. A horse without a rider creates alarm. But if neither show, alarm will be delayed, for there are many reasons the pair might not immediately return.*

His mouth dried as he waited to kill. He trembled agreeably at the thought of murder. And then it came to him: Reason, gnawing at the corners of his mind. Now he regretted giving in to his bloody inclination. He ought to have slipped back into the cleft and huddled there like a frightened rabbit until the man passed, but now he was trapped by his own bloodlust and curiosity.

On came man and horse.

The horse! Will he discover me when his master cannot? the Irishman wondered.

Closer came the dismounted rider, so close he came… and stopped short, looking over the cliff toward the water.

For an eternity the Irishman waited, wanting to feel the perverse joy at killing by surprise. Soon man and horse were above him, on top of him. The Irishman's grip tightened on his cutlass and skean as he lost his sense of balance and time. Only by his instincts could he see.

Now! Now! they shouted.

Soon the struggle was over.

A minute later the Irishman opened and closed one panel of the darkened lantern three times, making a signal to sea. A tiny light—the flash of a "false fire" ignited in a tub—winked twice in response. Lying by offshore was the *Mary and Martha*, a small merchant-galley whose pretended destination for trade was Portugal, but had, in fact, been the coast of France. Usually her hold would have been filled entirely with smuggled French wine and brandy traded for a cargo of English cloth and lead, but on this voyage she carried more than spirits; part of her hold was packed tightly with boxes of muskets, horse pistols, swords, and saddles, and with casks of powder and shot, all destined for Jacobite rebels—or patriots, depending on one's point of view—who waited in England and Ireland for the invasion that would restore King James.

The merchantman was commanded by an Englishman of Jacobite sympathy and apolitical greed. For several days and nights this late November of 1695, he had sailed the coast between Trevose and St. Agnes Heads, signaling by night off this and two other coves and awaiting reply.

As he did, he ran a dangerous gauntlet. Europe had been at war since 1688 when English Protestants deposed the papist King James II and put the staunch Dutch Protestant William III of Orange and his wife Mary, daughter of James II, on the throne. Louis XIV of France supported the dethroned James, and soon after the war began the French king helped the exiled English king invade Ireland as a stepping stone to regaining the English throne. But in less than two years the Irish campaign was over, and the defeated James was back in exile at Saint-Germain-en-Laye in France, plotting again to regain his throne.

Such plots and plans were but a part of a much greater campaign, for arrayed against France's ambitions were England and most of Europe, Protestant and Catholic.

The Irishman's purpose was to trade in smuggled goods and to see arms and ammunition safely delivered to agents in England and Ireland.

He signaled again, this time to acknowledge the Bristol merchant-galley's flash of light, set the lantern on the ground and uncovered a single panel so that the light would show to sea, and clambered down the hill.

"Is the trainband gone?" the Cornishman asked worriedly.

"Aye."

"What took so long?"

"One of them returned, a sly bastard."

"You killed him!"

"Sure now, and I'd spoil the enterprises of men in France, England, and Ireland." Having provoked an astonished look on the Cornishman's face, the Irishman grinned. "He's gone. But I almost forgot myself and killed him anyway."

"Damn you, Irishman, you *are* a fool," the Cornishman said and departed.

He returned ten minutes later with a long string of fat little horses in tow, hardy animals every one, yet none had ever known food other than local grasses and furze. With the ponies were a dozen or so Cornishmen, stout miners mostly, along with two or three fishermen, all skilled at the brutal sport of Cornish wrestling: a 'Cornish hug' and a cudgel awaited anyone who dared interfere with the night's work.

As soon as the ship's longboat was ashore, the Cornishmen went to work. The Irishman supervised the seamen from the ship, but the Cornishmen took their orders from their compatriot, for they could not understand the Irishman's 'brogue upon the tongue,' nor the Irishman their 'jouring speech.' Quickly and quietly they unloaded small casks—ankers, half-ankers, and firkins—of powder and shot, along with boxes of muskets and pistols, and packed them on the small horses. Twice more the Irishman had to shake off thoughts of his woman in Ireland, whose strange business it was to be constantly wooed by other men, no matter that she had promised herself to him.

Abruptly the Cornishman briefly stepped away into the darkness. When he returned he was accompanied by a stranger dressed as a common tradesman, yet who foolishly carried himself with the bearing of a Great Man.

"And who's this?" the Irishman asked with a hint of suspicion. A messenger, doubtless. The Irishman did not recognize this particular one, although he had met several during covert journeys from Ireland to England: once aboard the *Mary and Martha*, twice aboard a French privateer, and thrice aboard fishing vessels.

"I have come in haste from France by way of London," the stranger said, with no intention of giving his name. He was English, with the patronizing haughtiness of a nobleman or elite intellectual, and the Irishman hated him immediately. The stranger nodded at the Cornish smuggler, who stepped out of earshot.

"You are Michael O'Neal?"

"Aye."

"Then you will know what to do with this," the stranger said, passing to him a small but heavy package tightly wrapped in tarred canvas.

The Irishman took it but did not open it. He knew that inside were coins and also innocuous-appearing letters with secret messages written in cipher or penned between their lines in disappearing inks, some whose words would reveal themselves when heated, others when wet or with a candle placed behind the paper; and even these hidden messages might have hidden meanings. The money, an odd assortment, was to support James' agents in Ireland as they laid in arms, bought horses, and recruited fighting men for the anticipated invasion of England and the restoration of King James II to his rightful throne. Once already this year had invasion plans been quashed, but another was being readied. The Irishman slipped the package into a bag slung across his chest, opposite his cutlass.

"I have one more message," the stranger said.

The Irishman was silent.

"Sir George Barclay," the stranger whispered in a manner neither statement nor question. "He asks that you join him in London. He says there may be work soon—profitable work—for a man like you. He says it would be wise if you were there by the end of January, and even wiser by the end of December."

The Irishman said nothing.

"As you like, O'Neal, but Sir George urges you to London immediately," the stranger whispered, as if the wind might carry the words across land and sea. "You know the taverns to frequent while you wait. Sir George says you are well-suited to the affairs at hand, and well-acquainted with the ways in and out of London. He needs men like you. King James needs men like you."

The Irishman laughed softly and wickedly. "So the honorable old Scottish warrior intends to return to England one day soon as a secret soldier. It's a bloody business to restore a king, and a desperate business that would bring a poor Irishman to do the dirty work of the English and French. Or is it only the Irish and the Scots who have this sort of courage?"

"It's in your own Irish interest, as you well know," the stranger said forcefully.

The Irishman ground his teeth in return. "I've business in

Ireland first, landing the rest of this cargo. You may send word to your bloody-minded master that I'll come to London as quick as I can. If he's seeking me, he's seeking others and therefore isn't ready to strike, whatever his business is. My part alone is unlikely to breed or abort this—what shall we call it? Regicide?"

"Who speaks of regicide?" hissed the disguised gentleman sharply. "And Sir George is not my master!"

And indeed, there was no suggestion of regicide in Barclay's verbal missive. But plotting against King William's life was rampant in Jacobite taverns, sputtered by rum-sodden firebrands. Yet they had reason to hope: a very real plot against William's life had been suspended this past year only because the king had traveled outside of the country. The Irishman felt sure of his prediction. He had a habit of foreseeing the likely deeds of men, not to mention that he knew what sort of violence would be required to restore James to his throne. Barclay knew this too, even if the order had yet to be given.

"What else could it be, then?" he said, deliberately provoking the messenger. "To restore King James will require the death of Prince William. Surely even King James himself understands this much."

The Englishman fidgeted but remained silent. The Irishman might have the right of it, but speculation—were there indeed a plan—might foil it.

"As you please. Go then, *master-less lord*, and do *your* bidding," the Irishman said mockingly.

Even in the darkness he could tell that the stranger's blood was rising. He was not to be sneered at by any damn'd *Teague*. Yet the gentleman held his anger in check. Perhaps he knew better than to challenge this wild descendent of Irish kings and kerns, a man known, or at least said, to have been buccaneer and pirate, highwayman and rapparee, interloper and smuggler, duelist and prize fighter, cattle thief and black renter, spy and assassin. More likely, the stranger knew that the mission at hand was far more important than any personal affront that could be settled later with thirty-four inches of German or Spanish steel.

The Irishman snorted at his English Jacobite ally, then returned his attention to his business. Two hours later, the trade of smuggled goods and treasonable arms was done.

"A drink before you're on your way?" asked the Cornishman as Michael prepared to help launch the jollyboat.

"Where's the stranger?"

"Gone, too important to keep our company for long." The Cornishman nodded toward the sea. "God speed you, Irishman, among the hagboats and fisher boats, the herring and charcoal, the tin and lead and copper. You'll hardly be noticed among this sea of ships, and anyway, you have passes to escape the French, and the English shouldn't bother you."

Michael grunted his non-committal.

"We'll see you return soon?" the Cornishman asked.

"Not likely. I've arms and dispatches to deliver with my gang—"

"Your Irish raparrees, you mean."

"Highwaymen in the service of the rightful king," Michael replied, emphasizing each word.

The Cornishman shrugged. "As you please."

"And I've other affairs to attend."

"To the king across the water, then!"

The Cornishman took a swig from a jar of excellent French brandy, then Michael did.

"The true king!" Michael toasted.

As the gray glimmer of dawn grew behind them in the east, the Irishman and his gang carefully timed the rhythm of the pounding surf one last time, then, muscle and mind in unison, drew the jolly-boat through the waves, followed soon by the longboat.

Aboard the Bristol-merchant the Irishman's attention was soon taken by the sea and the future he had chosen with Barclay, whatever bloody intrigue it might turn out to be. As soon as he had done his duty in Ireland, he would head across St. George's Channel to England, and then to London. He thought of nothing else: not of other men alive or dead; not of enemies past or present; not of women and children innocent, not of those names he commonly invoked and abused, those of God, Jesus, Joseph, or Mary; not even of the woman he professed to love. The prospect used to lure him to London was a trifling pretense, and the adventure it would unlock was merely a passing, if likely profitable, excitement.

Beneath all lay an anger that had long since passed into a petard of black powder sheathed in cold iron, the hatred into a smoldering match set in a linstock poised above the fuse.

Chapter 4

By fate expell'd, on land and ocean tost...
—Virgil, *Aeneid,* 3rd century BC

Cows.

He was looking at cows, at small black cows in wet green pasture.

He could see big soft cow eyes, and small hummocks of grass grown up over piles of cow dung, and mist drifting across hills in the distance.

Cows? Cows.

From dark ships and fair women to cows?

And those sounds: lowing, yes, and clanking? Yes, clanking, again and again.

Cows and cowbells, he thought; then from a corner of his mind came a nagging questioning, an annoying denial of one of his senses, and as he followed its trail he realized the sounds came from beyond the edges of his private universe. Cows, pasture, and mist disappeared and he dreamed no more.

Edward opened his eyes, or thought he did, yet saw nothing before him but blackness, dull and without depth—a blind darkness. He felt movement, too, a simple motion, a gentle swaying to and fro.

No, two motions: his, and another in the background in all directions, yet somehow related to his. Stench was there also, not overpowering, but still there, foul, unclean, unlike that of the cows and pasture in his dream. He heard creaking, groaning, breathing, and snoring, all within arm's reach, and on top of it all, the obnoxious muted-yet-loud clanking of a cowbell, and he wondered for a moment if perhaps he still dreamed this bovine cacophony.

Every night for a fortnight the bell had interrupted his dreams and their shroud of sleep. Always an easy sleeper, he would have slept again shortly this time, as he did every time, his mind filtering the bell and smothering his annoyance, had he not heard movement at the small door in the nearby bulkhead where the bell hung. He rolled over, keeping his head down to avoid the deck beams above, and swung carefully out of his hammock and onto his knees, trying both to keep quiet and keep from falling through the rotting canvas that served as two of his four tiny cabin walls.

The small bulkhead door whined open, and he heard shuffling and muttering, barely audible. Quickly he reached between the two canvas partitions, found a small arm, grabbed it and yanked hard, and with the small arm came a boy of perhaps twelve years. Edward quickly covered the lad's mouth with a hand, but not in time to stop the beginning of an exclamation. He pulled the struggling boy close and whispered in his ear before the lad could pull a knife and shove it into his belly.

"Whisht and strike amain, laddie! 'Tis I, MacNaughton."

The boy stopped struggling. The bell had stopped clanking, replaced by woman's voice with a Dutch accent.

"Who is there? Boy? Are you there, boy? I heard you, boy!"

"Don't answer," the man whispered.

"Boy! Damn you, answer me! Bring me wine and water; I need to sleep!"

Other than the noises of ship and sea—timbers creaking under the force of the sea, rigging straining under the force of the wind, elm tree pumps vomiting bilge and sea water overboard—there was only silence in return.

"You pock-marked little sea heathen, where are you!" she shouted, her voice echoing.

"Elizabeth! Maria! Wake up! Are you awake?" she changed tack, more quietly this time, as she must be more mindful of her servants than of the ship's boy.

"I know you are awake! Get up!" she finally cried loudly again in exasperation, but heavy breathing was her only response and she was likely to get no other. The passengers around her were still drunk enough to render them senseless to her demands. Even her young son was deep in sleep, aided by a beaker of wine and water.

The bell clanked again. The man removed his hand from the boy's mouth.

"Is your heart still beating, Jack?" he whispered.

"Aye, sir, but you scared the devil himself out of me!"

"Faith, I rather doubt Old Roger would run from me," Edward laughed in a whisper. "I know him well, but he's nae friend nor family. What hour is it?"

"Just past eight bells, sir, the middle watch just ended."

"Listen carefully. I'll give you a pence each night, plus more reward when we reach Kinsale, if you find some oakum or other junk and silence the bell clapper, and you can get some sleep too."

"Aye, sir, I'll do it! Bless you!"

Into the black bowels of the small ship went the boy, and back to sleep went Edward, and though the Scotsman did not dream again of dark, swift ships and fair, disingenuous women, neither did he dream of cows, with or without bells around their necks. The bell at the small door clanked no more that night.

He woke at dawn to a sharp headache between his eyes, the result of a night spent breathing the fetid, uncirculated air of the tiny closed space.

Around him was a tight press of seasick humanity, five women and one boy, crammed within tiny cabins of rotting planks and rotting canvas on the tiny aft platform in the hold of a one hundred sixty-ton merchantman, the *Peregrinator* galley. The air in the berth stank of human waste, vomit, and ammonia, plus the counter-actives of liquor, sachet, and vinegar, and of the usual ship odors of wood, cordage, canvas, pitch, and tar. The small deck was littered with sea chests and portmanteaus, buckets and chamber pots, empty wine bottles and food scraps. Everything was wet, damp, or mildewed.

He yawned and prepared to force himself to his feet. His senses told him that the seas had quieted, and that the scuttle to the aft platform had been opened to let out the fetid air and let in the fresh, but the fire hearth in the cook-room was still not lighted.

He dressed, went topside, and passed his eyes first to windward to search the horizon, then aloft to see what sail was set, then over the small activities around him on deck and at the helm, and was pleased to hear the shout, "The pump sucks, the ship is free!" This was good news, for the ship had sprung a leak when she'd run north from a French privateer and into foul weather, and the pumps had been manned ever since, exhausting the small crew.

Edward looked out across the sea again and saw no other sail but a small, similarly built merchant-galley a league distant with her main topsail clewed up, then set, then clewed up again, perhaps as a signal, although a gun or a weft in a flag would have been more common, if indeed it were a signal at all. At any rate, the *Peregrinator* could not afford to lie by for her. Certainly the ship in the distance did not seem in distress. He wondered idly why she was fooling with topsails in this ugly, windy weather, whose misty rains hid both predator and prey.

For nearly two weeks—much too long—the *Peregrinator* had beat against wind and sea, patiently and slowly making progress, though often it seemed she made none at all. Captain and crew daily entreated the wind to veer and the swells to quiet, and coaxed the small frigate into the southwesterly winds without pressing her too hard. The ship now beat toward Kinsale Harbor, only two leagues distant, but those two leagues might mean hours, days, or even, if the wind and weather went relentlessly against them, weeks.

So very close, Edward thought, *but there is an infinity even in inches.*

Eight bells.

The tintinnabulous pairs broke his reverie.

"Captain MacNaughton! Nothing but this blowing, rainy weather. She's a good sea boat in bad weather, the *Peregrinator* is, a fine ship, as long as the pumps are manned, that is. And if the wind doesn't veer against us again, we'll come to an anchor in Kinsale harbor today."

Edward smiled at the man. Giles Cronow he was called, a Welshman born in Monmouthshire and bred to the sea.

"Good day to you, Captain Cronow. You'll win our wager if we do."

"Aye, twelve days *you* said, taking into account that damn'd picaroon first driving us north, then the damn'd weather driving us farther north. But this is the thirteenth day of December, so you're a day too short! Damn my eyes, what with all the French privateers cruising between England and Ireland, I'm surprised our luck has stood."

Edward was himself surprised that they had run into no other rovers during their passage. North they had run from a privateer in the late afternoon on their first day at sea after the long passage down the Severn River. By dint of good seamanship, Captain Cronow and his crew had prolonged the chase until darkness, where Fortune let her hide in the deep troughs of the sea amidst a moonless night. At dawn the French cruiser was nowhere to be found, but more foul weather was. After the dangers of sea and man-upon-sea were finally past, the small merchantman busily beat against the southerly wind and sea, turning the normally short passage into one far too long for Edward's liking.

A passing English merchantman, her captain's voice shouted through a speaking trumpet but audible over wind and sea, had informed them two days past that a French man-of-war of forty-eight guns and more than three hundred men had captured the English hired ship *Betty*, and that other French cruisers had captured the *Devonshire*, *Resolution*, and *Sussex*, the only three East Indiamen expected in England this year. Several of the *Peregrinator's* crew, just over their fright from being chased by a privateer at the outset, had grown fearful again at the news.

Indeed, it was sea rover heaven and merchant seaman hell. Waters around the world were swarming with privateers and cruising men-of-war hoping to get rich by plundering the trade of enemy nations, as Edward himself was on a quest to do. The twin missions of his trip to Ireland—delivering secret letters and soliciting an investor—would, he hoped, be the means of acquiring the funds necessary to secure of his own privateering commission.

Captain Cronow talked on. "But I'll have none of your damned French claret, though, when I win our wager. It's sherry-sack for me, Bristol milk by God, a dozen bottles you'll owe me."

"A few more than that, I think. I've drunk four or five from your store so far," Edward reminded the captain.

"You're my guest, sir, and better company than those poxy lubber bastards in the steerage—damn all soldiers and churchmen!—so I'll take nothing in return for what you drink in my company."

The youthful voice of the ship's boy interrupted the two men. "Your pardons, Captain Cronow, Captain MacNaughton, but I have a message to deliver to Captain MacNaughton, if it pleases you and him."

"Steer a direct course," Edward told the lad, "no need for a traverse when the wind is large. What's the message?"

"Aye, sir. The bawd below wishes for your company," said the boy.

"Bawd?" Edward replied sternly.

The boy's eyes darted quickly to Cronow. Seeing no corporal punishment coming his way—yet—he relaxed a bit. "The *lady* below wishes to see you, sir."

"You'll go farther in this world when you learn that it's wise to never call a woman a whore and always to call her a lady, unless she tells you otherwise, and even then I wouldn't believe her. You wish to have her favors, or those of her maids when you grow to man's estate? Then understand that she's a lady always, no matter her station. Whatever she may have done, it can be no worse than what most merchants and courtiers do every day."

"Aye, sir," the boy replied with a disbelieving smirk he could not control.

"Damn you, boy, you'll take Captain MacNaughton's advice and keep a respectful tongue in your head, or I'll take a rope's end and flay the skin from your young arse!" Cronow said sharply, smacking the lad upside the head.

"Tell her I'll come below soon," Edward told the boy.

"Aye, sir," replied the boy again, this time with a rueful, respectful grin as he rubbed the side of his head. In an instant he had disappeared below.

"Edward, my old friend," laughed the captain, "You're too kind, given how she pesters you. They say in Bristol that she *was* once a whore to Spanish merchants in the Low Countries before she married a papist English merchant trading there, a rich man who owned a Bristol trading company and an Irish estate. It's a cozy berth you have below. Surely a rich, widowed lady-whore would be useful in outfitting a privateer? The crew jests that you threw the young officer out who was giving you competition!" Cronow laughed.

But the captain had his facts wrong. An ensign, who along with an army lieutenant and an English parson was berthed in the steerage, had indeed made his way below, with less than honorable intentions. The widow Hardy, furious at the ensign's assumption that her favors and those of her servants were for sale, had routed him from the cabins. Edward had merely escorted the young officer topside. If anything, the Scotsman had preserved him from having his skull broken, no matter that he probably deserved it. Even so, the officer blamed Edward for his failure to secure the pulchritude below.

Edward smiled and shrugged. There was no malice in the captain's words or the crew's forecastle jests, only good-natured humor.

"I'll have the boy bring food to my cabin when the next glass is turned," Cronow continued, his eyes never losing track of the condition of ship, sea, and air. "Join me, sir, if you still have an appetite when you're through with your Scotch warming pans below. And take your time, sir—there's five of them!"

Edward returned below to the platform in the aft hold, a space not even twelve feet by eight feet, partitioned into four cabins, with only five feet from the planking under his feet to that of the deck above, and only four and a half feet to the beams themselves. He could not stand erect in the space, and moved about by stooping or squatting, and sometimes even by shuffling on his knees. The cabins were partitioned by port sail canvas rather than by bulkheads of light planks, giving rise to jokes about the gangplanks that must lie between Edward's cabin and those of the women.

As he entered he tried not to notice the disheveled and revealing condition of Mrs. Hardy's servant women. One of them, Maria, a very intelligent and attractive young woman, had flirted with him since he had set foot aboard the *Peregrinator* in Bristol, often joining him for cards and backgammon, along with two navy wives en route to rejoin their warrant officer husbands at the navy yard in Kinsale after visiting family in Gloucestershire. With the games came far too much indulgence in a liquor the Dutch knew as *jenever* for its juniper flavoring, and the English as *gin*, leading Maria more than once to try to crawl into his hammock. But that he had not wanted to discommode his neighbors in the tight confines of the small ship, and also that he did not want to cause any problems with her demanding mistress, he might have accepted her repeated offer.

"Get dressed, you hussies!" Mrs. Hardy shouted. "Captain MacNaughton, I cannot wait for this abominable voyage to be over," she said, as he turned away from the revealing condition of her servants. "I hope we haven't disturbed you too much, sir, with our pleas for assistance and attention? Would you mind helping us secure our cabin walls—furl them, isn't that what a seaman would say?—so that we may have some more air in here?"

Mrs. Hardy, born Janneke van Tienhoven in the Low Countries and now a denizen of England, was known as Jane by her adopted compatriots and as "the foreign papist whore below" by Parson Waters in the steerage above. Edward had no such prejudices of origin and faith, knowing from experience that both good people and Fortune appeared in many guises.

"I'm happy to help, madam, and in no way could the presence of several women so lovely disturb me. Nay, the robin's song would grow harsh long before my service to you could weary me," he said, bowing awkwardly in the confined space and hoping he adequately disguised his mocking tone. Too often had her damned bell awakened him in the night.

"Oh, Captain MacNaughton," she replied with sarcastic breathlessness, "are you a poet?"

Edward blushed at being so easily discovered. "Clearly not, nor much of an actor either."

"A soldier, then? Or sailor?" she laughed, clearly flirting. "Nay, an adventurer I think, a Gentleman of Fortune, for you are no supercargo or merchant captain, no matter what you pretend. I know men: their professions are invariably written in their figures and characters. Am I right?"

Edward, his self-confidence notwithstanding, blushed again. "You might be."

"An adventurer with business in Ireland, then, although it's no longer a place of adventurers, but of factors, lawyers, and thieves. It must be money you seek."

"Naturally. Adventure requires silver and gold."

"Much of the money in Ireland is stolen, sir."

"Indeed," Edward replied, acknowledging the truth. "But I intend theft elsewhere, and at the risk of my own skin."

"Good to hear, sir, that there may be at least some honor in your future adventures of armed robbery. I myself am also on a mission of money, or at least property: to defend my dead husband's Irish estate, now by law my son's, but I its guardian until his majority. It's a Catholic property, you see, one not yet confiscated by the papist-hating government, but in danger of becoming so."

"Yet Catholic properties are being restored," Edward said,

glancing at Mrs. Hardy's waking son. Clearly he was accustomed to women in dishabille; he yawned, ignored the women, then laid his head back down and closed his eyes in protest at having been awakened.

"Only some properties, sir. It's a profitable game: the blackguard authorities make accusations of treason, confiscate Catholic properties, then Catholic owners pay black-rent to get their title back. As I said, a place for factors, lawyers, and thieves, not stout-hearted adventurers anymore. Even the Irish adventurers, the Tories I mean, have fled. But surely we have more pleasant things to talk about? For example, why has so handsome a man been so aloof—isn't that how the sailors call it?—from your traveling companions?"

Edward looked at her, tempted for a moment less by her sudden, not to mention obvious, flattery and sexuality than by an intriguing side of her character he had overlooked: she displayed a comfortable, familiar perception, the sort that comes from years of experience and makes personal intimacy almost immediate. Then he remembered the bell.

"I'll be dining with the captain shortly. Would you please join us?" he asked out of common courtesy as he finished securing the rolled up canvas cabin walls to hooks in the low beams above.

"No, Captain," she replied, "but I do thank you. It's unfortunate that the sea kept of us from getting to know each other. Perhaps you will visit us in Ireland?" She noticed his hesitation, as if he were inventing an excuse. "I'm a much different woman ashore, sir."

Edward let gallantry take over. "Gladly I'll visit, madam. But if you will excuse me, I must retire for a moment." He bowed slightly again—an oddly dignified gesture, in spite of the fact that he was already bent half over—and shuffled toward his cabin but two feet away, bumping his head on a beam as he did.

"Oh, Captain MacNaughton?"

"Yes?" he replied as he turned to face her again.

"I do have one favor to ask of you, 'tis but a small one. Will you please fix the bell by the door, the one I ring when I need assistance? Or let me seek your assistance when I need it, if my maids won't wake? Oh, come now, don't blush again, I know you silenced the bell or bade the boy do it. I know men, Captain MacNaughton, and you may be as honest and honorable as they come, and I think you probably are, but you will have done it. I am not offended, for I am a demanding woman, after all."

She smiled, and he smiled in return, his sudden admiration outweighing his chagrin.

"Gladly, madam. Which do you prefer: the bell, or me?"

"Sir, I will leave that up to your discretion."

"I shall attend you, madam, when your servants are unable to."

"Thank you, sir."

"Your servant, madam."

Anything to keep that damned bell quiet, and it's only for another night at most, he muttered to himself, still amused by their sudden flirtation, as he climbed the ladder to the steerage above.

And here he ran smack into the army ensign.

The quieting seas had roused the young officer, as it had most passengers. A lubber at the best of times, the ensign lacked sea legs, both in the sense of being able to keep his food down as well as in the sense of being able to move easily aboard a vessel pitching, rolling, and yawing upon the sea. In other words, the collision knocked the ensign flat on his ass.

"Ah, Ensign Ingoldsby! My rutting young friend! You must excuse my hurry," Edward said pleasantly as he helped him to his feet, surprised not only that the young man was up and about, but also that the sea had not yet swept his feet from under him sooner, considering the amount of brandy on his breath. "And I see you're headed in the wrong direction again. So much to know about a ship, after all. Fore and aft, aloft and below, windward and loo'ard, within board, without board, by the board, *overboard*. So many strange names for places and things, no wonder you're so often lost, even on a such a small frigate as this. I think you and Mrs. Hardy agreed that you would not *go below* again, did you not? Come, we'll go to the great cabin and eat a hearty meal, add some belly timber and wine to your brandy-pickled stomach, and you may puke it all up later. This might even save your life, for Mrs. Hardy is in a fierce mood this morning, what with having been up all night seasick, and her maids too," he lied. "What say you, then, sir?"

"Twice, sir," said the ensign as he shrugged off Edward's helping hand and drew himself wobbly to his full height, "you have insulted me on this voyage! First you would not let me at the whores, then you would not move out of my way! Nay, thrice! Thrice, you have insulted me, for I can count and this makes three! This shall not stand! And now you have laid a hand on me! I shall fetch my sword and you will walk with me!"

Edward grinned in spite of himself. "You do know that we're still at sea? Come, Ensign Ingoldsby, you may trust me when I say that men do not fight duels above or below deck. There simply isn't room for them. Besides, you can barely stand anywhere, whether or not you intend anything to *stand*, as you said. Come, there's hot food waiting, and Kinsale and Charles Fort in the offing. Be a good lad, not a fool, and rethink your quarrel with me when you're sober."

But the officer did not move, and by not doing so blocked Edward's way to the great cabin. His look grew distant, and for a moment Edward thought the officer might pass out.

"Woman *varium et mutabile*."

"I'm acquainted with the phrase," Edward replied, amused

by the turn the officer was taking. "I am in fact a university bachelor."

"Indeed?" replied the Ensign, half in sarcasm, half in honest surprise. "It means women are fickle and changeable." He spat the adjectives.

"Actually, it means a woman is a fickle and changeable *thing* —the adjectives, sir, are in the neuter gender, implying objects —and here I don't agree with Virgil at all. Well, at least not of women as *things*. How much Latin have you had, my young Aeneas?"

"Two thousand pound, you Scotch bastard! Two thousand pound!"

Edward grinned. At least the officer had forgotten about seeking satisfaction.

"Well-portioned she was," Ingoldsby continued, his voice alternating between slurred words and emphatic exaggeration, "a stocking merchant's daughter in London. Her father had bought himself a knighthood. By God, what Irish estate I could have had with her money! She wrote letters to me! And when I came to London... to London, sir, the greatest capital in the world... we delivered him, the papist spy-priest, caught him in Kinsale we did, they'll hang him for treason you know, I kicked the Catholic traitor's teeth in when we captured him... and when we arrived in London, I would have made her my wife... But she had chosen a lawyer! A fucking lawyer!"

"I have no hope, you see, you Scotch bastard, no fortune. And she would not marry me, nor would her father make her! I would have spitted that law bastard on my sword, but Lieutenant Fielding, he who travels with me, prevented me. 'They'll hang you if you kill him,' he said, 'the lawyer's crony bastards at the Inns of Court will see you hanged.' The whims of Fortune, sir, the whims of Fortune. *Varium et mutabile*. Have you any Latin?"

Edward almost felt sympathetic. "Come, Ensign Ingoldsby, if you won't eat, then drink: wine makes women and the sea easier to forget."

But the ensign still refused to move and, like many angry drunks, took a darker turn.

"Ah, I understand now," the ensign said. "It's the beldam below, you're fucking her, and her maids too? Aye, she'd have given her maids to me if only I would take her first. But her flesh... too ripe, you understand? Or is it the stink and darkness down there that you like, it reminds you of home, you Scotch Highland bastard? I've not forgotten your insults, sir! But what is to be expected from a man who grew up with dirty floors and food, with dirty people half-dressed in their *plaids*, their women bare-footed, their *lairds* and *chiefs* herding cattle like peasant drovers, can't even make a chimney in your wretched hovels to let out the smoke—"

Edward frowned and struggled to control his rising temper. He had neither time nor tolerance nor even an inclination for foolish quarrels with drunks, and wondered if the officer were so intoxicated that he had no idea what he was saying, or if he were only half-drunk and his condition had simply loosened his tongue.

"Mr. Ingoldsby," Edward said slowly and coldly, "you're still drunk, or reasonably so, so once more I'll forget what you're saying if you return to your cabin. It's but a few feet away. I'll even walk with you there."

Edward received nothing in return for his offer but a stuporous stare. The officer would not budge. Quite possibly he was so insensible that he could not, but no matter. Edward's temper turned cold and his tongue regained the Scots of his youth. He grabbed the young officer by the throat, shoved him backward through the steerage, past the startled parson, and slammed the young officer against the door of the great cabin.

"Listen, you drunken cock-laird, my forbearance is usually served to a man but once, and I have now served you so *thrice*. I swear to you, I'll let my sword drink your blood if you're fool enough to press me again, drunk or sober."

"Take... your... hand... " sputtered the ensign.

"Easy laddie, easy," Edward said as he pressed the web of his hand deeper into the young officer's throat, cutting off voice and breath. "You'll make no more threats if I keep the wind from your lungs. Perhaps you need more rest—"

"A sail! A sail!"

The unusual urgency in the words from aloft drew Edward's attention. He let the ensign fall, leaving him to lie vomiting in his drunken, seasick, half-consciousness.

"Fortune spares you today, lad."

Quickly Edward MacNaughton strode to the main deck, ignoring Captain Cronow and Lieutenant Fielding, who burst forth behind him from the great cabin.

Southwest in the offing, breaking through the mist of low clouds and light rain, her hull showing now and again above the swells, was a full-rigged ship sailing under reefed main and fore courses. She was a swift, dark ship, just as he had dreamed.

Chapter 5

But for all his cheat we knew what he was,
and were in all kind ready to give him welcome.
—Capt. Tho. Phillips, *Journal*, November 1693

From the dankness below, the sailors of the larboard watch came topside to stare at the approaching ship through the shroud of rain. She was to windward, her course nor'east by north with the wind on her larboard quarter, and she appeared to be flying Dutch colors. A few fisher boats were also visible in the distance, but the small merchant-galley Edward had sighted earlier was nowhere to be seen.

As Edward stepped onto the quarterdeck he called to the ship's boy. "Jack, fetch my spying-glass, the large one; it's in my sea chest. Here's the key."

Soon Edward was squinting through his old, battered spyglass, three feet long at full draw, confirming her Dutch colors. Edward picked out black wales and upper works, and stern carvings painted to simulate gilding, as well as a number of men engaged in the business of sailing. Her compliment was as large as that of an East Indiaman—or a privateer.

Behind Edward, Lieutenant Fielding, by the Captain's invitation, climbed to the quarterdeck with a lubber's lack of balance. Sobriety, courage, and a finally-quiet stomach were evident in his firm expression.

"Is she English?" the army officer asked.

"Not likely. She flies the Dutch ancient and is Dutch-built," Edward responded distractedly. "Frankly, it's a bit curious that she's flying colors at all, unless she hoisted them recently, perhaps to identify herself to a cruiser, or even to us. But colors don't mean much these days. Your opinion, Captain Cronow?"

"A damned brandy barrel, a butter box, a Hogen Mogen. I fought in the Dutch wars; I can spot 'em leagues farther in the offing than this. If we still had wars with the Dutch, I'd swear she was a Holland caper. Times change; now we've a Dutch king of England." Cronow shook his head, then snorted deeply. "But no matter what the eyes see, gentlemen, my nose smells a foul-bottomed cruising French whore in Dutch skirts."

"She's as big as a large fourth rate; forty, fifty or more great guns, although it's hard to tell at this angle," Edward commented. "Maybe six hundred tons. The French would call her a frigate of the first order. She's as powerful as a cruiser gets; let's hope she's not one."

He surveyed her through the glass in detail, from sprit to rudder, from truck to waterline.

Cronow's right, his instincts told him, *she's a Dutch prize made into a French cruiser.*

"Could the French use a Dutch ship?" asked Lieutenant Fielding.

"Easily," Edward replied. "A ship's origin means as little as her colors. This one I think is a privateer, though, not a ship of the French navy; not that there's not much difference. King Louis is lately in the habit of lending men-of-war to investors—*armateurs*, the French call them—as privateers."

"The merchant captains who anchor in Kinsale complain of them often."

"And rightly so," Edward replied, "they're bold bastards. It doesn't matter that we've trapped the bulk of the French navy in its harbors; French privateers still slip out and wreak havoc, all for purpose of riches under the guise of patriotism. And then you have the Jacobite cruisers, too: Irish, Scots, and English who sail for Prince James."

Cronow, intently watching the approaching ship through his own spyglass, cleared his throat and spoke slowly. "Captain MacNaughton, you're an old friend and the only man I would trust to advise me in chase or fight. What do you make of this ship standing toward us?"

Edward did not reply immediately. Instead, he squinted again through his spyglass, then brought it down, rubbed his eyes, and took two deep, slow breaths. The motion of the *Peregrinator*, combined with the magnified view of the pitching and rolling ship in the distance, was starting to wear his sea legs down. He let his breath out slowly. Something about the dark ship disturbed him. She looked familiar, but he was certain he did not recognize her. There was an eerie directness about the ship, as if she felt she could sail with impunity anywhere she chose. *A figment of last night's dreams*, he thought, *still drifting in my head.*

"To be safe," he replied finally, "we've no choice but to run for Kinsale. Now."

"Aye, agreed, God be damned," Cronow said with sharp resignation. "We've plenty of sea room, but she's close by and has the weather of us, plus we're leaky and a bit foul. She'll just overhaul us if we show our heels to sea, and I won't risk my ship on the slim hope of disappearing into the weather again. Aye, we'll shape our course direct for Kinsale and hope Fortune favors us one more time."

"Before I left Kinsale for London, the Corporation had petitioned for a forty-gun guard ship to cruise between here and Saltash to keep privateers at bay," Lieutenant Fielding remarked hopefully.

Cronow spat. "The Corporation wants a guard ship but won't pay for one, so don't hold your breath, Lieutenant." He turned to Edward and cocked his head at the dark ship. "And if *you* commanded this stuck-up concubine who pretends to ignore us, Captain MacNaughton, what would you?"

Edward reflected for a moment. "If I were in her captain's place, I'd keep my course and do nothing suspicious. I might even make a signal for you to lie by and hail as if I needed help, a pilot for example, hoping the ruse would take. In any case, I'd wait until you made your next tack. That way I could close as much distance as possible. Then, when you're on the larboard tack, I'd suddenly stand to your forefoot with the wind off my beam and all the sail I could safely bear, and take you just before you reach Kinsale."

"We can't fight her," Cronow grumbled.

"Not in the conventional way," Edward replied, "but she can't open her lower lee ports in this sea, and they're the ones we really need to worry about. And she can't board us; the sea runs too high. On the other hand, she probably won't need to fire any of her guns. She can simply overhaul us, show us her upper teeth, and send a boat to board us."

"And blast us to hell with her upper battery and muskets if we don't strike," Cronow stated matter-of-factly. "Damnation, even her quarterdeck guns are a match for our broadside. Closed quarters will do no good; we're not stout enough to withstand her guns."

Edward lowered his spyglass. Cronow was silent as he looked back and forth from the dark ship to the harbor entrance to the lee shores and the islets off Oysterhaven nearby. He stared at the sky, then turned to his mate, raised his eyebrows, and rubbed his beard.

"Goddammit," he muttered with venom, then barked, "Mr. Foxcraft, let's find out what she is. Call the hands and standby to wear ship!"

"All hands on deck! Up every man! Smartly now!" the mate bellowed.

Within seconds the crew was mustered, the mate's years of practice with a rattan cane having raised many a welt on laggard shoulders.

"Standby to wear ship!" Foxcraft bellowed.

Lieutenant Fielding turned to Edward, not wishing to disturb the ship's captain. "Can you explain what we're doing, sir?"

"We're changing course," Edward said, as he passed his spyglass to the officer. "To 'wear ship' means we're making a long turn away from the wind to put the ship onto the larboard tack. This has advantages in our circumstances, but they're dangerous advantages. With this leaky ship and these seas, it's safer than tacking through the wind, which is the short and usually best way. And by changing course now we can head toward the harbor mouth *and* discover the unknown ship's intentions. But there's the danger that our leeway might put us on the Bulman rocks. Still, I think the advantages outweigh the dangers: if this ship means to take us, she'll have to change course when we do. We're forcing her hand."

"So we're between Scylla and Charybdis?"

"Captured or shipwrecked, if we're not careful," Edward replied matter-of-factly. "But we'll be careful," he continued with a smile.

"There's always Fortune."

"Aye, a grand goddess who proves the proverb."

"Which?"

"Hope for the best, but assume the worst and prepare accordingly."

"That's a fighting man's revision of the proverb, I think," the lieutenant said with a small grin.

Hands manned the braces. Edward took back his proffered spyglass and watched the dark ship. He paid little attention to the activity on deck.

The captain's commands came quickly. The crew responded eagerly, and soon the small ship was sailing as near to the wind as she could, larboard tacks aboard, her course toward the harbor mouth. Meanwhile, Edward saw nothing to indicate the unknown ship might chase the *Peregrinator*.

But we'll see, he thought.

Nothing.

The dark ship sailed her course.

Cronow glanced aloft, sniffed the air, and nodded his head. "I smell a stiff gale, Mr. Foxcraft; it over-blows no more. Heave out the tops'ls, reefed. If we can keep out of range a bit longer she might not think it worth the risk to come this close to the coast."

The mate sent hands aloft, and all went well until the fore topsail weather sheet parted as the yard was hoisted to set the sail, sounding like a musket shot and leaving the weather clew of the sail flapping out of control. Cronow cursed, Foxcraft shouted: there was enough ice in each man's voice to shiver any man's spine.

"Clew up the tops'l, you damn'd jackanapes!" came one shout, then, after the crew backed the sail, lowered the yard, and got the canvas under control, came another: "Splice the sheet and be quick about it, damn you all!"

The ship was soon orderly again in its disorder.

Edward had largely ignored the mysterious vessel during the commotion on deck and aloft, but now turned his attention to it again. *Here she comes.*

The dark ship changed course. A long puff of whitish smoke appeared from one of the quarterdeck guns, followed a few seconds later by the sound of a distant cannon, un-shotted, reverberating over the water.

French bastard! he thought, his jaw tense.

"Damn!" cursed Cronow. "A change of course and a signal, as you predicted."

"Aye. She *could* be a Dutchman looking for a pilot, but I'll bet you my share of a Manila galleon she's French and wants us for a prize."

"If so, Captain MacNaughton, you'll likely arrive in Ireland later than the rest of us. You look like better surety than anyone else aboard," Cronow said, with a grim gallows grin. Edward doubted, though, that the owners would give a damn about ransoming him, or even the ship's captain for that matter. "Shall we eat then?" Cronow continued, now nonchalant. "We've time before she comes in range, and there's little else we can do at the moment."

He turned to the helmsman: "Have a care! Touch the wind and wear no more; we don't want to run aground on the Bulman rocks and become wreck-goods for the Irish!"

And then to Foxcraft: "Have the crew eat quickly in their watches, and call me immediately if she does anything other than sail her present course!" And in a low voice: "And keep an eye on the crew!"

"We have time to eat?" Lieutenant Fielding asked Edward.

"Aye, plenty of time, even for a short chase like this one. That's the thing about chases at sea: lots of waiting, requiring lots of patience. It can take all day sometimes, or even days. Skill and a good ship are vital, but Fortune loves a contest too, so you can never be entirely certain how it will end. Probably a lot like a siege on land, waiting and waiting until it's time to fight."

Fielding nodded his understanding; he'd had experience of sieges.

Edward, Cronow, and Fielding ate quickly in the 'great

cabin'—actually a very small one which could barely seat six at the table—aft of the steerage. They discussed the peripherals of war at sea: lost cargoes and high insurance rates, prizes and privateers and impressed seamen; they spoke hardly at all of the approaching French privateer. Parson Waters snored loudly next door, having, as the seamen put it, returned to his blankets to pray in his sleep as soon as he realized an enemy was nearby. The ensign, tossed back into his cradle by a pair of grumbling seamen, snored loudly too.

Edward's hopes rose when the three returned to the quarterdeck, for the privateer was not sailing as well as he thought she would. She had surely been too long at sea; her bottom must be covered with enough weed, barnacle, and worm to strip some speed from her.

We might yet outsail her, Edward hoped cautiously.

Then to his dismay she shook the reefs from her courses and hove out her topsails. He watched the main and fore topsails billow and the dark ship heel even more. If she could carry this canvas in the present winds, he realized, she would surely overtake them.

"Do you mind, Captain Cronow, if I look at your guns?" Edward asked.

"They're yours, sir! You're as fine a gunner as I've ever seen, and we're too small to ship our own. Our first mate does what he can; he was a gunner's mate once. Mr. Foxcraft, give Captain MacNaughton any assistance he requires! We may need the great guns, and he's the best man I know to command them."

Edward left the quarterdeck to examine the guns, known more commonly as cannon to lubbers and soldiers, in the waist. A distant observer would see eight, but only four were real. The others were fashioned of wood, fake barrels on fake carriages. The real guns were a pair each of old iron minions and falcons anciently cast during the reigns of Elizabeth and James I. Of roughly three and two-and-a-half pound shot respectively, they were too small to do any real damage, except to sails and rigging, or to men at close range.

Joseph Foxcraft looked quizzically at Edward, smiled wryly, and then looked at the captain.

"So we're hunting Goliath today? Well, my guns will sling a small shot or two."

The mate, born to an English father and Genoese mother, had a pragmatic, if at times sarcastic, optimism that Edward admired.

"With the Captain's permission, then," Edward said, not looking at him but at the French ship, "I'd like to let fly a few times. We might part a stay and discourage him from bothering us so close to a rocky lee shore. What shot do you keep in your lockers, Mr. Foxcraft?"

"Plenty of small shot, partridge and burrel that is, plus a fair amount of bar, and maybe a dozen or two cast double-head. We've a few dozen round shot also, not that they're much use in these guns, except maybe against a small, thin-hulled privateer at pointblank."

"We'll use the minion just abaft the main mast; it should be the most stable of the two larboard guns," Edward stated matter-of-factly. "We'll let fly a few times with the double-head or bar, and if we don't escape we'll tell the French captain we were just firing a badly pointed salute and hope he has a sense of humor."

"*Us* firing on *him* will make him laugh. Hell, he might die laughing and save us all," Foxcraft noted wryly, then looked at Captain Cronow.

"Make ready the ship, Mr. Foxcraft," the captain said.

"A clear ship! A clear ship for engaging! All hands to quarters!" Foxcraft shouted sharply.

He assigned a gang of four seamen to work as a gun crew,

while the second mate and the rest of the small crew scrambled to make the ship clear for a fight.

The gun crew quickly cast off lashings and began positioning the designated gun, which had been secured alongside the bulwarks, in line with its gunport. They struck open the port lid, which had been wedged shut with oakum, and they brought loading and firing tools up from the gunner's store. On Edward's order, because he wanted a fresh cartridge in the gun and different shot, they drew the tallowed tomkin, or plug, from the mouth of the gun, drew wad, shot, another wad, and the old powder cartridge from the bore, removed the lead apron, and drew the waxed oakum fid from the vent. The gun crew cleaned the vent, checked the breech rope and training tackles for wear, and greased the carriage trucks.

And there was still more to do. They moved shot from the bulwark locker to a rope garland on deck near the gun, double-checked the caliber of the shot by measuring it against a shot gauge and comparing it with the roman numeral III painted above the gun port, hung a wad-net filled with wads nearby, and placed a linstock in one of several notches cut for the purpose into the rim of a small tub filled with a couple inches of sand to catch embers. Close by the gun, they placed a large tub of water to wet a swab and cool the gun if it got too hot, unlikely as this was today, and one more amidships, with blankets next to it, in case of fire. Edward ordered the crew not to reload the gun until he had decided which shot to use.

Clearing the ship was time-consuming for the small crew, even augmented as it was by the two navy wives who had rushed on deck as soon as they heard the order to make a clear ship. Both had seen action aboard the ships their husbands served on: they had carried cartridges, helped serve guns, loaded muskets, and assisted the sea surgeon. Captain Cronow's opinion of women was offset by his pragmatism, and any hand lent in battle was a hand well-received.

Edward held a similar view. Even so, he could not always suppress the superstition, central to his philosophy, that women and Fortune went hand-in-hand. He hoped the women on deck would incline the goddess toward the *Peregrinator's* cause and not turn out to be, as some seamen believed they were, bad omens.

Edward looked the gun over carefully when the mate and his crew finished readying it for its furious purpose. It was in better condition than he had deemed upon first glance; but he wondered about its accuracy and whether any of the crew had fired it enough to become familiar with its peculiarities.

"Don't worry, sir, I've inspected all my guns for honeycombs and flaws. They're old, but they won't blow up in our faces, and this minion is a fair piece," Foxcraft said, noticing his concern.

"She'll be in range soon," Cronow called over, as he grabbed the ship's boy by the collar. "Captain MacNaughton, will you need some brandy?"

"Aye, for the crew."

"Jack, my lad," Cronow ordered, releasing the boy, "bring out a pannikin of brandy and sugar. And if you drink any of it before it's issued, I'll flay your hide with the salt eel!"

The boy, indentured to the captain but happy to have such a tolerant master, grinned and ran below.

The dark ship slowly, insistently, gained on the smaller vessel. Then, gone was the Dutch ensign, and soon in the wind flew the white ensign, jack, and pennant of France.

"Aye, look at the white rags Monsoor calls his fighting colors," sneered Cronow.

"He means to attack, then?" asked the lieutenant of no one in particular.

"It's their signal for us to yield," Edward said. "At least he's being lawful and honest, raising his true colors before he shoots at us."

A gun boomed in the distance, loaded this time with a round shot, intended as a warning, which splashed and drowned in the sea.

"And this is his way of telling us that he'll shatter our hull and rigging if we don't."

So much, thought Edward, *for my venture.*

Part of his mind remained calm and analytical, calculating the distances between the vessels and their relative speeds. He considered the likelihood of doing any significant damage to the Frenchman's rigging before the small ship was forced to strike —probably be after the Frenchman fired his first real shot at them. There was no point in angering the French crew by firing in desperation. A few shots would satisfy both honor and sense.

But in another part of his mind, a storm raged.

God's blood, why of all days, just at the point of completing this tedious voyage, does Fortune send her here? So close, dammit, I was so close!

First a foolish *rencontre* in Bristol and now this, as if Fortune were toying with him. He had business in Ireland, money to raise his venture. For months he had worked for this, months of trying to break out of the tedium his life had seemed reduced to, months of taking reduced positions while he planned the forthcoming venture, not to mention the time waiting for the prohibition on his travel to the colonies to be lifted. Nothing infuriated him as much as being so close to an object of desire, so close he could smell it, see it, almost touch it, to have it remain tantalizingly just out of reach. He thrust his frustration into one of the small rooms in a distant corner of his mind and concentrated solely on the immediate situation, step by step, moment by moment. The past was useful right now only for the experience it provided, and the future did not exist.

"What?" he said, glancing down at Jack, who was trying to get his attention.

"Sorry, sir, I only asked if you'd want your sword. I'll fetch it for you."

"Aye, do that, though it won't be that kind of fight. No use hiding the sword if we strike; they'll strip us and search the ship anyway. Fetch my backsword, not the smallsword, if you please. And my cartridge box, horn, pistols, and buccaneer gun too. You can't miss it, it's longer even than I'm tall. You still have the key?" The boy drew it from beneath his shirt where it hung from a length of tarred marline. "Good. Oh, dammit, bring my leather wallet too. And while you're below, tell the passengers not to come on deck unless the ship is sinking."

"Aye, sir."

Edward would not go below himself, for fear his absence might be construed as cowardice. Within minutes the boy returned, comically overloaded with weapons. Edward immediately took the leather wallet with the confidential letters inside and tucked it beneath his waistcoat.

"I'll pitch it into the sea if the French capture us," he told the boy. Of the arms, he took the backsword first, the boy cocking his head sideways as he did. "What's the matter, lad? Surely you've seen a backsword before."

"Not like that."

"It's Highland, and a bit unusual at that."

"It has devil faces on the hilt."

"Two of something with horns, for sure. I imagine one is David Jones, that Scottish sea devil who rules hell under the oceans, and the other Old Nick himself, who rules hell under the earth." The boy frowned. "Better two devils in one's own hand than one in the enemy's, don't you think?"

The boy smiled. "Why do you wear it like that?"

"Like what?"

"Over your shoulder."

"It's a baldric. You've never seen one?"

"Only on soldiers on horses."

"Well, when I was a lad your age they were common everywhere. Now mostly only Highlanders and horse soldiers wear them." Edward re-tied his Scots plaid sash over the baldric. "To let them know who I am," he said with a wink, "and also to keep my Ferrara—that's what I call my sword—from bouncing about."

He buckled a belt and cartridge box over his sash, keeping the box to his left front. "Now the pistols, young sir, the large ones. You know how to prime a pistol?" The boy nodded. "Good. Take my horn and prime the small ones, if you please." The boy did as he was told. "Now, tuck them into your belt like this, use the belt-hooks, here, on your right, one in front, one on the side, locks against your body, butts pointing left, half-cock only." Jack did as he was told, then stood tall, one hand on each pistol butt. "Good lad! Now you're ready for a fight, buccaneer fashion."

The boy grinned proudly.

Edward leaned over and whispered, "Do you see how some of your crew are looking really scared, like they might run below?"

"Yessir!" the boy whispered back.

"Well, men like that might run, but they also might mutiny and try to take over the ship. If anything happens, stand by your captain on the quarterdeck. Understand?"

"Aye, sir," he replied, wide-eyed yet resolutely.

"Good lad."

Edward stood up straight. With his left hand on the fish-skin grip of his basket-hilted Highland backsword, his right resting on the butt of one of his pistols, and the boy imitating him at his side, he watched the dark deadly ship approach.

Chapter 6

I was still in hopes some lucky Accident
would facilitate our Escape...
—Capt. Nat. Uring, *Voyages and Travels*, 1727

"She's well within range," Lieutenant Fielding noted to Edward, once more inspecting the enemy ship through his spyglass. The lieutenant, following Edward's example, had also armed himself.

"If this were land, aye, but not at sea," Edward replied. "We like to fight close, that way we can shoot straight at our target. This privateer captain will wait until his ship is within pointblank range of the guns on her upper deck. They're probably eight pounders; say three hundred yards. We don't waste shot at sea by firing at longer ranges. I prefer to fight even closer, at pistol shot: yardarm to yardarm we call it."

"Not today, I hope."

"It's quite something to experience, Lieutenant, but no, not today. We wouldn't survive a single broadside. We'll have a short running fight, nothing more."

Edward subtly pointed out a crewman casting his eyes toward a scuttle that led below, and then nodded in the direction of three nervous seamen who had the look of a cabal among them.

"They know as well as we do," he resumed, "that we're

between Scylla and Charybdis, as you put it, and they'll prefer being taken prisoner to being killed or maimed in a fight they think we can't win, or drowned in a shipwreck trying to escape a fight. If there's a mutiny, it'll probably be of men fleeing below deck or refusing to obey orders, and we'll see it coming. But if the crew tries to take over the ship and surrender to our enemy, they'll do it suddenly when we're distracted. Your best place will be on the quarterdeck, the high ground so to speak. Can you rouse the ensign to join you?"

"He's unconscious."

"My fault, I expect."

"I'm sure he deserved it; of his own doing he's not a popular young man. Just do me a favor and don't kill him until we're back in Ireland; I'm under orders to keep him out of trouble until then. If I weren't under this obligation, I'd have let him risk his neck in a duel with a damned lawyer in London. But the parson's up, I heard him praying frantically in his cabin."

"The more the merrier," Edward said dryly. "We can shove a blunderbuss in his hands if necessary."

The crack of a second shotted gun was followed by the captain's cursing.

"Dammit, Mrs. Hardy, I need no more petticoats on deck! You and your maid go back below, now!"

"I have come to help, sir!" she shouted back, followed by a phrase or two in Dutch.

"Madam, you're a damned fool in a dress!"

"Maybe, but I'm no coward!" Mrs. Hardy retorted, then proved she could curse as well as any seaman in English or Dutch. "If those two women can be on deck, then so can I! I'm no weak vessel!"

"Madam, they've been in action before; they can help us fight this ship. You and your maid, however, are useless to us. To be plain, the only Dutch I want to see on deck right now is

'Dutch courage!'"

"That, sir, is a slander! A dishonorable calumny! The Dutch don't need brandy to make them brave, but I guess the English do! You should name it 'English courage' instead, that brandy and rum you drink to make you brave!"

"I fought in the Dutch wars, madam! Do you remember who came out on top?"

"I remember the Dutch fleet in the Medway!" she swore back.

"A clean palpable hit," Edward said aside to Fielding.

"Hell of a woman," replied the lieutenant. "Are you married?"

"No, my present philosophy won't permit it."

"I hear she's wealthy."

"I've a theory that until I've made my fortune I need to steer clear of fortune-hunting women and of hunting women for their fortunes," Edward said, watching the crew carefully to make sure any likely mutineers did not attempt to seize the ship while Cronow and Mrs. Hardy argued.

"Maybe Captain Cronow should marry her, then."

"He's already got a wife. You?"

"Yes. And two mistresses."

"You live dangerously."

"Indeed? So says the man who's about to fire on a ship that outnumbers us by how much?"

"At least twenty-five to one in guns, probably fifty to one in weight of broadside, and at least a dozen to one in men, probably more."

"And you think wooing a rich widow is too dangerous? It's a strange philosophy of yours, Captain MacNaughton," the lieutenant said, shaking his head in friendly disbelief.

"It's a matter of perspective, Lieutenant. When we fire on the privateer, she can only bring her two bow chasers to bear.

In other words, the odds right now are much more even than they appear. On the other hand, Mrs. Hardy will have the odds greatly in her favor in every circumstance. You can see that Cronow has her desperately out-gunned and out-manned, yet she may well carry the day. Further, to woo Mrs. Hardy for her fortune might make Fortune herself angry; to woo her for her beauty might make Fortune jealous; yet to woo Fortune—to follow the sea as a gentleman of fortune—while also wooing Mrs. Hardy might make the widow angry and jealous."

"I wish we had more time to discuss your philosophy and its curious logic, Captain. Perhaps when victory is ours; or if not, then in a French prison. Good luck; may your aim be true!"

As soon as Lieutenant Fielding took his place on the quarterdeck, Mrs. Hardy, red in the face, strode three steps to Edward and struck a commanding pose, hands on hips.

"Captain MacNaughton, will you be my champion in my dispute with this Julius Caesar on the quarterdeck?"

"Mrs. Hardy, I can't, because I happen to agree with him. You must obey his orders and go below," he said politely, suppressing a grin. "There's nothing you can do here, and it will be quite dangerous soon."

She made no reply, suddenly busy shoving her upset maid to the rail while berating her.

"The leeward rail!" Edward said sharply. Seeing Mrs. Hardy's questioning look, he stepped quickly to the maid, grasped her around the waist, and carried her on his hip to the opposite rail, where he held her so she would not fall overboard. The ship rolled suddenly over the crest of an unusually large swell, dipping the maid's head and shoulders in the sea and soaking her head to thigh as seasickness got the better of her. Edward did not escape a partial drenching either, but ignored it, concerned only with the priming of his pistols.

"I'm soaked!" Maria cried, "I'll catch my death of this cold, wet ocean!"

"But at least you'll have had a bath," Edward noted wryly. "Mrs. Hardy, take your maid below now, and remain there!"

Gone was any pretense of being polite.

"I will not! Let her make her own way below! If nothing else, I'll take charge of the brandy—by God, I'll show the lot of you what Dutch courage is! I *will* do something useful here, sir!"

Edward glanced knowingly at Lieutenant Fielding, as if to emphasize that he had just proved the point of his philosophy.

"Goddamn you, woman," Cronow shouted, "stay if you please, for I've no men to spare to carry you below, but I swear to you that if a bullet takes off your head, I'll by God have one of your maids swab your blood from the deck, for I won't waste one of my jackanapes on it!"

Edward firmly moved Maria, her voice trembling with fear and cold, yet her eye alluring, toward the hatch and told her to go below and dry off, then turned his attention once more to his duty.

"The gun is yours, Captain MacNaughton," Cronow said finally, glad to avoid further address to the doughty widow.

"Thank you, sir," he replied, then, noting with surprise that the parson was now on deck too, said, with just a touch more honesty than sarcasm, "Ah, God's servant is finally here. You impress me, sir. I feared you would leave us entirely to ourselves to plead our case with God, sea, and enemy."

"God will always send me where I am needed," he replied with timid dignity. His knuckles were white, like bleached bones, where he gripped the rail. He could not take his eyes off the large French ship.

"Doubtless," Edward replied. Likely the man had never been in harm's way before.

"Let us pray—"

"Damn your prayers, sir!" bellowed Cronow. "Or keep them

to yourself! My crew have bloody work ahead and need no distractions! David never fought a more one-sided battle than we do against this Goliath today, and God helps those who help themselves, or so I hear you black-coated, dark-visaged, Malmsey-nosed soul-drivers preach! I'll have no public prayer aboard my ship! When the wind is good it's not needed, and when it's storm or battle my crew have more important things to listen to, namely me!"

"In a calm, pray or pick oakum," Edward intoned, quoting a well-known seaman's proverb, "but in a storm, serve God, serve devil. Pray as you please, sir, no man will fault you for that. But do so in silence, for the crew have duty enough to occupy them." A fair number of seamen were in practice an agnostic lot, religious only in ceremony; others, though, were quite devout.

He joined the gun crew in the waist to supervise a business he knew all too well. The seamen under his command grumbled to themselves about the parson, muttering that he was a Jonah and all would be better off if he were thrown overboard to test his standing with God. That the parson considered the seamen a pack of heathen jackanapes had not gone unnoticed.

Edward felt much the same as they did. He preferred to rely upon courage, skill, and intellect, and upon the demonstrable reality that Fortune usually favors the bold, although she may later seize payment in return; thus his philosophy of leaving her, and her messengers, out of his plans as much as possible.

The mate turned to make his report to Edward, linstock with lighted match in hand.

"'Tis loaded with double-head, and my gang have drunk their spirits and are ready to fight."

"Very well. Perhaps 'Dutch courage'—your pardon, Mrs. Hardy—will see us through." Edward called to the captain on the quarterdeck. "Your permission to fire when I please?"

"Aye, sir, aye. May your aim be true, God willing, and if not, let the Devil himself take up our cause."

"Captain Cronow, I object to your impertinent wish!" ejaculated Parson Waters. "It's bad enough that you allow women on deck to do a man's work! And one of them a papist, too!"

"Shut up, sir," replied Cronow. "Today I'll accept help from any who offer it, women, papists, Jews or David Jones, or even that God-damn'd Old Roger himself. If you don't want to meet *that* soul-buggering, cleft-footed Leviathan today, then make your prayers heard—but silently!"

"Mr. Foxcraft, let's see how this wandering sea maid can claw a buxom vixen," Edward said. "The range is more than pointblank, but it won't be a waste of powder, since we're shooting at her rigging. Point at her foretop, perhaps we'll part a stay or put her topmast by the board."

He stood back to give the mate room to do his job. His gun crew was not as well-trained as one aboard a man-of-war or privateer, so he gave commands for each step.

"Handle your crow and handspike!" he ordered.

Two of his gun crew stood by with the levers.

"Haul up the port and belay it!"

One seaman shoved the port lid open with a handspike, while another hauled on the port rope until the port was fully open, then belayed the line. The next commands and actions came quickly:

"Run out the gun!"

"Lay the gun to pass in the port!"

"Point to dismast!"

One of the gun crew employed a hand-crow lever to raise the breech as another drew the quoin aft. A third then used a wooden handspike to shift the carriage slightly, per the mate's signals. Here the mate took over. He blew on the lighted end of the match, removed the lead apron over the vent, and waited to time the roll of the ship for the required elevation, then stepped back and placed the match to the small train of crushed gunpowder that led from the base ring to the vent.

The powder flashed into the vent, then again like a vertical blade of flame. The gun made a loud, ear-ringing Crack! as it jumped back, spewing forth flame, smoke, and iron. The carriage creaked and whined as the breech rope took the strain, and the wind blew a cloud of thick, whitish smoke across the deck. It was a moment before Edward could follow the shot. Unfortunately, an errant swell had struck the ship just as the gun fired, sending the shot wide. From the dark ship came the sounds of jeering Frenchmen.

"God's blood! Ream me with a marling spike!" the mate cursed. "Begging your pardon, sir, but I look the fool now. It won't happen again."

Edward sniffed the air, breathed deeply, and smiled. He liked the smell of burned powder, and could not comprehend those who did not.

"You need make no apology, Mr. Foxcraft. Try again."

"Aye, sir." Foxcraft waited as his gang reloaded the minion. Again, he timed the roll. Again, he fired the cannon. It was a fair shot, but it did no apparent damage and the ship sailed on.

"You've let some daylight through her mains'l, but that won't stop her. Make ready your piece, we'll fire at least twice more," he ordered.

Foxcraft reloaded the minion himself this time and again gave fire.

Again, a hit.

And again, nothing.

Edward was not surprised. Indeed, he would have been amazed if they did do any significant damage. Ships of any size could take quite a battering to hull or rigging before being distressed, much less put out of commission. He put his perspective glass to his eye and could see the French crew jeering, laughing at them, waiting to pounce, a cat playing with a mouse until she tires and crushes its skull in her mouth.

The *Peregrinator* fired her fifth shot. Almost immediately one of the Frenchman's chase pieces returned the compliment. Edward caught a glimpse of a black speck, then his hand flew up from the rail, numb. The eight pound shot had passed through the bulwark beneath the rail where his hand had rested and was lodged in the opposite side. His heart pounded, excitement tinged with fear surged through his body. He made a fist; his hand was stiff, but had no broken skin, no blood. His fingers and wrist still worked, although painfully. He pretended nothing had happened. Several of the crew looked surprised, and several more were unaware anything had happened. Splinters lay across the deck and a jagged bit of wood jutted out from the bulwark an inch from his groin. He took a deep breath, held it, let it out slowly. It was always good to be reminded that this was no game.

"Captain," he called, "with your permission I'd like to salute the Monsoor twice more."

"Twice more, then I put up the helm if nothing comes of it."

From aloft came a sudden cry: "A sail! A sail! From Kinsale! Nay, two sail of ships!"

Immediately Edward put his glass to his eye and made out topsails. Men-of-war, surely! Lookouts at Charles Fort would have alerted any navy ship in harbor. But his elation quickly passed, as did the crew's. It would take too long for the men-of-war to sally from Kinsale.

"Ne'er mind them!" barked Cronow. "They can't help us—can't you see which way the wind blows? But stick to your quarters, my hearts!"

By now the French privateer was within one hundred and

fifty yards. Within minutes, French musketeers would begin firing their long-barreled *fusils boucaniers,* and it would take only a volley or two to clear the *Peregrinator's* decks. That way, they could capture the valuable prize with hull intact—mostly— and full cargo.

"Mr. Foxcraft, this time give fire when your piece comes to bear with the foretop," Edward ordered, as he climbed onto the gunwale, steadying himself with one of the main shrouds. He wanted to get a better look at the privateer, to find any conceivable way out of their predicament.

"Aye, sir," Foxcraft replied.

"Bougres anglais!" Edward heard, among other vulgar insults as the French crewmen brandished muskets, boarding pikes, pistols, and cutlasses. Their commander waved with his sword, an order to strike amain—to lower topsails as a signal of submission, of surrender. Out of habit Edward drew his backsword and waved it in defiance. By way of reply, a musket ball whizzed over his head, then another. One bounced off the mainmast with a thunk!, then off a yard and ricocheted again off some unknown spar above, like a lead die rattled in a wooden pannikin. His pride would not let him abandon his post on the gunwale, even though he was making himself an obvious target. He must wait a minute or two to prove he scorned their shot. He swore he could hear the pounding of his heart.

On the heels of the musket shots came another round shot. It struck the bow and sent splinters across the deck, but both shot and splinters missed everyone—good Fortune, indeed. Splinters accounted for more injuries in battle than did the round shot that caused them, but lubbers seldom believed this until they witnessed it.

Edward wondered why the privateer was not firing at the rigging instead, then thought he shouldn't question Fortune too closely. Quite possibly, the privateer's captain realized that if he shattered the *Peregrinator's* rigging, he wouldn't be able to repair it before the sallying English men-of-war appeared on scene.

Some of the crew now looked frightened to the point of inaction, or worse, of fleeing below the deck. Edward glanced around for the parson, intending to order him to say a bold prayer aloud or, barring that, sending him below to rid the deck of a perceived Jonah. But the soul driver, as the seamen called him, had already retreated below to the hold, probably after the first round shot struck the ship.

"Follow my commands and load the gun, Goddamn your eyes!" the mate shouted suddenly at his gang.

Edward looked down at the gun crew, then dropped to the deck, his left hand instinctively seeking the butt of one of the pistols hooked in his belt. He kept his sword in hand, but let the back of its blade rest casually against his right shoulder.

Three of the crew stood mutinous, refusing all orders; most of the rest looked to be unsure which side they might take.

At least none has yet laid hand to their weapons, Edward thought.

Cronow cursed and drew a pistol from his belt and drew it to full cock, while Foxcraft picked up a hand crow from where it lay on the deck and brandished it menacingly. There was no doubt Cronow would use his pistols if necessary, and surely the crew knew that the mate had no compunction against crushing heads with the hand crow. After all, wasn't his nickname Kill Turk, earned defending a Portuguese slave ship against a Sally rover hoping to turn the crew of white slavers into white slaves? Foxcraft, cutlass in one hand and hand crow in the other, had cut and bludgeoned a dozen Barbary corsairs down as they tried to board.

"Avast!" Edward ordered. "At least for the moment, Mr. Foxcraft. Cracked skulls can't man guns, and these men didn't sign aboard to fight a fifty-gun privateer."

He feared the blatant threat of force might cow these men into complete inaction, and inspire others likewise, long enough for the Frenchman to capture them all. Swift persuasion, backed by the veiled threat of force was needed, and quickly. He opened his mouth, but he was cut off by one of the navy wives.

"And you call yourself English seamen!" she sneered at the men whose fear had overcome their alcoholic courage. "Jack tars, you pretend to be! By God, a crew of women could give that poxy French whore more cause for fear than you have! Stand off, then, you cowardly hussies, and leave the women to make the slaughter!"

The men said nothing, their faces red.

"Here, lads," Edward said confidently, taking advantage of the pause. The woman's sneer had turned shame to anger, and now he wanted that anger aimed at the Frenchmen, and not at the women or officers. "What's this across the water but a Monsoor about to run himself aground and keep the wreck-mongers busy? Keep to your piece, we'll be no worse off for warming our hands on a gun barrel. Kinsale is in sight, a pair of English frigates venture forth to fight, and the *Peregrinator's* owners will reward you for your brave service."

His firm voice, combined with his height, martial appearance, and reputation, not to mention his one hand on a pistol butt and the other gripping a sword, topped by the woman's scorn, all aided by the menacing sight of Cronow, Foxcraft, and Fielding, quelled the immanent mutiny. Edward was pleased to note that the ship's boy was at Cronow's side, hands on pistols.

In spite of their fear, two of the three shamed men prepared to load the gun again. The third stood red-faced and unmoving, for the woman who had spoken had already seized the rope rammer from him and stood by to load the gun.

"Can't we sweep their forecastle?" she asked Edward militantly. "There's so many men there, we couldn't miss. Bar shot is what they liked to use on my husband's ship."

Edward smiled sympathetically. "Any other time I'd agree with you, but today we can't waste a shot. Killing a dozen French seamen won't stop their captain from chasing, and it might make things worse if they capture us. Still, let's make a change, as you suggest. Bar shot this time, Mr. Foxcraft," Edward ordered, "but keep pointing at the foretop." He picked up his long musket, loaded at the same time he had primed his pistols, and nodded to the woman using the rammer. "In honor of your suggestion."

He brought the musket to full cock, aimed, and fired. The two dozen French seaman massed on the forecastle all dropped to the deck.

Edward laughed and shouted to the crew. "See, they're not so brave, are they? Mr. Foxcraft, let's get this gun loaded!"

The mate, to ensure there was no skullduggery, picked up a load of bar shot himself, in this case three iron bars square in cross-section and "armed" with rope-yarn at each end. Under his close supervision the navy wife rammed charge, wad, bar shot, and wad home.

"Why don't you lay the gun this time, sir?" he suggested to Edward, who, having quickly reloaded his musket, set it aside, took the linstock, stepped forward, laid the gun carefully, blew on the match, removed the lead apron, checked to make sure all was clear to rear of the gun, timed the roll, and fired. But the shot, though another good one, was also another disappointment, the iron bars doing little more than ripping through the foretopsail. The gun crew loaded the final shot.

The privateer fired again, this time parting one of the larboard fore-shrouds.

"Pray louder in silence this time, damn you—if you please!"

Edward shouted before he remembered that the parson had retreated below. This was it, they must strike. The privateer crew would board, hopefully not too annoyed by the noble attempt at defense, and take possession of the ship in sight of the harbor, barely a mile from safety.

He laid the gun again, and the *Peregrinator* fired her final shot. Three iron bars spun into the rigging and sails of the foremast.

Damn you, fly true, hit something, part a stay!

Nothing.

"You may lash your gun, Mr. Foxcraft. My apologies, Captain Cronow."

Edward, in vain hope, fired his musket a second time, certain he knocked down a French seaman waving a cutlass. He set the gun aside, raised his spyglass, and stared at the Frenchman, furious disappointment in his chest. It had been a fair try, but no contest; it rankled that he had won at longer odds in the past, admittedly in situations reduced simply to win or die. That comparison did nothing to dispel his inner fury.

Wait.... There, French crewmen racing aloft, the topsail sheets veered! One of the bar shot had parted the foretopmast stay! The French ship immediately bore away, lowered both topsails, and steered before the wind to take the pressure off the foremast. Edward looked carefully at her stern as she changed course, for he wanted to remember this ship. Centered beneath her taffrail was the carved image of a black tulip.

The *Peregrinator* would escape after all. The privateer's rigging was otherwise little damaged, and in most circumstances she might still have captured her prey. But not today, not so close to a hostile lee shore with a foretopmast that might go by the board. A simple, small, sure victory had suddenly become much too expensive.

The crew of the *Peregrinator* jeered from the tops and the

rails at the retreating privateer, their fear changed to jubilation. Edward had one anxious moment more, wondering if the Frenchman might fire her upper battery out of spite. But the gun-ports remained closed.

"My compliments, Captain MacNaughton," said Lieutenant Fielding.

"Thank you, sir, but the credit belongs to Captain Cronow, his crew, these valiant ladies, and, much as I hate to say it, Fortune. And perhaps to the men-of-war in the offing as well."

"No, Mister MacNaughton," the parson interrupted, having returned to deck once he heard the cheers and realized they had escaped the Frenchman. "It was not Fortune, but God's Providence. O, how the mighty have fallen! O Lord, thy powerful arm hath smote thine enemies!"

Edward ignored both the parson's insulting use of Mister instead of Captain and his vacuous bombast.

Foxcraft rolled his eyes. "To hear him speak, we must have sunk the French fleet! Surely he was in command, too."

The mate's remark irritated the parson. "The wind, Mr. MacNaughton, look about you! God sends the wind to blow for England!" he responded, refusing to stoop to the level of a heathen seaman.

Edward could no longer ignore the man. "The wind, sir, blows for none but herself." He caught the Captain's eye. "May I buy some of your brandy and sugar for the crew?"

"You may not *buy* it, sir, but you may *have* as much as you please. Jack! Have the cook pour more brandy, tell him to light the fire hearth as soon as the deck is cleared of powder, tell him to heat the brandy and sugar, we have thirsty lads here! Take the anker of good Nantz brandy from my cabin this time. And good work," he yelled proudly at his crew, "good work, all of you, my hearts!"

His crew responded with three resounding "Huzzahs!"

which brought Mrs. Hardy's servants and son to the deck. Only the ensign remained absent.

Edward looked back one last time at the disappearing French privateer. His fingers tapped quickly on the rail, then paused abruptly.

With his spyglass he examined the small merchant-galley. Lost in a squall of rain during most of the chase, it had appeared again to windward of the privateer. There was little chance she could escape, given how close the two vessels were to each other. The privateer would soon be under full sail, and would surely set her sights on the new prey.

"The *Mary and Martha* Galley, Bristol," Cronow noted matter-of-factly. "By God, the Frenchman will have her instead; she'll not be able to escape in time. It'll be two hours at least before the frigates from Kinsale work their way across the bar. At least we'll be at anchor under the guns of Charles Fort before long."

From a distance the merchant-galley could be mistaken for the *Peregrinator*, even to her reefed topsails. Then, as Edward watched, she clewed up her fore topsail then hauled the sheets home again, as she had done earlier.

I'll be damned to hell! he thought as he grinned a strange grin of admiration, anger, and sheepishness. *A coincidence? Maybe...but maybe a signal!*

He watched back and forth as the privateer, still setting up her foretop stay, fired a gun across the bow of the *Mary and Martha*.

Of course that bastard privateer's gunnery was poor at first! he thought. *She wasn't trying to capture us—she thought we were the* Mary and Martha*!*

He smiled at the likely possibility of the French captain furious at the risks he had run by mistake. He put down his spyglass. Few would believe this tale. Instead, everyone would believe the unlikely story that a small leaky merchant-galley fought off a formidable fifty-odd gun privateer. It might even merit a line in the *London Gazette*. And why not? Everyone aboard had believed the fight to be a true one, and near the end of the chase it *had* been real.

Suddenly the French privateer bore away, leaving the *Mary and Martha* alone. For a moment Edward was perplexed: the ships sallying from Kinsale were still in the river. But soon the answer was apparent: out of the rain squall appeared an English man-of-war, colors flying, starboard broadside run out, surely drawn by the sounds of gunfire across the water.

"The *Shoreham*, by God," Cronow shouted. "I know her by her topsails. Only thirty-two guns, but she'll bugger this French bawd even if the frigates in the river can't get out in time."

Edward took two steps away from the rail and let out a deep breath. Only now did he realize how truly tired he was. Time to put away his sword and pistols, drink some brandy, celebrate with captain, crew, and passengers, then sleep and dream again. Perhaps in his dreams would come the closure he still needed? Their escape should have been enough to convince body and soul that they could rest now, but lingering questions of possible intrigue assailed him and would not let him relax.

Below he found the aft platform unusually quiet and, in a way, even clean. The cheers above had brought all topside, the widow's son and servant included. Much of the platform's filth had washed into the bilges when the ship took seawater over the deck and down the open hatchway. Fresh sea air had replaced the fetid atmosphere.

Hearing a small noise, a sniffle perhaps, he pulled open the canvas partitions of his cabin, and there in the cradle below his hammock he found the maid Maria, all shivers and giggles and winsome smiles.

"I thought you were on deck," Edward said.

"I was, but now I'm back. It's all over, then? We're safe?"

"We are. And soon we'll be at an anchor in Kinsale."

"And there we part ways."

"And there we part ways."

"I'm cold, Captain MacNaughton. Can you not help me?"

He smiled twice, first to himself, then to the waiting woman. She giggled again. Knowing full well the obligation he would be under to the demanding Mrs. Hardy—and wondering if it would have been the ensign here instead had he not offended her—he shook his head and stepped into his cabin anyway; and for the first time since he had come aboard he lay in the cradle, wrapped in arms, legs, and petticoats, in sweet lips and salty breasts, and earned more knocks and bruises in the narrow bed in ten minutes than the Irish Sea had been able to serve either of them in nearly a fortnight. By the time they finally timed their rhythm with that of the sea, they came almost together, she pulling him even tighter, he trying to withdraw that he might not leave her with child.

Their passions sown and reaped, they lay together for a few moments more, half-dressed and embarrassed in the intimate unfamiliarity that Hogarth, a few decades hence, would depict so well.

Edward knew he must soon return to the quarterdeck. He was likely missed already, and probably the object of various vulgar musings. And he would have to meet Mrs. Hardy's eye. No longer a bawd in the social or financial sense of the word, Mrs. Hardy still understood the *moments* in the lives of the persons around her, and would doubtless claim such a moment for herself at a more appropriate time and place, the thought of which did not displease him, even as he lay in the fatigues of fight and fornication. Maria had given him the physical release the day's events had so far denied him, and he likely gave her the same.

He rose, licked the salt from his lips, and buttoned his breeches while Maria arranged herself and scampered to her own cabin, asking him in a saucy voice to send her a bottle of *anything*. The intimate spell was broken; relations had returned to normal. Mrs. Hardy would quickly quash any of Maria's pert post-coital familiarity, and he returned to the quarterdeck feeling like a bit of a fool, albeit a much satisfied one.

The French privateer receded into the misty distance, and the *Mary and Martha* lay her course north.

"He must have a heart of oak and balls of brass!" muttered Michael O'Neal aboard the *Mary and Martha*.

He stared through his glass at the *Peregrinator* and at the tall man who had apparently commanded during the mock fight, and wondered what sort of fool had the nerve to fire his puny guns against *La Tulipe Noir* and come close to sending her foretopmast by the board!

He scanned the rest of the sea around him. The French privateer was now in full flight, having chosen the better part of valor. The *Shoreham* pursued, and the frigates from Kinsale had passed the river bar and would soon be in pursuit. From near the Old Head of Kinsale, a small fisher boat and its crew of sympathizers had earlier set a course for *La Tulipe Noir* to provide her captain with intelligence of the shipping in the harbor, but she'd fled at the sight of the *Shoreham*.

The *Peregrinator* tacked away from the dangerous lee shore, then soon again into the harbor. Darkness and the turn of the tide found her lying peacefully at anchor beneath the guns of Charles Fort, and Michael O'Neal landing the smugglers and their cargo ashore at Oysterhaven only a league away.

Chapter 7

Women are of the extremes,
either better or worse than men.
—La Bruyère, *Of Women,* 1691

The next morning found Edward MacNaughton at the *Peregrinator's* starboard rail, one hand gripping a shroud to steady himself even though the harbor was as flat as glass. The sea inside his head, however, pitched and rolled like the Bay of Biscay in a storm. *Too much damn' Sherry sack,* he thought. *I'd almost rather be seasick.*

"Ahoy there!" he called to a burly waterman not ten feet below, but got no answer. "Ahoy there, damn you! Is that cockleshell yours?"

After a few idle moments the waterman looked up. "Aye, Cap'n."

"Do you know me, or do you address everyone as Captain?" he barked, making his head hurt even more. *Hellfire, I know better than to drink that much!*

"Aye, sir, I know you. This morning the whole of Kinsale knows Cap'n Edward McNutt, the famous buccaneer."

"MacNaughton," Edward replied severely. He squinted against the sunlight, too bright after more than a dozen cloudy days at sea, not to mention for a hangover.

"Ah, indeed, Cap'n MacNorton it is."

"Jackanape," Edward muttered under his breath. "Will you row me to the quay?"

"Aye, sir, the ship's boy said you'd want a wherry."

"When do you shove off?"

"When you're ready, sir. The customs officers are staying aboard until the ship takes the tide; I can come back for them later."

"I'm ready now, I'll have a couple of seamen lower my baggage."

"Very well, Cap'n MacScot. Oh, almost forgot, I have a message: you're to meet Mistress O'Meary at the town square an hour or two before noon, her servants said, and they'll pick up your baggage at the quay. Oh, and you're to pick up a horse at the stable near Fryar's Gate."

"O'Meary?"

"Aye, from Ballyderreen, Sir William's manor, not far outside Kinsale."

"How will I know her?"

"Ah, she's a fine looking woman, rides a fine horse, always has a couple of fine fierce wolfhounds with her. A striking sight, you can't miss her. She's Sir William's ward, or his niece, or whatever he claims she is to him, if you take my meaning. Some say she's—"

"Watch your tongue."

"—wild Irish on the side, riding barefoot and astride on moonshiny nights doing wicked, unlawful things. It's not hard to imagine her kissing her saddle with—"

"Hold your tongue, waterman!"

"Aye, of course, Cap'n MacHighland, no offense intended. I figured you'd have a seaman's sense of such things, but I see now you're a gentleman of sorts, so in that case you should know that hardly a gentleman for miles around doesn't try to woo her and wed her. That's all I was saying—she's a handsome, propertied woman, that is if they don't take her tattered estate from her for treason."

"Treason?"

"She's Irish, there was a war, the Irish lost, that's reason enough. But marriage to the right man would save it, for sure. Are you a papist, Cap'n? If not, you should clean yourself up a bit if you want to stand a chance; you've got lots of competition. Right now you look a bit too salty and stink too much of tar to impress a lady. Rough night?"

Edward picked up a bottle of claret, two-thirds full, from where it sat on the rail. He tossed it to the waterman. "See if this will shut your mouth," he said lightly, but with enough of an edge to make the warning clear.

The waterman drew the cork and took a big swig. "Ah, thank you, Captain MacNaughton! I'll love you like a brother now. Share? You look like you could use some hair of the dog."

"I tried, it didn't work. Drink up, waterman."

A few minutes later, after saying goodbye to Captain Cronow, who was busy supervising preparations to break bulk and unlade some of the ship's cargo into a lighter, Edward pitched his riding boots into the boat below. Only a fool would wear the stiff leather footwear except on horseback, and anyone who wore it shipboard would be a laughingstock. He clambered nimbly over the side in spite of his hangover and the brace of pistols in their holsters hanging over his shoulder.

Edward surveyed the harbor and city as the swift wherry skimmed the surface at the hands of the skilled waterman, causing a grey seal—*rón mór* in Irish—to duck quickly beneath the water. He saw fisher-boats lying "at a grappling" and also tied up at the quays, waiting for the bell to sound so they could sell their catch to the joulters, or middlemen, for the law required that they first try to sell it to local residents. He knew they also sold their catch cheaply to the garrison at Charles

Fort. This bribe kept the fishermen from being pressed into the English navy, and kept the soldiers from foraging—plundering, that is—across the countryside, or at least as much as they otherwise would, for their pay was not enough to keep them fed.

He spotted a lighter and a yawl under sail from the naval yard across the bay where the men-of-war *Shoreham*, *Pearl*, and *Dolphin*, along with the *Green-fish* store-ship, lay at anchor. A sand lighter, with its load of sand dredged from the harbor by a complicated-looking machine and destined for use inland, rested at anchor some distance away, waiting for the tide so it could wallow back into the harbor. At anchor nearby lay vessels provisioning for voyages west, and several others waiting for convoy to Bristol and other English ports. Farther away, there was construction or repairs underway at Charles Fort, a vital bastion against the French.

Edward came ashore at the customs house quay. It was crowded with goods, in particular the beef, butter, and other ship provisions with which Ireland competed with England. When he finally did have his privateering commission and ship, he would probably provision here, as it was much cheaper.

Half the barrels, crates, and sacks were stacked in orderly rows, and the rest lay on sledges, each drawn by a garron, the small native horse. Still, in spite of the impressive merchant chaos and cacophony on the quays, Kinsale, or Cionn tSáile in Irish, did not seem as prosperous as he thought it should be. Cork overshadowed it economically, and English laws prohibiting the export of beef to England and the colonies, other than as provisions, hurt it as well.

Long gone were the days when there were two Kinsales, one Irish, one English; it was solely an English town now. The native Irish lived in Scilly nearby, or in cabins on the edge of town just beyond the market. The Corporation prohibited Irish papists from doing business or living within the town walls, and required its approval of papist servants.

He tugged absentmindedly at his waist where his secret correspondence lay secured beneath sword-belt and waistcoat, leading thoughts of Jacobites to enter his head, for here in 1690 James II had fled Ireland after his defeat at the Boyne. The Duke of Marlborough captured both Kinsale and Cork soon after, and Kinsale, given its fortifications, became a navy yard. Open warfare in Ireland was now effectively at an end, and this thankfully had also ended the extensive pillaging and rapine that both sides had engaged in, leaving deep scars. Now only a petty guerrilla war remained, much subdued, and much of it indistinguishable from common highway robbery.

Edward hired a small boy to carry his boots and pistols, asked him for directions to a barber, then took a different direction, south first, then west. He admired the handsome houses on the hillside, and yielded to the temptation to climb to the summit of Compass Hill to view the harbor and river. With the boy following and cursing under his breath, Edward headed north through Fryar's Gate, his stride rolling a bit larboard and starboard as he did, his body convinced that he was still at sea and not ashore. He strode to the summit of the Hill and back again, past almshouses to a walled-up gate he last remembered being open, then back toward the quays. He idly noted a ducking stool for petty malefactors, those who sold goods on the Sabbath, for example, or were otherwise caught in socially inappropriate behavior during the Sabbath rounds, or those who blasphemed. Even so, he heard many of Kinsale's residents cursing with apparent impunity. *Acting like damned pious hypocrite Puritans!* he thought cynically.

He continued toward the market square, near Water Gate where tax collectors levied a portion of goods brought into town to sell, and paused before a blue and white striped wooden pole.

Ashore he usually saw a barber every second day, at least

when he could afford it, but at sea he seldom shaved more often than twice weekly, and he had not shaved in five days. He rubbed his beard and stepped into the shop.

"Rapparees? Yes sir, they're still around," the barber said, as he scraped away whiskers, "but they're not the problem they used to be. Bantry's still a nest of Jacobites, though, plotting in high places and thieving on the roads; you should be careful if you head that way. You'll be safe enough around here. What else can I tell you?"

"I saw a local boat stand toward the French privateer yesterday."

"Aye, some of the buggering Irish still spy for French privateers but swear they don't. And there's bigger spies too, sir. Some say there's one right here in Kinsale, someone high up, helping prepare for another French invasion. I'm not sure I believe it, though. They caught a spy here not too long ago, a papist priest, sent him to London they did; I hope they put him to the rack before they hang him."

"In my experience, dead spies usually get replaced," Edward said as the barber wiped his razor.

"You know something about spies, too, Captain? I thought you were only a buccaneer."

Edward smiled. "Just making conversation."

"Well, sir, some do say there's a new spy, others say that one will soon arrive from Dublin, London, or St. Germain."

"If everyone knows there's a spy, he wouldn't last long, don't you think?"

The barber paused, deep in thought, then shrugged. "Maybe it's just gossip then. Still, everyone around here knows everyone's business, and the damned Irish still hope Prince James will save them. Speaking of privateers as we just did, what luck that those convoy frigates were here when you braved that privateer yesterday, Captain! And greater luck that you, a famous buccaneer, were aboard to command the guns of the *Peregrinator!*"

Edward scowled uncomfortably at the flattery but said nothing, figuring it was at least half sincere.

"But there's not much else going on around here," the barber continued. "Just the usual, you know, more new royal Acts for Ireland and that sort of thing. A damned increase in customs duties, an Act for better observing the Lord's Day, an Act for better suppressing Tories and rapparees—but like I said, you'll be safe on the roads around here."

Edward nodded politely as the barber droned on with more of the useful and useless. His face shaved and his hair and periwig combed out, he next had the barber scrape his teeth, first asking if the barber knew how to do it well, and what he charged for it. When he finally stepped into the street again, he felt a new man, a clean face above clean linen, teeth well-cleaned, his hair and campaign wig well-combed.

A suitable counterpoint to martial poverty, at least when meeting a woman, he thought, then suddenly recalled Maria, the maid.

He smiled and put himself mentally on guard. He must behave and remember his own philosophy: never engage too closely with Fortune's minions. This O'Meary woman was a lady whose reputation reached wide, and deservedly, if the waterman were to be believed, making her far more dangerous than mere maid or man. The last thing he wanted at this time was to be taken as a fortune hunter, or worse, to be taken in as a potential husband, at least until his fortune was made. And he did not intend that a woman make it for him, fully believing that if she did, her mistress Fortune would take it back soon after.

He quickly discovered the stable between a small inn and a busy smithy, and found himself surrounded by the clear, painful peal of hammer on iron on anvil, by the sweet odors of fresh roast mutton, beef, and baking bread, and by the deliciously acrid odor of a charcoal-stoked forge. Betwixt all these odors and sounds were those unmistakably equine: horse sweat on worn leather, sweet earth and straw, dusty oats and sedge, pungent stalls and manure piles, and the nickering, stamping, kicking, blowing, whinnying, and squealing of bored, restless horses.

The hostler pointed Edward to a mare left there earlier by Sir William's servants. The Scotsman pulled his boots on and saddled the horse quickly, in spite of her habit of taking halter rope and reins into her mouth, and nipping at him when she was not busy with rope and rein, and mounted.

"She's still young; she doesn't like too much leg or hand; she's soft-sided, and she can be hot-blooded" the hostler warned with a direct look at Edward's spurs.

"Not to worry," Edward replied, "I won't use them," knowing that if he did, this high-tempered horse might very well buck him into the mud, serving his vanity a rude check. "My thanks to you, sir." He turned the mare toward the road, pulling a coin out of his pocket as he did.

"I don't want that, sir. Sir William pays me well to care for his horses when they come this way."

Edward doubted the man was paid as well as he claimed, Sir William's generosity notwithstanding. Wages here were half what they were in England, but Edward wouldn't argue with honest pride.

"Good morning to you, then," he said and squeezed the horse into a trot.

"Don't ride her like an Englishman—use her with care!" the hostler yelled.

Edward waved his hand in acknowledgment and, as an afterthought, shouted, "I was born a Scot!"

As he approached the busy market square he felt he was being watched, a sensation he put down as a phantom left over from last night's wine-inspired dreams in which he had lost or forgotten something.

But maybe people really are watching, he reasoned: the past day's adventure was the talk of the town. Both the waterman and the barber had known immediately who he was.

Edward reined in his mount when he espied a woman sitting sidesaddle on a bay gelding near the Green Dragon coffeehouse. She wore a riding habit of fine green camlet that, except for the petticoats, might have been a man's. Two enormous wolfhounds sat nearby, panting and awaiting command.

The woman moved her horse slowly forward, her dogs following. Their horses came head-to-head and greeted each other by rubbing noses and nipping muzzles.

"Captain MacNaughton, I know you by your mount. I am Molly O'Meary, Sir William's papist Teague-lander niece, as the local English call me, here to lead you to my uncle's, and you are to give me protection on the way. My uncle said I would find you well-prepared to do so, and I see that you are," she said, glancing at the pistols at his pommel and the sword at his side.

Her easy smile and introduction did not quite eclipse a reserved manner. He doubted it derived from aloofness, for she seemed neither shy nor arrogant. He considered for a moment that he might simply intimidate her, given that he was a stranger with an arguably infamous past, but he cast this idea aside and settled for the moment on the possibility that she might regard him as a threat, although it was far too soon to come to any conclusion.

"Good morning, Mistress O'Meary," he said, touching his hat and bowing slightly from the saddle, trying to make his manner as unintimidating as possible. She nodded in return but said nothing, as if taking the time to examine him more closely.

He likewise took the moment. She was above average height, but he realized it was the commanding carriage of her head that made her appear even taller in the saddle. He considered her face beautiful in no single feature, yet attractive in the sum of its parts. He suspected that a man lacking sophistication might call her plain. Her sunburn and freckles proved that she was often outdoors, and that she rode without a mask, unlike many gentlewomen. Certainly she had no mask in her hand, nor was there one at the pommel. Her hair was more brown than red, subtly streaked with bronze and blonde. Her eyes were grey-green, as if in imitation of coastal Irish hills on a misty morning, and her mouth was firm, with hints of small wrinkles on the upper lip, suggesting she scowled at least as often as she smiled.

Or maybe she just smokes a pipe when no one's around, he thought humorously.

Something about the combination of eye and mouth made him suspect even more that she was hiding something: he tentatively concluded that her mouth hinted at aggression, her eye at fearful outrage.

She in turn saw a man lean and spare, yet sinewy and vigorous as a hungry wild cat, and more than two yards tall. He was well-dressed, with an obvious taste for fine clothes, reasonably elegant yet simple, not overdone, with a martial aspect: he was no fop or dandy. His hair she assumed was brown like his wig, and his eyes showed variously as brown to green, as if his character could not quite be pinned down. His mien was stern, and his sharp, hawk-like face, though not as bronzed as a seaman's, was unfashionably dark, swarthy even, like olivewood or mahogany, with prominent Celtic cheekbones and a partly hidden scar on the forehead.

Doubtless he belonged to that odd, dangerous minority race of dark Scotsmen and Irishmen whom some said were anciently descended from selkies. In his face she saw all the savage arrogance of Highlanders who bowed to no man, except occasionally a Stuart king, and all the dour stubbornness of the old thieving Border Reivers who, until James I had them crushed, would have no way but their own, not to mention all of the horses and cattle of their English neighbors. Yet, when he smiled he appeared a different man: gentle, calm, and friendly.

"Shall we go?" she asked. "Sir William is expecting a parson as well, and I've no mind to travel with him."

"Parson Waters? I had no idea Ballydereen is his intended post. He and I had little intercourse, but I think it's fair to say he won't like you, being both papist and woman as you are."

She turned her horse toward the nearby gate, but made no reply. Edward followed at her side, observing both her and the locals, some afoot, some mounted, others on sledges loaded with goods or in two-wheeled carts, all observing the pair of them. As they rode through the town, Molly noted that he put off his hat to lady and serving girl, English and Irish alike, suggesting a gentleman either of commanding regard for all women or one lusting after all of them—or even both. Beyond Fryar's Gate they headed northwest on the muddy road.

"You're not much for talking," Molly said after a minute of silence.

"Nor are you, I think. In my defense I'm slightly adrift today, but it'll pass."

"Too much punch last night?"

"In my case, sack, both sweet and dry, although there was plenty of punch to go around. I have a weakness for Spanish wines and brandy." She made no comment, so he felt compelled to keep talking. "The captain of the *Shoreham* invited a few of us to celebrate our escape. So we celebrated."

Molly replied only with an inscrutable look, leaving him to wonder whether he stood condemned or was simply under evaluation. His present state was hardly unusual in most men, at least at times, and in many women as well.

"So the sun has finally appeared," he said awkwardly after another minute of disconcerting silence. "It's a blessing after the stormy weather at sea."

"Such an astute observation of the weather could come only from a mariner," Molly replied in a tone of such dry declaration that Edward thought she must either be entirely honest, or an excellent actress.

"You're mocking my discomfort," he said with a smile, gambling on the latter.

"Discomfort?" she asked, and this time there was an obvious hint of raillery.

"The effects of sack and your company."

"Are you afraid of me, Captain? I'm sure I'm the one who should be afraid. I've heard of your piratical ways."

"*Privateering*," he replied sharply, without thinking. "I was never a pirate. Accusations are only allegations until proved, and even then not always true." His hangover had left him more irritable than he wished, although otherwise he was in a pleasant humor.

"A privateer, is that your claim? I've heard you were not only once a buccaneer, and they're one and the same, buccaneer and pirate, but also twice a pirate. And since the spots are never known to change in leopards, how can I know a leopard is not a leopard anymore, much less that a rover has abandoned his trade?"

"Ah," he said, then shook his head and immediately regretted it.

"That's quite a riposte, Captain. I hope you're quicker with your sword than your tongue, otherwise why carry one?"

He laughed lightly, causing his head to pound again.

"I see that you need more time to gather your wits, sir," she continued. "I suppose I should apologize. I'm in a mood and you're within reach."

"No need to apologize. Too well do I know the dangers of 'mere' woman, Mistress O'Meary. Indeed, I consider your sex not only the more dangerous of the two, but by far the more intelligent. It's in my best interest to cross swords with you another day," he said, smiling and touching his hat once more.

She laughed this time, without any of the usual pretense of gentlewomen. "Come, Captain, I'll help you along; it would be a waste to ride in silence. Tell me what led you to a life of crime upon the sea," she suggested a bit impishly. "It's not often one has the chance to talk to a famous sea rover."

"First, I deny that I was ever, but once, a true pirate, and was never brought to trial for that honest occasion. So why to sea to plunder lawfully? I wanted money, perhaps to buy land, to raise a family, or perhaps just to have it, and it seemed to me more interesting to steal with the sword than with the pen. Too many do so with the latter, and I've never followed the herd. The sea is the only place left to plunder sword-in-hand, not to mention that it has always called to me."

"And you found your wealth and family?"

"No, or at least never for long. Today I own only my clothing and arms. I've no family of my own, although my parents are alive and settled in Virginia."

"So now, Sir William tells me, you intend to return to sea again to cruise for wealth, to take again from others by the sword."

"It's what I know, and it can be quite profitable. And anyway, I'm unsuited to employments where other men take all the risk and I all the reward."

"How noble, sir, to preserve others from both risk and reward."

"Sharp words, Mistress O'Meary."

"A pirate accuses me of being harsh? You have no other way to seek your fortune?"

"It's in my blood. My father, a Highlander whose seafaring uncle persuaded him to go to sea, was with Penn and Venables at the capture of Jamaica. He later sailed with Myngs and Morgan against the Spanish. His father had waged war with Montrose in the Highlands during Oliver's Usurpation, and his mother's family were of the Scottish West March, known in the years before the first King James for raiding the English across the border. My mother's family are of Aberdeenshire, and some of them took up arms with Montrose as well. And then there are the old rumors, too, that there is some renegade blood in my veins, French or Spanish, Dutch or English, maybe all of them."

"Rogues, rovers, reivers, and renegades, then—you come honestly by a dishonest trade. And your intentions in Ireland?"

"It's my turn, Mistress O'Meary—"

"You may call me Molly if you like, and I may call you Edward?"

"As you please."

"You were telling me of your intentions in Ireland."

"No, I was saying that it's my turn to ask you a question."

"'Questions and commands,' is it?"

"And it's my turn to play commander."

"Ask or command, then."

"I hear you're wooed from far and wide."

"Don't believe everything you hear. I'm betrothed."

"He's a good man?"

"He's rogue and rover, sir, like you."

"You must introduce us."

"He's much too far away."

"At St. Germain, perhaps?"

"You should know how foolish it is to blithely suggest a man is a Jacobite or Tory without evidence. Sir William tells me you were once a Jacobite, yet now you serve King William."

She did not wait for his reply, but cantered ahead for a few hundred yards, then slowed to a trot. They rode silently together into the countryside for an Irish mile, Edward bumping up and down a bit to his mare's short strides, Molly sitting comfortably and moving easily with her gelding's undulations. Edward and his mare often lagged behind. Several times the mare broke into a canter to keep pace with the gelding, who each time took up the canter himself, was restrained by Molly, tossed his head in annoyance, and reached over to nip the mare for trying to take the lead, often missing her shoulder and biting Edward's boot instead.

"Damn animal!" swore Edward.

"You curse much, Captain MacNaughton—I mean Edward."

"The curse of being a mariner."

"We're not aboard your ship, sir," she said, smiling, then gently pulled her horse to the right. "Three more miles is all you need tolerate my occasionally sharp tongue, and only at supper afterward if you'd rather avoid me. You won't be with us long, and have affairs of business to manage, so Sir William says. Why make this journey, then? Few travel so far for so short a time."

"Sir William surely told you: I'm here settle his investment in my privateering adventure."

"But this you could do via letters and solicitors. You don't need to travel yourself."

"Don't you know well that a Scot, a rat, and a Newcastle grindstone—"

"—travel all the world over," she laughed. "But you have merely crossed St. George's Channel, not the world over. As I said, correspondence would suffice. I think you must truly be a messenger bearing important news or questions."

Damn this head! I hardly think straight, Edward cursed inwardly. "You've caught me out, Molly. In truth, I'm taking the opportunity to visit with Sir William while on another errand, whose nature I can't disclose."

"I see, sir—an intrigue!" she replied in the same tone of friendly conversational disinterest masking interrogation. But Edward dismissed his incipient suspicion, just as he did his sense of being watched, as the mere byproduct of the wine bottle.

"Nothing so adventurous, merely matters between great gentlemen and lesser noblemen whose affairs they prefer to keep private," he replied.

"And doubtless you hope they will invest in your adventure in return for your service?"

"You're a quick one, Molly."

"Well, if you need my help with your errand, secretive though you are about it, you can call on me. I know everyone around here."

"My many thanks, but I'm sure I'll manage."

His mare stumbled slightly, then tried to canter briefly as she caught her balance. Molly's gelding immediately leaped ahead, thinking it a race, but she quickly restrained him.

"Easy, girl, easy," Edward said as he reined his mare up and patted her on the neck.

"It must be difficult, though, this begging of gentlemen and noblemen," Molly said more seriously, once both riders were back on course.

"I don't beg," he replied.

"Truly?"

"No."

"Not even God?"

"Not even."

"A woman, then? Every man begs at least one woman in his life for love, lust, or money."

"Not any woman for any reason."

"Then it's a very hard head you have, for I'm sure it's taken many hard knocks as you've made your way alone in the world."

Edward laughed. It felt good; he had not laughed so honestly in weeks.

They passed a man and woman walking on the road. Something about the pair, a hint of their scorn perhaps, drew Edward's attention, but upon examination they seemed harmless enough, if aloof and surly, and he saw no one else about. The letters he was to deliver were safely on his person, and he doubted anyone here knew of them.

"The roads are safe this close to town," Molly said, noticing his sudden military inspection of his surroundings.

"So the barber told me earlier. Yet you seemed grateful for my armed protection."

"Mere flattery, sir. Praising a man's martial virtues, whether he has any or not, puts him at ease."

And off his guard, Edward thought, idly at first, then more seriously.

"Does this work with all men? And what need do you have to put men at ease if you're betrothed?" Edward replied too bluntly. His hangover was wearing off and his apprehensions of women and Fortune got the better of him. Immediately he regretted his words.

"You've already heard that men seek me from far and wide. Where did you hear this? From Sir William? I doubt it. On the quays? From the barber? Or from some clacking hens in the market square? Perhaps you'd like to join these would-be suitors?" she said with a thin smile. "If you do, know that you must seek me for my land, for any other maid or spinster in the county can imitate me in the dark. Know that, if you believe the local people, you'll pursue a wild Irish woman who will have no master and whose promised lover is a rogue. She rides by night with smugglers and rapparees, or so they say. Like the gossips, you'll wonder why I'm not married in spite of my many greedy suitors. Am I Sir William's secret mistress, perhaps? Does he—a Whig, an Englishman, a loyal servant of the English church and of the Dutch king in London—find perverse attraction in bedding a papist? They're all certain, of course, that I'm a fornicatrice, and therefore wonder why I'm never pregnant. Perhaps I know potions, perhaps I'm barren, perhaps I'm used contrary to nature? But these are trifles that do not matter: property is everything. Better a shrew with property as a wife than a saint with none."

"And your betrothed?" Edward asked carefully.

"Is Irish and an outlaw. If I marry him now my estate becomes his, and the English will seize it."

"So, like the Irish-hating Elizabeth, you play at being wooed while biding your own time?"

"Aren't you the quick one now!"

In an instant she was off across the countryside at a gallop, and so was Edward's mare before he had cued her. Molly rode skillfully and aggressively with a loose rein over the troubled ground, using her hands only when necessary to guide the horse or slow him down. She and her mount gained two hundred yards on him and his. Near a copse at the crest of a low hill she slowed to a hand gallop, then a canter, then to a trot and finally a walk. Her gelding was annoyed at having been reined up and showed his displeasure by bucking, snorting, and throwing his head. Molly waited for Edward, walking her horse in small circles. She laughed as he drew near. The bitterness, real or pretend, was gone, but for a hint in the partly hidden hard line of her mouth and jaw.

Fortune's Whelp

"You are no true horseman, sir. You ride with more boldness than skill. But you sit a horse well enough and don't interfere with her."

"Thank you for the compliment."

"Sir William's manor house is just beyond, as you probably recall," she said. "I must apologize for my outburst. I know you're not like the others—the men who court me—because you haven't asked me why I live with Sir William when I have my own estate. In other words, you haven't wondered at our relationship." When Edward replied only with silence, she continued. "Sir William is an old family friend who took me in after I returned from France. My father was dead by then, and Inniskilling dragoons had burned our home. Only rain saved it from entire destruction."

Edward stiffened noticeably in the saddle. He had briefly served with the same dragoons during one of the many side adventures in his life.

"I don't hold you responsible," she continued. "Sir William tells me you were with the Inniskilling men only under duress, and by the time they burned our property you were no longer one of them. Again, I apologize for my outburst."

Quickly she leaned over and kissed him on the cheek, then immediately cantered away, preventing him from returning the salute if even he had thought to do so. She seemed embarrassed, whether for her outburst or the kiss, or both, he could not tell.

Edward followed, and soon they arrived at Ballydereen.

"My thanks for your company and protection, Captain MacNaughton," she said after releasing the wolfhounds to run to the kitchen. She rode away before he could reply.

Edward shook his head, bewildered. He began to wonder if his philosophy of Fortune's messengers was flawed, that there was no escaping Fortune after all; or if his hangover had simply left him vulnerable.

Damned sack!

He could not fathom whether he had just had an innocent conversation in which he had said a foolish thing or two, or if he had been quite subtly manipulated for reasons he could not identify. The woman who finished the ride did not seem to him the same who had begun it.

For a minute he sat on his mount alone before the house. Once more he looked around and about, for the impression of being watched had grown stronger rather than weaker as his hangover diminished.

And for an instant he spotted what he had suspected: a glimpse of a dark rider quickly disappearing into some trees just below the crest of a hill.

He turned to follow, discarding his brief urge to inform the house first of his intentions, when he heard the unmistakable voice of the grand old gentleman Sir William Waller who hobbled strongly, cane in hand, from the house.

"Spurs! Damn, you didn't use your spurs on her, did ye?"

Chapter 8

But the Natives of Ireland,
over and above that publick quarrel of Religion,
have a private one of Revenge...
—"An Answer to the Late King James's Declaration," 1689

All afternoon the Irishman shadowed his quarry, in spite of the urgent need to deliver smuggled arms. To date, he had handed over only two of five stores of arms, and he had other pressing tasks as well. Five days had passed since he had come ashore at Oysterhaven, and he must depart as soon as practical for London for service under Barclay. He had no time for accidental discoveries on the road, yet he indulged himself.

In the past, Michael O'Neal had often tracked travelers on and off the roads, sometimes simply out of the need to line his pockets with someone else's coin, sometimes as part of his duty, as he called it, to Ireland. Often he carried a coded letter of instruction: whom to rob and when, or, more rarely these days, which house to burn and when, or what messenger needed protection, or what ships were sailing from Cork and Kinsale, and roughly when, and what their cargoes were. Sometimes his task was merely to handle the secret post sent via French smugglers or privateers, making him no more than a common messenger on a dangerous mail route. In the past his instructions had come from his cousin, a papist Irish priest. But with his cousin's capture—the brutal beating of the man had burned Michael to his soul—the routine had changed. A new spy was to give him instructions. To give *him*, Michael O'Neal, who hated to be commanded, *orders*.

He had almost come to blows with both of them, Molly and the spy.

"You may not kill the English officer, the ensign who abused your cousin, the one named Ingoldsby," the spy said.

And Molly said much the same.

"It will raise suspicions," both she and the spy agreed.

Michael, angry, acquiesced but silently reserved the right to revisit the issue later, on his own terms if necessary.

"And what of the Scottish buccaneer?" he asked both the spy and Molly.

"Nor him," the spy said.

"Yet surely by now the Scotsman has the letters," the Irishman had argued. "Hasn't he already met twice with the viscount and baronet? In my experience, it's easier to steal letters from the dead than from the living."

The reply was patronizing and sent Michael's temper nearly to a blind fury.

"You're a fool, but for your sake and mine I'll explain this to you one more time. A Jacobite agent in Bristol bungled the attempt to get Lord Deigle's letters from MacNaughton, even bungled something as simple as preventing him from sailing. But the Scotsman is here now, so we'll wait until we know for certain he has the replies from the viscount and baronet. Do you follow me so far? Good."

Michael ground his teeth, his face empurpled.

The spy continued. "Both men claim allegiance to King William, yet both once supported our cause, thus both have intelligence of our cause. In particular, before Viscount Brennan claimed to have abandoned King James, he met with the Duke of Berwick, who is gathering support for King James. Both replies are important, but the viscount's is vital: he knows of plans being laid in St. Germain. He claims that he won't help us anymore but also that he won't betray us. Even so, until his reply to Deigle is in our hands, we won't know whether he's telling the truth or not. Is this too difficult to follow?"

"Damn you," Michael sputtered. "I endure much for you!"

"And I for you. Remember that this cause is greater than both of us."

"And when MacNaughton has their replies?" Michael spat.

"We'll rob him on the road if we can, but we'll let him live. Our cause can't afford the attention his murder would draw."

"And if we miss him on the road?"

"We'll have other opportunities, you know this."

Michael swallowed his fury and stayed his fists. It was easier for him to obey the spy than it was to obey Molly, for the spy also took orders, therefore Michael was not as much obeying the spy as he was obeying the spy's superior.

Molly herself said much the same, likewise ordering him, who had sworn never to be commanded by a woman, not to settle the old score.

Does she not care that he marooned me once, leaving me to die of thirst or madness?

She was adamant. "It would draw too much attention to Sir William, thus to me, thus to you, thus to our hopes."

He began to disbelieve her excuse for letting other men woo her, that by this her estate might be saved until James was king again, and then they could marry openly. He began to suspect that she planned for multiple contingencies, including the failure of the Jacobite cause. The obvious conclusion was that she might one day abandon him, rather than her estate, should Fortune choose the wrong side.

Still, for now he had no choice but to obey. She burdened

him with love as the price of sex and eventual estate, in return for which he, sometimes petulantly, often angrily, always hating it, must at times do her bidding.

So today he would pass on vengeance, for it was a luxury, and luxuries must wait until King James ruled again. He glanced at his quarry below, a mounted English officer named Ingoldsby. Among his other sins, the officer had pretended to woo Molly, as did many men from miles around. Or at least he had before he traveled to London, escorting Michael's cousin for trial.

The Irishman's horse snorted and shook his head, as if afflicted by his rider's mood.

Too much to do, no time to waste, a *king is likely to die*, Michael thought. Yet still he tarried.

The thought of regicide—his prescient guess that Sir George Barclay would be tasked to kill the Dutch king of England—gave him no pleasure except in the details. He despised Prince William but did not hate him, for the Dutchman was too removed from Irish history. Michael did hate most Englishmen, though, or claimed he did, but had a curious ability to work with them for profit by stealth or violence.

He trotted his mount for a hundred feet in order to keep his quarry in sight, then settled him back into a slow walk.

The ensign below was well-mounted on a foreign animal, nimble and of good wind. The Irishman's own sturdy mount might better handle the forage and weather of Ireland, but whether it could best the Englishman's in fight or flight was an unknown. To ride him down, this man, this Englishman, this officer, in broad daylight was too dangerous, given the circumstances. Were the officer to escape he would raise the *hutesium et clamor*, the hue and cry, drawing attention to those who laid in arms and prepared to rise again against the English. Even his death, his killer unknown, would raise the alarm, as would his disappearance. In this Michael had to agree, although he hated to do so, with Molly and the spy.

And they will be furious, both of them, if I kill the officer!

Nevertheless, how he wished to gallop down the slope, pistols in hand, and shoot Ingoldsby at close range, the powder and wad singeing his coat, the balls and shot penetrating his organs, the empty pistols then bludgeoning his brains, knocking him from the saddle, to lie in the mud until his head was severed from his shoulders.

Today this was only a fantasy.

His quarry below paused at a fork in the road.

Off to seduce another young woman and abandon her with child? wondered the Irishman, not bothering to consider that this was also often his own way. He laughed quietly to himself. *Aye, going farther afield now that you've returned from sending my cousin to London to be hanged, after you broke his teeth and head with your boot. Do you know, boy, that some of the English and all of the Irish laugh at how you were passed out aboard the* Peregrinator, *too drunk to fight the French off Kinsale and cover yourself with glory? Surely you've heard the tales, Englishman, so how do you still hold your head up so high?*

Michael recognized the curious synergies of man and Fortune that put him here on this road at this nexus of important events, patiently observing a quarry who had committed two sins, one of desire, the other of politics. It was almost as if Fortune herself had arranged it.

The officer changed direction, toward a small ordinary in the Irish village nearby, a place frequented both by the Protestant English of Ireland—who hated being called Irish, especially when visiting in England—and the native Irish themselves, and where decent French claret and brandy were served. Doubtless the officer would refresh himself before heading to one of the nearby homes of English landowners, in pursuit of one of their daughters if their fathers were so foolish as to admit him.

Michael followed the officer to the village. Most of its poor lived with their livestock and poultry in small huts they called cabins, and survived on bonny clapper and potatoes. They commonly spoke Irish, these *Teagues* and *Bog-Landers* and *Dear Joys*, and those who did speak English rarely used it, often pretending they did not know the language.

The Irishman heard the faint cries of wailing and knew thereby that most of the villagers were attending the visitation for some poor soul recently departed. A dozen or more women mourned over the body, some of them hired to do so. All shared a pipe and tobacco to cover the stench of the corpse as they drank poteen, sounded their grief, and enumerated the deceased's personal and material virtues.

Suddenly the Irishman smiled. Fortune, being a woman, was therefore to be commanded, not served, and not treated with for terms. And by Mary, Mother of God, he knew now how to command her, and her servants too. There would be no hue and cry. If he were lucky, he would kill two men with one stone. But if only one fell, he could bide his time for the other. And neither Molly nor the spy would be the wiser—a doubly satisfying revenge.

As soon as the officer was out of sight among the village houses, the Irishman turned his horse down the hill and rode slowly to the ordinary. Here, while most villagers were paying their respects to the deceased, the Irishman introduced himself as William O'Sullivan to the English officer, and engaged him in local gossip he modified only slightly from the truth.

"Have you heard," he asked between swigs of claret, "of that slander on the docks, of some English officer who hid in the hold during the fight between that merchant ship—What's her name, *Peregrinator*?—and the French privateer? Surely you know who he is? I can't believe it myself, but I overheard it from the Scotsman who was aboard, MacNorton his name was, or MacKnight, something like that, used to be a buccaneer, said the officer was a damned coward, nothing more than a base ignoble coward. I can't understand what sort of man lets someone abuse his honor like that."

And now, the fuse lit on the luxury of a common revenge, Michael O'Neal could devote his full attention to killing a king.

Chapter 9

Such tempting Charms what Mortal can avoid?
—Ned Ward, *The London Spy*, 1718

"Is that all?"

The voice, a bit scornful and much bewildered, drew him from his slumber.

Edward opened his eyes. Before him he saw two breasts, well-shaped, large yet surprisingly delicate. Behind them lay a body neither too slender nor too full, with smooth skin but for tiny wrinkles at the corners of the eyes and juncture of the breasts.

The widow Hardy, for the crimson-flushed body was hers, sat astride, gripping his loins and hips with her thighs, her breasts parting and meeting as she breathed in and out in time with the pitching of her hips. She wore pale blue silk stockings gartered above her knees and a linen shift unlaced from breast to waist and torn open from waist to hip.

"Mrs. Hardy. Good morning," he said slowly.

"Good morning? That's it? I've known many men—well, not *too* many—but I never expected the cursory treatment of this morning from you, not after last night! I could have had this brief moment from some fat merchant! Only hours ago you were in a fever for me, I hope not just because of the whiskey.

But now? What the hell, sir?"

"Mrs. Hardy, I humbly beg your forgiveness," Edward said, gathering his wits. "I'm afraid last night's celebration left me slow under the moon and quick under the sun. Rest assured, your attractions have not faded with the sun's rising and my setting."

"Don't use your tongue on flowery words that would fool only an ignorant maid. That's not what I expect it to be used for." She was quiet for a moment, then softened and smiled. "I know well enough not to take a man to bed with his boots on. And anyway, two out of three in a night isn't so bad. Excuse me, my darling adventurer, but the sun is up and I shouldn't be seen undressed."

She slipped from the large bed. Edward sat up.

One week more, he thought, *one week, certainly no more than two, and I sail for Bristol.*

He had been in Kinsale for more than a week now, and not for a single moment had he been entirely at ease. The phantom of the dream that followed him to shore—the sense that he was being watched—had only grown with each passing day. To reassure himself he went well-armed everywhere. Three days past, while taking care of the business Molly had identified correctly as an intrigue, he'd felt certain he was being followed, but even after circling around and waiting in ambush above the road, he could not confirm this. If someone were following him, he was good at his trade—and probably knew something of his business as well.

The meetings themselves had left him annoyed, almost angered, but he suppressed his emotions for the sake of his purpose. This favor of letters and information for Lord Deigle should help him in his quest for his privateering commission.

The first meeting had not gone well.

"You may go, sir," Viscount Brennan had said, without

looking at Edward after he'd delivered the secret letter.

"My Lord, I am under instructions from Lord Deigle, who informs me he acts on behalf of the Crown, to remain here while you read the letter, and not to go until I receive your verbal answer to the main question. This is his insurance in case your written reply is stolen. However, I'm to pick up your written reply later, for I must have it before I sail."

The viscount had walked up a short stair, then, with all the arrogance of a man born to privilege and fully believing in his entitlement, turned, looked down at Edward, and smirked.

"You may tell my friend Lord Deigle that I have no relationship with Tories or Jacobites, that I will provide him with what I know of them and any plans they may have, which will be little enough, and that I will happily engage in the trading adventure he proposes. *Now* you may go, sir. My servants will show you out."

"As you wish," Edward had replied, refusing to use the man's title. "I'll return in five days for your letter." Unconsciously he'd put his hand to his sword.

The second meeting had gone better, at least in terms of polite address. Sir James Allin, Baronet, had been more than cordial, perhaps because as a baronet he was a member of the gentry, not a peer. But along with his pleasant manner was a disquieting fascination with Edward's past.

"You, sir, were once a Jacobite, isn't this true? And so was I, but times change, sir, times change. It is sad, sir, sad. A new king, what is it now, seven years almost? Yet Tories still plot. Tories, that's what we call Jacobites here, you understand? You do? Of course you do. I trust I can trust you, sir?"

"If I could not be trusted, Lord Deigle would not have sent me."

Here again Edward had seen, albeit only for an instant, the patronizing smile he had seen on Lord Brennan's lips, and he'd wondered if Deigle were to be trusted.

"Can you imagine, sir, the import of Lord Deigle's missive?" the baronet had said, waving the letter around. "He wishes help gauging the loyalty of the local gentry and nobility in case there's another Irish uprising in anticipation of another French invasion! And he wants a list of Irish conspirators, too, if I can provide it. And in cipher! I love ciphers, such an exercise in words and mathematics! One day, sir, my loyalty shall make me a peer."

Edward did not trust men or women who were fascinated with intrigue, especially not those who talked about this fascination. Not only could they not keep secrets, they were otherwise untrustworthy: invariably they were the first to run when things went sour, leaving honest fighting men behind to hold the line and die. Edward had briefly pretended to share the baronet's fascination, then excused himself.

Jane Hardy interrupted his reverie.

"I take it you've completed your affairs here? There's talk that you and Sir William intend to buy a ship to seek the French. Aren't there enough investors in Bristol?" she asked, as she pulled on her mantua and sat down upon a chamber pot just out of his sight.

"There are interested parties in Bristol," Edward replied, "but not enough, nor do I have enough money of my own to purchase a ship or outfit it, and for a commission I need a ship. Investors are cautious right now, and most don't believe I can secure a commission, or that I'll make a profit if I do. It's been two years since a privateer sailed from Bristol. It's not easy anymore. After all, it's France, not Spain, we're fighting, and the French don't do as great a trade by sea as some other nations. But I intend to sail to West India again, a grand voyage, not a mere summer's cruise as a Channel privateer."

"That'll be expensive to outfit."

"With Sir William's money to help guarantee a ship, I'll be able to convince other investors, and also an influential noble or merchant to back my petition. It's a long process, full of the sort of pandering I despise, but worth it to get to sea again."

"And if this doesn't work out?"

"The world is full of opportunities."

"Of Fortune, you mean."

Edward smiled. "Of late I prefer to see it as opportunity made at my own hand, and not at Fortune's. At any rate, just in case my main plan fails, I'm already in contact with the Spanish for a commission to pursue smugglers along the Main; I'd also take anything else, French ships, I mean, that might come my way. Spain has a long history of hiring former pirates under the idea that it takes a thief to catch a thief, so my 'piracies and plunders against Spain,' as they put it, shouldn't keep them from considering me, at least as long as I'm willing to pretend to become a papist. I could also take a cargo and get a commission as a letter-of-mart ship, permitting me to take prizes along my trade route. I could also seek a commission from one of the English colonies in America."

"What of Scotland? Can't you seek a commission in Glasgow?"

"Probably, but I suspect only to cruise Scottish seas. I briefly commanded a Scottish privateer once, but I won't bore you with the story today. All's not lost if I can't get a commission in England, for I will somewhere create the opportunity. One way or another I'll return to sea and to America again, armed and plundering."

Jane stood up, brushed her fingers lightly across Edward's shoulders, then called for wine and a brand with which to light her pipe. Maria arrived moments later, bearing both and grinning broadly.

"Would you like a cup?" Jane asked as she poured some

wine for herself. "No?" She put the pitcher down, then lit her pipe. "I don't expect your having once been a buccaneer will help your cause. Or will it? You stood trial for piracy, didn't you?"

"Twice. In my defense, I was sailing under a French commission, albeit a very dubious one, when accused the first time. I was acquitted of piracy, yet was likely to be found guilty of manslaughter for the associated killing of a man in a duel. Thankfully, our former king pardoned me because he suspected their lies, and perhaps because he didn't like their politics. The man I killed was a thief and a coward. He challenged me, not the other way around. But he also had friends willing to lie and pretend he was an honest gentlemen whom I murdered in an affray."

"What profitable purpose did it serve to accuse you of murder?"

"I see you're well-acquainted with mankind. The man's embezzlement had enriched my accusers, and if I proved this, they'd have been accused as well. Unfortunately, I ended up embargoed for two years from the Americas, so I took my sword to Scotland, Ireland, Hungary, and Transylvania, even had some intrigues in Spain believe it or not, before heading back across the sea to America, only to find myself embargoed yet again, this time for honestly plundering a Spanish pirate."

"Maybe you should embrace Fortune, and not shun her."

"Embracing her hasn't worked; it's only gotten me into various affrays and misadventures."

"So it's true what I hear, you're still not immune to, what do you call them, rencontres?"

"Indeed?"

"A passenger who arrived here two days ago spoke of you. In fact, there's a rumor that you lugged out and whipped a man through the lungs in Bristol just before you left. And that you did so over a woman."

"Damned gossips and their tongue-clack. I did pink a fool, but only in his ass as he turned his back in a fair fight, or at least it was fair on my part. And a woman may have put him up to it, but she's no lover of mine, or at least not for some months, and had no cause to send a ruffian to stick me with his bilbo."

"Lydia Upcott."

"You're well-informed."

"A trim frigate, as I recall."

"You know her?"

"Not well, but in Bristol I cast a wide net in spite of my reputation."

"Trim indeed, she is, and with a sharp set of teeth. The boarding of her is easy, but then she springs her closed quarters, and damn, her suitor catches a Tartar. She was best rid of, and quickly."

"And thus her revenge. Edward, darling, be careful around women."

"Thus my philosophy!"

"Yes, Edward, you've already explained your theory of women and Fortune to me once, and that was more than enough. Frankly, it sounds like nothing more than an excuse to avoid marriage; or, God forbid, a means to pretend to treat women well, but only in passing. That is to say, in bed and conversation. And while you may be able to avoid wedded bliss —I'll be honest and say I've indulged in marriage twice, but found its bliss to be brief and will never wed again—you can't avoid women or Fortune for long. You proved this with me last night."

"I don't intend to *avoid* women," Edward replied, enjoying the fencing. "I intend to avoid their entanglements, especially in regard to Fortune."

"With one the other, Edward. They're inseparable, women

and entanglements. Yet I agree with you in part: the combination is either fortunate or unfortunate, almost never in-between. You can't separate women from entanglements, nor from Fortune. And you shouldn't try."

Edward shrugged. "My instinct disagrees and my philosophy requires a practical test. Damn, what's the time? I need to get up, I promised Molly O'Meary I'd escort her to the race meeting this afternoon. If I don't leave soon we won't arrive in time. Sir William is racing two horses."

"Be careful, my tall man."

"Indeed?"

"There are dangers around here you are unaware of, in spite of your vast martial experience."

"I can look after myself," Edward replied, unsure of her direction.

"You can begin by looking after yourself around Molly O'Meary."

"Her?"

"Don't be a fool. Word around here is that she's been at your side since you arrived. Your own philosophy argues that you should keep your distance from her."

Edward grinned. "I think you're jealous."

"I'm sure it's only my bed you're in, lad, and I'm too experienced to be jealous of anyone. I know what I have and what I can have. My old trade was an honest one, and my payment up front—I let *you* lie with my maid in advance in return for lying with me. If I'm not jealous of my maid I'm not going to be jealous of Mistress O'Meary."

Edward smiled, then shrugged. "I would have lain with *you* anyway. As for Molly, she's promised to another."

"So she says, and he a man rumored to be jealous and a scoundrel; some say he was a rapparee in the North, and a pirate before that. He's surely a Jacobite. Don't you find it curious that he's never around, yet is said to tolerate her dalliances?"

"You make it sound as if she's playing all men one against the other."

"And maybe she is. Or perhaps she's increasing her odds at finding a rich husband. Or trying to make her betrothed jealous. Or trying to trade him for a man worth more money. Or distracting herself from her anger by playing coquettish games. Or wanting a man made of parts of several. Or tangling you up in some other net all her own. Some women are best kept clear of, my dear."

"How do you know so much about her? You've only been here a week."

"One can learn a lot in a week, and I've known *of* her for a long time. People gossip, and I read their letters. You forget that my husband owned this estate for many years. I've lived here before, if only for a short time."

Edward sat fully upright, the result of a minor epiphany. "Wait—you condemn me for my philosophy, yet tell me to avoid getting entangled with a woman. Isn't this the same as telling me to practice what I preach?"

"*Varium et mutabile*, Edward."

"The young officer, Ingoldsby, quoted this to me the day we were chased by *La Tulipe Noir*."

"How clever of him to show his education while drunk. With most men it's the other way around," she said sarcastically. "I suggest you keep your distance from him, too, if you don't want delays in pursuing your venture. He's a hothead, and we already know him for a drunk. It's a bad combination. And I hear he holds a grudge against you."

"Whisht! Let him fume in the barracks and taverns. But back to our philosophical discussion: I think you're jealous of Molly, in spite of your denials."

"Always a possibility, I'm a woman after all. More importantly, you need to recognize the flaw in your philosophy: you lump all women together, and Fortune with them. But we're not all alike, nor are Fortune's interventions. You should have learned this already from Lydia Upcott in Bristol, and surely from others like her. An adventurous man can hardly avoid meeting a few such women in his life, not to mention Fortune in her many guises."

"I still think you're proving my philosophy, not gutting it."

Mrs. Hardy smiled broadly but refused to engage. She changed the subject.

"You haven't finished telling me about the second time you were accused of piracy."

"There's nothing more to say. I was acquitted again, but King William's ministers yielded to the Spanish ambassador and placed me under an embargo for two years to the Americas. For my part, I was merely doing my duty, this time under an English commission. The fact is, there are some who consider my alleged unlicensed privateering an excellent credential, and others who do not. Some of the latter would have seen me hanged if they could, the Spanish especially; although they'd gladly forgive me if I offered to serve them as a privateer, especially a pirate hunting one."

"Well, darling mariner, I saw only one character flaw this morning. Otherwise, I think you are magnificent. Is there anything I can do to help? I have money—"

"My dear Jane, I'm not here for your money and won't accept it. As *you* said, one explanation of my philosophy is enough."

"Well, if you need anything, let me know. I maintain a regular business correspondence with Bristol, one quite secure, should you need to safely post anything."

Edward got out of bed and began dressing. "Again my

thanks, but I'll deliver my own correspondence, Lord Deigle prefers it that way." He paused for a moment, suddenly lost in thought. When he finally spoke, his demeanor had changed. "Forgive me, but you said you know of Lydia Upcott?"

"Yes?"

"Then forgive me for assuming also that you must have heard of me also, not that I consider my fame or infamy great. Yet during the passage you didn't know me at all."

"Darling Edward, of course I knew who you were. Everyone in Bristol knows the name of the buccaneer and fencing master Edward MacNaughton, even as aloof as you are. I had hoped to have seduced you by the end of the voyage, but that old bastard Neptune refused to cooperate. And even I won't play the card of the innocent wide-eyed fool in awe of the great man just to get his attention. I'm neither an innocent nor a fool—you wouldn't have believed the fiction. You'd have simply thought me a widow desperate for a man's hard touch, like the widows on stage in the theater. Rather than be my friend, you'd have had me once or twice on my back and then away with you. So instead I gently lured you to me. I hope you haven't minded."

Edward returned her smile. "Obviously not at all, although your seduction wasn't as gentle as you claim."

"You haven't complained until now, and you certainly enjoyed it last night. Must you go to the race meeting?"

"I must, for I also promised Sir William." He pulled his shirt over his head, but stopped suddenly halfway, leaving the garment to cover his head for a few seconds. He finished putting the shirt on, then cocked his head at Jane. "Wait a minute...the bell! It was part of your seduction, wasn't it?"

"Ahh!" she said, smiling broadly.

"I've been unable to reconcile your shrewishness aboard ship with your charm ashore. I tried to rationalize the difference in character by blaming your behavior at sea on seasickness. Suddenly it's clear."

"How clever of you, Edward!"

"I think you should warn me to steer clear of you as well, Jane."

"But you won't, no matter what I say."

"Women playing games is a sign Fortune will become involved."

"My games are innocent."

"So you say."

"Well, I won't warn you to keep away from me, but I will warn you to watch carefully on the roads. There are eyes upon you; there's much talk of you in town and country, by those who take too much interest in you, your visits to a countryside manor or two. Your visits to a local viscount and baronet have set tongues clacking, in spite of your pretense that you went there to tell stories of buccaneering and privateering, and to seek their money for a venture. They are each involved in local intrigues, and by your association with Lord Deigle—yes, word of that has reached here, too—you may be suspect in some eyes. They will see, not a messenger bearing business terms, but one bearing secret correspondence."

Edward shrugged.

"And there will of course be talk of your visit here," she continued. "The difference, though, is that everyone already knows why you came here. I really think you should avoid the races today."

Edward smiled at her concern. "I'll have what I came for soon enough, and then be away, out of the dangers of Irish women and rapparees—and of Dutch widows."

He finished dressing while Mrs. Hardy watched. She leaned over him as he reached for his cravat. She smelled of perfume and musk. "Enjoy the races, if you must go," she said, as he tucked the lace ends of his cravat into a buttonhole. "I'll send a groom to hold your horse at the door." She wrapped her arms around his waist as she called for her maid.

"You, my dear Jane, are mad," Edward said, growing hard again. "But I have to leave, you know." He stepped away, bowed low, kissed her hand. "Don't think ill of me. I promise to improve my performance."

"You take your leave much too formally. Having taken me twice in one night—I don't count your half-effort this morning— you should be more familiar," she said, putting her arms around him and kissing him. "You owe me a third."

She stepped back, took a swallow of wine, and kissed him again. He kissed her back, tasting the wine on her tongue. She pressed her body hard against his, her breasts tight against his ribs. She put her glass of wine to his lips. He drank, then kissed her, knocking the glass and spilling the wine. She threw the glass across the room at the fireplace but missed it. The glass shattered against the wall. Edward kissed the spilled wine from her chin, from her neck, from between her breasts where the purple streams were dammed.

He pulled her mantua off, she unbuttoned his breeches, he pressed her back into the wing chair and himself upon her and into her. The door opened, Maria looked in and saw nothing but a chair alive with blue stockinged legs bending and stretching until she looked into a mirror and saw the glazed eyes glancing at her, saw the heaving breasts, the boots and spurs, the small hands entwined in hair, then working up and down a strong back and buttocks, and heard a few spoken words amid the coos and grunts of passion:

"Ma... ria... go.. .away... damn you... O! More... Go... away... now!"

But Maria did not go away and Mrs. Hardy did not really seem to mind that she did not.

"Hurry, Edward," Jane said half an hour later as he

buttoned his breeches, "you'll be late. Can't you stay here today?"

He shook his head 'no'. Already he was failing to keep to his principles—and although he had told her nothing important, she already knew too much about him, and she had asked too many questions. Still, he realized, she had also answered all of his.

She sighed. "Then go. I did my best to keep you here. But remember my warnings: don't let your manhood do your thinking for you. Better me or one of my maids than Mistress O'Meary. Trust not the roads! And avoid the races!"

Jane watched from the window as he rode away. "Maria!" she called when he was out of sight, "Maria, I'll have a word with you!"

Chapter 10

To avoid those Desperate Combats, my Advice is for all Gentlemen to take a hearty Cup, and to Drink Friends to avoid Trouble.
—Donald McBane, *The Expert Sword-Man's Companion*, 1728

Edward rode at a canter to the stable at Ballydereen. Molly awaited, mounted on the chestnut mare Edward had ridden the day he arrived. She held the reins of a large dark bay gelding.

"I thought you might like to ride Rocinante today," she said, an odd look, almost of mistrust, in her eye.

Edward dismounted his own mount and took the reins of the extraordinarily tall horse, two inches more than seventeen hands. He adjusted his stirrups, then noted their height above the ground; he thought it too high for him to reach in his stiff boots.

"Shall I give you a leg up, sir?" asked a groom.

"No, thank you," Edward replied.

He grasped reins and mane with his left hand, pommel with his right, and, hoping the horse was not skittish, with a small leap swung himself into the saddle. The gelding took several steps forward as Edward clumsily gathered his reins and found his stirrups.

Molly turned her horse away and squeezed it into a trot.

Edward followed, uncomfortable. A walk or canter would have suited him better, given his hangover—at least it wasn't as bad as the first—but Molly's mood seemed to say he could follow or be damned for all she cared.

"I've been advised," she said as they trotted away from the manor, "that I should make you apologize and pay for being a notorious rake."

"I'm not a rake," Edward replied almost indignantly.

Molly laughed in that stinging way of some women when they wish to manipulate or have their revenge. "Come now, what gentleman would have your reputation?"

"What gentleman wouldn't, or at least wish for it?" Edward asked, quickly recovering his sense of humor. "And what reputation are we discussing? Anyway, I'm not sure I've ever been a gentleman, at least not in the sense of beating lackeys, refusing to pay my tailors, and cringing in front of noblemen great and small. Are you angry with me for some unknown indiscretion?"

"Yes, and jealous, too," she said daringly, "but I'll pretend I'm not. Come, I'll race you to the currach, we can make a double celebration there of your business success and Sir William's victories, for I'm sure his horses will win, they always do."

"My business success?"

"Sir William said you and he had reached agreement, and that your other business—your *intrigues*—were coming to a close too." Her tone changed, combining the jealous doubt she had displayed moments before with an almost Puritanical, judgmental haughtiness he had never seen in her. "I thought it must be to celebrate that you spent the night with that Dutch harlot who pretends to defend her son's estate. Isn't that what men do to celebrate—get drunk and lay with a woman?"

"You've no need to be jealous, Molly. Haven't you enough

suitors already?" he riposted cuttingly.

"I'm sorry," she said quickly.

She's quick to apologize, he thought. *Too quick. Maybe Jane's right and she's a husband hunter, no matter that she's betrothed. But you can't blame her, not in her circumstances.*

"I'm sorry," she repeated. "There's been much on my mind lately, nothing that need worry you, though. I was being selfish —I thought you might have told me if you had something to celebrate."

"In fact, I'm not quite ready to celebrate anything. I still have some minor business to settle with my correspondents, but it's nothing of consequence."

"Come," she said, "ride off to the countryside with me and leave the races for another day. You can tell me all the details of the privateering adventure you plan, when you will go, where you will go, how you expect to bring profitable violence down upon your French enemy. It would certainly be more interesting than listening to the local wives and their dull husbands. Here one only hears of how much an officer paid for a horse, or whose cargo made a profit, or who is bedding whom."

"I can't; I promised Sir William. Besides, you're the one who told me that we must be on time."

"Sir William won't mind much, and I, a woman, may change my mind as I please."

"You're not the first woman to try to keep me from the races today."

"But I didn't use the lure of my bed to do so!" she replied, and cantered ahead before he could see the expression on her face. He quickly caught up with her. "Please," she said, "let's skip the races anyway."

"It's one thing for everyone to gossip that I visit a widow, quite another that I'd ride off with a woman betrothed to another, and at a time when everyone expects us to be somewhere else. Your reputation might well be ruined. I won't be a part of that."

For an instant he thought he saw a hint of fury, then of acceptance. But between the two he thought he saw something else, some other emotion he could not quite identify.

They rode on, cantering this time until they saw the currach —the racing ground—in the distance, then halted in order to get a sense of the course. Not once more had Molly suggested they avoid the sporting event. For some reason this put Edward doubly on his guard. He touched his waist, but his wallet was not there. It was at Ballydereen, empty, waiting for the replies from Lord Brennan and Sir James Allin.

Edward and Molly walked their horses until they reached the crowded field. Much of the local population had already turned out for the races: the first between Irish hobbies, the following three heats of well-bred racing horses of English and Irish extraction, each carrying ten stone. They wove through a crowd that ranged from tenant farmers to noblemen, from fishermen and seamen to local tradesmen, from middle class merchants to soldiers and their officers. Amidst this mass of humanity, near a stone marker designated as the starting point for the several two-horse races, they found Sir William with his retinue of grooms, other servants, and friends. Given his gesticulations, he was doubtless describing the ancestry of his horses, as Edward had already heard him do a dozen times, repeating the genealogies as if he were reciting the sons of Adam.

Molly cantered toward Sir William, but before Edward could follow, two army officers, afoot but leading their mounts, stepped in his way.

"Good day, sir. Are you Captain Edward MacNaughton, the pirate?" asked one with a brusque sneer.

Edward regarded him curiously.

"I am Captain MacNaughton, a son of Neptune and Mars," he replied after a moment. "However, I'm no pirate, but if you want to quarrel with me, you may make the accusation again."

"We will speak with you privately, but first you must dismount."

Edward smiled. "Thank you, but I enjoy my station and prefer to keep it."

The two officers looked at each other, then mounted their horses. Edward laughed softly.

"Sir," said the officer on the left, "I'm Lieutenant Woodcock, this is Ensign Tillbury. We are here on behalf of Ensign Ingoldsby, to whom you have done a grave disservice by casting doubts upon his courage in the face of an enemy."

"I've done no such thing, and any man who says I have is either grossly misinformed or an arrant liar," Edward said calmly.

Woodcock flushed with anger, swallowed, and resumed his rehearsed speech. "It's bruited around the town and villages that you said repeatedly that Ensign Ingoldsby was not only drunk, but hiding in the ladies' quarters of the ship during the fight with the Frenchman. That, in fact, he is a coward."

"I've said nothing of the sort," Edward replied, still calm.

"Sir, we are well-informed by an unimpeachable source that you told these lies. Ensign Ingoldsby believes an apology is not sufficient for the injury he has received, but will accept one—if it is made with an abject admission that you have lied, for he feels he should in fairness show you mercy. Thus, sir, to avert bloodshed you must apologize *and* admit that you lied."

Edward laughed softly, then spoke loudly and clearly. "Gentlemen, I've never said any such thing regarding the ensign. In fact, I've hardly thought of him since I debarked the *Peregrinator*. But in case you're unaware of the facts, you should know that he was unconscious during most the fight, having had the misfortune to drink too much and knock his head, as I'm sure Lieutenant Fielding has told you. Even so, he wasn't hiding from the enemy. His timing was just poor. Rumors often have strange sources, and people will gossip and exaggerate in any case. Whatever the misunderstanding here, I won't apologize for something I haven't done and I'll never declare myself a liar except truthfully. But I'm sure you knew this before you came to me." He paused, then looked each officer fiercely in the eye. "And if either of you suggest again that I'm a liar, I'll fight you here and now."

Woodcock flushed again. "It doesn't matter what words you use now, sir, for the offense is in the words you used previously."

Edward's smile in reply was one of bemused contempt.

"So be it," the officer said, clearly annoyed. "We are therefore instructed to deliver this message: 'Having abused the honor and integrity of Ensign Ingoldsby, you are requested to meet him at your soonest convenience to satisfy this question of honor.' We'll serve as his seconds. Lieutenant Fielding has said he'll serve as one of yours if it pleases you."

"The lieutenant honors me. I'll inform him that I'd like to have done with this butcher's business as soon as possible. Is tomorrow too soon? Or should I let the lieutenant tend to this?"

"Tomorrow is quite satisfactory. The choice of weapons, of course, is yours. A gentleman's sword, or broad or back, is appropriate."

"No, by God!" interjected Sir William who had cantered up unnoticed, Lieutenant Fielding at his side. "Not tomorrow! Not tomorrow at all, by God!"

"You know about this?" asked Edward, somehow not surprised that Sir William had appeared.

"Everyone, lad, everyone knows about this—except you,

apparently, until now, for you've been busy with women, business, and *intrigues*," said Sir William in a low but excited voice. "The rumors have been flying for three days. Damn, lad, I know you need to get back to England, but there is no avoiding this, and when you kill Ingoldsby it will secure your reputation around here. Damn, lad, the Irish money's on you, both that you will accept and then kill the young officer. I'll be your other second, if you don't mind. Here, then, let me speak for you."

He turned to address the two officers, both of whom were red-faced from Sir William's blunt speaking. "The encounter will take place in a week, not tomorrow, and according to local custom. That is, on horseback on a marked field, with pistols and then broadswords if the pistols miss their marks. I trust this will suit your officer, for he's an officer of horse and this should suit him well." He turned to look at Edward. "Do you agree?"

Edward shrugged. "As you please." He had a feeling he was involved in something quite out of his control.

"Lieutenant Fielding and I will take care of the details if you want to do something else?" Sir William said, prodding him to leave.

"Of course, Sir William," Edward replied, and turned to ride away.

"Wait!" called one of the officers, "There is another matter we must settle before you leave."

"What is it that my seconds can't settle?" asked Edward as he slowly turned his mount about.

"It's a delicate question, sir, but one we must resolve now. We assume, sir, that, pirate though you were, you are once again a person of honor?"

Edward, who had remained calm, almost detached during the formal challenge, felt his heart begin to beat faster and his stomach to twist, sure signs of his growing anger.

Easy, he thought, *slow down, relax, there's never a time to lose your temper when involved in any part of a duel. Keep your temper cold, for in cold anger do you fight best.*

"You ask if I am a gentleman? You wish bona fides of some kind, a certificate of pedigree, a sworn statement as to my ancestry, perhaps?" he replied. He was not controlling his anger well, and his accent of Broad Scots combined with Virginia and Jamaica became more pronounced with each word, as it always did when he was angry or drunk. "Well ...—I'll handle this, Sir William—where should I begin? I canna truly say my antecedents are as prominent as the young Ensign's, but then, as the wise men say, what man truly knows his father?"

The two officers flushed at the insult.

"There must then be other criteria for a gentleman," Edward continued. "An education? I hae one, from the College of King James in Edinburgh, not Oxford or Cambridge, but many gentlemen are nae Bachelors, so I canna see that an education is necessary to be a gentleman, though many believe it makes a man so. The King's Commission? I hae held commissions under three kings—but then so hae many knaves, as knaves have in all armies of all kings. As gentlemen are never knaves, so I'm told, my commission canna serve as evidence. These things are but paper: a man is flesh, blood, and bone.

"Land? I own none, but I could; yet many who are nae gentlemen own land. Coat armor? A title? I bear none. But a man can buy them, yet a gentleman, they say, canna truly buy his nobility, great or petty. Travel? The Grand Tour? I hae seen more of this world than most gentlemen, but haena gone buggering in Florence like many a *gentleman* has. Gentle manners? They are unrelated to birth: I ken many a peasant with them, and many a gentleman without them. Courage? I hae known noblemen to show base cowardice, and base men to show noble courage."

Edward paused, his gaze fierce. When the officers blinked nervously, he spoke again. "In all my travels I hae never seen a man's birth to be a restriction on whether another man could or couldna kill him—except, of course, in the courts of law. A man dinna need be a gentleman to make a gude fight. But something must serve to satisfy you; I canna give you a paper. Hae ye forgotten my name? 'Tis MacNaughton, and proud I am of it, for a MacNaughton, mud on his boots or nae, is as gude a man as any in the Kingdom and I'll fight any man to prove it!"

He paused again. Seeing that none would reply, he continued. "You may be satisfied I'll provide Ensign Ingoldsby with much honor if he fights me, for I hae skill enou' in arms to challenge him. If he kills me, he may glory in having bested me, and if he dies, no one can say he died by a weak or dishonorable hand, for I'll fight him well and do my best to kill him. Will you *gentlemen*," he said sarcastically, "now be satisfied I'm of suitable cloth to face my challenger's pistols and sword?"

Woodcock replied as if he were biting his tongue. "We are satisfied. But, sir, you are arrogant in your ways—"

"Shall I take the measure of your bilbo too? We are discussing a duel, nae a minuet, and I see nae need to tread lightly when a man hae decided he must kill me. If we must fight, then let us do so and hae done with it! We are nae dogs sniffing and growling at each other, nae wee lads daring each other to step across a line!" Edward said arrogantly.

"Easy there, gentlemen!" said Sir William, "One duel at a time! We must be civilized as we prepare to kill each other. Edward, go and look after Molly, we'll take care of the details."

Edward rode away, coldly furious at the questioning of his ancestry and almost as furious at his own temper. It was a killing mood, a cold blooded thinking-without-thinking mood. Had he to fight the Ensign right now he would likely prevail, his cold hand thoughtlessly but effectively managing pistol, horse, and blade. He would calm down soon, and would be quite cool when it came time to fight, his nerves under control but still providing the edge he would need.

He looked for Molly among the crowd. Eventually he noticed a woman he thought might be her, speaking, or perhaps arguing, with a cloaked man. Both were mounted. Edward pulled a small perspective glass from his pocket and inspected the twain. There was nothing suspicious about them other than that they were alone, some three hundred yards or more away from everyone else, and may have been speaking to each other heatedly. He was certain the woman was Molly, but could learn nothing more of the man she was speaking to. His mount was sturdy, his clothing plain. He appeared unarmed. Edward watched for a minute more, then walked his horse toward them. Eventually Molly looked his way but seemed not to react. Moments later the man rode off at a canter, his hand waving in the air.

Molly turned her horse toward Edward and met him halfway.

"There's talk of a duel," she said when they met. "Is it true?"

"It seems everyone here except me knew about it. I certainly didn't expect a crowd to know about it before I did. As a matter of fact, I think even you knew of it before I did."

She ignored the obvious accusation. "Don't duels usually draw crowds?"

"Not in England, because they're against the law, even though a fair number engage in them—soldiers, drunk lawyers, gentlemen and noblemen with nothing better to do."

"So you'll join these fools?"

"I'm sure I'm not yet done with playing the fool. But better a fool than a coward."

"You don't have to fight this duel."

"What you mean is that you don't want me to. Why?"

"For practical reasons that mean a lot to Sir William: if you die here your venture dies too."

"That doesn't seem to bother Sir William."

"Perhaps I have other reasons."

"You're betrothed and I'm not looking for a wife."

She flushed angrily. "You assume too much! Don't take my suggestion earlier that we avoid the races as anything other than concern for a friend, to keep him from foolish harm."

"I'm suitably chastised, Mistress O'Meary," he said.

"I doubt it, sir! Good luck, Captain MacNaughton," she said and rode off without another word.

Sir William and Lieutenant Fielding arrived before Edward could follow her.

"The betting continues, lad!" said Sir William, grinning widely. "Two or three months in advance would be better, but there'll be plenty of interest as it is. You'll have a grand audience, sir! I'll make certain the constable and his hired officers don't interfere, and the magistrate has already made some wagers, on you of course. I hear the betting among the soldiers will likely be evenly divided between the two of you. Their commanders won't be a problem as long as the issue is settled honorably. Of course, some of them will prefer it if their lad wins, but that's not the outcome I foresee. Kill the officer, or at least put him *hors de combat*, and I can then prevail on others to invest in your venture. Don't disappoint me!"

"I'll try not to disappoint myself," Edward said wryly.

"Do that. We'll speak more later; the first race begins soon. I'm running a horse against the Viscount Brennan, and I want you at my side for luck. Mine's an evilly fast one, sired by the Turkish mount Colonel Byerly rode at the Boyne. When the day is done we'll ride home together and speak some more. There's much to prepare." His countenance changed. "And, strictly between us, I don't think you should spend too much time with

Molly, at least not between now and the day of the duel. It's your business, of course, but beware. She has strange ways sometimes, even for a woman. She's seen hard times, not that we all haven't, but they've affected her more than most of us. You need no distractions. Keep to the Dutch woman instead, she won't play any games."

"Of course, Sir William. But if you'll both excuse me for a few minutes, I need to think a few things over."

"Certainly, my friend, certainly."

Edward watched as his seconds trotted off to attend the next race.

Something's not quite right, he thought, *something's just not quite right.*

But he couldn't put his finger on whatever it was, and for the moment he settled on the hypothesis that his misgivings were due to nothing more than his engaging too closely with Jane and Molly, and thus with Fortune.

She's trying to beguile me again, he thought, *but this time it's my fault.*

He drew a flask of Spanish brandy from a pocket, took a swallow to warm his insides, and suddenly felt certain there were hostile eyes upon him—and not all of them belonging to Ensign Ingoldsby and his seconds.

Chapter 11

So in their own sense Duelling cannot properly vindicat[e]
any opprobrious epithet, but that of a Coward.
—Wm. Anstruther, *Essays, Moral and Divine*, 1701

A week later Edward was on the currach, well-armed and
well-mounted for single combat. An eager crowd looked on, for
here was an adventurer who was or had been buccaneer,
privateer, naval officer, dragoon, hussar, fencing master,
duelist, and pirate—an experienced if sometime reluctant killer
ready to kill yet again, this time with an audience. Huntsmen
and gamekeepers held the surging tide of four or five hundred
spectators back.

It's like a race-meeting or fair, he thought.

Many of the spectators were women. Most of those of the
gentry and nobility were masked and remained in their
carriages or on their horses at a distance, but those of the poor,
working, and middle classes consorted unmasked in the crowd,
although a few did celebrate in small groups in coaches hired
for the purpose. Like the men, they had come to see a bloody
adventure. Both sexes drank, many smoked, all talked and
laughed loudly. The celebratory atmosphere was at odds with
the melancholy air played by two fiddlers, "Once I Had a
Sweetheart."

Edward knew Jane was there, and Molly too. A handful of

men stood apart from the crowd while trying to look a part of it, and if Edward were still a soldier he would have looked them over. He had no time for such military curiosity today, for his adversary already faced him at the opposite end of the field.

The county trumpeter, known best for his duties at the county assizes, sounded a levet, the trumpet's notes commanding silence. When he had the crowd's rapt attention he put a ship's speaking trumpet to his mouth.

"Oyez, oyez, oyez! Today for honor Captain Edward MacNaughton, famous Scots buccaneer, swordsman of renown, breaker of Spanish heads and despoiler of Spanish riches, will fight Ensign James Ingoldsby, brave soldier to His Majesty King William!"

Poor bastard! Edward thought as he watched Ingoldsby receive the small accolade. *The crowd's already against him, not that it will make much difference once we come to blows.*

The trumpeter continued. "These brave men will fight for honor under our Irish rules: two passes at the hand gallop with one pistol each pass, and then with swords on horseback if neither brave man falls, is badly wounded, or begs quarter! The arms of these bold warriors are a brace of pistols loaded with single ball and five swan drops, a cutting sword, and a skean, dirk, or other short blade! I do note one exception to our ancient Irish rules: there will be no distance separating the riders! They may pass as close as they please!"

And thereby be more likely to wound or kill each other, Edward thought cynically.

Under the common rules, the duelists would have ridden against each other at the gallop, separated by posts roughly eight yards apart, and would fire a single pistol at each pass, making it unlikely either would hit the other, except perhaps with a swan drop, which was unlikely to do serious damage. But Edward and the ensign had no need of such humanitarian protections. The ensign intended to kill Edward, and Edward, who cared not whether he killed the ensign, only that the ensign fell and he did not, felt such rules only postponed the quietus.

"Gentlemen, prepare yourselves for battle!" the trumpeter ordered. The crowd looked on in animated silence.

Edward stood in his stirrups to double-check their proper length, having shortened them so that he might stand the taller in the saddle, of great benefit at swords. He settled back into his saddle, tugged at the stiff leather cuffs of his gauntlets, and prepared his arms.

In his mind he checked each step as he made it. *Draw and hang your backsword from the right wrist, make sure the sword knot's secure. Draw and cock the pistol in the right holster, put it back. Draw the left, cock it, hold it in front of the lock with thumb and forefinger, barrel to the left, hold the reins with the smaller fingers and make sure to shorten the reins on the left, as Rocinante pulls to the right, done. Draw the right pistol, point it skyward, flints are new and sharp, vents are clear, we're ready, Goddamn it, we're ready!*

His heart pounded harder and faster, his mouth was dry and he felt butterflies in his stomach. Rocinante pawed the ground, shook his head, and shuddered. A horse in the distance whinnied. Rocinante whinnied back.

Edward touched his right pistol to the brim of his hat. His adversary, one hundred yards away, returned the salute in the same manner.

He's showing some panache, or at least replying to it, Edward thought. *He's not so scared that he can't fight.*

"Are you ready?" shouted the trumpeter.

Edward checked his feet in his stirrups and breathed deeply. Rocinante stamped the ground and tossed his head, then moved his forefeet to and fro as if he were dancing in place. Edward pulled slightly on the reins and Rocinante threw his head powerfully back, restrained only by the martingale.

Easy, boy, no time for an argument with you now; it's the man and horse down the course we need to fight. We'll be off in a moment; I hate waiting too. We'll do this in one pass, all right? Steady there, steady, my Quixotic comrade-in-arms.

Edward raised his right arm, pistol in hand, straight up over his head to signal he was ready. Ingoldsby did the same.

The trumpeter raised his speaking trumpet to his mouth and his smallsword, a red handkerchief tied at the point, to the sky.

"Gentlemen! At the gallop... Charge!" he bellowed and sharply swung his smallsword down.

And they were off!

Give him spur, lean in but keep out of the saddle, use his head for cover, cluck to him, there we go, we're almost flying!

Fourteen hundred pounds of muscle, breath, and bone raced down the course. The wind teared Edward's eyes and only the weight of the skull cap stitched inside his hat kept it on his head. He could only imagine what he must look like on the huge, dark horse whose wide nostrils blew white fire like some demon from hell.

Head down, keep your head down! Keep the horse off his forehand ... Go! Go! Go! Here he comes!

Edward brought his pistol to bear.

Ready .... Edward prepared to suddenly cut across the ensign's path. *Fire to the left, force him to do the same, he's probably not comfortable shooting like this .... Damn him!*

The ensign had ridden just a bit wide, forcing Edward to fire conventionally, to his right. He saw the ensign's pistol aimed at him.

Almost there, wait, wait ... Fire!

Edward fired a hair before they came abreast, as did his enemy. A tight column of invisible flame passed his cheek;

smoke burned his eyes.

Something's on fire! Dammit!

He flung his empty pistol away and rubbed his gloved hand over the smoldering tow he discovered on his coat.

Christ, a good coat almost ruined, he realized, *I'll have to patch the damned thing*, then wondered at the absurdity of the thought under the circumstances.

Quickly but carefully now, come about, get your other pistol ready!

He gripped his second pistol and pulled Rocinante swiftly about to the left on his haunches.

Hellfire, the little bastard's got a nimble beast, he's already charging at me!

Edward spurred his mount forward, pulling slightly on the reins as he did. Rocinante reared in response. Edward released the reins, touched him again with the spurs, and with a jump and buck Rocinante leaped to the gallop.

The horse raced ahead furiously, less under control now and more on his forehand than he ought to be.

Let him have the rein, Edward cautioned himself, *he'll buck if you pull him back.*

Edward brought his pistol to bear; this time he intended pass so closely their boots would touch. Yet suddenly the ensign cut across from right to left as Edward had himself intended to do on the first pass!

Edward was neither novice nor fool on horseback. From Hungarian hussars he had learned such tricks and their counters. Immediately he pulled Rocinante around to his left, but the great horse was not nimble enough and his head blocked Edward's aim.

He saw the twin flashes of vent and muzzle, heard the crack of pistol, and was blinded by gun smoke.

What the hell! he cursed as he felt two dull blows, followed immediately by pains sharp yet dull in his left thigh and buttock. *Only small shot!*

Rocinante had not yet spun entirely about, but the ensign had already ridden past. Edward aimed his pistol to the rear over his shoulder, hussar-style, and fired, but to no avail. A small flash and smoke followed from the vent, then, slightly delayed, a larger flash and plume of smoke from the barrel.

Damned hangfire!

But he was not likely to have hit the young officer anyway.

Already the ensign, more skilled on horseback than Edward had anticipated, had turned swiftly about, backsword now in hand, and was charging at the gallop.

Edward pitched his pistol away, flipped his hand down into the basket-hilt and around the grip of the backsword, and only cantered Rocinante toward the oncoming rider.

No need for a gallop at swords.

The ensign held his sword high and threw an outside cut, screaming as he did. Sparks flew as Edward easily parried it, his blade high and outside. The ensign passed swiftly, leaving the Scotsman to settle for a back stroke that cut through coat but otherwise did no damage.

I've paid you for my coat, sir!

The men rode three strides, turned to face each other, spurred their mounts to an easy canter and flung their blades again, each attack parrying the other, the blades sparking brightly.

Edward pulled Rocinante quickly to the right to try for the officer's crupper, but the ensign did the same. Again they cantered three strides to open the distance, again at each other they came, again at an easy canter.

The ensign stood suddenly in his stirrups and brought his blade down hard toward Edward's left cheek, but the mounted Scotsman, far taller in the saddle, parried the attack with a prime, and thrust quickly, his point low, to the ensign's upper chest.

Flesh and bone! Edward thought as his blade struck.

He spurred Rocinante to the right, again to gain the crupper. Ingoldsby, clearly injured, thrust his backsword twice into Rocinante's haunch. The great animal squealed once and bucked twice.

"Keep under control, damn you!" Edward cursed under his breath.

The ensign spurred his mount away for several strides, then spun about and halted.

"Will you yield?" Edward called.

"Damn you for calling me coward! Never!"

"On my honor I never said such!"

"You lie!"

"You are sore hurt, sir!"

"It's nothing! I'll do far worse to you, sir!"

The young officer advanced again, but now only at the trot. Edward waited. Soon the combined weapons of man and horse stood side by side.

No more sweeping strokes for you, ensign! he thought grimly.

Neither duelist could now safely make the broad cuts suitable on horseback at a gallop or canter, but must make tighter, less damaging cuts, or thrusts to the throat or belly— easy in, easy out, and usually fatal. A sweeping cut now, if parried or slipped, would leave the swordsman vulnerable to a counter stroke.

Ingoldsby threw a tight high inside cut. Edward parried it with his hilt high, his point low and immediately riposted with a thrust which the young officer only just escaped by moving his mount sideways.

Why doesn't the fool yield? Edward wondered. *He's*

bleeding hard, he can hardly parry anymore; on the next exchange I'll probably kill him.

Men and horses spun to the right around each other. Noting the ensign's lowering guard due to his injury, Edward threw a fast, hard outside at his ear. The ensign barely parried it in time: Edward's blade cut through his hat and across the bridge of his nose.

The ensign turned swiftly and rode three strides away to the jeers of the crowd. Clearly the spectators did not know he was wounded.

"Yield, lad! Yield before you bleed to death!" Edward shouted as the ensign's seconds, more alert than the crowd, galloped toward the injured officer. "Damn, laddie, you've proved your courage! Let's drink friends and have done with this foolish butcher's business!"

"Never!"

Edward shook his head. *You damn fool, you're bleeding so much that before long you'll fall from your mount. All I need do is keep away from you and thereby spare you, but damn if you deserve my mercy, you fool.*

But before his seconds arrived, the ensign dug his spurs into his mount and came at Edward at full gallop, hand and sword held high. The Scotsman had no time to slip aside as the young officer aimed a sweeping blow at Rocinante's head, leaving Edward to lean forward and thrust his blade out over his mount's head just in time to prevent the ensign's blow from splitting the animal's skull.

The ensign's blade glanced off to his left. Edward stood tall in his stirrups and from shoulder and elbow brought his own blade across in a powerful backstroke, over his mount's head and straight at Ingoldsby's ear. He spurred and pulled Rocinante to the right as he did, and caught a glimpse of the ensign's blade cutting back toward him.

Shit! he thought as his blade struck and bit, and he knew immediately that it was impossible for him parry the officer's exchanged stroke.

Rocinante hurled into the ensign's horse. The great animal squealed as he did, then stumbled, threw his head, and broke the martingale. Something smashed hard into Edward's face, stunning him, and something else into his foot and ankle. Or was it was the other way around?

The ground is coming up! No! My horse is going down!

Images one after the other filled his eye and mind while a small detached part of him wondered in these few short slow seconds just what the hell was happening.

Am I hit? Is the horse? The ensign, too? Shit-fire!

He slammed into the ground.

Pain, in the ankle, pain in my face, my leg—did the horse land on it? No, it was there before, a pain like an ax biting into my leg....

Dirt and mud flew everywhere. He saw the sky, he saw the horse. His face, something had hit him in the face.

My front teeth, do I still have my front teeth? He couldn't get his hands up to feel them. *You're on the ground, fool, can't you smell the mud and grass? Get up! The horse, he's on your leg, he's kicking, don't move, cover your face, I can't, wait for him to get up, can he get up? He's moving, get out from under him, get up, get up.*

My Ferrara! Where the hell is my sword! Draw your dirk, draw your dirk! Where's the ensign, damn him! He comes afoot, sword raised, get up you fool—he's going to kill you! Close with him, command his hilt and thrust, now thrust again... damn, can't pull the dirk from his armpit, he's down now, don't fall... too late.

What the hell's this around me? People running, the horse kicking on the ground. Copper, a sweet penny in my mouth, no, blood, whose blood? The horse, up now; get up, remount. I'm up again, on my feet, the horse, he's in pain, go to him, wait, canna, my ankle, did the horse land on it? Where's the ensign?

One step, another, I can walk, I'm not hurt that badly, take care of the horse, is that blood all over my face? And water, warm water in my boot, how did it get there? The ensign, where's the ensign? My Ferrara, damn, what happened to my sword? Rocinante, that's his name, restrain him, he's bleeding, but he's on his feet, that's good, he must be all right, and I'm all right....

Edward's right leg collapsed and his vision narrowed.

Damn! he thought as he hit the ground, *I might finally be killed ....*

Chapter 12

Wounds cut and hackt in heat of Fight by a broad Sword...
—Richard Wiseman, *Several Chirurgicall Treatises,* 1676

"Edward! Stay down, lad, stay down, let us help you!" shouted Sir William as he dismounted and stumbled on his game leg.

Now that his head was down, and his body splayed upon the ground, Edward's vision and head began to clear.

"Yes, I'm fine, fine, don't worry about me, Goddammit. The horse, how's Rocinante?"

"Easy, Edward, lie back, stay where you are."

"No, I'm fine, Goddammit, I need to see the horse!"

"Damn you, Edward, lie still where you are or I'll take a stick to your damn stubborn head! Surgeon! Surgeon!"

Edward tried to stand in spite of Sir William's restraint, but his ankle immediately gave way. Blood squished and oozed from his right boot. Someone fiddled at his right wrist—his backsword was in fact still there, hanging from the sword knot. A surgeon walked quickly over from a group of bystanders inspecting something on the ground.

"Cut off his boot," he ordered, and someone began cutting the boot away.

"Pull it off, damn you, I don't want it cut!"

"It's already cut, lad."

"What? What's wrong, the horse landed on it, so what?"

"Just be patient," the surgeon said.

"A pun," Edward muttered through the shock of the blow to his head.

Sir William cut through the thick leather, exposing the bloody flesh beneath.

Damnation, thought Edward, *it wasn't the horse, I felt the ax before we fell. Hellfire, my leg's been split open! Don't let it make me a cripple! But I'm alive, I'm still alive.*

"Is it shattered?" he asked, fearing the surgeon's saw.

The surgeon did not answer.

Sir William looked at Edward and grinned. "Split his head open from side to side, never seen a prettier blow in my life, except once when I was in London—one of only three times I was ever in London, in fact—I saw a Highland soldier strike off the head of a Dutchman. I don't know which the ensign died of, your backsword or your dirk, but by God, for a moment I thought he might kill you in spite of all when he came at you dying and gurgling and spitting blood. Good that you had the instinct to dirk the bastard when you couldn't find your sword."

"He's dead? I don't remember... yes, I do now, of course he's dead. How did I get hurt?"

"Ingoldsby struck your mount in the face just as you struck him. The horse threw his head back, breaking his martingale and striking you hard in your face, then stumbled. I'm surprised the blow didn't knock you unconscious. Damned if that ensign didn't stay in the saddle for a moment and take two more swings at you as your mount slipped and went down. Lucky Rocinante didn't land on you, but your seat is light and you fell away."

"How is he? The horse, I mean."

"He's got a long cut in the face and has been stabbed in his right shoulder and haunch. I don't think his wounds are serious, though. And I warned you about his forehand!" Sir William grinned again. "But by God, what a day! And you, lad, you'll be fine, I feel it in my bones. Hell, this surgeon can fix anything! He's fixed all my wounds, and my horses' too, and I won't let him carve anything from you unless there's no other choice—understand? You'll be fine, lad, you'll be fine."

The surgeon finished his examination. "You're lucky," he said, "for you could be missing your foot or even your head. I've stanched the bleeding for now, but I can't work on you here. You're cut deeply in the ankle and shin, well into the bone. You're lucky your adversary hadn't much strength left, otherwise he might've taken your foot off. Amazing what a dying man can do. You've a couple of small shot in you too, but I think only in the flesh." He turned to Sir William. "I'll work on him at Ballydereen."

Several bystanders lifted Edward clumsily onto a two-horse sledge. One of Sir William's servants climbed on as well to keep an eye on the Scotsman and keep his leg secure.

Edward looked where several men stood about, some shaking their heads. The young ensign lay dead before them on the wet ground. A crowd of spectators had approached yet kept its distance. An English officer held the ensign's broadsword, its hilt of ornate chiseled iron surrounding an image of King William. The air was filled with mutterings in Irish and English.

Ensign Ingoldsby lay on his back, his periwig gone. His eyes remained open, glazed as if by tears, and his pupils were wide, one more so than the other. Though much of the blood on his face had been wiped away, much still remained, and the ground around his head was a moist, deep purple, almost black. In the middle of his face was great split that began below his right ear and stopped just beneath his nose; a grotesque wound, yet it seemed at first merely an abstract defect, like a rend in a painting. Only after a moment did the mind recoil.

His limbs had been moved from their splayed positions into those more natural, leaving the body looking passive and relaxed. It exuded a surreal quality, unlike sleep, unlike death, unlike the unnatural quality of bodies laid up for viewing at a wake, unlike bodies in rigor mortis, but rather a sort of detached reality, the body still warm and pliable, as if with the addition of a single spark it might live and breathe again, in spite of the wound in its face and the dirk thrust to the hilt through armpit, shoulder, and throat.

Edward viewed the corpse distantly. The vulgar game was finished, the petty play of expensive consequences was done. The duel had proved only that both men were valiant at arms, that neither was a coward; but such virtues were better proved on the battlefield. Only, perhaps, in his dreams would the finality of this man's death become truly apparent to Edward. In his waking hours he had neither the time nor inclination to grieve over every absurd death. Too much grief, too much morbid contemplation, and a man was dragged down, unable to live even day by day.

Damn the young fool, Edward thought. *Twice I offered to let him yield.*

"Let's go, damn it," he called to the sledge's driver. The pain in his ankle remained tolerable, even if excruciating. He had been hurt before. Pain was never so bad as it seemed, or so he always convinced himself so that he could manage it better.

Edward and his swelling entourage departed, but it was nearly an hour before they reached Ballydereen. Along the way, a crowd gathered to follow the sledge. They cheered, they wished him well, they called him a hero. A small crowd remained outside the manor house as Edward was carried to the kitchen and laid upon a table. Someone slid a rolled-up cloak beneath his head. His pain was worse now, nearly ninety minutes after the original injury. What had been quite tolerable at first was becoming increasingly distracting. His legs trembled and twitched, as if by kicking or shaking them he could toss away the pain. He ground his teeth and attempted to maintain a stoic disposition.

Fortune, he thought, *you fickle bawd, you deserted me today, but I should've expected it. Maybe Jane's right, maybe you're having your revenge because I ignored you twice.*

One of Sir William's servants brought two bottles.

"Local poteen, Captain MacNaughton, or Irish *uiscebagh*?" he asked.

"Whiskey!" Edward almost bellowed. He took several swallows, stopping only when the arriving surgeon, his sleeves bloody and rolled up, his hands wet, took the bottle from him.

"A drunken Highlander—and I know you to be a Highlander, or mostly so, for Sir William tells me you are—will hurl my assistants across the room. Best you were sober and awake. A sleeping or drunken patient can't have his wound cleaned and ligatures tied without risk because he can't answer questions his surgeon ask. As a fighting man, you know this. I'll admit, though, that whiskey is often a better cure than my rusty steel," he said with a hint of a smile.

"I'm not entirely a Hielander," Edward muttered.

"Even so, it's my belief that you'll survive my surgery, but don't blame me if Fortune decides otherwise. Do you need a parson or priest?"

"Nae, keep the bedrals away. I'm nae papist, nae Presbyter, nae even of the English church."

"Of which, then? Not that it will matter to my surgery."

"Of the church of pen and sword, of woman and wine, of wind and weather."

"As fine as any, I dare say."

"Another patient?" Edward asked, nodding toward the

blood on the surgeon's sleeves.

"Rocinante."

"Indeed? He's well, I hope?" Edward asked sarcastically.

"Quite. I've directed an assistant to finish tending his wounds. He'll soon be under the care of Mistress O'Meary, who, by the way, sends this message: she thanks God for your deliverance, and will attend you as soon as I've finished my business with you, and she can't bear to think of you in pain."

"Probably likes the horse better."

"Probably. Mrs. Hardy also sends her well wishes, and I hear there's a gaggle of young women and older widows outside praying for your recovery. You'll be well-tended to, sir, and doubtless pleasantly distracted while you heal. Now to your wounds."

The surgeon drew several steel and pewter instruments from his bag: straight and curved incision and dismembering knives; probes, forceps, and incision shears to spread and penetrate wounds; bone saws whose teeth grinned and wanted to eat flesh.

"Put this musket ball between your teeth, bite down, and do not move. Doubtless you've done this before." He nodded to several men surrounding the table. They grasped Edward by his arms and legs and held him down.

"Ughn!"

"Don't swallow it," grinned the surgeon as he began to spread apart the wounds. "Cut and splintered bone, sinews partly severed, much bleeding but not florid. Still, it ought to have stopped by now. On the other hand, a good blood-letting will do you no harm."

Edward stared at the ceiling while the surgeon washed his hands in his blood. He tried several times to watch the procedure, but his view was obscured by the grimacing faces of the self-appointed assistants.

The whiskey helped to block the pain. It did not remove it, but it made him care less about it, made it seem farther away than it really was. When the surgeon was not probing or cutting, the pain felt merely like a great weight pressing/crushing/smashing his throbbing foot and mind. But when the surgeon probed the wounds, when he pushed and pried at bone, when he pressed, pulled, tugged, and cut, Edward was forced to grip the sides of the table until he could not feel his hands, forced to bite deeply into the lead bullet between his teeth, forced to curse dully, twice, through the bullet as the pain seared like a sharp, hot knife forced between his bones; it felt as if his foot was being twisted, pulled from his socket, shattered, splintered, torn away bit by bit, muscle by muscle, tendon by tendon, shard of bone by shard of bone, and his mind saw nothing but a burning sun and his voice choked as he tried a third time to shout through his clenched teeth: "Goddamn! Goddamn! Goddamn!"

"I've almost finished," the surgeon said finally. "So that you may know what I've done so far, I'll quote from memory of my study, for you're an educated man and can thereby increase your knowledge: 'The first is, in careful and diligent taking away all such extraneous bodies as by their interposition may hinder the true agglutination of the disjoined parts, whether they be concrete blood, hair, sand, dust, pieces of bones, cartilages, or pieces of weapons, rags, etc.' That is, I've cleaned your wounds of splinters of bone and scraps of skin and flesh.

"'The second is, in bringing the lips of the wound even together, which were separated.' In other words, I've made sure I've trimmed the lips of the wound such that they will fit together well. 'The third is, in retaining the lips so brought together, that they may by consolidation be restored to their former figure.' This should be obvious enough: I've sewn you up, one stitch per finger's breadth of wound. None of the

Spaniard's glover's stitch for me except in your face, although I see by one of your scars that you were likely once already sewn up this way. By a Spaniard?"

"By a Spaniard."

"Surely an interesting story; you must tell it to me one day, assuming you survive my ministrations." The surgeon smiled. "I was a sea surgeon once, thus my gallows humor. But I'm sure you're more interested in your prognosis than my surgical history. In sum, your shin and ankle are not as bad as thought, though you have two good sword bites to the bone. You were lucky, for the sinews are mostly intact, and none of the bones were broken through. You should heal quickly, in other words. I've also removed the swan drops from your leg and buttock, and I've sewn up your upper lip where you put your teeth all the way through. I've done your vanity a favor and used the glover's stitch on your lip so the scar won't be too large. Still, you might have to grow mustachios if you're vain." The surgeon pressed on his front teeth. "Not too loose; you likely won't lose them. Hard teeth, hard head."

"Are you sure you dinna just push them out?" Edward retorted weakly.

"If I made false teeth in addition to sawing bones and sewing up wounds, I might have considered it, but I don't. Lie still now and be quiet, sir. I have more still to do."

The final procedure completed, Edward lay on the table in his shirt, bandages, and splint, soaked in sweat, the pains in his leg and foot almost intolerable. He did not even notice the ache in his teeth.

It's not that bad, he thought, *and in two, three days it will no longer be bothersome. Best to sleep 'til then.*

"How soon before I'm healed?" he asked, his eyes closed.

"Hard to say, but, unless you wake up one morning to find your lower leg missing, you should be able to bear weight on your foot in a month or so, and be completely healed in eight or ten weeks, maybe more, maybe less. You'll have a bastard gout in the foot and ankle, I dare say, and you may limp to some degree, at least for a few months. Bloodletting, by the way, is a seasonable remedy for the wandering pains you'll have in ankle and foot. We'll know better in a few days whether mortification will set in. If it does, I'll take your leg off below the knee."

Eight or ten weeks, Edward thought, *eight or ten weeks. Much too long, much too long.*

Soon he was asleep, the pair of wolfhounds at his feet and Molly eyeing him from the door.

Chapter 13

The Kernes, the Rapparees, those wild Irish, Who are not yet reform'd...
—Solomon Bolton, *The Present State of Great Britain, and Ireland,* 1745

"We need to get going," Edward said. "We've finished the wine, it's growing late, and the roads are not safe, no matter what you say. It'll be dark soon, and we won't make it to Ballydereen with light to spare even if we leave now."

"I know," Molly said with a sigh and a smirk, "there are rapparees and wolves and things that hide in the night. But I'm safe with you, aren't I, with your sword, handsome furniture, and bad leg?"

He groaned. She had teased him all day, taking nothing he said seriously.

"If we're confronted, I'm only one man—"

"And I'm but one woman. That's two of us, and if the sum is greater than the parts, then we two as one would be formidable."

The clichés, drawn perhaps from bad poetry, annoyed Edward. Somewhere in his head a voice warned, calling him to arms against women with agendas of seduction.

"Poetry is for the fireside, not dangerous roads at dusk," he said.

"You're growing cold and boring again, like a winter rain," she said, continuing the refrain. "Why are you always so serious?" She grinned. "It's safer to travel by night anyway. People worth robbing travel only by day, because they're afraid to travel at night."

"Sir William will flay my hide if anything happens to you," he said, then limped to the horses. He untied the leather hobbles securing their front legs, stood up, and suddenly Molly was there, an inch in front of him, a horse at his back.

"Don't move, Edward. If you press the horse he'll move aside, and then I'll be your only security. I could let you stand or fall as I please." Her voice still teased, more subtly, yet with a sharp edge.

He looked at her green-grey eyes, her long hair hanging down about her pretty neck, and thought her a selkie or nereid changed to sylph in the twilight.

She kissed him, then he her. He pulled away.

Inexplicably his hand itched for his sword and he felt eyes upon him again.

"I was going to say that you kiss well enough, even with a fresh scar on your lip," Molly said after he stepped back.

"We have to go," he said. "If you're not concerned about wolves or rapparees, then at least be concerned about your reputation and Sir William's ire."

Edward, fool though he often was where women were involved, suddenly realized she had been subtly arranging her activities to coincide with his since the day of the duel. The answer appeared obvious: there were signs that her estate might be seized, so she had abandoned her pretense of letting any and all men woo her until her estate was safe, and resolved to marry one who could save her—either him or any other of the many who best suited her purpose. She was laying a trap, one without malice or ill intent other than self-interest. Yet he could not set aside his growing suspicion that something malicious was at work somewhere.

They mounted their restless horses and trotted down the road.

It had only been a month since the duel, and Edward's more serious wounds were not yet entirely healed. His leg remained weak, and a corner of one wound still oozed a drop or two of blood each hour. The rest had knit neatly, leaving thick purple scars. He and Sir William made quite a pair when together, limping along, yet no one made too much fun of them, at least not in their presence.

"Another month and you can cast the cane aside," the surgeon had said, only a week ago, but Edward had proved him wrong within the hour. He had to return to Bristol, and within a week more, wind and tide permitting, he would.

Edward's recovery, however, had been precarious. On the fourth day the surgeon had been pleased, as laudable pus appeared in his most severe wound, indicating that it was healing. But two days later the wound was greatly inflamed, and the surgeon feared mortification had set in. In order to keep Edward quiet and still, he bled him repeatedly, over Edward's obscene objections, putting his life more in danger than it had been during the duel. Fever made him hallucinate: a cutlass pierced his throat as he prepared to leap forward from an ambuscade, yet he felt no pain. He barely escaped from a raging sea, an ocean which let him approach the shore, then drew him back, a living being of great water who, as soon as he thought he had escaped, tossed him toward a dark ship. Suddenly he was cornered in Scotland, surrounded by soldiers, then rescued by an officer, whose rescue had a price of service in Ireland, bloody Ireland.

Ireland! he had thought, *I must be awake! I remember now, I'm in Ireland!*

The ship exploded, and he would have sworn he was truly awake. Yet as he looked about him he saw nothing but tombstones, barrows, and cairns, and graves in the shape of men, and he was wrapped in a woolen shroud, with shrouds or mists hanging above. He also saw furniture, and sconces on walls, and great beasts lying nearby, and all was gray, and all was real, and he thought himself in the land of the dead.

A horse!

He heard a horse, he found a horse, two horses, and he leapt to them, to and fro, but found neither to his liking as he rode on one then the other, and suddenly he heard the sound of trees again, and out the window he saw green everywhere, and hills, and he smelled air filled with rain, and he knew again that all was well, and he realized he had not been riding two horses but had been shifting his injured foot back and forth, trying to find a comfortable place to rest it.

Edward vaguely remembered Molly visiting while his fever raged and his hallucinations tormented him. She appeared an angel to him as she came to see him during the night, candle in one hand, the other hidden. He thought he had asked her one night not to leave, but perhaps he only dreamed this. In his fever, he thought she touched his wounds, a soft, magical, healing touch. After his delirium began to clear, she became his constant companion, bringing his meals and tending him until he could get back on his feet. He enjoyed the attention, yet it also made him uncomfortable. And when others visited, officers from the garrison at Charles Fort, for example, she was attentive with them instead, even, if he were not mistaken, flirting with some of them.

Curiously, this made him jealous. Sensing his discomfort, she always maneuvered to distract him by having him describe to her the business of merchantmen and privateers, of their comings and goings, of the gossip of Bristol, of all the details of places and things she had no experience of.

Only Jane and the surgeon had come close to being as solicitous of his health. The lady and one or both of her maids—the latter variously giggling and smiling rapturously, the former appearing confident yet vulnerable, and all of them overtly sexual—came every other day to sit at his bedside, engage him in conversation, read to him, play cards with him, and invariably offer to aid him in any way they might. Molly despised their visits. The surgeon came daily, always commenting on Edward's progress. He changed the dressings only every three days, and once quietly cursed the poultice someone had applied in his absence.

"Still bleeding from one wound, I see, even after cauteries of hot iron and styptic which I only use as a last resort. Well, don't worry, Scots blood runs thick, so the bleeding will stop eventually. It always does, one way or another, it's a surgical maxim," he said one morning, smiling as he squeezed the bandages and watched the blood ooze through the linen fibers. Then, on another morning, "I believe you're healing, sir; I have brought my saw for nothing." But Edward knew him to be a fine surgeon in spite of his necrotic sense of humor.

A physician had also once come to visit, to clyster him: "You've been long abed, sir, and must be purged of your intestinal irritability." Notwithstanding that clysters were commonly used in many treatments, Edward clapped a pistol to the man's breast and invited him to insert the large metal syringe into his own backside. The physician never returned. From a lifetime of adventure Edward knew that he healed best when physicians kept their lancets and clysters at a distance.

Likewise Parson Waters, now employed by Sir William, who never would have ordered prayers for Edward until the parson vowed he would never pray for a heathen Scot who might be a Presbyter or other Nonconformist, or worse, a papist, or worst of all a free thinker. Sir William, anticipating Edward's reaction, had promptly ordered the parson into Edward's room to pray. The Scotsman had sent him out, as he had with the physician, never to return. Sir William had smiled for two days. Edward, however, no matter how amused he was with the joke, did not trust the parson. The man in black often hovered nearby, especially when either Molly or Jane was in Edward's company. The Reverend Waters smelled of something more than a mere busybody or gossip: he had the stench of a troublemaker.

As for the duel, the forms had been followed and the coroner's inquest had cleared him: he would not stand trial. It helped that he was a Scot and his opponent an army officer, the challenge and fight well-witnessed and honorably fought. Even had there been a trial, Edward would likely have been acquitted.

His thoughts returned to the present. The shadows had grown long and Molly seemed pensive in her irritation.

Is she in love with me, he wondered, *or is it something else —the tactics of marrying me to save her estate?*

Edward was not in love with her, and now that he was no longer an invalid he considered it unlikely he would fall in love with her; nor did he wish to be inconvenienced by the curious madness of love, or even of mere infatuation. The duel had clearly proved his philosophy, that dallying too closely with women and Fortune often led to ill-fortune.

Molly had met him on the road today, as he returned from receiving the written replies from Lord Brennan and Sir James Allin. She'd told him that she had a mind to ride with him as they had done the day he arrived in Kinsale. She'd seemed a touch jealous, in spite of her blithe manner, saying she had met a messenger who sought Edward in the name of Jane Hardy. Molly had sent him on his way, justifying this to Edward by telling him he ought to keep better company than retired bawds.

As they trotted down the road, Edward noticed that Molly's mood changed yet again. She was more introspective now, something more than common pensiveness, and wished to walk the horses rather than trot them.

"If there are rapparees on the road, as you suspect, we can hear their approach better if we ride at a walk," she said to placate his objection.

"And they can more easily catch us," he replied.

Edward sensed an irritability, or perhaps what he sensed was in his own mind, not hers, and was simply his suspicions taking root.

Twice Edward paused. The second time he was certain he heard the sound of a horse snorting in the distance. His horse's ears were now in constant motion, much more than usual. But Edward heard nothing else, and so they walked on.

"It's nothing," Molly said, each time he halted.

Yet soon Edward thought he heard horses again, and this time voices too, as if they were brief shadows or whiffs of whispers that might exist only in the mind. He slowly turned his mount around, squeezed he horse a few steps forward, and casually gazed about. His eyes noted the wisps of shapes—heads of men and horse, an arm, legs and flanks—of riders in shadows down the road, visible only to someone whose eyes were long accustomed to searching into dusks, dawns, and darkness.

He trotted to Molly where she waited a few yards away.

"We must go, and quickly," he said, slipping his hand through his sword knot, then drawing his Spanish colichemarde and letting it hang from his wrist. He drew a pistol, brought it to full cock, and passed it to her. "In case you need it. Keep it pointed up until you need to use it. There are riders behind us."

He drew his other sea pistol, cocked it, and held it pointed toward the night heavens. He made sure his wallet and the letters within were secure beneath his waistcoat. Cued by

Rocinante's ears, he pulled his mount around in time to discern the outlines of two riders spurring their mounts from a walk to a canter.

"Ride!" he shouted at Molly, as he aimed his pistol at the dark shapes of man and horse. "Ride, damn you! Ride! I'll keep them at bay!" he shouted.

Immediately Edward fired his pistol and tossed it away, spun Rocinante around, grasping his colichemarde as he did, and with the naked blade whipped Molly's mount—which had yet to move in spite of his order to her—to the gallop.

The two rapparees came at full speed.

Edward spun Rocinante back around, leveled his sword, and spurred hard.

"For King James!" he shouted to confuse his attackers, one of them several yards in front of the other.

After a brief hesitation, a brace of pistols flashed from the lead rider, flame licking several feet from their barrels and illuminating a masked face as Edward, charging, lost his hat and right stirrup. A flash and a crack came from the right, a shout from the left, another flash and noise to the front, hot breath against his cheek, and then the crash and spark of steel on steel as he rode Rocinante upon one of his enemies, then a crash of horse on horse, a thrust and bite of sword into an enemy, foul breath on the air, a cry of pain, another of anger, the sense of something thick and heavy caught on his sword, then of something flung from sword into air, then...

Nothing. The two men were gone into the night. For a moment Edward thought the rhythm or number of hoofbeats changed. Approaching again? Or retiring?

Retiring.

Edward regained his stirrup, cantered off the road, and for several minutes waited in silence, sword in hand. He ought to have ridden already toward Ballydereen, for Molly was alone on the roads with these thieves and murderers. By the light of the moon he could see several inches of his blade smeared with blood, but lightly, as if it had been partly wiped clean.

Soon he heard more vague sounds in the distance, an argument perhaps, or just the wind. Then came a tiny flash, followed by the faint crack of a gun, a pistol he judged it. He considered waiting a few more minutes, but realized this was too dangerous. There was something he had to find, and if it were valuable, the rapparees would soon return for it.

Quickly he dismounted and searched the ground, sword in hand, his heart pounding as he expected to meet the highwaymen again. When he'd realized during the fight that his sword had lifted something from one of the men, he'd thought at first it might be a small pistol; then it occurred to him it might also be a wallet, carried in the same way he carried his own. His guess was correct: he found a small package trampled into the mud. Edward scraped away the wet earth to reveal a leather wallet of the sort used to carry correspondence and other important papers. He had no light by which to examine it, and it would be too dangerous to do so here anyway, so he tucked it under his waistcoat. Moments later he found his empty pistol in the mud. He sheathed his sword, drew the reins over Rocinante's head, and prepared to mount the suddenly skittish animal.

"Easy, lad," he said, gently stroking the horse's muzzle before putting boot to stirrup. "We'll be away soon."

As Edward settled into the saddle, Rocinante shied sideways and almost bolted. The Scotsman quickly got the animal under control. He drew his sword, fearing another attack. Again the horse shied, and this time also began to back away. Edward realized it was not man the horse feared, but beast.

Fifty feet away, barely visible except for his shining eyes, was a rangy wolf slinking along the tree line.

You're a bold bastard, Edward thought; *the shooting should've scared you away.*

"Away with you, fool, if you want to live!" he shouted. "Away with you!"

The wolf trotted a few steps.

"Still making your reconnaissance, are you?" Edward asked. "Well, then!"

He shortened his reins and spurred Rocinante, forcing the horse to charge the wolf, who this time turned and raced away.

Edward laughed quietly. The confrontation had lightened his mood.

And then a cold shiver started at the back of his neck and ran down his spine.

The dogs! They would've discovered a wolf long before it got this close—as they would the rapparees.... His instincts would not let him ignore the glaring absence. *She never rides without them: where the hell were her wolfhounds?*

Coldly furious, he galloped away to raise the hue and cry, trusting his and his mount's senses and instincts to guide them safely through the darkness.

A horse and rider skidded to a halt by the two rapparees.

"Damn you!" the rider cursed in Irish, voice quavering with anger and fear. "I ordered you not to attack him! I said to rob him as if you were after his valuables so no one would suspect we were after the letters! I wanted him left alive!"

"Hell, only the letters matter! If we'd killed him, we'd have them now! He'd not have parted with them without a fight, anyway!" one of the rapparees argued back.

Michael O'Neal, who had so far been silent, grabbed the man by the shoulder and shook him hard. "Shut up, you fool! You disobeyed orders, you failed to kill him, and you didn't even get the letters!"

"Christ, Michael, leave off! I'm hurt bad; I'm bleeding all over my saddle!"

Michael handed the man a handkerchief. "Stuff it with this. And give me the wallet."

"I don't have it; I lost it when I took his blade to my gut."

"What the hell?" Michael shouted. "*Now* you tell me? Shit!"

"We've lost all the letters, his *and* ours?" the newcomer demanded incredulously.

"Aye, apparently," Michael replied, biting his lip in shame and anger. "But they're probably still on the road."

"Michael, I need help, get me to a surgeon, Christ, please," his companion pleaded.

"Shut up, you damn fool."

"By God, if we had killed him, we'd have the damn letters and we wouldn't be arguing while I'm bleeding to death!" the wounded rapparee retorted.

"Kill him? Kill him and they'll hunt us all down like dogs! There's too much at stake! Kill him and we'll all hang!" the other rider said, furiously.

"Are you sure that's the only reason you don't want him dead?" Michael asked, his voice cold and threatening.

"Why the hell do you take orders from her anyway, Michael? She's a Goddamn woman; what does she know? I told you this business on the road is a man's work—that a woman would get us killed. Just fuck the bitch, she's proved that's all she's good for," his companion said between sobs of pain.

The rider raised her pistol.

"Dammit, give that to me! I'll break his Goddamn head with it," Michael hissed as he reached to grab the barrel.

Crack!

The pistol flash startled the Irishman so much that he drew back hard on his reins, almost pulling his horse over as it reared.

His wounded companion, however, never recovered from

his own surprise. In moments he had slipped dead from his horse, with nary another word of criticism.

"What the hell? You're mad!" Michael shouted.

"I didn't shoot him, you did!"

"Whose bloody finger was on the trigger? It wasn't mine! Christ, he was right, you'll get us all killed!"

"You would have clubbed him to death for what he said!"

"He was mine to punish, not yours!"

Michael dismounted and quietly inspected his companion for several moments. He kissed the man's forehead and arranged his arms across his chest.

"He's dead, though I'll admit he may have deserved it for his disobedience," he said quietly.

"And for what he said about me?"

"What he said was true."

"You want truth? Here's some: you're profoundly lucky it was him in front when you attacked," she replied, voice still trembling in anger and fear, hand with pistol still shaking from the shot. "Otherwise I'd swear it was your idea to disobey me!"

"To hell with you!" Michael snarled. "You find a way to get the letters now."

"By Joseph and Mary, you'll help me clean up this mess," the rider commanded. "Get this body out of here, then get back up the road and find those letters!"

"Oh, I'll take care of my man; I know a useful purpose he can serve. As for the rest, it's your problem, it always was. I'll do your bidding this one last time and search for the letters in the mud—and then I'm off and away, whether I find them or not. *Slán leat!*"

"Where do you think you're going?"

Michael came close to Molly, leaned over, and whispered coldly.

"I'm going to kill a king."

Chapter 14

But the unhappy contriver of this nefarious Treason, expiated his Crime with his Life, being hanged on the next tree.
—Sir Roger Manley, *The History of the Rebellions in England, Scotland and Ireland,* 1691

From an old tree the pendant corpse hung, an ancient life proclaiming recent death. The great oak directed a diminishing stream of water from leaves to branches and thence down the rope, cleansing the body of the dirt and sweat of having lived.

If a man must be murdered by hanging, Edward thought as he stared at the body before him, *let it be in the rain, for the spectators won't stay long, and the compassionate will remove the empty flesh.*

Edward, tracking on his own, had spotted the body from a distance that morning soon after the hue and cry. It was difficult to miss, standing out from the wet grays and greens as it did, a striking image.

"How's your foot?" Sir William asked after several minutes of silence, interrupting Edward's dark perusal of the day. The two men were taking their rest, one sitting on a stump, the other on a fallen tree. The old gentleman was fatigued from the chase, and Edward was keeping him company while the two posses, one of combined militia dragoons and the constable's hired men, the other of royal dragoons garrisoned at Charles

Fort, had ridden off together to investigate suspicious riders noted by a traveler on the road.

Edward, doubly troubled by the night before, to the point that his cold-blooded temperament needed a distraction while his mind worked to find answers, said nothing until Sir William passed him a serving of cold rabbit and venison pie. The old gentleman always traveled well-stocked.

"Well enough," Edward said slowly. He pulled off his right boot and massaged the thick scar tissue on his foot and ankle, then took a bite of the pie. The morning's search had rubbed his scars raw, and tired his leg to the point where he could just barely use it. "I lost our men's tracks in the rain, but at least I found my hat."

"Why'd you go off alone this morning?"

"Posses make too much noise, and they trample on footprints."

"Ever the hunter, even ashore." Sir William said, and took another bite of the rich pie. He pointed at Edward's ankle. "Warned you about hard riding."

"You warned me about riding with a bad foot, not about meeting rapparees on the road," Edward said dryly, as he pulled his boot back on.

"At least it's a man's weapon you're carrying on the road now, and not that gentleman's tilter you had last night, nothing more than a damn'd porker suitable only for sticking pigs and simpering gentlemen," he said, motioning with his piece of pie at the basket-hilted backsword Edward now wore. "Hell, a smallsword's not even that: it's a bodkin, nay, a tooth-picker, and yours is a damn'd Spaniard one at that, although I do like their blades. Keep your broad Highland fox with you instead, at least when you ride."

"My Konigsmark blade served its purpose and held up to that Irishman's, but I know what you mean. At Killiecrankie I cut an English officer's smallsword clean through with my backsword—broke it would be more correct, I suppose—and smashed his skull cap into his brains with the same blow. It's not the best weapon for the battlefield, the small rapier, even one as sturdy as the one I carried last night." Edward took another bite of pie and spoke as he chewed. "And how did your own search go?"

"It was almost as much fun as a wolf hunt, this hue and cry, riding headlong into who knows what," Sir William said, strangely unexcited. "Had quite a go. We followed some tracks, the militia and I did, but like you lost them in the rain. We stopped several travelers, but all could account for their activities. You found more than we did: the dead." He paused and nodded toward the corpse. "I wonder who hanged him."

"More importantly, *why* was he hanged?"

"You said you think he's one of the rapparees who attacked last night?"

"I think he's the one who took my blade to his belly," Edward said matter-of-factly, entirely devoid of any emotion but curiosity.

"Then someone found him, dead or alive, and hanged him for the villain he is."

"Maybe. Or maybe his companion wasn't as friendly as he thought he was. Let's find out if he's the same man."

Edward walked through the light drizzling rain to the tree, drew his backsword, and cut the rope from which the body hung, swaying and spinning gently and so very slowly in the wet air. The flesh hit the soppy, soaked ground, splashing more mud across Edward's boots.

Edward noticed that something was stuffed in the mouth, a handkerchief probably.

Quite a message! he thought.

He ripped open the shirt beneath the coat—*Curious*, he

thought, *that the coat wasn't stripped from the body*—and there it was, as he suspected: a sword wound next to the navel... *and a bullet hole about ten inches above*, which he examined closely. He wondered which was the wound that had killed the rapparee.

"I can't tell if he was alive or dead when he was hanged. Wouldn't someone seek the reward for killing a highwayman or rapparee? Forty shillings, is it? Or why not? Fearful of retribution?" Edward pondered as Sir William joined him.

"Looks like you pinked him twice, once with ball, once with blade. He was one of O'Hanlen's men, I warrant, and probably a traitor to his brethren," Sir William said, nodding at the hanged man now lying in the mud.

"Who?"

"Raver O'Hanlen, our local rapparee or highwayman. They call him the Black Captain, or just Captain O'Hanlen. They're false names, of course. A few poetic idiots even call him Captain Manannan after the Irish sea god, and his horse they call Splendid Mane, or whatever it is in Irish, after the name of Manannan's steed, all because some say he was once a pirate. But it's mostly romantic nonsense; he's just a damned thief and murderer now, though he fought for James during the war here. Pity no one's sure what he looks like—or at least, none will tell."

"It wouldn't have helped me to know what he looks like; I couldn't see either of their faces. What do you think of this, Sir William—a bloody handkerchief is stuffed in his mouth."

"Odd thing to do. You know, I remember a man hanged on this same tree; the gossips said O'Hanlen did it, hanged him as an example to others who might *surrender* to King William. Yet that didn't stop King William's courts from finding him guilty of treason after his death and ordering his lands confiscated. 'Tis a mad world. I've even heard that O'Hanlen hanged one of his own for disobedience. But the war here is over; I don't know why he'd hang anyone now, if that's even who did it. Perhaps this dead man talked too much, or said something he shouldn't have."

"There's no reason to remind a dead man not to talk," Edward said dryly. "The handkerchief in his mouth is almost certainly a warning to others instead. Maybe even to Brennan or Allin."

"Stay out of politics, Edward, no good ever comes of it to honest men. But I think you're grasping at straws to think this is a political message."

"Those weren't common highwaymen last night, Sir William."

"Nonsense. What else would they be?"

"Tories doing secret business. And the handkerchief in the mouth a reminder not to interfere—and for Tories not to turn traitor."

"Or just a reminder to mind one's own business, or else," Sir William grumbled. "Still, it's an odd sort of thing to do to one's own unless, perhaps, he ran his mouth too much."

The old gentleman hobbled to his saddle, filled two large wine cups from a squat bottle tucked in a saddlebag, and sat down again on the stump, gesturing for Edward to join him.

"Damn, my ass hurts. It's not my game leg that gives me pain, it's the ass it's attached to. Here," he said, passing Edward one wine cup and raising his own, "to a life free from old age!"

"To a short life, then?"

Sir William laughed. "A long life, then, with no more pain than necessary to live it well."

"That, sir, I will drink to," Edward said, wondering at the philosophical turn in the conversation.

"By the way, were you a natural son of mine, I'd have flayed you alive for sending Molly home alone last night."

"I had no choice," Edward said.

"Never again leave her like that. I love her like a daughter, though we're often of opposite minds and loyalties."

"You have my word."

"I intend you keep it."

"And I will. But I do need to talk to you about something. About her."

"Not now, lad, I'm too tired."

"Sir William—"

"Edward, not now! Forgive my temper, I'll explain it all to you in good time." The old gentleman poured more wine. "Now, lad, you said you think these weren't common thieves. What were they then?"

"Tory agents, Jacobite agents, however you want to call them."

"Your evidence?" Sir William asked as finished his piece of pie and got another.

"First, they attacked at night and at the gallop from behind, rather than by day and from ambush. And then they argued after they rode off, at least it seemed so to me, and there was the flash of a pistol," Edward said.

"Scared, stupid highwaymen who buggered a robbery. Probably snapped the pistol by accident."

"I'm sure they knew I was carrying important letters from Brennan and Allin."

"Maybe, and maybe not. That's it?"

"No. There's this," Edward said, holding up the large leather wallet. "I doubt they missed it until too late, but for certain they came back to look for it; I found boot tracks other than mine where it was lost last night. I saw the tracks this morning before the rain washed them away. The wallet came from the man I pinked with my sword, he who now lies in the mud over there."

Edward passed the wallet to Sir William, a flat hole punched through it and the letters front to back.

"What are they?" Sir William asked, as he briefly inspected the correspondence.

"Three letters from France, addressed to persons, known Jacobites I'm sure, here in Ireland. One pretends to be sent lover to lover, but I'm sure the names are false. Do you know 'Mrs. Sullivane of Bantrydereen?'"

"No such person or place around here."

"The second and third are merchant letters. In both are identical lists pretending to be signatures to a warrant against a debtor—but no warrant needs three dozen signatures. I think it's a list of code names of men in England willing to rise in rebellion, or of men around here to be recruited or to have their loyalties tested. Nothing too unusual here, we both know rebellion is still planned behind some doors. Yet there's something more."

Sir William, his mouth yet again full of pie, nodded at him to go on.

"Last night I found a secret message in the love letter; it was revealed when I wet the paper. I've dealt with spies and their ilk before, I know their ways. The heat of a fire didn't work, nor a candle behind the page, but water did. Alum dissolved in water would make an ink that water would reveal. Fire and light are too obvious."

"Nothing unusual there; lovers often hide secrets in their letters," Sir William said, but starting to look concerned.

"We both know this isn't a lover's letter—highwaymen aren't post riders, and messages that reveal only when wet are too sophisticated for green-sick romantics. In the letter is a cryptic message that the 'blessed event' will occur only if 'what each of us hopes for' also occurs, and that the 'blessed event' will surely happen by Easter. In both merchant letters, in plain writing, is a similar message, but more dangerous: the writer is exhorting another to 'have faith and prepare' because what they hope for *will* occur by Easter!"

"Business dealings. Smuggled goods, perhaps."

"In secret letters smuggled by rapparees?"

"Smuggling is still a crime, even if a popular one, and secrecy is necessary to maintain it. However, I'll pretend to see from your point of view: an invasion, then."

"No, Sir William, I don't think so, or at least I don't think that's what the letter refers to specifically. Rather, an uprising, keyed to an event other than an invasion. The Irish won't rise again in open war against the English unless the French come, and the French won't come unless William is first overthrown and significant forces rise for James. The French can't get another army past the English fleet, and even if they could get one to England, Scotland, or Ireland, they can't survive ashore without traitors turning out in great numbers in support. They can't pin their hope on Jacobites rising when a French army lands. They must have the uprising first—and this will occur *only* if King William is dead."

"I still don't see what you want me to."

"It is simple: someone plots to kill King William."

The old gentleman was silent for a minute. Then he shifted, stood, and walked about.

"There are always plots against King William," he said eventually.

"I'm not talking about common tavern-room plotting by drunken Jacobites, nor of a few arms laid in secret by wishful thinking Jacobite loyalists. I'm talking about a real plot, a planned assassination, one that will indeed be attempted."

"I suppose I see your logic, but who else will? Those you must convince will see many explanations. They'll doubt that plotters would forewarn so many people, because someone always talks. Not all those sworn to secrecy can keep secrets, and others may surmise an assassination from events we ourselves know nothing of."

"Exactly: if someone at St. Germain has let this slip, even a hint of it, even to only one other person, it would pass to a dozen or more. People don't keep secrets well."

Sir William picked a crumb from his cravat. "Logic and evidence notwithstanding, no one here will believe you. And even if some do, they'll still debate for weeks on the information before they do anything, *if* they do anything. The best you can hope for is that they'll forward them to London. Of course, some spy among them will warn the local Jacobites." Sir William shrugged as if annoyed. "Even so, it's your duty to turn them over to the sheriff or to Captain Waller, the lieutenant-governor at Charles Fort."

Edward's jaw tightened. "No, I don't think so."

"What?"

"I'm not going to turn them over to the local authorities."

"What's got into you, Edward? You must turn them over. These are letters of great import, if what you say is true."

"I know that. And if the best they might do is to forward them to London, well, that's something I can do myself. After last night, I don't trust anyone around here anymore, excepting you, of course, Sir William. But even my trust in you isn't enough to sway me. I'm sure I've been followed since I've been here; I'm sure I was followed and betrayed last night."

Sir William's brow began to darken. "Edward, you had damn well better not be insinuating what I think you are."

"Easy, Sir William, you'll be struck with apoplexy! And if you know what I'm thinking, then you've been thinking it yourself. At least hear my argument. It's not my intention to accuse Molly, but to clear her name," he lied, even while hoping he might prove his suspicions baseless. "And I certainly don't accuse her of trying to have me killed, only robbed. But dammit, someone knew when and where to find me on the road. And only you, Molly, and apparently the widow Hardy knew I was off to see Brennan and Allin. And Molly—"

"Must you accuse her while pretending you're not?" Sir William said angrily.

"It was by her doing we were where we were. And Molly, well, she gave me back my pistol this morning—unloaded. It had been fired."

"My God, you think she shot that bastard you just cut down from the tree!"

"No, Sir William, I don't, but—"

"Molly told me this morning—damn, she was still distraught —that she fired your pistol last night, she thought rapparees were after her. So maybe she hit that bastard you found hanging from the tree; hell, maybe it's your bullet in him, that's all there is to it."

"Please listen, Sir William: if between us we prosecute the case against her, we'll prove why it won't hold up. Consider this: why weren't her dogs with her yesterday? There'd have been no ambush if she'd had the wolfhounds with her."

"Well, I damn well don't know why she'd leave her dogs behind. But leaving her dogs behind and having a picnic with you and firing a pistol because she was frightened is no proof she tried to have you robbed or murdered for some damned secrets. For God's sake, Edward! Do you really think she set you up?"

"Dammit, Sir William, someone did, at least for robbery."

"And no one else saw you on the road?" Sir William asked pointedly, already knowing the answer.

"A few, surely."

"And of course none of Brennan's or Allin's servants saw you?" he continued sarcastically. "There you have it, lad, rapparees do have their spies among the common folk. Hell, maybe Brennan or Allin set you up; either could be a traitor pretending to back the king. These damned intrigues of yours, wanton and otherwise, are going to get you killed if you're not careful. And who's to say that widow woman isn't involved? Didn't you say she knew you were on the road?"

"You're right, Sir William, I'm sorry. It may be my imagination running away with me. I'm just tired of being a pawn in these Irish intrigues. I swore I was done playing games with Fortune, and now it seems I've fallen right into her arms," Edward said, half sincerely and half to placate the old gentleman.

"I forgive you, lad. I'll admit I was myself concerned for a brief time this morning. But I know Molly; it would make no sense, no matter her ties to Jacobites and Tories. I'll look after her."

Edward was silent in thought, worried that further discussion would antagonize Sir William and jeopardize both their friendship and their business relationship.

Aye, Sir William might even be right, it could be anyone. But dammit, if Molly's involved with Jacobites and rapparees, Sir William himself may be in danger.

"What about the letters?" Sir William said eventually.

"I'm going to deliver them to the Crown myself. In London."

The old gentleman shook his head. "I think that's foolish, but it's your business. I'll pretend I know nothing of it. But have you considered that maybe they killed this man for losing these letters? If so, you'll be in even more danger now."

"I sail soon enough, and they can't be sure I have them. For all they know, they were discovered this morning by one of the posses."

"But you said there's evidence they came back to search for them last night. And if there are spies around here, and I'm damn sure there are, they'll soon know whether or not the authorities have them. And if the authorities don't have them, the Tory spies will assume you do. If you're going to take those letters to London, you can't leave Ireland soon enough, not if you really do have evidence of assassinators or plotting rebels in hand."

"I'll keep on my guard. I didn't come to Ireland to seek out traitors, only to further my own cause—and maybe these letters will help us both. The Crown would look favorably on anyone who brings evidence of a plot against it."

"How many pistols do you keep on your person?" Sir William asked, his brow darkly furrowed.

"Two at the saddle and two in my pockets."

"Good. Don't travel anymore unless you absolutely must, not until you venture to Kinsale to set sail. When is that?"

"As soon as I can. Hopefully within the week; perhaps in a day or two. I'll see if the captain will let me come aboard now; the letters will be safe that way."

"We can lock them in my strongbox until then. We've still some business matters to discuss, and this way you won't have to hide aboard ship."

"I intend to keep all the letters on my person until I sail, Sir William."

"That's dangerous. If you're robbed again …. By God! Damn you, Edward! You really don't trust Molly! What now, you think she'll break into my strongbox and the steal the letters? Friend or not—damn you!"

Christ, not now! Edward thought. "Sir William, calm yourself, you're going to have a stroke, for God's sake."

"You don't know what this means, Edward, you don't know what this means."

"I do, Sir William, I'm sorry, but I do. The facts are against her. She acted last night as I've seen traitors do when they try to lead an enemy into an ambush. And even you can't explain why her dogs weren't with her. And dammit, there's a couple things you still don't know: I only heard one shot afterward, and with it I heard voices. And worse, that bastard laying in the mud over there, there are powder burns on his coat, even a few unburned powder corns not yet dissolved by the rain. Whoever shot him did so at close range, closer than when I fired, and certainly closer than a woman fleeing on horseback. I'm not saying she shot him—"

"I don't want to hear your evidence! You misunderstand me, you don't understand at all."

"No, Sir William, I don't. You're my friend and business partner, but I can't avoid telling you the truth as I see it."

The old gentleman shook his head. Edward swore he saw tears in his eyes.

"She's my daughter, Edward. She's my bastard daughter."

Edward flushed.

"I'm sorry, Sir William. I didn't even suspect. What a fool I've been. Does she know?"

"No, and by God if you tell her I'll fight you and kill you, old and crippled as I am." Sir William stood and wiped away his tears. "If Molly were a part of the attack on you last night, it was no choice of hers, I'm sure. She's trapped, hell, we're all trapped. If I declare her my daughter, she'll lose her estate because she'll no longer have legal right to it. And I have little to leave her when I'm dead, even if I acknowledge her. My shit of a greedy, ungrateful brother will inherit. I don't even speak to him or of him anymore. He covets my estate, he despises Molly, probably suspects she's my bastard, and he hates all papists. That damned parson of mine—never take on a man, Edward, until you've tried him—has been trying to reconcile us, but I told him to go bugger himself; he's only trying to insinuate himself with my brother against the day I die."

"I'm sorry," Edward said again, at loss for other words.

"It gets worse. O'Hanlen? I'm sure he's the man she's betrothed to; O'Neal is his real name I think, and I've no doubt he's around here again. Likely enough it was he who attacked you last night. I've tried to marry her off, to no avail, for she loves that scoundrel, or so she says. And now I hear rumors they're going to accuse her of treason in order to confiscate her estate. Someone's been feeding lies to the prosecutors lately, or maybe just the truth, that she won't wed anyone but her betrothed. So if none of these fine, upstanding local asses can add her estate to theirs, why not let the law seize it and sell it below fair value?"

"Sit down, Sir William. There's been too much excitement today. You need to rest."

"What the hell am I to do, Edward? It's far easier to invest in a privateer, or search the sea for plunder, than it is to navigate this mess ashore. Ah, hell, the soldiers return, we'll talk more later, my friend."

Edward tucked the packet of letters beneath his waistcoat under his sash as Lieutenant Fielding rode up and dismounted.

"So, Lieutenant, now that you've ridden him in chase, are you ready to buy that gelding?" Sir William asked jovially. It was, Edward perceived, an act, a means of putting the past moments out of his mind. "He has lungs, he does, and is far more handsome than that ugly bay you usually ride. Are you hungry, sir, will you take some pie? Edward, the lieutenant's stomach is as bottomless as yours, I think."

"And yours, Sir William," Edward replied, also jovially, in keeping with the pretense.

"I'll give you twenty-five pound, sir, for the gelding and some pie," replied the lieutenant with a grin.

"Excellent, sir, excellent!"

"Can you join us this afternoon, Captain MacNaughton?" the lieutenant asked. "We're going to reconnoiter the north countryside and see if we can't find a thief or traitor to hang."

"I can't, my leg needs rest, and I've some last minute affairs to settle before I depart on the *Virginia* Galley, wind and tide permitting."

"Another time then," the lieutenant said, as he finished his bit of pie. He directed his men to tie the end of the rope hanging around the dead man's neck to a horse to drag the body to Charles Fort.

"Careful you don't pull his head off!" shouted Sir William.

"It's what we intend anyway," Lieutenant Fielding shouted back.

Edward, his mind on the new letters beneath his waistcoat, watched them work and sensed dangerous eyes upon him.

Chapter 15

...and when the wine-presse is hard wrought,
it yields a harsh wine, that tastes of the grape stone.
—Francis Bacon, *Essays*, 1601

The next three days were quietly uncomfortable for everyone. Molly kept to herself, pretending—or so Edward thought—fatigue and anxiety caused by the attack on the road; then he considered that her stress might be authentic no matter what role she had in the violence that night. Sir William put the house under heavy guard and confined Molly until, after a raging tempest of an argument, he agreed to let her ride close by once daily, and only under armed escort. After some brief resistance he got Edward similarly to agree not to go abroad without an escort of two or three armed servants. The Scotsman did not fear traveling, no matter the threat. In fact, he hoped he might encounter O'Hanlen, or O'Neal if they were the same, and by killing him solve Sir William's problem—and perhaps Molly's too.

The letters were another matter. Both Brennan and Allin sent frantic inquiries regarding the safety of their missives, to which Edward would not reply by message or messenger. Sir William reassured him of the security of his large iron chest, so heavy that it would take six men to carry it out and a cart to run away with it, with double locks so well hidden that not even

Molly knew how to find them, but Edward would not be moved. The letters must not remain where either Molly or armed thieves could get at them.

And so on the third day Edward rode out, armed with a backsword, dirk, four pistols, and also his long buccaneer gun, a sling hastily rigged to it. In one of his saddlebags was his writing box. Two of Sir William's most reliable servants, likewise well-armed with swords, pistols, and musketoons, rode at his side.

He made his first visits to Brennan and Allin, telling them plainly that they had nothing to fear, that the letters were safe. Brennan's arrogance was insufferable: Edward immediately knew he was nervous about something but had no idea what it might be.

"Damn you, sir, what impudence to come here after what has happened! Everyone is gossiping of an intrigue, and now you confirm my role! Leave now, sir, leave now!"

Allin, on the other hand, was even more talkative than before, almost reveling.

"Swordplay and pistol shots on the road! A Tory hanged as a message to the others! Desperate times, sir, desperate times!" the baronet said almost gleefully. But otherwise he seemed unconcerned and only wanted to know that the letters were safe.

Edward's third stop was to visit Jane Hardy. He dismounted, left his musket with one of the armed servants, both of whom were tactful and disciplined enough not to give him any sly looks, tossed his saddlebags and pistol holsters over his shoulder, and entered the foyer to be received.

"Edward! I've missed you, you rogue. Mistress O'Meary keeping you busy? I think I warned you, didn't I?"

"I need something," he replied, ignoring the jibe.

"I'll not be taken to bed that easily, sir. It'll cost you

conversation in the salon and at table."

"I haven't time for that, and anyway it's not your bed I'm asking for, at least not yet."

"Indeed?"

"I want fine flour, water, a basin, some rags, and to be left alone."

Jane cocked her head, then called for a servant to tend to him as requested.

"I'm surprised you trust me, Edward."

"Shouldn't I?" he said, more coldly than a friend ought.

"Considering your philosophy and recent events, I'm surprised you trust any woman. But then, you already know my opinion on the subject: it's always best to keep your friends and enemies close."

"I'll bear that in mind after I disengage and get some distance to reflect. And don't let anyone leave the house; my servants are under orders to stop anyone, to shoot if necessary."

"My, what a mistrusting soul you've become. But I have a remedy for that," she said, smiling as she closed the door and left him alone in the room.

When his materials arrived, Edward went to work. On the table he placed his naked sword and his four pistols, fully-cocked. With flour and water he made molds of the seals on the letters sent by Brennan and Allin, and dried them by the fire. Thanks to some brief experience in the past of petty craftsmanship in the trade of espionage, taught to him by an expert in the trade, yet not so expert—or perhaps not so lucky—that it kept him from being hanged, Edward was able to open the letters, read and copy them, and re-seal them, although it took him almost two hours to get the seals right, even with the aid of much cursing. If Lord Deigle suspected he had opened the letters, Edward would explain truthfully that he'd opened and read them because he feared their being stolen.

But in the letters he found nothing of note, unless there were messages hidden in code or secret ink. Neither described plots, but were only lists of persons thought to support the Jacobite cause or to support the king, none of whose names he recognized. Nor was any spy's identity speculated on, and, significantly, Molly's name was not listed. Edward was disappointed at first, then realized the lack of intelligence on Jacobite plotting made the letters he had stolen on the road all the more valuable.

He tucked the letters into his saddle bag, tied it down tightly, and called for Jane.

"Your servant, sir," she said mockingly.

"I've an hour. Your son's away, I trust?"

"He is."

"Good. To bed, then, if you please," he said, a cocked pistol in his hand.

"And what games are we playing today, Edward?" she asked as she ran her fingers gently along the barrel.

"Games that please me."

"Then let's to them, sir!" she said flirtingly, patronizingly, and irresistibly, and led him to her bedroom.

Almost exactly an hour later, Edward was in the saddle again, ignoring Jane's bawdy jests about exchanging one saddle for another. It was late afternoon when Edward finally returned to Ballydereen, after having made one last stop in Kinsale. All of the letters, including their duplicates, were now safely locked in a strongbox aboard the *Virginia* Galley, whose captain was a solid supporter of King William.

"Should anyone try to get at these letters, you may shoot him," Edward advised the captain.

"I'll shoot anyone who tries to open or steal the box," the captain replied. "I've my own poor fortune to be made in there."

At Ballydereen the house was in an uproar, and at first

Edward thought it might have been attacked, so bloodthirstily angry was Sir William.

"Edward! It's come to this, finally. The magistrate did me the courtesy of sending a rider to warn me in advance. They're accusing Molly of treason, by God! Come, now, to the inner hall, if you please."

"Constable Rutson is still waiting, sir, with his hired officers," a servant interrupted. "He wishes to speak with Mistress O'Meary."

"Bugger that scoundrel. Let him cool his heels a little longer, I'll call you when I want to see him."

Edward, his foot aching from riding all day, followed Sir William to the inner hall, a dark, cold, and imposing room whose walls were covered with arms and armor, some of ancient origin, some of recent, much of which had been either hidden or used during the late Irish conflict, or recovered afterward.

Sir William stamped his walking stick hard on the floor.

"You know, Edward, it offended me that you came so late seeking my assistance. It seemed that you had forgotten that I was the principal investor in your venture commanding a letter-of-mart ship a few years ago."

"A venture from which I returned no profit to anyone; ship, cargo, and plunder all lost. I didn't want to burden you again if I didn't need to," Edward said, trying to reassure him.

"It was Fortune, nothing else; there was no shame in it. It's an odd sort of honor among you Highland men, much the sort I imagine as among your freebooting brethren and American Creoles. Still, of whatever sort, you're a man of honor, or at least as much a man of honor as any, and you're a better Christian than most Christians I know, at least in how you treat people, though you'll disavow believing in any religion. Oh, you've your vices, I suppose, but I've never seen any to fault you for. You won't take the food from a poor man's mouth and you'll even give him your own, I've seen you. It's much the way you are with women. You take what's given, but you're no seducer or forcer of women; you won't take advantage of a woman for your own profit, meager or great."

"I'm not sure where you're going with this, Sir William."

"I know you don't trust Molly—Hell, man, you think she's plotting with Tories and rapparees!—but she's my daughter, whether she knows it or not, and I'm going to protect her come what may. I need your help. I ask you two favors."

"And if I disagree?"

"You owe me, Edward. Not as your investor, but as a man of honor to his friend. I ask nothing of you but what you can do in good faith and honor. If that turns out to be nothing, then so be it."

"Fair enough."

"They're going to accuse her, Edward. She'll be arraigned at the Assizes in a week. I suppose the local bachelors have grown tired of waiting for her to marry one of them, and now prefer to have the law seize her estate so that one of them may have it cheap." The old gentleman was silent while he ran his fingers along the fireplace mantle. "I've heard rumors that someone accuses her of having Jacobite ties, that she waits for James— they call him the 'king across the water'—to regain the crown. She can then safely marry that bastard she claims to love, and her estate will no longer be in danger of forfeit. Thus, I believe, the charges. At any rate, I want you to stand with her at the bar tomorrow. The judge is a friend, I think he'll allow this even though the law doesn't." He sighed. "I grow too old and ill-tempered for some things, and it will look bad if I advise her at the bar. As I said, the judge is a friend. So, first, will you stand with her such as you can? And second, will you help her in any other way you can, duty and honor permitting? It's not much to ask, and you'll soon leave these Irish politics behind you anyway."

Edward sat down with his chin on his chest. *Sir William is right*, is thought, *we're all trapped by Fortune. Is Jane right, too, that there's no escaping it? No matter what he says, if I don't help Sir William I may lose him as an investor and a friend. But if evidence is found against Molly, it may taint Sir William too—and even me as his friend, not to mention I might be tainted as Molly's counsel. Christ, what a mess. So much simpler is the sea.*

"Of course, Sir William," he said eventually. "Assuming I'm still here. You know that I hope to sail before then. And you also know I was only educated as a Scots lawyer, and not in the English common law, though I did study it for my own defense against charges of piracy. And I never practiced law—I preferred lawful theft upon the sea instead. The only lawyers I've dealt with in years have been those who prosecuted me and those I've run through with a sword."

"Thank you, Edward. You never were one to fear anything, not even Fortune, and I'm sure she'll keep you here long enough to help Molly."

"Sir William," he replied gravely, almost reversing their roles, "I'm going to help Molly because the fundamental accusation is a false one. And because she might yet be innocent of other accusations, in spite of my suspicions. And because you're my friend and I wouldn't hurt you for all the world. I would shatter our business agreement long before I'd harm the friendship and honor between us. But I swear to you, as soon as I set sail it's back to my philosophy. It's my own damn fault I'm in this mess, but I know now how to adjust my hypothesis and make it work."

"You're a smart, brave, loyal man, Edward—and you're also a damn fool. Let's get that little bastard constable in here; I'll give him a show he won't forget soon!"

And surely the constable never would: Sir William's verbal broadside shivered the pompous Constable Rutson to splinters in less than a minute. He departed almost at a run, more red-faced than a Scottish seaman. Afterward, Sir William brought Molly into the inner hall and asked Edward to explain the charges to her while he tended his race horses at the stable.

"It will come to naught," Edward said uncomfortably, after shouting at Parson Waters, even now still loitering around when they were together, to get the hell out. "Some of the English here in Ireland are merely out to lawfully steal property from the native Catholic Irish. There's nothing unusual in the charges against you, even though baseless. To the victors go the spoils is how they see it. Fear not; Sir William is a powerful man, and besides, you're innocent of the charges. More importantly, you're here to defend yourself. If you were abroad they might outlaw and attaint you, and seize your property without trial. Again, fear not: already some confiscated estates are being returned to their original owners."

"But high treason!"

"They're only words intended to scare you," he said calmly, hoping to mollify her.

"Then why only me?" she asked, mollified at least enough to wonder why other estates were not being threatened with confiscation along with hers.

"I don't understand."

"Sir William warned me ahead of time, but he also said I am the only one being charged and in danger of losing my estate. Why not that Dutch bawd, too?"

"A good question. I hear she's wealthy, with friends in England. There's always one law for the wealthy, another for the rest of us. I can ask her for advice, if you like."

"No!" she answered sharply, then softened. "But thank you

just the same," she said.

"Are you sure?"

"You and Sir William have comforted me sufficiently to keep me from worrying," she lied. "Again, I thank you."

Edward thought she sounded reassured, although her manner in general suggested otherwise. "It was nothing," he replied casually, fearing a trap.

"No, I mean to thank you for the other night."

"It was nothing, too," he said, more plainly matter-of-fact than casual.

"Sir William has told me that you suspect I had a part in it."

"Did you?" he asked coldly.

"No!"

"How, then, would you explain what happened that night?" he continued as coldly. "Your wolfhounds left behind, you leading me into an ambuscade on the day I receive important letters, not to mention the curiosities and inconsistencies of pistol shot and a hanged man?

"I can't, except to say it's all coincidence and mistake, and that I'm sure they were only out to rob you."

"Obviously."

"I think," she said, softening her tone, "they suspected you had more on you than arms and some coin."

Edward was momentarily taken aback. *Clever*, he thought: *If she's guilty, she's unlikely to be so bold. Yet bold she is.*

"Then they were fools," he said, giving nothing up in case she were fishing for the letters he had found. "And you shouldn't give me more reason to suspect you. I'm but an impoverished soldier of fortune, one who makes his way in the world by his sword: I am the heir of mine own right hand, as the Spanish say. There is only cold steel to be had by trying to rob me."

"Have you considered that that widowed whore knows your

comings and goings better than anyone around here?" she said spitefully.

"I've considered that both of you do. If you'll excuse me, Molly, I'm going to read through some of Sir William's law books."

As much a pretense as intention, he sought the most recently published law book he could find in the small library—*The Young Lawyer's Recreation*, 1694—and began flipping through it by the fire. He had to get away from Molly. Each conversation left him conflicted, simultaneously even more convinced of her guilt yet more doubtful of it too.

But perhaps this is what she intends, he thought.

A week later they rode early to Kinsale: Edward, Sir William, four of his servants, all heavily armed, Parson Waters, and Molly. Trailing behind one of the servants was a mule loaded with Edward's baggage, for the Scotsman hoped to finally sail for Bristol on the morrow. The ill-timing of ships and the vagaries of wind and tide had delayed departure.

Molly and Edward took rooms at a boarding house in Kinsale, and a servant ferried Edward's baggage to the *Virginia Galley*. Afterwards, the entire party met up at the courthouse.

"Molly O'Meary, hold up thy hand," ordered the clerk of the arraigns somberly, yet with a twinkle of humanity. Years of repetitious procedure had not entirely effaced his personality.

Molly hoped her face did not show her fear, hoped her voice was not weak. She raised her hand.

"Thou standest indicted by the name of Molly O'Meary, also called Magdalene O'Meary, an unmarried woman who lives near Ballydereen in the county of Cork and who owns property in this county."

The judge looked down upon her from his high seat. He was a ruddy, round-faced man, with deep-set eyes and thick eyebrows that made them appear even deeper. His wig was crooked.

"My lord," she said, before Edward could stop her, "there are many things I don't understand, and I want to ask your lordship questions. Indeed, I desire you to permit me counsel," she declared, her spirit bold, her voice tremulous.

The judge glared, then sighed. "You may speak, Mistress O'Meary, when I ask you to, or indicate you may. As I was saying... what *was* I saying, Clerk?"

"*I* was speaking, my lord. The indictment for foreign treason, and so on," said the clerk.

"Yes, er, foreign treason against his Majesty King William. The clerk will read the indictment."

"My lord," Molly interrupted.

"What? Mistress O'Meary, let us get through this, I'll explain everything you need to know. There are no matters of law for which you need council. Continue, clerk."

"My lord," interrupted Edward, stepping forward.

"What! Who's this now! Is this a court of law or a coffeehouse?" thundered the magistrate. "Ah, you're that pirateering rascal who's been visiting Sir William. Great sport, that duel of yours, by the way, and I hope your wounds have healed. Have they? Good, sir, good, but pray, use that Highland bilbo of yours on the French, if you please, and no more on English officers, no matter how deserving one or two might be. Now, what do *you* want?"

"If my lord will permit—I know it's an unusual request—I wish to stand as counsel for Mistress O'Meary in order to help her understand these proceedings."

"Are you a barrister-at-law?"

"I studied to be a Scots lawyer, my lord."

"Humph. Scots law, eh? Roman law, you mean, and French and Dutch nonsense, begging His Majesty's pardon."

"I did make something of a study of the English common law, my lord."

"Doubtless when you were accused of piracy. Have you taken the abrogated oath?"

"No, my lord, for I don't practice law. I was merely educated as a lawyer long ago. In fact, I take as few oaths as possible."

"You prefer not to take oaths, is that what you say? You're not perchance a Quaker, are you? For they will take no oaths. Nay, a rascal like you couldn't be a Quaker. They may invest in piracy but they won't swing a cutlass."

"I'll take oaths as necessary, your lordship, for example in order to receive a privateering commission."

"More practical than political, I see. Do you read Epictetus? You look like a man who seeks solace in Roman philosophers who believe that a man should be free of oaths, or at least as much as possible. Tell me, do you acknowledge the right of King William to the Crown of England?"

"I've no intention of hindering him, my lord."

"You didn't answer my question—perhaps you truly were trained as a lawyer. And you're also a Scotsman? Are you a Presbyterian Dissenter, then, who perversely believes we should not be ruled by kings chosen by God, but instead by a leader chosen by men?"

"My lord, matters of kings and princes are for greater minds than mine. I am but a loyal subject of King William—who, as it happens, was chosen by men to be our King."

The judge grinned. "Well, rascal, when you do answer a question you answer indeed like a lawyer. Tell me, did you become a rascal before or after you became a lawyer?"

"I think, my lord, I first became a rascal when I studied to become a lawyer."

"A witty rascal, too! You're fortunate, sir, that my humors make allowance for other's wit. Yet you may not approach. I'll tell her all she needs. And you, sir, as a lawyer, or something of one, should know that no one accused of a felony is permitted counsel at bar. And though there's a new Act in England that will remedy this in cases of treason, it doesn't apply to cases of treason in Ireland. So please, sir, content yourself with silence."

The recorder raised an ink-stained hand.

"Does my lord wish this to be noted in the record?"

"Of course not!" The judge returned his stern gaze to Molly.

Edward made as if to speak again, but Sir William gripped his arm tightly and whispered, "Say nothing. He's on our side; he won fifty pounds betting on you in your duel. Trust me, he'll let you stand with her, just be patient."

"Read the indictment," the judge ordered.

The clerk read the litany of tortuous ineloquences and obscure legal redundancies. The several pages could be summarized in one sentence: Molly was accused of high treason in parts beyond the seas, namely, she withdrew allegiance from the King and late Queen and levied war against them. It did not mention how she levied war against her sovereigns.

The judge addressed Molly when the clerk finished reading the indictment. "Mistress O'Meary, you've been accused of *laesae majestatis*, that is, high treason. Ah, you must hold up your hand again. Now, how do you plead to the indictment?"

"How can I plead when I do not understand?" she asked rather too pointedly.

"Captain! Sir! Pirate or privateer, whatever you are! I appoint you to be the accused's council. There, you have council now, Mistress O'Meary, so we do not need to read the law to you. Captain MacNaughton will explain it to you later." The magistrate paused to adjust his wig. "But understand this," he continued ominously, "if you don't plead we must pass judgment."

Edward stepped to the bar, whispered "Not guilty," in Molly's ear, and then stepped back.

"Oh. Not guilty, my lord," Molly said loudly.

"The general issue, good and simple. Clerk?"

"*Cul prit*, my lord," he said, then, addressing Molly somberly yet paternally, "How wilt thou be tried?"

Again Edward whispered in her ear.

"I was just told to say 'by God and the country,' but, I ask, by which country?" she asked, much too pertly.

"What!" exclaimed the judge.

"I am Irish, my lord."

Sir William groaned.

"You are a subject of King William, for you are within the dominion of his Crown, and therefore not only must you be faithful and bear true allegiance to him, but you must also be tried by the laws of the England!" thundered the magistrate, as much to impress the audience as to frighten Molly.

But she was not swayed. "Didn't your lordship just say the laws of an Englishman don't always apply to an Irishman? Or Irish woman?"

"Infernal woman, Ireland is a dependent state by right of conquest! Just say the words! You are not yet even on trial! This is a very simple procedure!"

Edward shook his head.

She's either decided she can't win, so she's having her revenge, or she's being bold because she's innocent, or wants it to look that way, he thought.

He was still unsure if her previous boldness had been authentic or pretense. He suddenly felt strangely compelled to defend her, perhaps by the natural result of his mistrust of all courts of law.

"Molly," he said firmly, "this is just a formality. Say the words, please, and we can go."

She shrugged. "I will be tried by God and country," she said loudly and, apparently, sincerely, all questioning truculence absent from her tone.

"Good, Mistress O'Meary. We thank you," the judge said,

too weary to thunder anymore.

"God send thee a good deliverance," the clerk said.

"God send us all a good deliverance," the judge said, to a few laughs from the audience. "Mistress O'Meary, you will post a bond and enter into recognizances to appear at the Court of the King's Bench in Dublin. As you seem intent on understanding the law instead of leaving your defense to the judges before you and to your own truthful words, I suggest you avail yourself of another lawyer before trial, for Captain MacNaughton is not truly even a Scots lawyer, much less one of ours, although I suppose he might advise you well in spite of his official deficiencies. I do know of a good man here in Kinsale, Cormac his name is; he just had a bastard daughter by his maid, or so I hear, name of Anne, not that this matters in any way. Don't note that in the record, mind you, clerk. Or any lawyer in Cork or Kinsale will do, if you must indeed have counsel. I warn you, though, most won't understand the law as it relates to criminals and treason as well as your judges will. It is the jury who will decide the facts of the case, and a judge who will see that law and justice are done." The judge looked up from Molly and cast his eyes across the room. "Sir William!"

"My lord?"

"I'll see you tonight?" the magistrate asked as if there were nothing indecent about the obvious conflict of interest.

"Of course. My servants have already dropped my baggage off at your house."

"Excellent. How many guests did you say? Twenty? A nice round number indeed. I'll quickly dispense with these next issues and we can open a bottle or two before your guests arrive."

Sir William, Edward, Molly, and the remainder of Sir William's entourage headed out the door as the magistrate took up his next case. On the courthouse steps Edward excused himself, slipped his arm through Parson Waters', and drew him down the street in opposite direction to the rest of the party.

"Walk with me, my faithful friend, if you please," he said pleasantly.

"Sir, I must see Sir William!" the parson replied, his voice filled with the indignation of the coward made bold by badge of office or patronage.

"Sir William won't miss you, nor would he help you in any case. He's none too fond of you, you know."

"What do you want, sir? I am not a man to be accosted in this way!" the parson replied, his face red.

"You know I'm not a Jacobite," Edward said, less pleasantly.

"I don't know that for certain, sir."

"Well, you may take my word for it. But I've been accused of it before, and struck the accusation down with a sword," Edward said, as if simply reciting a common truth. Parson Waters stiffened and tried to pull away. "Relax, parson: your faith is too small to give you the strength to escape my grip."

"You're threatening me, sir!" the parson hissed, showing incipient signs of angry panic common to the entitled when confronted by their own impotence.

"Not yet. But someone's been pretending Mistress O'Meary has been playing up to Jacobites, including her betrothed; thus this sudden arraignment, which does seem to be little more than an attempted land grab. Someone close to her. Someone too conveniently present, too watchful, too interested in others' affairs. You, in fact."

"I don't know what you're talking about. Now release me!"

"Sir William is often in ill health, you know."

"I don't know what you're talking about."

"And his shit of a papist-hating brother will inherit when he dies. I think you've been talking out of turn to that ungrateful wretch, telling lies about Molly in order to make sure you'll keep your position when the brother inherits. Certainly Sir William is no friend of yours, no matter that he's given you employment. From experience I know you to be afflicted with a cowardly nature quite incurable even by your pretended faith. Therefore, by simple deduction it's obvious that you're acting under the protection of his brother. You may have the intelligence to perceive a base opportunity, but you lack the courage to undertake it except under someone's aegis. You spy on Sir William and his household for his brother, you get to feed your papist-and woman-hating hungers, and in the end, when Sir William dies, you get your reward. Or so you hope."

"All lies!"

"No matter, I simply want you to know how *I'll* reward you if we ever sail together again. I'll make sure the crew knows exactly what you think of them—and that they'll be better off letting you play Jonah with the fishes. It might even change you for the better. It did Jonah, or so the Holy Bible says. I have read some of it, at least the nautical parts and the Song of Solomon." He paused for the length of several seconds. "And I also want you to know that if you give any testimony against Mistress O'Meary, or cause any to be given against her ...." He let his voice trail off.

"You'll murder me?" the man whispered hoarsely, panic setting in. "I'll have you arrested for these threats, sir!"

"Calm yourself, parson. You must collect yourself."

"Damn you, I'll see you arrested!"

Edward leaned in to whisper in the parson's ear. To any observers the Scotsman seemed a man suddenly taken with religion. "I'll kill you? No, I'll be putting this Irish mess behind me soon, I won't have the opportunity. But Sir William will. You may trust me, Parson Waters, when I say that only the bold may test their standing with Fortune."

Chapter 16

...by which Means we were in hopes to have outsailed
the Privateers, but one of them still came up with us...
—Capt. Nat'l. Uring, *Voyages and Travels,* 1726

The next morning, with the luck of fair wind and tide, the *Virginia* Galley finally sailed, alone, from Kinsale harbor, intending a quick passage to Bristol. She had already made a swift run from Jamaica, stopping at Kinsale, intending only to seek shelter from a French privateer. Unfortunately, the captain of an English man-of-war had sent a press gang to impress several of her crew. Several more had deserted to a lighter just before the warship's boat boarded, but they were soon captured by the garrison at Charles Fort and turned over to the man-of-war, forcing the *Virginia* to seek more crew in Kinsale while she waited on wind and weather. She was still shorthanded, and had wasted two weeks in port, just shy of her destination.

Edward stood tired and ill at ease on deck as the ship made its way across an untroubled sea under a clear sky. The various letters and their import, not to mention troubling events of the past evening, held his attention, but hand-in-hand was his concern that a French privateer or privateers might still be cruising the area. Although he had no status aboard the ship, he felt it his place to be on the quarterdeck and ensure that a proper watch was set and that all appropriate steps would be taken in the event of a chase. And yet he knew he had little cause to be worried: the *Virginia* Galley, formerly a small French man-of-war and now an English *runner* or *running ship*, was swift and weatherly, perhaps as much as any ship he had known. As soon as they had enough sea room they would be safe from most privateers.

"Coffee, sir?"

Edward took the stoneware mug from the cook and nodded his head.

"Thank you."

"The captain said you looked like you needed it."

"Please send him my compliments," Edward replied with a smile, then turned and nodded at the grizzled commander near the helm.

Edward needed the stimulation, given his mere two or three hours of sleep in his tiny cabin—practically a kennel, one of a pair aft on the quarterdeck—after the events of the past day and night.

Sir William had arranged an important dinner at the magistrate's house in support of Molly's cause. The company had been eclectic and included a dozen local notables, including Jane Hardy, several army and navy officers.

While they waited on supper, they were entertained by a blind traveling minstrel whose skill with the great Irish harp was unsurpassed, and whose array of songs of his own composition ranged from the celebration of whiskey to the laments of body and soul. Turlough O'Carolan was his name anglicized, Toirdhealbhach Ó Cearbhalláin in his native tongue. Poet and bard, he had been taught the harp from the time the smallpox had blinded him, a common practice in Ireland. One of the airs he played, of his own composition, was "Once Upon a Sweetheart." Edward recalled hearing fiddlers play it the day of the duel with Ingoldsby.

How ironic, he thought: *If Ingoldsby's sweetheart had married him in London, he'd still be alive. On the other hand, if he hadn't been such a pompous ass, he'd still be alive. Better to blame him than a woman, even one in the service of Fortune.*

The guests were soon called to eat. They filed past the fireplace, its intemperate glow lending them sinister countenances as it illuminated their faces from below. Yet when they sat down, the gentle flames from the candelabra and sconces made them look warm and friendly.

The conversation ranged from war to sea stories, from business to politics, and all in-between. Edward found himself called upon often to describe his adventures, something he seldom felt comfortable doing unless he'd had a few glasses of wine, and tonight he was trying to maintain his sobriety among the merry band of drinkers and soon-to-be drunks.

The gathering had moments, some curiously unforgettable. Mrs. Hardy flirted outrageously with Edward off and on, at least in the eyes of the wives present, who were probably more the object of Mrs. Hardy's intentions and devices than was he. Molly stood silently by, tense yet newly alluring, with a curiously subtle hint of instability, the wine perhaps. And perhaps jealousy, too.

Edward's surgeon, Dr. Cross, drunk enough to be garrulous, but not so drunk that he could not walk a straight line, gave Edward advice.

"Be bled, sir, be bled! At least once more to manage your occasional pain. I have my lancets with me, sir, I can bleed you now."

"Thank you, doctor, but I've spilled enough of my own blood already, I won't waste what's left."

"As you please, sir—but remember, I wouldn't tell you how to sail a ship, and you shouldn't tell me how to practice surgery!"

"Don't worry, doctor, it's likely someone will soon enough take your advice and try to bleed me," Edward replied wryly.

The doctor raised his glass in salute. "In that case, make sure you bleed him too, and well!"

The army and navy officers, as expected, spoke of war, warfare, and women, and waited for an appropriate moment to take leave and visit their mistresses—after, of course, the pickings of politicking or provender were consummated or consumed. A visiting businessman wondered aloud whether the Hollow Sword Blade Company, in which he was a significant investor, might not make more money buying confiscated Irish properties and selling them off in smaller portions. The only thing that stood in the way of his grand idea, or so he proclaimed, was that the Crown had not yet granted permission for their purchase.

The large meal, normally eaten earlier, but had been postponed for this gathering. Each dish served was delicious, if simple in preparation, and rich in fat: shoulder and rack of mutton, a haunch of venison (the best course by far), Neat's tongue, marrow bones, veal hash, fricasseed chicken and rabbit. Wine was abundant: claret, Malaga, Canary sack, sherry sack. Attendants and servants not busy serving dined in the kitchen on roast veal and mutton, washing the meat down with beer and common wine.

When the meal was finished—but never the drinking—everyone retired to play at cards.

"Edward! Come join us! What say you, hombre or whisk?" called Lieutenant Fielding. His mistresses could wait: games of chance were afoot.

"Piquet, sir," Jane informed the officer. "I prefer to take everyone's money one at a time. Someone bring pen, paper, and ink."

"Twelve penny, then?"

"Six penny, sir: this is Kinsale, not London."

"Six, then. Edward?"

"Start without me, I'll join you in a moment."

"Hurry! There soon won't be anyone left standing!"

Eventually Edward obliged, and so it went, port and piquet first, followed later by wine, whisk, and whiskey. He grew weary of the games long before everyone else and intended to take French leave. He must be early aboard the *Virginia* Galley, his adventure in the offing. Edward glanced around to see who might seize on his escape, and noticed Molly missing from the company. No one could tell him when she had departed. Sir William and the magistrate were now each asleep, or passed out, in tall carved leather-backed chairs by the fire, and Edward did not want to ask too many questions of the guests still awake, if not entirely sober, for fear of starting more rumors.

"Careful, there, lad."

"What?" Edward asked, the silky, wine-soaked voice catching him off guard.

"Lay where you please, sir, but remember my warning: she's no simple maid. Beware the allure of consorting with the enemy."

"I'm not sure how many of my enemies I've consorted with so far here in Ireland," he replied, wine making the accusation a bit too obvious.

"You'll hurt my feelings if you keep that up, Edward."

Still jealous? he wondered.

Jane Hardy recognized the look. "No, sir, not jealous, as I've told you before. But do be careful of her and hers—she might want to marry you now, or worse. It's her last opportunity and her tail's in the air. I hear her betrothed has gone; some say he's really Captain O'Hanlen, and he fled after the hue and cry. Whether rumor or truth, Sir William's sot of a parson is spreading it around."

"So I've heard. As a matter of fact, I discussed this with the good reverend."

"Was he amenable?"

"I think so."

"Whose part did you take: Mistress O'Meary's or Sir William's?"

"Whose do you think? By the way, I've also heard that there's a spy in Kinsale."

"Spies, I'd say."

"In this room, perhaps."

"Foolish man, I'm a gossip, not a spy. One day we'll have to revise your philosophy in earnest—you can't keep aloof from women and Fortune, at least not if you want to weather their outrageous whims. Ireland just taught you that."

"And in a few hours Ireland will be behind me."

"Alas, sir, alas!"

She slid her hand around his neck, pulled his face to hers, and kissed him in front of three wives, all still sober enough to note what they saw and gossip about it later.

"Off with you then, lad, to bed and to sea, with a good ship and an easy gale! And don't forget to write!" she said, then whispered, "Unless you wish to slip away with me one last time!"

"I'll consider it, my darling Jane—but don't wait up."

A hint of annoyance, even of anger flashed briefly across her face. Then, lustful again, she whispered close into his ear: "You know where my room is when you change your mind. I'm sure the innkeeper is already sound asleep; he'll never know you came to me."

And with these words Mrs. Hardy, her skirt and petticoats swirling as if suddenly animated, slipped away, smiling at each of the three wives, one-by-one, as she did.

In this brief confusion of startled semi-sobriety and

common drunkenness, Edward also slipped away in the opposite direction.

Once outside, he kept alert, watchful for an ambuscade of assassins. More than once had Jane been astutely prescient in her warnings: did she know something now too? The thought of her indirect and implied warnings gnawed at the edges of the still-lingering kiss, as did the new idea that she might be, in fact, an enemy. After all, she knew more of his comings and goings and business than anyone, with the exception of Sir William.

And her prescience? It was a sign that she had good intelligence. She knew of his duel in Bristol, even that it was occasioned by an accusation of being a Jacobite, and that by a man who was strongly rumored to be a Jacobite himself. And she knew of Lydia Upcott, whose father had been a Jacobite— the same Lydia Upcott who may have sent a *spadassin* to wound or kill him in a duel. Edward was half-tempted to return and carry the merry widow off to his room and have her, or she him, until the first light of dawn, in this way discovering whether she were indeed the spy, and if not, at least pleasurably allaying or distracting his sense of watchers, spies, and assassinators.

But he was only half-tempted. The lure of danger ahead kept him away. At his waist was his Spanish-hilted smallsword, and in each coat pocket was a loaded and primed turnoff pistol. His left hand rested on his sword hilt, and his right on one of his pistols. If the letters he had recovered on the road indeed suggested an assassination, wouldn't Tory and Jacobite plotters try to have them back at any cost before he left Ireland? And wouldn't this be their last occasion to obtain them? It didn't matter if he no longer had the letters on him; they would have to make one last attempt just in case.

But he arrived safely at his door, accosted by none save for a dog, who came up silently and jumped at him, a friendly begging. Edward had sensed the dog as it came, so the startle died at birth and he kept within his skin. He patted the dog, who then followed him to his lodging, never giving sign of man or beast lying in wait, save only a cat at whom the dog only growled and who in return only hunched down, hissed, and made a petty roar, but never retreated a step. Each then ignored the other, the dog perhaps sensing that there was greater reward in following Edward than in chasing a cat who might fight instead of run. At the boarding house, a gray-haired old man opened the door, still awake in spite of Mrs. Hardy's assurances.

"Any visitors tonight?" Edward asked.

No, the old man shook his head.

"A bone or scrap for the cur? He kept watch for me tonight."

"A good dog, I'll give him something."

Edward nodded and ascended the nearby narrow stairs. At Molly's door he paused, wondering if he should check on her. Most of the visitors to the magistrate's were staying here, and by the very nature of the place everyone knew who was there and which room they were in. Gossip would not be far off if he were caught at her door, even if only by the innkeeper.

In the end he chose not to knock on her door, less for fear of gossip than for fear she might think he came to seduce her. He walked the few short steps to his own room silently, and as he came to his door he thought he heard a sound inside: he was certain of the candlelight leaking from beneath the door.

What to do? he wondered as his body tensed, then relaxed slightly as a bit of adrenaline hit. *Wait outside until whoever's inside grows weary and steps into the hall? Force my way into my room, not knowing who's there, if anyone? For that matter, am I sober enough to fight if I have to?*

He had no illusions about defeating more than two simultaneous adversaries in any circumstances, and only then if he had luck and surprise on his side, not to mention sobriety, and a bit of incompetence on theirs. Only in tales could one man defeat two or more attackers, if they attacked at the same time from different sides. But the old man had said no visitors had been by. It was unlikely any of the guests or boarders were threats, and Edward's windows were barred from the inside. Yet there it was again, another quiet sound, someone moving about.

Edward made up his mind. He quietly drew his smallsword with his right hand, a pocket pistol with his left, then paused, wondering how he would open, or if necessary, force the door with his hands full. He returned the sword to its sheath, drew his other pistol, cocked it and held both in his right hand, then carefully tested the door. It was unlocked and unbolted. He cracked the door open slightly, quickly shifted a pistol back to his left hand, then kicked the door open and moved swiftly into the room, pistols raised and following his eyes.

"Edward!" whispered a female voice sharply.

He passed his eyes over the woman in the dimly lit room, then kicked the door closed behind him.

"Why are you here?" he demanded as he lowered but did not put away his pistols.

"Edward! Are you still drunk?"

"If I were, I'm not anymore. Again, why are you here?"

She's about to cry, he thought. *Perhaps even for true. I must be scaring the hell out of her.*

"Waiting for you. I couldn't bear the thought of your leaving without my seeing you one last time. And I want to thank you again for your assistance at the Assizes. I also have letters to give you, for England, from some local correspondents. And I wanted to warn you."

Edward glanced about the room again. He set his pistols at half-cock and put them in his pockets, then bolted the door. He thought his room might have been carefully searched, yet could not put his finger on any single thing out of place. Molly's words had come across as both sincere and trite, and the combination irritated him. The sense that she was out of character seemed oddly in character. After all, she hadn't been waiting in his bed, but perhaps that was too obvious. She had never given him any look that suggested she might sleep with him, yet some women never did, until you suddenly found them in your bed. Still, she seemed both too timid and too manipulative. An alarm was sounding, and he neither wanted to ignore it nor tread too closely to its object.

Damn Jane Hardy and her suspicions!

If Molly were here to search for the papers, she now knew he was on his guard about something, and it could only be about what she sought.

"Warn me?"

"Just to be careful, to keep yourself safe."

"Is someone threatening me? If so, they haven't much time left while I'm in Ireland."

"You may only be a messenger, Edward, but there are dangerous men about, Jacobites and others, who're surely still interested in your correspondence. You have it safe, I trust?"

"Quite."

She passed him a small light-colored sack, inside of which was a bundle of letters tied with a ribbon, and outside of which were directions indicating mail to be delivered to Bristol, the assumption being via the *Virginia* Galley. Edward untied the ribbon, glanced quickly over each letter, and set them on the table, wondering if Molly wanted to see where he might put them. She said nothing more, but put a hand to her dress at her breast as if to begin undressing, or perhaps simply to send a signal. Edward pondered the consequences, but before he could make a decision, or have one made for him, there came a soft knock at the door.

"Who's there?" Edward called as he took a pistol from his pocket and cocked it fully.

The answer was quiet, soft, confident—and a woman's.

Edward opened the door at arm's length so that, should someone force the door as he unlatched it, he wouldn't be knocked to the ground.

Jane Hardy stepped in, and with her forefinger she pushed the barrel of his pistol gently aside.

"Edward, dear, you and your pistols! This isn't the weapon I'd have you point at me. Hello, Molly, dear," she said. "I thought I'd spare both of your reputations at the expense of mine. There are guests about downstairs, they've just returned from the magistrate's and it wouldn't do for Mistress O'Meary here to be caught with you alone, Edward dear." She glanced at the letters on the table. "Of course, I'm sure Mistress O'Meary is only here to deliver the post. Come, Molly dear, let's away with us before your reputation is further harmed. After all, you're accused of high treason. Best you avoid any further hint of a stain on your honor that might harm your case."

Edward put the pistol back into his pocket and walked into the hallway with the women. Molly, clearly angry, entered her room with scarcely another glance at Edward.

"It seems I'm jealous after all," Jane said in a whisper. "I came to see that you weren't lying murdered in your sleep, accused of rape, or kidnapped by rapparees. Or worse, in bed with that woman. I don't trust her; there's something of madness or the spider's web about her."

"And you're here to protect me?"

"I consider you an investment, Captain MacNaughton."

"Indeed?"

"Don't worry, sir, I'm not looking for a husband. But you have the potential of one day being well-placed to do me profit, and a well-placed *honest* man is hard to come by. I'll deal with most anyone, but I'll partner only with those I trust well. We might one day be in position to help each other."

"And this is why you came here tonight? I've no letters worth stealing."

"Fool, it's too late for words tonight. I came foremost for your strong hands and hard, at times ungentlemanly, body."

Edward, although not quite up to the task as Jane might have liked, given how much he had drunk, still managed to please her. Or perhaps more correctly, she in her practiced way brought forth his broadside, as she liked to call it, to her satisfaction.

And the process left him quite spent and soon deep asleep.

When a servant boy woke him two hours later at three of the clock in the morning, he felt for a moment a sense of panic. His alert nature taking over, he searched his room and his effects, and all were as they had been. Even the letters Molly had delivered were still on the table, along with an added one from Mrs. Hardy, addressed to a factor in Bristol. He dressed quickly, berating himself for being a fool. But the ship would not sail before dawn, giving him an hour to do what he needed.

He added coal to the embers in the small fireplace, and put a small coffee pot, begged earlier from the kitchen, along with some coffee powder, onto the grate. As the water heated, he examined the correspondence, seven letters in all. Three were from Sir William to business associates in Bristol. All were clearly in his secretary's hand, and all were sealed on the outside with wax. These he disregarded, for he trusted both Sir William and his secretary, and anyway he did not have the resources here to counterfeit the seals.

When the water boiled, Edward one-by-one opened the other letters, each sealed between the folds with a common wax wafer. He held each letter over the exhaled steam until it softened the wafer, then slipped his narrow-bladed pen knife between the sealed pages and slit the wafer. He read each letter, then held it first to the flame of a candle then to steam to inspect for secret ink, then folded and re-sealed each with a new wafer. He had several sizes and colors in his writing box, and could closely match each of the wafers he had destroyed. He slightly botched one re-sealing, but covered the error by writing additional details of address over the spot where the wafer lay.

He felt a bit ashamed at having read the letters—like a poulterer, one who slits letters open to steal the money or valuables within—and a bit disappointed as well, for there was no value in them. All were common personal or business correspondence. Even Jane's letter was dull reading. If there were any secret messages in any of them, they were hidden in cipher.

Edward quickly finished his coffee and gathered up his property. He headed down the stairs, carrying only a small portmanteau into which he had tucked the writing box and new letters, the rest of his baggage being already aboard.

Everyone was asleep, including the innkeeper. Edward opened the door—and immediately dropped his portmanteau and reached for his sword.

Yet just as quickly he relaxed. Waiting outside were the two servants who had lately been his armed escort.

"We're sent to keep you company to the customs house quay, sir."

"And I thank you," Edward said. "Draw your swords, and I'll draw mine," he said to settle his slight suspicion that the men might have been bribed against him. "Lead on, then."

If an ambush had been set, the ambushers got cold feet. At the quay the servants roused a waterman by kicking him thrice in his backside.

"Ah, Cap'n McNutt! Fore and aft we meet! We're going to miss you here in Ireland, sir, but we won't forget you! In a hundred years they'll be talking of your fighting and fornicating!"

"Just shut up and row me to the *Virginia* Galley, you damned glorious whoreson."

"Aye, Cap'n, aye, right away."

In minutes they were alongside the ship, its crew busy making preparations to get underway.

"Stand by, waterman," Edward said, after he paid him. He climbed aboard, his foot causing him only a little trouble as he did, and from his cabin he fetched a bottle of sack and tossed it down to the waterman.

"And for what do I owe this pleasure, Cap'n McNorton?"

"For your damned good intelligence."

"Women will be the damnation of you, Cap'n! Fair winds!"

"And smooth waters to you!"

The *Virginia* Galley was soon under sail. The morning passed quickly, then the day, as they finally made their way upon the open waters, the sea entrancing Edward, as often it did when he had nothing to do but breathe it in. Even better, it distracted him from his raging suspicions. A brief trip to Ireland, which should have resulted in no more than a letter of credit and two private letters, had turned into a nasty nest of intrigues, the sort he'd hoped he had finally gotten past and which he had no interest anymore in seeking.

But no matter; he was at sea again, even if only for a short passage. The *Virginia* Galley sailed smoothly on, the voyage that day interrupted only once when the captain lay the ship by and queried some fishermen for intelligence of French seekers, and bought some of their catch as well. The *Virginia* shortened sail overnight, for it wouldn't do to find herself aground on any of the shoals and rocks of Cornwall or Wales.

When Edward came on deck soon after dawn the following day, he found conditions nearly the same. The wind was nor'west by west, the current northerly, and the *Virginia* Galley sailed with the wind over her quarter on a course of west by north to put the ship to the south of Lundy Island, the safest passage into Bristol Channel. She pitched and rolled with the swell, making excellent, exhilarating speed. Several fisher-boats were in sight, and also one other vessel, by its appearance a small merchant flute, known by the English as a pink: short-masted and seaworthy, but nowhere near the heels of the swift running ship. Edward admired the galley frigate's sailing qualities. Light, stiff, weatherly, and fast, she would make a fine privateer.

"She's a bit foul."

Edward looked from sea to soul. The ship's commander, Tom Cocklin by name, had grimaced much but said little the day before, and in general kept much to himself. He suffered from intense, periodic pains in the gut, but today they took their rest from persecuting him. He seemed a skillful-enough master.

"She goes faster, then?"

"By two knots or more when she has a clean pair of heels. She's a former French sixth rate who cruised against our privateers and merchantmen, but was captured after a fight with two privateers who trapped her against a lee shore. Our owners bought her at auction. Even now she'll outsail anything but a few of the French privateers. The Monsoors have never caught us except by circumstance."

"Profitable, then, most voyages?"

"No, and it's left her owners nearly bankrupt. Bad cargoes, bad luck. We were captured by the French more than a year ago after we sprung the mainmast. But the Frenchman's crew was too small to man the *Virginia*—they had taken too many prizes, couldn't spare any more crew, and there was a stout English cruiser looking for them—so they ransomed us and let us go. Six months ago we were chased again. We escaped, but not before we took four feet of water in the hold from a shot betwixt wind and water that damnified much of the cargo. Even this voyage won't save the owners but for a few months at most, if at all, and then the creditors and their shit-hounds will be at their doors again. The bill of bottomry's liable and chargeable since the owners didn't pay off their loan at the end of the first voyage. They can seize the ship anytime. We've a cargo of logwood, as well as some indigo and poor sugar from the last season, but I fear it won't be enough. Damned privateers. Damned creditors. Damned Fortune and her wiles. Ah, damn, Fortune forgive me for that last oath!"

Edward grunted. "Become a privateer."

"No, I'm not a man made for a trade that must rely so much on Fortune. The merchant trade is already too much that, and I haven't the strength or weakness of will to grant her a greater part in my livelihood."

"Well spoken."

"But you've managed well enough at the trade, or so they tell in the taverns," Cocklin replied.

"I've little to show for it."

"Tales to tell at least, and as the seeker, not the chase."

"I've been both. I would've given a fortune at times to have had a hull like this beneath my feet when chased," Edward said, continuing to admire the galley's clean lines and easy motions.

"Aye, she'll—"

"A sail! A sail!" came the sudden urgent shout of the lookout.

"Nay!" continued the lookout, "Two sail of ships! Small ships, aye, small ships!"

"Where?" shouted the commander.

"One point aft of the starboard beam!" shouted the lookout in response.

"How stand they?"

"They've no sail set. Wait... their courses might be brailed up."

"Bugger me!" muttered the commander. "No sail set? Privateers, then, wouldn't you say Captain MacNaughton?"

"Two small ships in fair weather with bare poles? Only cruisers lie with no sail set, trying not to be descried until close aboard, leaving their prey little chance of escape. Ask your man aloft if they're changing course and crowding sail. I'll warrant they are or soon will."

A few minutes later they heard the lookout's grim words.

"Courses, tops'ls, and t'gans'ls! They stand northeast to our forefoot!"

"Damned Fortune!" cursed Cocklin, rubbing his belly, then the stubble on his chin. "To continue west toward Bristol or stand north betwixt England and Ireland?"

"A gamble either way," Edward replied, unsure whether the commander sought his counsel. "Four, maybe four and a half leagues distant on our present courses, they'll speak with us; but you said none could overhaul the *Virginia,* even foul as she is. But if,—*if* mind you—they have the heels of us by two knots, then they'll speak with us in six hours or less."

Captain Cocklin said nothing.

Edward had the impression the merchant captain was weary of it all. Edward resumed his assessment of their situation, in hopes of inspiring Cocklin to action.

"If you stand north now on a bowline they might not overhaul us before dark, when we could escape, but it can be a treacherous passage. You could also run for Milford Haven. But if you wait too long to choose, you'll have to work the ship to windward, and they'll have us. If we run, no matter the direction, they'll chase; they'll know we're no seeker, although they probably don't care anyway, given there are two of them. In other words, you can't scare them by running at them. We're more likely to find aid on our present course, more likely to escape if we stand north or northwest."

The *Virginia's* commander rubbed his chin, fuming. His decision was a tough one: if he chose the wrong course, his owners might well sue him for the loss of the cargo and try to withhold his pay and shares, given their current financial state.

"Northeast," he muttered after a few moments, "Milford Haven. I hate the idea of running when the owners need this cargo in Bristol, but twice is enough, I'll not be taken a third time."

He turned to his mate and gave orders to change their course to north by northeast. They would now sail closer to the wind, but the *Virginia* sailed swiftly, both by and large. Cocklin shouted orders to his mate and the helm to change course.

"A sail! A sail!" came suddenly the lookout's shout again.

"Damn, and damn again!" muttered Cocklin, then shouted "Where?"

"Larboard abeam! She sets sail!" And a few minutes later: "She stands southeast to our forefoot!"

"Avast there!" Cocklin shouted to his mate and helmsmen. "Keep your present course!"

Edward smiled grimly. The lookout, distracted by the two ships to the south, had missed the ship to the north. Edward's gut told him the third ship was another seeker who'd kept her sails furled with rope yarns or in brails, waiting to sight a likely prize. Now it was a pair to the south and one to the north. Those to the south could cover anything heading from the Atlantic to the south of Britain or Ireland, and the one to the north could take or delay anything that ran in that direction. There was no chance now of running north, certainly not to Milford Haven.

Capture seemed inevitable, and by their manner half the crew and passengers already looked ready to surrender.

Chapter 17

Fortune aids the bold.
—Virgil et al, 3rd century BC

"Perhaps she's not a privateer, the third, I mean," Captain Cocklin suggested hopefully.

Edward discounted the wishful thinking. "There's almost no chance she's an English cruiser, much less a common merchantman. And I'll warrant those two to the south sail well by a wind. French privateer or French man-of-war, it makes no difference. Respectfully, assuming you intend to run, and I think you must, you should lighten ship as a precaution. She's foul, after all."

"She's no more foul than the privateers in these waters, and even fouled she can outsail just about any ship, even one with a clean hull," was all Cocklin said.

Edward stared at the man, incredulous. *A West India voyage, and he thinks his hull is no more foul with weed and barnacle than French privateers who've been on short runs in cold waters?*

Soon the hulls of the two southern ships, now under full sail, could be seen from the deck. Cocklin set their courses by the compass. Both stood to the *Virginia's* forefoot, on a course to intercept the galley-frigate. Before long it was obvious that the *Virginia* would outsail one of the southern privateers, but the swifter kept on the same bearing and slowly closed the distance. Not only was the *Virginia* on her best point of sail going large, but the privateer was probably off of hers by two points. This left but one conclusion: she would "speak" with the swift galley-frigate before dark. That is, she would soon enough order the *Virginia* Galley to bring to and be boarded.

"Look," Edward said quietly to Cocklin, after fuming for two or more hours, "the slower ship to the south is already bearing to our wake and the ship to the north stands to our windward quarter under as much sail as she'll bear. Soon we'll have one ship on each quarter and one in our wake, or worse, one on our bow. You must lighten the ship!"

"With her trim right she'll outsail anything, by and large—on a bowling or quartering."

"And how is her trim?" Edward asked sharply.

Cocklin refused to reply.

Damn, thought Edward, *she sails two knots off her best when out of trim the bosun said yesterday. We're going to need every advantage. He must lighten ship!*

He wondered at the captain's not even setting a water sail on the flagstaff, for the wind was light relative to the time of the year. He wondered at the captain's not abandoning everything unnecessary to the sea.

Noting the rising fear and discontent among a few of the crew and passengers, including a former colonel of colonial militia, a former naval officer, and two or three of the planters, Edward slipped into his tiny quarterdeck cabin and armed himself with sword and pistols. He stuffed all of his correspondence, having earlier retrieved it from the captain's locked chest, beneath his shirt in case he needed to throw it overboard, tucked his perspective glass under his arm, and grabbed his buccaneer gun, un-wedging it from the diagonal stowage necessary for it to fit in the tiny cabin. Back outside he caught some of the crew looking nervously toward him.

Good, he thought, *let them fear me more than the French.*

After another interminable hour, one of the French privateers to the south was but six miles away, still standing to the *Virginia's* forefoot. The second of the pair was seven miles away and falling aft. The ship to the north was ten miles away. Although there was no danger of her overhauling the *Virginia*, she had closed and locked the door of escape in that direction. Cocklin was clearly wrong about the *Virginia's* ability to outsail anything, even foul: the privateers, or at least one of them, had the legs of her by almost two knots.

An hour later, Cocklin ordered a few of the water casks staved and the ensuing water pumped from the hold to lighten ship, worried now that he had waited too long. Edward suggested he cut loose the ship's boat, which was a drag on the ship's speed, and so he did, after fuming about the cost to the owners. Edward himself fumed that Cocklin did not do more to lighten the ship, but perhaps he thought it would do little good, or he had greater faith in the *Virginia's* speed than was warranted. By now it was clear that the *Virginia* could not outsail the swiftest predator large, and to set by a wind was too dangerous with an enemy to the north and another to the west. There was an enemy in every direction but one: home.

Five glasses later—two and a half hours—the chase had turned grim. The swiftest seeker, her lines much like the *Virginia's*, had come within four hundred yards, not yet within point blank of her bow chasers, nor yet close to the practical range of her small arms. But soon enough she would be. She hoisted the white French ensign and fired a shotted gun wide of the *Virginia*, the call for her to strike.

"Not yet, my hearts!" shouted Cocklin, "We've still the heels to run!"

He did not make his ship clear for engaging. Doubtless he

thought this futile, and running his only chance.

All the usual tactics of the chase—try different points of sail until you discovered the one that worked best against the chase, prolong the chase until nightfall, slip to the opposite tack if the chase was not paying close attention, run the ship ashore—were useless with three ships chasing from three directions.

Lightened, the *Virginia* Galley eked out a bit more speed, but the closer privateer still slowly gained, and soon was within the two hundred-fifty yards or so known as musket range. Her companion stood southeast, to keep to the *Virginia* Galley's quarter and prevent her from running south. But in the *Virginia's* wake would the swift seeker remain, Edward knew, or on one of her quarters, to avoid the *Virginia's* own great guns, small and of little worth though they were.

She carries only ten guns, he thought, *and three pounders at that. She could carry eighteen sakers or six pounders, and should, and four smaller guns on the quarterdeck, plus swivels. Why don't these fools of merchant owners arm their ships as they ought!*

Soon the privateer astern would open fire with small arms. Eventually she would range along the *Virginia's* quarter, fire a broadside, slip back into her wake to reload, and then repeat the process. If the *Virginia* tried to bring her own small broadside to bear, the privateer would be aboard in an instant.

"She still gains, Captain Cocklin," Edward said quietly, now raging inside for action, for anything. As a prisoner of the French his hopes for command of a privateer would be destroyed.

Has Fortune decided to stand against me forever? he wondered. *Twice now she has gone against me in this channel between England and Ireland. But no, no, I escaped last time. She presents an opportunity—so seize it!*

"You must lighten the ship even more—you've no other

choice," Edward now coldly insisted to Cocklin. He was half tempted to knock the man in the head and take command himself, but that would be mutiny, a hanging offense.

The sound of another shotted gun preempted Cocklin's answer.

And his life as well, for this was no warning shot, but one well-aimed for the seven hundred foot distance.

Bits of Cocklin's brains, jaw bone, and teeth struck Edward in the face and shoulder. At his feet was a headless, twitching body painting the deck scarlet with a rapidly diminishing fountain of blood.

For a few moments there was silence as the crew, in shock, stood staring. Recovering, one of them shouted, "Strike! Strike!"

Edward drew one of his long pistols, brought it to full cock, and pointed it at the seaman.

"Get below, damn you, if you've no stomach for the business here! Below, now, or I'll pistol *your* brains!"

Gone in a moment were several seamen, and all of the passengers on deck save four, one of them a stout-bellied old planter who had marched with Morgan on Panama, another a Jewish merchant who had recently borne arms in Jamaica against French incursions. Each had cargo aboard, and by trick of fate were traveling to England. The ship's cargo was a combination of goods owned and freighted by planters in the Indies, and goods purchased by a factor in the Indies on the behalf of English owners and investors. This latter system of trade was slowly replacing the former. Standing with the planter and merchant were a merchant master who had lost his ship and a former army officer who served occasionally as a volunteer. Otherwise only three seamen and the ship's boy remained on deck.

"It'll be hot here soon," Edward said to all. "A quarter hour and they're in small arms range, and they'll ply them well. Cover your commander with a tarpaulin, then overboard with the spare spars and all of the sweeps, they're useless to us. Over with them, now! The boat amidships, too, then the anchors, all but the kedge! Fetch some hands up from below if any are brave enough; the French aren't yet in small arms range!"

Edward had assumed command, and no one opposed him. About half the crew and passengers heeded his orders, while the rest hid below in fear, or in the cowed pragmatism that proclaims that it is always better to choose the surety of life, no matter the conditions, than risk one's life for something better, including freedom.

He ordered each man to his quarters.

By the time the dutiful among crew and passengers had done all he had ordered, the privateer was within musket range. Long, narrow puffs of smoke shredded by the wind began popping from her deck, foretop, and foreyard, followed by sharp striking sounds of musket balls punching into planks, masts, and timbers, or ricocheting off them and rattling among the yards. The privateer had stopping shooting its chase guns, probably out of concern for the bit of speed lost each time the guns fired. Even so, three of the half dozen fired rounds had passed through stern cabin and steerage, sending many of the crew and passengers to hide in the hold.

"A steady hand at the helm, squat down, keep low!" Edward ordered as balls passed nearby. He was glad of the high transom and the adjacent small cabins, for they gave extra cover and concealment—otherwise they would likely have been killed already. He grabbed one seaman, suddenly retreating below, by the collar. "Cut up all but one of the anchor cables, pass them up to the forecastle, and toss them out a gunport!" he ordered. Better those men below were at least of some use.

"Shouldn't we fight rather than run?" asked the former

army officer and occasional volunteer. Like many soldiers, he had far less fear of fighting than of drowning in the sea.

"We can't fight, as much as I wish we could," Edward replied. "They overmatch us at least sevenfold in arms and men. Had we more men and guns, I'd cross his path suddenly and rake him bow to stern, but as close as they are we would never escape, no matter the damage we might do, and they'd be on us in an instant. We might fight seventy or more boarders from stout closed quarters, but this ship lacks them, and we don't have time to fix them up properly. The French would hack through our decks in a trice and flush us with grenades and firepots."

"The ship leans much: won't it run under the sea?"

"Nay," Edward replied with a friendly laugh at the landman's concern, "this ship is a swimmer, not a sinker. She'll heel even more if the wind grows. Think of her as a race horse stretching her neck forward the swifter she runs."

A moment later the merchant master's arm was shattered by a musket ball and he was carried below by two stout foremast-men who promptly returned to deck. The occasional volunteer refused to help carry him below for fear Edward might think he were running away to hide.

Now but seven men remained on deck.

No, eight, the lookout is still aloft, using the topmast to shield himself. Good man! thought Edward.

The *Virginia* sailed a little faster now, but the privateer still gained, if more slowly.

Damn, if only she weren't yet in range! fumed Edward.

The wind grew a bit, and Edward feared it might carry the topgallants by board, perhaps even a topmast, or spring the main. The deck had grown so hot from the fire of more than a hundred French musketeers that soon none would be safe on the open decks. The shot buzzed like a swarm of bees and hammered like a hundred carpenters.

We here on the quarterdeck will all soon be dead if something doesn't change, thought Edward.

His gut was in a knot. Part of him wanted to squat under cover, wanted to retreat out of the path of the hot musket balls. But if he went, so would the helmsmen, and then the rest. He must stay, and stand as much as he could, and he would.

A musket ball passed through the skirt of Edward's coat, barely missing his left leg. As a seaman might put it, his ass puckered so tight he couldn't have shit anything, even if he wanted to.

Damn!

He rubbed his wet palms on his coat, and they came up sticky with Cocklin's blood. He wiped them on the gunwale.

Three more seamen came on deck, encouraged by the example of others. But two were soon shot down, one of them killed, and no more came up from below. One of the seamen on deck dragged the headless body of the captain and that of the dead seaman to the bulwark and heaved them overboard.

"Dead weight," he said with a shrug, a wink, and smile.

Soon one of the two helmsmen went down, wounded. Another took his place nervously.

"Keep low," Edward ordered, "steer with the relieving tackles!"

"Some say you would sail a ship out of hell!" the new helmsman shouted at Edward. "But this is as close to hell as I want to get! Can you do it, Captain MacNaughton, can you sail a ship while the devil has his teeth in your arse and his nasty yard out and ready to bugger you?"

"If you stay at the helm, then by Fortune and my Ferrara we'll sever Satan's cold cock and sail right through the gates of hell!" he shouted back. Edward wasn't sure if the man were terrified, sarcastic, or serious. Or all three. "Do you have a short tiller in the great cabin for emergency?"

"Nay!" came the reply.

"Then we must steer on deck, and be damned!"

Edward desperately wished to fight the privateer chasing them, but half of the crew and passengers would not, and those who remained were too few. The *Virginia's* commander and owners had relied too much on her speed. She had a pair of chase ports beneath the stern lights in the great cabin, but the shot flew so thick at the stern that none dared open them.

The guns, Edward thought, *we might as well heave them overboard too*, and so he gave the order to abandon all but two in the steerage. Two seaman armed with iron crows, handspikes, and a jack, and doing their best to keep under cover, bravely went from port to port, back and forth from larboard to starboard, and soon sent eight three pounders into the Deep.

"Sir!" Edward shouted down the ladder to the Jamaica planter just below, where he and the merchant worked one of the elm tree pumps, drawing the last of the staved water from the bilges. It was exhausting work and both men looked ready to collapse. "Find the feckless gunner, get his keys, and fetch the rest of the arms from the locker! We may need them if they try to board! And tell the crew below that they must work the ship or fight, that anyone hurt will receive a gratuity as smart-money out of the owners' pockets."

The planter waved his hand and went below. By now the wind, although it had not veered, had picked up significantly.

"T'gans'ls!" shouted one of the helmsmen. "The wind will carry away the t'gallant masts soon!"

"It's the devil's wind and it does my bidding!" Edward shouted back. "I'll put her gunwale in the water before I take in any canvas!"

And the *Virginia* gunwale was indeed flirting with the sea.

Nor did the French privateer take in any canvas.

The report of a pistol came from the waist, then another. The planter and two seamen surged retreating up the ladder from the steerage.

"Mutiny!" the planter shouted, "They intend to give up the ship!"

Edward drew sword and pistol, cocking the latter against his wrist. Up the ladder from the steerage rushed the colonel of militia armed with an old mortuary sword, its point catching at the rear of the hatch. Bunched behind him were others, number unknown.

As the colonel paused to release his sword, the planter struck him in the head with the butt of a pistol, knocking him down the ladder. Edward rushed to the quarterdeck rail, a pair of French musket balls passing through the skirt and a sleeve of his coat as he vaulted to the main-deck, just missing the capstan. His bad foot and leg gave way as he landed.

"Shit!" he cursed as he stood up and rushed into the open steerage, the planter, merchant, former army officer, and two loyal seamen with him.

Here the fight dissolved as quickly as it had started. There were but five actual mutineers, three of them passengers, two of them crew. The colonel of militia lay unconscious on the deck. His companions, now only passively mutinous, stood hangdog in the open steerage except for one argumentative fellow.

"You gain nothing by this sham of running!" shouted the naval officer at Edward. "The French will butcher this crew for its resistance! There's a time to resist, and a time not to! You waste men's lives!"

"Including perhaps your own? Had been on the quarterdeck with me I'd receive your words with more respect. But doubtless your mother paid for your commission," Edward replied cuttingly. "Pity she didn't understand what a naval officer's duty is before she sent a perfumed wisp of a cringing fop to do a man's job. There's more to it than smuggling goods, bedding whores, and substituting brandy for courage." He prodded him with the point of his backsword. "So below, damn you, into the hold where you belong. And curb your tongue or I'll cut it out!"

Edward had known army and militia men who, brave enough in a fight on land, had cowered below decks during a sea fight, and had more than once seen notorious duelists flee from battle—in Edward's mind, the common soldier and naval seaman had far more courage than the common duelist—but he could never forgive a naval officer for retreating from deck.

The Scotsman pointed at one of the mutinous seamen. "The gunner. Fetch him, now, or when I find him I'll cut off his balls —and yours—and nail them to the mainmast. You, and you," he said, pointing at the two seamen who had followed him into the affray, "can you manage to get more small arms on deck and beat any of these curs out of the way as needed?"

"Aye, Captain!"

Edward raced up the ladder to the quarterdeck. The closest privateer still gained, but thankfully more slowly. Ahead lay Lundy Island. Edward knew they should be shortening sail, but it was far too dangerous to do so yet. The quarterdeck was still a hail of lead and small splinters. Edward now crouched at the windward side of the quarterdeck with the two helmsmen there. All three men joked nervously and cursed vehemently about the balls passing nearby and overhead, especially after one passed through the stern planking and between one of the helmsman's legs.

"You French bugger, you can have anything but those!"

The helmsman on the opposite side laughed nervously, then turned green and vomited on the deck, wisely not daring to put his head over the gunwale or taffrail. He gave Edward a sheepish look as if to apologize. This was his first action.

"Many a man below is puking his breakfast," Edward said. "The difference is that you're here, not there. That's all that matters."

The helmsman next to Edward smiled and nodded. "I pissed myself in my first action," he shouted over the sound of wind and thumping musket balls, "but I never left my quarters. Anyone who says he's never pissed himself in action is a liar, a fool, or a madman!"

More balls flew past, and all three men hunkered down even lower. Cocklin's blood was sticky beneath their feet. Edward wished he could stand tall, but it would serve no purpose: he would be killed almost instantly, so thick flew the shot.

But enough is enough, he thought angrily.

Keeping his head low, he picked up his long-barreled buccaneer gun from where it rested along the transom.

"Boy!" he shouted down to the ship's lad tucked away under cover of a gun carriage on the main-deck. "Bring me a loaded musket! Or two, if you can! Quickly, lad, but keep low!"

One hundred yards astern was the French corsair, too far on a pitching deck for anything resembling accuracy, but Edward could certainly put a ball or two among the large crew. He took careful aim with the musket, elevating the muzzle well above his target and timing the rise and fall of both the *Virginia* and the privateer.

He fired. He swore he saw a man among the many fall. From the main shrouds a French seaman waved a cutlass in angry defiance. Edward passed his now unloaded musket to the ship's boy and its place received a loaded common English musket of much shorter barrel. He aimed and fired again, this time at the foretop where three musketeers crouched. He hit one, as much by luck as skill, and watched him fall.

To no one in particular he said, "I'll be damned if I'll have it said of me I never fought back against an attacker. Two dead here, no, three, and several wounded—we owe them."

Now there was nothing left but to hope a sail did not split, critical rigging did not part, a mast did not spring or go by the board. In Fortune's hands they lay.

What the hell keeps us going? he wondered. *Duty? Greed? Or just fear? Does fear send some to action, others to hide? Is it for fear of a French prison? The officers, merchants, and gentlemen would be easily enough ransomed, eventually. The fear of death? Of maiming? Of the loss of hand, eye, arm, foot, finger, leg, testicle? Of the various consequences of futility? Or do they do this for many reasons? No matter,* thought Edward, *we've done what we've done, and under Fortune's gaze.*

"A sail! A sail!"

By God, thought Edward, *the lookout's still doing his duty!*

He cupped his hands and shouted aloft. "Where?"

"Dead ahead! At anchor in the lee of Lundy!"

O Fortune! Please let it be an English cruiser!

"And another with her!" shouted the lookout.

Edward stood up, ducked again, much too late, as two musket balls passed by. He stood again and made a crouching run to the quarterdeck rail.

"You!" he shouted to a seaman. "Pass the ensign up here and help me raise it at the staff—nay, we'll *nail* it to the staff, I'll have no one strike our colors. We'll let the strangers know who we are!"

Edward and the seaman rove the flag to the base of the staff then hoisted it aloft, then, braving French fire, nailed the bottom few feet to the staff. The ensign stood erect from the staff in the stiff wind.

"They bear away!" the lookout shouted.

And so the privateer astern did, altering to a southwesterly course and signaling to her companions.

"Men-of-war, I'm sure of them! Fourth rates at least!" shouted the lookout.

"Huzzah!" shouted those on deck.

"Aye, huzzah," Edward muttered under his breath.

Twice saved by Fortune in as many passages, he thought. *But as much by our own efforts as by Fortune*, he reminded himself, then remembered something he'd heard someone say: *Fortune often aids valor when it's a bit reckless.*

Yes; he smiled suddenly as he stared at the retreating Frenchman—the words of a French privateer captain.

The ship's surgeon lay dead below; his occasional apprentice, to his credit, tried not to mangle his wounded charges until a woman passenger, her brother a surgeon, took over for him. Under her surgery and care for the next two days, none of the wounded died of their wounds, not even the pair who lost limbs. Edward, the ship now in one of the mate's hands, slipped into his cabin to write a letter to the owners describing the chase. As he took off his coat he noted holes where seven musket balls had passed.

Late that afternoon the *Virginia* Galley begged a bower anchor from a merchantman in the lee of Lundy Isle: Bristol Channel was extremely dangerous without a good anchor, or even two, to stem the tides. The kedge she had kept would have served only as a last resort. The next morning, the *Virginia* came to an anchor in King Road and would wait another day to put herself in order before ascending the Severn. Edward could not afford further delay and went ashore. As soon as he had dealt with the usual officials, he took passage on a ferry up the Avon to Bristol, the tide favoring the short journey.

He was confident he had escaped Fortune's last Irish grasp. The road ahead lay straight, and ill-Fortune's handmaidens lay far behind.

Chapter 18

[A] pox of poverty, it makes a man a slave, makes wit and honor sneak, my soul grow lean and rusty for want of credit.
—Aphra Behn, *The Rover,* 1677

Edward, still flush from his second escape from a French privateer while crossing St. George's Channel, pushed through the door of the Black Swan coffeehouse on Tower Lane near the Old Bowling Green and stepped into a large room busy with the clatter of word and cup.

Before him were sea captains and merchant traders growling and grumbling as they smoked their pipes and drank their coffee, about why they could not get enough convoy protection, about how the French were damnifying English shipping, about how it was safer to sail under Swedish or Danish colors. Some quietly puffed at their pipes and read the news posted beneath stained paintings, lottery notices, and various broadsides on smoke-smudged walls.

In a tobacco-smoke darkened corner, an investor, owner, and captain signed articles of agreement on a table mottled by spilled liquids, ink, and candle wax. A notary public stood by to put his seal on the agreement and sign his name, abbreviating his title as *Not's Pub'cus.*

A wily old investor who had just returned from the Tolzey— the local Exchange or stock market—kept an ear open as he listened both to supercargoes just returned from West India as they discussed goods and profits, and to several members of the West India and Chesapeake Trades as they complained of Scottish and Irish interlopers.

A sea surgeon and a captain-owner discussed sailing a slaver from Guinea to West India independently of the Royal Africa Company, and thereby illegally. The captain-owner delayed discussing wages, and instead cursed high insurance rates and bottomree, how they were keeping him from making a profit.

"Damn, a good surgeon would help me keep a few more slaves alive and so make the voyage more profitable. Are you a good surgeon?" the captain-owner asked. "I warn you, though: when the war's over I won't be able to interlope on the Africa Company's territory, the goddamn navy will start protecting the Company again. An honest man can't hardly make a living while the Company has a monopoly on slaves to the West Indies. So, are you a good surgeon?"

Nearby, a reasonably well-dressed young man—or he would never have been granted entrance—pretending to be a merchant's son but revealed by eventual admission as a member of the strolling trade and a penniless poet, sat with a foppish old gentleman and told him he was tired of playing roles written by others and wanted, so he said, "to his own self be true." At the old gentleman's suggestion, the young man made his way to a tavern on the quay to meet a woman who could, so the old gentleman said, help him. A day and several bottles of wine later, he found himself trepanned, spirited, and indentured aboard a pink bound for Virginia, having learned just how mystical wine, woman, and a cudgel can be.

All had come to the coffeehouse to conduct business: most of them sober men making sober transactions, reading and discussing yesterday's post, and generally conducting themselves as men were coming to do in the nascent Protestant ethic world of trade. Coffee now reigned as the drink of worldly men conducting business, although some suggested that coffeehouses turned men into womanly gossips, and that the brown Turkish water dried men up and left them limp, and if not limp then still unable to give fire. Wine, beer, and strong spirits were not served here, and neither loud dispute nor lover's woe were tolerated, or so the posted rules stated. Here all men were considered equal; here common merchant might engage nobleman without begging leave to do so. And here women, other than those serving, were commonly refused entrance in order to avoid distracting men from the business at hand, or so the argument went.

Edward wended his way through tobacco smoke and loud but not boisterous conversation.

"Pardon me, sir!" said a serving woman carrying a wooden tray loaded with cups and pint coffee pots as she gently brushed him aside.

"Ah, Captain MacNaughton!" called a merchant trader and acquaintance, who then turned to his companion and spoke in a low voice. "This man is a buccaneer, duelist, and occasional lawyer—three rogues in one! And never, unless you know him well, as I do, call him a lawyer if you value a whole skin. You don't want to get his Scots blood up. His father was a roving Highland man who sailed with Henry Morgan, so there's a streak of savage blood in him as terrible as a West India harrycane."

Edward drew near and nodded his greeting.

The merchant captain continued more loudly, now directing his voice as much to the room in general as to Edward. "We heard about your duel in Teagueland from Captain Cronow, and he heard about it in Cork, or was it Waterford? It even merited a line in the *Gazette!* At any rate, my congratulations, sir, on your survival, and on your two successful rancounters with the French. I've heard you intend to be away to sea again, and I wish you luck on your venture, whatever it may be. Have you heard? Seager is likely to have his commission for the *Danby* Galley as a private man-of-war. One hundred tons, ten guns, forty men."

Edward frowned. The news annoyed him, although Seager was not truly a rival. What really annoyed him was that the man had the support of the peer Thomas Osborne, First Duke of Leeds, and of his son, the peer Peregrine Osborne, Earl of Danby, Marquess of Carmarthen. Both men had rejected Edward's petitions, albeit politely. No matter, it still might be months before Seager had a signed commission and could head to sea. This reality, the time it took to get commissions granted, made Edward frown again.

"Come," the man continued, "sit with us if you have the time."

"Thank you, I will later if I can, but business first."

"Of course, sir, I understand. Business first always, unless your pleasures be business also."

Edward walked to an enclosed counter projecting into the main room. On it sat candles and candlesticks, cups without handles, and a box filled with long churchwarden pipes.

"Mrs. Williams," he asked, as he put a coin into a small box to pay for his coffee, "do I have any mail?"

"You've returned, sir! And alive! Heard all sorts of tales about a duel in Ireland, how you'd lost your foot and were running around on a wooden leg, even that you might be dead, not to mention tales of taunting and then escaping French privateers. We heard this morning of your adventure aboard the *Virginia* Galley; it's all anyone is talking about. And it's still rumored you fought a duel here in Bristol, too, the day before you left!"

Edward was accustomed to hearing tales of his adventures upon arriving home or abroad. A man who gloried in his own image would be pleased with such foreknowledge and attention, but for Edward it was a curse. Two trials for piracy, along with various misadventures, several of which had been noted in newspapers, printed single sheets, and the occasional broadside, had made him variously famous and infamous. If he fought a public duel in the morning, the deed was on everyone's lips by afternoon. If he fought a private duel—and most were— and wounded his adversary in the morning, by afternoon he was suspected of being involved. News traveled as fast as man or woman could talk, walk, ride, or sail. And men, he had found, gossiped at least as much as women, although they pretended such speech had a manly purpose and therefore could not be gossip. All of this made his pursuit of a commission much more difficult, for the facts and exaggerated fictions of Edward MacNaughton, privateer and pirate, invariably preceded him, siring far too many preconceptions.

"Whatever my adventures, I'm not yet dead, nor do I even have a wooden leg," he replied with a smile.

"You've a limp, though—you've been up to some mischief!" she said, her eyes twinkling.

"Will you never stop flirting with me?"

"Captain MacNaughton, sir! You seem to think every woman in the world would lie with you, likely because you've had more than your fair share of success with women. But some of us have principles," she said, and laughed.

"Mrs. Williams, you'd make a better wife than lover, I think. If you and your husband ever tire of each other, let me know—I might let you make an honest man of me."

"Oh, Captain, Captain," she clucked as she shook her head and rummaged through bundles of letters, each small bundle tied with a string. "Here you are, sir, seven letters."

"Thank you," he said as he paid her twelve shillings five pence for the postage. "But mind what I said."

"Go away now and read your letters, my young friend! And you call me a flirt!"

In return Edward handed her the pack of letters Molly had left with him in Ireland, some to be delivered to the royal post office at the Dolphin Inn, others to merchant traders and factors here at the Black Swan, and also gave her a note to have made into a notice for the wall, to wit: *Capt. Edw. MacNaughton is Available Once More to Give Lessons to All True Sword-Men.*

"Have you seen Jonathan Graham today?" he asked.

"Aye, he was here this morning, said he was going to meet someone at the Three Cranes and then must ride to Bath, something about a meeting to arrange. I'm to tell you he'll meet you at your apartments tomorrow before noon, said it's important. So you'll be having coffee, sir? Oh, forgive me, I watched you pay already, of course you'll have coffee."

"Yes, thank you, and a pipe and tobacco—sacerdotes or Oroonoko if you have it, otherwise some good Virginia."

Edward took his letters, pipe, and tobacco and sat down in a high-backed bench chair near the coal fire, one of the few chairs in the room. Most men sat on long benches at long tables.

A serving boy came by with an ember to light his pipe, then a serving woman with a pint coffeepot of rich, dark liquid and a cup to drink it from. Another lad roasted beans at the hearth, tended the copper kettle over the fire, and ground the roast beans into coffee powder which, as this a reputable establishment, was never reused. As called for, the boy ladled coffee from the kettle into the coffeepots.

Edward opened his letters. No good news, but no bad either. No word from Spain. There was an offer from some members of the Bristol Merchant Venturers, of assistance at a steep interest rate, larger than he was willing to agree to. Edward snorted. These were the investors who had once tried to throw him in debtors' prison after he returned from imprisonment in France, having lost ship and cargo to a French privateer. His share of the ship's cargo had been uninsured—he could not afford the fourteen percent the insurers wanted—and this had left him deeply in debt.

From France he had escaped to sea, returned home, and put his investors off long enough to return to sea again, this time as a volunteer to lead boarding parties. He'd saved the ship from capture by the French after her captain was killed. In the process, he'd captured the French corsair. For this, these same powerful investors had rewarded him, first by making him a Freeman *Gratis* on the nomination of the Mayor, and then denying him loans and investments in his present venture. But perhaps they had heard of Sir William's likely financial support and were now more willing to invest, as long as someone else took most of the risk.

Edward tucked his mail beneath his waistcoat and fell asleep, chin on chest, feet stretched out before him. It was late afternoon when he woke, grumpy as ever he was from afternoon naps. He bid his farewell to the coffeehouse, walked swiftly yet circuitously to his apartments on narrow New Market street—he could almost stretch his arms out and touch the buildings on each side—just off Tower Lane, was pleased to see his baggage had been delivered, greeted his landlady and housemaid, gave each gifts of Irish linen, and went straight to bed.

He was awakened early the next morning by his landlady, who delivered him a letter brought to the door by a boy.

Edward broke the seal, read it, and cast it into the fire.

An hour before noon she interrupted him at his desk.

"Sir, there's a *lady* to see you," she said coldly.

"Indeed? Unfortunately, I rather expected a visit after the letter you delivered this morning. Lydia Upcott, is it? Show her in, please."

"I know you don't like to hear it, but I don't like this woman, even if she is supposed to be a lady! I don't like her sluttish ways, though I'm sure it's why you tolerate her company; and I don't like the people she keeps company with, actors and actresses, and those gallants and highwaymen at Bath, not to mention those notorious lords and such."

"Some say I'm notorious."

"Ridiculous! There's a difference between a rake and a legitimate gentleman of fortune! You only rob the Spanish of their silver, not young women of their virtue."

Edward laughed. Mrs. Barlow had been his landlady since he first made Bristol his home port. She was also his liaison for the mending and washing of his clothing, the purchase of his necessaries, and his wigs being sent out to be combed. Formerly a housekeeper, born and raised in Bridgwater, she had moved to Bristol after she'd inherited several apartments, not long after the surgeon who'd employed her was arrested as a rebel in the aftermath of the Monmouth Rebellion and was transported to the West India colonies, from whence he had escaped and, some said, turned pirate.

Mrs. Barlow showed Lydia Upcott and her maid from the tiny foyer into his parlor-cum-office. Edward received them casually, wearing a somewhat threadbare quilted Calico morning gown.

"Good morning, Lydia." He nodded at her maid, Bridget.

"Edward," she replied softly, smiling and cocking her head slowly to the right.

She was tall and slender, too slender almost, and pale with blonde tresses. She resembled Elizabeth Barry, the great actress whom he had once met in London, or perhaps even more so

Marie Louise, later known as Maria Luisa, queen of Spain, for whom Edward had once done a secret service. Her forehead and cheekbones were prominent, eyes and eyebrows dark, nose aquiline, lips full and sensual. Her resemblance to these famous women may have been much of the attraction, although her willingness to be bedded surely added to it.

"Edward, I've been so worried. So many rumors! I wrote a letter this morning as soon as I heard you'd returned. I had a boy deliver it here," she said, then whispered, "but I don't trust your landlady; I hope she gave it to you." Edward remained expressionless. In her normal voice she continued. "I feared you might not receive it, so I rushed over here, which I know a woman of my station ought never do. To be frank, I want to reclaim our friendship, and then I want to hear all about your adventures in Ireland!"

Edward cleared his throat. "Lydia," he said blandly, "thank you for coming to wish me well. I received your letter, which I interpret to say that your recent gallant is off to the wars or another mistress, that you've heard that I'm in a better situation with my creditors and investors, and that you wish to tease me into courting you again, even as you're doubtless spending time with some other man, and even though you persuaded a bully to seek me out and stick me with his sword before I left for Ireland."

Her cheeks flushed slightly. "Iain, you always were direct with me, but always in silent action, not words."

Edward ignored her use of his middle name. His parents had given him two names, unusual in those days. "If the Stuarts, kings though they be, can have more than one name, then surely a MacNaughton can, too," his father had said. The name was reserved only for those close to him, family primarily. She used it to bait him, to draw him into an argument or petty confrontation which would end up with both of them tearing at each other's clothes and the neighbors muttering, with a knowing wink, "There goes that she-cat again."

For some months prior to his trip to Ireland, Lydia had off and on again been his mistress, always with an eye for men of greater wealth and station. She played the game well: she was slightly too sophisticated to be a coquette, slightly too willing to be a tease, and slightly too discriminating to be a whore. She wished to possess what she did not have, and then cast it aside once possessed, wishing for something else—an endless cycle of desire, possess, discard, desire.

Alas, having no fortune herself, for her father had lost the last of his when he backed King James over King William and Queen Mary, and had then died of apoplexy soon after his arrest, she was not desired by men with fortunes, but only by those who would be fortunate with her. The few lovers who would perhaps have spent more than their seminal passion upon her, she abused their favor with inconstancy, her carnal allure ultimately failing to dissuade her lovers from taking their passion elsewhere.

Another woman who's lost her place, he thought, *trying to survive like the rest of us.*

Even so, Edward knew to keep his distance, and was even more so inclined after his Irish adventures.

"You shouldn't believe everything you hear, Iain," she said. "I didn't send that beast Lynch after you. I would never send one man to harm another. He's just a jealous fool, and for no reason—I've always kept him at distance." She paused, pretending to look embarrassed, then continued. "I've come to ask if you will escort me to Bath tomorrow," she said. "I know you might be busy, but surely you could use some rest and pleasure after your long trip, and the waters might help your wounds. It is all about the town how you've killed another man in a duel, in Ireland this time."

"So I've heard," he said dryly, and thought, *First attack, then flatter my sense of valor.* He knew her too well.

He knew she sensed his annoyance and disinterest. Now she would attempt to wear down his defenses, using a liturgy he had seen employed worldwide by prostitutes and fortune hunting ladies on reticent men. She would begin with flattery, the innocent young virgin standing in awe of the hero. When this did not work, she would move on to various other forms of feminine attraction, playing the roles, one after the other until one found its mark, of friend, mistress, sister, mother, damsel in distress, teasing coquette, dominating woman, and brazen harlot. Failing all these, she would scorn him, usually subtly, as a man socially and sexually inferior, a pale shade compared to all other men she knew, finishing with, "I don't know why I waste my time on you, all other men I know are greater men than you—*bigger* men than you."

And then she would look away and wait for him to come to her, to take her and screw her, to show her off in the city and screw her again.

But not today. He had meetings to plan, a commission to seek, dangerous letters still in his possession, and a philosophy to prove. Her association with Lynch, whatever it was, had almost waylaid his plans.

"Lydia, I won't accompany you to Bath and I won't forget that, in spite of your protests, you may well have sent that fool to name me a Jacobite and so challenge me, for whatever perverted purpose your jealous mind invented or for whatever other intrigue you might have been up to."

Anger, and what might have been a hint of pain but probably was only injured pride, flashed across her face. After a moment she was smiling again.

"Bridget, go away; keep Mrs. Barlow company in the kitchen." She looked at Edward, her face all innocence.

"Edward, you know well that my father was a Jacobite until his death. It's not so shameful a word. I didn't send that jealous fool after you; he challenged you of his own accord, using me as an excuse. I told him not to, that you would kill him. But if you're sure you want me to go away, Edward ...." she said, slipping back into the use of his first name.

She sat down on the day bed, then leaned backward, half-reclining. She raised the skirt of her dress several inches above her ankle, revealing a long, fine, delicate leg in a pink silk stocking.

Edward was disappointed, although as usual her wanton displays did arouse him. He had expected, or at least hoped, for something more subtle from her this time.

"Mrs. Barlow," he called, "please send Lydia's maid in here, as she will be accompanying her mistress out shortly."

Bridget entered the room; Lydia sent her out again.

Edward strode directly to Lydia, looking hard into her eyes.

Lydia smiled broadly. She knew that he would kiss her, and take her right there on the day bed, oblivious to her maid and his landlady in the kitchen, deftly removing only her dress and petticoats, leaving her shoes, stockings, shift, and jewelry, her long legs wrapping around him as he pressed himself onto her and into her, kissing and caressing her lips, her neck, her small, delicate, pink-nippled breasts that peeked at him as he slid his hands down her back and across her flat belly and round buttocks, ignoring her cries and moans of pleasure.

"Mrs. Barlow!" Edward called again loudly, mind overruling flesh, sense overruling lust. Almost immediately his landlady was at his door. "Please show the ladies out. Mistress Upcott, Bridget, a good day to you."

They departed, Lydia livid, an act perhaps, and her maid glaring, not an act at all. On the way out Lydia struck a vase of flowers on a side table, knocking the vase to the floor.

Edward regarded his landlady. "Don't give me that 'I told you so' look," he said, then laughed and shook his head. "I'll replace the vase and flowers."

"Then I'll say it, sir; I told you so," she said, and called for the maid to clean the mess. Moments later, she was called to answer the door, and escorted Mr. Graham to his room.

"Jonathan!" Edward said warmly, "I could have used your counsel in Ireland."

"Looks like you could have used it a quarter hour ago," he replied. "Did the baggage strike you?"

"Just knocked a vase over. You don't see any blood, do you?"

"You've a hard head, my friend, and besides, you might not have any more blood to give. Beware: it was a woman scorned I saw leaving here. I've already warned you once about her. I'll say this for your jades, they're never submissive. I thought you had done with this one, especially after she tried to have you killed."

"Not scorned, it's just a squall. She'll be back within a fortnight at most, more likely within a day or two. She's up to something, I don't know what, but I'd like to find out," Edward said, leading Jonathan into the long, narrow room that served as his *salle d'arms*. They stopped by the fireplace, where there was a small table with glasses and several bottles of wine.

Above the mantle and below a pair of crossed swords was a certificate attesting to Edward's skill as both swordsman and fencing master, inscribed "Society of Sword-Men in Scotland" at the top and signed "Wm. Machrie" and "Wm. Hope Kt." at the bottom. Next to it, from a ribbon hung the society's badge. On the fireplace mantle lay several copies of Edward's book on swordplay, published a year past in small quantity, much at his expense, with a handful of decent copperplates: *The Practical Sword-Man: Advice for the Novice and Artist for Fencing with*

Sharps in Duells, Affrays, Battels, and Sea-Fights. It was to his knowledge the only fencing book that gave advice on the use of the sword in a sea fight.

Each man poured a glass of claret. "To the swordsmen and privateers of Scotland!" Edward toasted, raising his glass first to Jonathan, then to the certificates and swords above the mantle.

In this room, and also in the narrow courtyard next to it, Edward gave the fencing lessons that produced the small income that helped get him by while he sought his privateering commission. His students varied from gentlemen, merchants, tradesmen, and the occasional nobleman wishing to learn true dueling technique as opposed to mere "school play," to sea officers and seamen who wished to learn the aggressive offense and defense of swordplay during boarding actions, to the occasional military officer who came to refine the technique of thrust, cut, and cut-and-thrust. Jonathan Graham—friend, factor, agent, supercargo, swordsman, Scot, and expert in all matters of maritime business affairs—often assisted him.

"Is that a good thing that she'll be back, that damn woman?" Jonathan argued as he inspected Lynch's sword where it still hung on the wall with three other smallswords for sale. "She's too lean anyway, not enough ballast in her narrow beam, nor enough sail on her yards. But I suppose a man must have his wenches, even those who try to have him killed. Anyway, how are your wounds? Nothing to prevent you from going to sea for a year?"

"I'm well enough, and a few more weeks will see me entirely healed."

"Excellent. Hearing yesterday evening that you'd returned, I procured an audience with Lord Deigle tomorrow at Bath—you did write me that you must see him immediately about the business you conducted on his behalf in Ireland, didn't you? I don't know what private matters are between you, although I have my own ideas, but he's now more keen on the idea of our venture. He has influence in London and is also a close friend of Lord Bellomont, the governor of the New York and Massachusetts colonies. Bellomont recently supported the outfitting of a ship to pursue pirates, the *Adventure* Galley, I think she is called, captained by a man named Kidd. Such a venture should've belonged to you. Perhaps if you hadn't offended Thomas Wharton in Bath last year? I've heard he's a silent partner. By the way, why did you fight with him? Two successful duelists and superior swordsmen—it must have been an impressive display."

"A successful duelist may be a superior swordsman, but he must also be a fortunate one, this I know from experience," Edward said indifferently. "And I don't recall the nature of the offense."

"Of course you remember why you crossed swords with him. Only a swashbuckler or *bretteur*"—he pronounced it breeTOOR in spite of the fact that he could speak French well enough when necessary—"never recalls and never cares why he fights. A woman is my guess," Jonathan said dryly.

"I don't fight over women," Edward responded just as dryly. "But back to the matter at hand, this pirate-chasing is a bad idea of Bellomont's, and is in the hands of an arrogant fool. No good will come of it. Indeed, no good will come of it no matter who the captain is. I know Kidd. He's an able seaman but no true leader of men. He's the sort who can lead well only when his crew are of his own mind."

"Well, Handsome Harry, as Deigle's taken to calling himself lately, they say he invented the name himself, wants to be associated with a similar venture but lacks money, as many noblemen do. He can only provide influence, but we desperately do need influence. Speaking of money, did Sir William send a bill with you?"

"A small goldsmith's note to help with expenses, but otherwise no, he had some business to clear up first, said he would send a bill of exchange within a fortnight, three copies to ensure arrival. He did send me with a letter promising to help finance the expedition," Edward replied.

"We'll need a ship, obviously, or there's no point to the rest."

"I've one in mind, the *Virginia* Galley."

"I thought you were trying to convince the Marquess of Carmarthen to design and build a privateer for you? Or that he might lend you his *Bridget* Galley?"

"Peregrine Osborne, a marquess since when, '94? How nobly advance these nobles, Jonathan. I served as a volunteer with him at Brest, yet he's ignored my inquiries."

"He wasn't interested in helping a former comrade-in-arms?"

"It seems he's too busy designing a new swift ship, a sixth rate or yacht. Plus his duties as a naval officer—is he an admiral now?—keep him too busy to deal with new projects. A man can have only so many mistresses."

"Maybe you inspired him in his new design."

"Doubtless he'll try to sell it to His Majesty rather than waste his effort on a common privateer."

"No matter," Jonathan said, dismissing the speculation. "The *Virginia* Galley is a swift ship, and her owners are in trouble with their creditors. A French *frigate légère,* as the Monsoors call their sixth rates, I think her name was *Mermaid* or *Siren*, or *Sirène* I suppose, designed by Cochois or something like that; the French do this sort of little cruising ship well, as well as Carmarthen, so bugger him. She was purchased by some investors as a letter-of-mart ship but ended up only being used for trade. Surely we can make a deal for her if her owners want to sell. Otherwise, to Bath, then, tomorrow."

"Has Deigle hinted at his terms?"

"No, but terms there will be."

Edward scowled. "He can't have too many, not if he has no money to invest."

"We'll work on it, Edward, but you must realize we may have no choice but to accept many of them. How long have you been seeking a ship and a commission? How long have you gone begging to merchants and noblemen? Call it what you will, it's still begging. By the Heavens, Edward, I don't know what's worse, your Highland pride or your Lowland stubbornness. I'm a Scot myself, I know of what I speak!"

"Go on, my friend."

Jonathan sighed. "You must realize that your reputation precedes you. God's wounds, you've been refused so many times already, no one wants to risk on a man others decline to back. A buccaneer, after all. An accused pirate, too. And amidst a pack of frightened merchants who recall that not long ago a Bristol ship, the *Charles the Second*, sailing to the Spanish Indies, turned pirate last year near the Groyne, sailed instead to the Red Sea, and took one of the Mogul's ships, causing one hell of an uproar. Man named Every, or something like that. So you can't blame them; they wonder if you would do the same. Indeed, perhaps some fear that a man who could change sides so quickly from James to William might offer his ship up to James as a Jacobite privateer—"

Edward's cold stare cut him short.

"I didn't it mean it that way, Edward. No one questions your loyalty. Damn it, I'm a Jacobite at heart, if not in head. And anyway, your Jacobite past has surely inclined some of our Bristol investors toward you, fond as they were of King James."

"And apparently turned others, like the Lords Osborne, against me, in spite of my recent service to the crown," Edward said.

"The Duke of Leeds is an ungrateful wretch. Nothing comes from his ass but stinking corruption. He's a damned assassin, too, or so I hear, or was, back during the Popish plot and Godfrey's murder and all that. You'd be left with nothing but hands full of shit if he were your patron and partner."

Edward laughed out loud.

"And now you laugh at me—may I continue without fearing for my life?" asked Jonathan.

Edward laughed again. "You may," he answered lightly, then more seriously, and over two more cups of wine apiece, he described his Irish intrigues in detail, including the letters and what he intended with them, to which Jonathan replied with his usual wise counsel.

"Tomorrow, then," Jonathan said, encouraged by the opportunity of the letters. "Some polite ass-caressing words to Deigle and we can make a clear ship for engaging, so to speak, and soon be away to sea. By the way, that backstabber Lynch has disappeared from Bristol, gone to London I hear, but I swear I saw him in Bath not long ago. And he's got a new nickname: Double Bung! Damn, that reminds me! You'd best watch out for that Upcott wench. While you were gone I saw her two or three times at affairs Deigle was lording over; she was trying to catch his eye. Not sure she ever did, there were entire flocks of gentle whores trying to alight upon his cock. Heed your advice and mine, lad, and beware of her!"

Chapter 19

How is this! A picaroon is going to board my frigate!
Here's one chase-gun for you.
—Aphra Behn, *The Rover*, 1677

The next morning, Edward and Jonathan were greeted by the sounds of splashing water, children playfully screaming, and young women laughing. They caught whiffs of sulfur as they climbed the stairs to the gallery overlooking King's Bath and smaller Queen's Bath beside.

Edward glanced down at the ancient green-water pools filled with bathers of all ages. The men wore breeches, the women yellow garments whose sleeves and skirts ballooned around them, and the children were naked. Here and there, tied to a woman's arm with a ribbon, was a floating lacquered dish, on which were perfume, a nosegay, and a few small patches to serve as beauty marks. A few children dove into the baths from the galleries before the sergeant, whose duty it was to keep order, could prevent them. Spectators—gentlemen gamesters, merry widows, chaperoned young women, penniless suitors, rakes and Hectors—lined the galleries and watched as the bathers floated, swam, and flirted.

At the center of King's Bath was the pump house with crutches hung from its supports and roof by those whom the waters had cured. Edward, however, had a theory that exercise had been the cure, not the waters. The exercise of both body and mind was a better cure than a physician's nostrums, he believed, a notion curiously similar to that of a Puritan preacher he had once met in New England, although in all other ways the two men differed entirely.

And it's time to exercise my brain more and my lust and sword less, Edward thought, *for now I enter again a world I despise, of patronage and pandering, of begging and bribery.*

The two Scotsmen paused before they approached Lord Deigle, whom they spotted standing with two other noblemen by the gallery rail, with his secretary and servants in attendance.

Viscount Deigle leaned against the rail of the gallery above King's Bath, his legs crossed to display his muscular calves. He stared and smiled at every woman who walked past. His face and figure were superficially imposing, with squinty, deep, narrowly set eyes, Roman nose, permanent smirk, and, in spite of being almost as tall as Edward, a small hitch or heel-bounce in his step when he walked, as if he felt he were not quite tall enough.

Around his party, at a discreet distance, fluttered obsequious humanity who had come to see and be seen, all of them bedecked in lightly powdered and perfumed periwigs, with scented gloves, fur muffs, beribboned canes, gilded and plated smallswords thrust fashionably through coat pockets, and hats in-hand in order not to 'offend' their delicately coiffed wigs. Silver and gold snuffboxes clicked endlessly as wits, fops, and sycophants sniffed, dripped, and, figuratively, drooled.

Edward felt like a beggar asking for a handout as he approached Viscount Deigle, but at least he did not entirely look like one. He was dressed in understated martial elegance. His periwig was un-powdered, tied at the back, and of a style almost out of fashion. His smallsword today was a French colichemarde with silver hilt and copper wire grip, quite serviceable as well as *à la mode*, hanging from a sword belt buckled over a sash over his coat. His cravat was of white *point de Venice,* casually tied and tucked into a button hole in the French military fashion. His hat was black with a white feathered edge, his coat blue with gold lace, his waistcoat buff-yellow and similarly laced, his breeches and shoes black, his clocked stockings white. For the occasion he even carried an elegant but sturdy walking stick made of a hard tropical wood. Some of the nearby fops might sneer at his dress, but they would do so in private.

Or so he thought.

"Hardly *au courant,*" he heard one man say to his companion, deliberately loud enough to be overheard. "Such a shade of blue as my whore might wear on Sunday, or a butcher might wear in his trade."

Perhaps the pair of well-born gentlemen—'painted, powdered, and patched,' not to mention 'simpering, apish, and cringing' as one scathing wit put it—thought themselves free from retribution, given Edward's obvious position as supplicant to a Great Man.

"Edward…" Jonathan whispered as his fellow Scotsman strode directly toward the two men, his face. He could not care less that he was too poor to keep up with fashions that changed monthly, nor would he have followed them even if he could. But he could not abide such impudent cowardice. If a man must insult him, let it be to his face.

The fops lost their grins as Edward approached, left hand on his sword, right hand gripping his walking stick like a basket-hilted cudgel.

"We don't know you, sir," said one as he fumbled to close his snuff box, his voice rising in pitch.

Like a fart held in too long, Edward thought.

"You lie, sir," Edward said quietly and coldly. "You know me well enough to comment on my favorite shade of blue, and of the trades it represents. I have indeed been called a butcher, yet unjustly, although I've covered myself in plenty of my own blood and that of others as well. I've never been called a whore, although I've known a fair number of women whom you would so consider; yet I found them of far more gentle breeding than I do you. Please honor me with your presence away from here, so that we might discuss the color of my coat further, not to mention my real occupation."

"I take not your meaning, sir," stammered the wit whom Edward's coat had offended.

"I mean for you to walk with me with your sword. I have one that sets my blue coat off well, and your coat...what is that color, sir, of your coat? Yellow?"

"It is gold-brown, sir, gold-brown."

"It needs a crimson trim."

"Sir, sir,…. I have only my walking sword with me, not my fighting. And your leg, sir, well, you limp a bit, sir, it wouldn't be fair to fight you today."

"You may consider my slight limp to your advantage then, even though it didn't stop me from killing a highwayman in Ireland or a French privateer or two at sea," he said, so calmly that the fop grew even more afraid.

"I am sorry sir, we must wait another day," the fop answered, trembling. That the man was scared to death was obvious to everyone nearby. Surely no one had ever called him out so publicly and with such obvious martial superiority. Edward knew his sort too well, and he had nothing but contempt for him and his.

"And where is your *fighting* sword?"

"In London, sir," stammered the sweating fop. One of his three beauty patches began to slide down his cheek.

"Then, sir, perhaps you'd prefer a taste of my walking stick instead? No? Then, sir, with your walking sword *walk*, and do it *now*, and do not return, ever, while I'm here, or come anywhere else I am, or we'll see how well *my* fighting sword will fit up your backside to give you the spine you lack."

Both men walked quickly away. Edward turned his back on the retreating pair, noting a pair of rather badly dressed gentlemen who had inexplicably escaped commentary on their own appearance. The pair turned quickly away as Edward's hawk-like gazed raked them.

Jonathan, who had behaved with extraordinary reserve while Edward threatened the fops, tugged at Edward's elbow and nodded in the direction of Viscount Henry Deigle. The nobleman soon noticed them, but continued his assessment of local pulchritude for several minutes more before addressing them. Edward fumed in silence.

More waiting, he thought, *always waiting for some damned fool to pull his fat head out of his ass!*

"Graham!" Viscount Deigle said eventually and flatly, "So glad to see you. And Captain MacNaughton; I knew you at once even, though the distance was great and I could not yet make out your face. You see, sir, I can spot a naval man anywhere. And these gentlemen," he said, directing their attention to the men at his side, "are Charles, Lord Mohun—you may have heard of him—and Sir Robert Wordsworth."

Edward knew Mohun. The young man, about twenty-one years old, was a notorious duelist and a murderer as well, but had enough influence at Court and in Parliament to protect him. Except for the unmistakable aura of debauchery, he did not look the part of a rake-hell, but rather of a self-indulgent and cunning backstabber, albeit a noble one. His face and lips were fat, his fingers delicate, his eyes weak but intelligent. He looked Edward over with an air both arrogant and tactical, notwithstanding that the two were already acquainted. Edward bowed—really more of an implied bow, something more than a nod and far less than the scraping of fop or courtier, and as much as he gave any man except a king—then ignored him.

"By God!" Deigle exclaimed suddenly, looking down into King's Bath, "look at that one down there! I had my carriage bring her here from Bristol; she's been after me almost since we first met some months ago, just before you sailed for Ireland, Captain. I had her the night we met, but not since then. Damn, look at that, almost three feet of cleanly sculpted leg, damn, now it's gone, you can't see her fine lines now. I hate the way the damn garments they wear float away from the body and conceal all that lies beneath. But I assure you she's a fine wench, trim and fast. I wonder how she'll look spitted on my yard tonight?"

Edward looked down at the woman, looked again, and bit his lip. He was certain she was Lydia Upcott. Alarms began to sound in his head.

"I think she'll suit my lord well. She's not married, but her father was a notorious Jacobite and lost all he had."

"Married or not married, Jacobite or Whig, of what concern is this to me? I don't care if a husband wears horns, nor do I care what politics or faith a woman has—women don't rule the world. The only things they can contribute are wealth, sons, and delightful entertainment. Do you dance, Captain? I'm thinking of holding a dance tonight at King's Mead."

Edward wondered how well Viscount Deigle would wear horns: probably not well at all. The timing of Lydia's pursuit of the pompous lord was of more concern to Edward. Still, it might be nothing more than coincidence. He had seen many curious coincidences in his life, and there had been nothing more to them than mere happenstance.

Lord Mohun and Sir Robert excused themselves, Mohun

first pausing to whisper in Edward's ear.

"It has been two years since last we met, sir. Since then, words have come to my ears about you from my friend Tom Wharton. And the wench below, my intelligencers tell me, is yours."

Edward refused the invitation. "I've no claim upon her," he murmured back.

"Ah, then she'll not do, sir, not at all. We must meet later, sir, I must have more words with you."

Mohun walked away, leaving Edward wondering at his cryptic speech. Those nearby whispered to each other, wondering if an affront had been given.

Edward heard Mohun tell his companion loudly, "We were together at Brest, with Lord Carmarthen when he reconnoitered the French defenses," as the two walked away.

The peripheral whispers ceased.

"Well, Captain," Viscount Deigle continued when Lord Mohun was gone, "you've returned from Ireland with more maritime adventures. It seems you are indeed the great mariner they say you are."

"Thank you, my lord, but I am a mere adventurer by sea. To call me great is to give me a compliment I don't deserve. I *am* an able seaman and navigator, and know how to fight both at sea and ashore," he said, combining honesty and as much ingratiation as he could stomach.

"I, too, am a man of adventure, but alas, I can't desert my duties in England—what think you of this pinnace steering her course toward us, Captain? What were we speaking of? Oh, yes, stipulations; if I am to use my influence in your quest for a commission, I trust you will also agree to my stipulations? Indeed, you must. We'll come to terms first, then I'll consider whether to support your petition. I must give it thought. Bunion," he called to his secretary, "have someone bring a bottle of sack or Langon. Oh, my correspondence from Ireland, you do have it, Captain? Yes? I'm sure the letters hold what I think they do. Please give them to Bunion, I'll read them tonight. I hope they hold great news for me."

Viscount Deigle watched a young lady—his pinnace—pass shyly by. He was anything but shy about his desire for her.

"Truthfully, my lord—" Edward began.

"My lord," interrupted Jonathan, "there are but few details to work out, details to put in order as is customary among men who follow the sea. If I might sit down with your lawyer and secretary we can draft the necessary agreements and sign them tomorrow. I have Captain MacNaughton's confidence."

"Excellent, sir, excellent: I loathe these matters of lawyers, contracts, and agreements. Your pardon, Captain," said Viscount Deigle, "but I see my little yellow bird prepares to fly from the pond. I must escort her part-way to her lodging. She has flirted my way all day, excessively, I must say."

"My lord," Edward said, stepping in front of Deigle, incurring thereby a glare which clearly conveyed that the lord was unaccustomed to anyone interfering with his intentions, however slight.

"Captain?" he said slowly.

"My lord, a word. I have matters of State to discuss with you privately, matters of grave importance regarding the safety of the King, and thus of England herself; matters beyond those you tasked me in Ireland on your behalf, whose letters you say will not read until tonight. The matters I speak of are even more urgent."

Deigle turned to watch long-legged Lydia disappear into her close chair and be carried off to her lodging. Edward saw her look up just before she did, and was certain she spotted both men. Deigle seemed to have an itch he must scratch immediately, yet Edward's words held him back, and in doing so, angered him.

"Captain, what mean you by this? And among so many common persons!" His voice dropped to a whisper. "Know you not the ways of managing secrets? Later, sir, later!"

"My lord," Edward persisted, "I have letters from Ireland, taken by accident from rapparees who were surely also Jacobite agents."

"And why do you have these letters, sir? Why have you not turned them over to the King's officers in Ireland?"

"Because, my lord, I feared none would act soon enough upon them, and because there is good intelligence that there is a spy among them at the highest level. I feared, my lord, that only a man of your experience, stature, and intelligence would understand their import, and act upon it," Edward said cunningly.

Deigle's arrogant intransigence had forced Edward to breech his own rule against flattering a fool. The man was no deep thinker, but he was politically shrewd and in need of capital in the forms of hard currency and political power.

Handsome Harry bit his lip.

Edward continued. "My lord, surely with your standing at Court someone would heed these letters. You might take them yourself to the King or to the Earl of Portland. Or if not, send me with them, under your own hand."

Edward intended these last words to give Deigle a way out, should Edward's fears be unfounded, and a way for him to take credit should Edward's fears be founded.

"I must read the letters," Deigle said.

"Of course, my lord, immediately. They do not leave my person. Surely there is a private apartment here where you may read them," Edward said, then thought, *By God's Wounds, the man hesitates. He's debating whether to lay with Lydia or save his king!*

"I do not see it, sir, I do not," said Deigle a quarter hour later, upon reading the letters. "Further, sir, if there were something here, some plot as you see, wouldn't Lord Brennan or Sir James have noted this in their letters? Lord Brennan in particular was once well-placed to know of these things; I'm sure he would have mentioned a plot if there were one. Indeed, this is one of the reasons for the letters you carried to him."

"My lord, you haven't yet read the letters from Brennan and Allin."

"*Lord* Brennan and *Sir* James Allin," Deigle corrected him severely. "Bunion, damn you! Bring me the letters from Brennan and Allin!"

Deigle read both letters, then Brennan's again, more slowly and carefully the second time. There was no hiding his disappointment. Edward, having read both letters, knew there was nothing of great import in either. Deigle reread the rapparee letters again and shook his head.

"I still do not see it."

"Even so, my lord, what harm? You must admit the possibility. If the letters do speak of regicide, then the king will owe you much; and if they don't, raising the alarm won't harm you. If I may, my lord, it would appear from your reaction to Lord Brennan and Sir James's letters that you have not received what you expected. If this indeed is the case, the rapparee letters may take their place. You might even send all of the letters together. If it turns out there is no great substance to them, the king would still owe you for looking after his person."

"The King would owe you as well. Is this what you're after?"

"I do seek a commission, my lord."

"If not by my influence, then by that of the King himself?"

"I've brought the letters to *your* attention, my lord," Edward said, thinking *Damn the fool! Doesn't he see what he holds in his hands?*

Deigle, his hands behind his back, walked back and forth for several minutes.

Surely he's not considering whether to send the letters to London, Edward thought, *surely he's only deciding how to present them and what gain he may have from them. Surely.*

"You should also know, my lord, that the men who attacked me were intent on stealing the letters I carried for you," Edward pointed out. "And one of them, whom I wounded in the affray, was hanged, I think because he lost the letters you hold in your hand. They must be of great import."

Deigle snorted, opened the curtains in front of a window, and stared into the street below.

"I will send you, Captain MacNaughton, with all of the letters," he said ten minutes later. "I will also send a letter of introduction and other correspondence with you, which you may present to the Earl of Portland. It's too late to depart today. Tomorrow morning then, and I'm sure you can afford the expenses of the journey. I recommend you purchase a horse and not rely on the post. I would offer you mine, but I have none here to spare."

Damn you! thought Edward, *You won't even pay for horses or lodging! Cheap, squinty-eyed bastard! Thankfully, we have Sir William's goldsmith's note for expenses.*

"Good," continued Deigle, taking Edward's glare as acceptance of his terms. "Bunion will have letters delivered to you at your lodging in the morning. God speed, Captain MacNaughton."

Handsome Harry turned on his heel and was gone, doubtless to find Lydia or some other woman. Edward shook his head.

"Well, Jonathan, what now? Will you come with me to London?"

"I can't keep up with you on horseback, Edward, and

anyway, I've business with Deigle's secretary and lawyer in the morning."

"I'd forgotten already."

"Relax a little, Edward. Chasing this venture has lately made you ill-humored. Hell, man, take the waters, they might even help heal your wounds."

"You already know my theory on that subject. And anyway my wounds are fine, and I'm fine. Just get me away to sea!"

"Well, it's to London first for you. I say it's cards tonight after you buy a horse or two, and with luck we'll have Deigle entirely on our side by noon tomorrow, with written agreements to back us up. Until then, forget about whatever's on your mind. I'm going to find a tavern, probably the one nearest our lodging."

"I'll meet you there after I tend to the horses I need," Edward said, suddenly feeling both lonely and a bit melancholy. His mind passed to Molly and Jane, probably the result of seeing Lydia and knowing Deigle would have her tonight. He noticed a maid selling oranges in the distance, a woman who had briefly flirted with him earlier and whose conversation had been surprisingly invigorating.

Jonathan, noticing Edward regarding the woman, retorted, "You won't meet me there, damn you, but I'll wait up for a few hours anyway. Let Deigle have that Upcott woman. You're moping like a dog who's lost a bone he never chews. She's poison, Edward, she's not the sort of adventure you need right now—she's luring you in by keeping her distance. Find a good woman soon, one quiet and quick on her feet, screaming and scratching on her back, and marry her, otherwise you're bound to be clapped sooner or later."

"I won't be long, Jonathan. Horses first, then a few words in the company of a woman."

"It's never words I need from a woman. Bring your purse if

you have any silver left after your purchase of horseflesh; I'll have the cards ready."

Edward saluted Jonathan with his walking stick and headed out to find a reputable horse jobber. As he walked, he tried not to obsess over the curious paradox Jonathan had alluded to.

Chapter 20

Familiarity encourag'd my Friend to a further Freedom ...
—Edward Ward, *The London Spy,* 1718

Edward spent an hour with a horse jobber, haggling over the price and quality of two horses more expensive than he really could afford. On the other hand, he could travel more swiftly with his own horses, and time was now vital. He would bear the expense because he had to.

He had considered hiring post horses, but they limited him to roughly ten miles before he must hire new mounts; and independent horse hire required him to stop at designated inns en route. Both of these means would slow him down. He might have taken the flying coach—two days to London in good weather—but it had already departed. The stage coach at three or more days was too slow, and carrier wagons were simply out of the question.

For an hour afterward he ambled into dusk, then darkness, pausing to procure a link boy with his torch of pitch and tow to light the way, another expense he really could not afford but tonight was willing to allow. He wended his way toward the location he had last seen the young orange woman, but she was gone.

Edward knew exactly what he was looking for as he wandered the streets idly: he wanted pleasure within his reach and beyond it as well. Something to distract him until morning. An unusual conversation. An adventure. A woman. Cards would not do. In this distraction of mind he would likely lose to Jonathan's sharp playing, so he wandered off, not to find what he sought, but to let it find him. He was no longer concerned about an ambuscade, certain that he had left that possibility behind in Ireland. And besides, until tomorrow the letters were in the hands of Deigle's secretary, a man far more likely to preserve them safely than even Deigle himself.

Not even Deigle's mistresses could get their hands on them, Bunion had told him privately.

This made him think of Lydia and suspect her as Jonathan did, which led to thoughts again of Jane and Molly, which brought to the surface a conclusion he had been wrestling with deep amidst his sense of morality. If Molly or Jane were a spy, or even simply associated with Jacobite plotting, as he believed Molly surely was, if not Jane, then the letters he would carry to London might ultimately destroy their lives.

And others' lives too. Sir William's life would certainly change by his association with Molly were she involved—not to mention the loss of his daughter, Molly.

Edward indeed required a distraction! There were solutions to his mental state; as his father used to say: "Fighting or fucking is always a better answer than drinking your woes away."

Aye, conflict or copulation it is, Edward thought. He had resolved not to drink himself even mildly insensible until the letters were safely in the hands of the Earl of Portland.

He wandered another block, down Horse Street, and paused at the River Avon. Clearly there was nothing more to see in this direction. He took a right turn along the quay, intending to take a turn down some of the smaller lanes that led back toward the baths. He heard the sound of quick steps behind him, but no voices, and instinctively turned halfway around to assess whether or not he need be concerned.

Two men stopped just within the light of the link boy's torch. Edward recognized them immediately as the two sallow gentlemen from King's Bath earlier that day, the pair who had disappeared after Edward threatened the fops. One was taller than average, the other likewise shorter. If they were footpads, they were obviously new to the trade, the sort of down on their luck gentlemen or pretend-gentlemen who would challenge others of their class to a duel and rob them instead.

"You rudely jostled my friend here," the tall one said, "and made no apology."

"That's a damn lie," Edward said plainly. If the Scotsman were looking for a fight, one had just found him.

"No man speaks to us that way, sir!" the tall gentleman replied.

"I'm sure that's a damn lie, too," Edward replied provocatively.

"You will give us satisfaction for that, sir!"

Before Edward could answer the challenge, a third gentleman, laughing with an older bawd who had lighted his way down the stairs with a candle, staggered from a darkened door nearby.

"Now why do you want to go looking for a pair of strolling strumpets when you've a house full of fine whores here?" laughed the woman, dressed in velvets and bright calicos, to her companion.

"Who's this?" Lord Mohun shouted when he realized he had an audience. His hand strayed playfully to his sword. "By God, it's that pirate MacNaughton. Sir, I believe you insulted me earlier today."

"I did not."

"Ah. Well, do so now," Mohun ordered, apparently

delighted with the world, or at least with the liquor he had consumed.

"Not tonight. Perhaps when I've more reason and you less claret. And besides, I'm already accosted."

"You refuse me? An insult! Indeed, a double one, for you accuse me of being cup-shot! But first, sir, I and my *bon ami*— where the hell has my companion Sir Robert gone?"

"Back to the coffee room, my lord," said the bawd.

"Damn him! Does he actually prefer the allure of pliant pulchritude to my own fine company?" Mohun said gleefully. He glanced at the two men confronting Edward. "And who are these penniless gentlemen clearly gone on account?"

"Who we are is none of your business, sir," said the taller.

"Well, sir, my name is Jack Killdevil, and this is my friend Edward MacNaughton the famous buccaneer. If you're planning on meeting him then you must also meet me!" Mohun said loudly, then leaned over and whispered in Edward's ear. "A sharp rum-bite, my false name, eh, sir? They wouldn't meet me if they knew who I really am."

"You're drunk," Edward whispered back.

"'Tis no matter, sir, I fence as well in my cups as when sober. And besides, I want to continue our conversation about Tom Wharton," he whispered.

"Sir!" said the tall sallow gentleman loudly. "You first insulted my friend and then the both of us! You will walk with us to the Ham or we'll draw on you here!"

"Well then, lead on, sir!" Mohun said, grinning.

"Let the link boy light your way, we'll follow you at distance so none suspect," replied the tall gentleman.

"Like hell—" Edward began, but Mohun cut him off.

"As you please, you pitiful gentleman!" Mohun interjected.

"Are you mad?" Edward asked him severely, and wondered *Is this an ambush? And Mohun a part of it?*

Mohun slipped his arm through Edward's. "Trust me, sir, I'm your friend tonight," he whispered, and, led by the link boy, turned toward the Ham, a large field in the bend of the River Avon. "Follow us, fools!"

"Where are you off to, my lord?" the bawd called after them. "Come back, follow your friend back up the stairs! My wenches are finer quality than any pair you'll find on the street!"

"We're going to meet a pair, my sweet dove, and we're going to spit them not with our cocks but with our swords! But I promise we'll return!" he shouted back.

Mohun interrogated Edward as they walked along the quay and turned onto Horse Street.

"So you did indeed meet Tom Wharton some months ago here in Bath, sword-in-hand?"

"I did, and on the Ham if it matters."

"You challenged him, then?"

"I did not."

"He sends no challenges, but refuses none," Mohun said accusingly.

"Are you calling me a liar?" Edward said calmly, and, but for the pair of armed men behind, would have been darkly amused by Mohun's boyishly murderous enthusiasm.

"If it suits my purpose. Yet you haven't answered me."

"It was mutual, and sudden. An affray, you might say."

"Over a woman!"

"I don't fight over women."

"But *for* them, I warrant, when necessary. Some actress Tom was debauching?"

"We kept the quarrel between us."

"How did you fare?"

"I didn't sleep in a whole skin that night."

"A pity, but not unexpected."

"Nor did he."

"Truly? Truly!" Mohun almost shouted for joy. "But perhaps

it's as I thought. I'll chastise him for this, I will. He told me the pain in his groin was due to a pocky wench, he said he received no hurt from you. You're surely the first man to put a hole in him, and I wanted that honor for myself. Perhaps one day. Tell me, how did you receive his point, and he yours? Together? Did he try to disarm you? He is a master of the disarm, you know."

"No man has ever disarmed me in single combat. We pushed together, his but barely through the flesh of my shoulder, mine likewise through the flesh of his hip. Both wounds were slight, and we considered honor settled," Edward said, as he cast an eye again at the gentlemen footpads some fifty feet behind.

"Unwise, sir, unwise! A *contre-temps*! Perhaps you sought his blade but were hasty? You committed to the attack as he deceived? Or he sought yours, in seeking to disarm you, but you deceived? Neither of you is fool enough to receive an exchanged thrust, but I can't account that either of you were fool enough to make a contre-temps either. Such accidents are common, but true swordsmen avoid them. It's mere chance that you were not spitting up your lung and he spilling his gut. You were careless, sir, careless, and he too!"

"Hold, gentlemen!" called the tall, sallow gentleman.

Edward and Mohun waited until their two adversaries came up with them.

"You must leave your link boy here," warned the tall gentleman.

Edward told the lad to go away, tossing him a coin and reminding him to tell no one what he had heard. Even with the loss of light, making skullduggery more likely, it still was better to have no witnesses to whatever end lay ahead. The four turned right and walked down the street between the gardens on the left and the Ham on the right.

Edward became coldly furious at the situation. He

considered the very likely possibility that he had walked into a trap. Logically he knew it was impossible that Mohun had set up an ambuscade, for there was no way he could have anticipated Edward's movements. Further, for what reason an ambush? The letters were not now in his hands. On the other hand, he realized, it might be a trap that Mohun had nothing to with.

The Scotsman felt an involuntary flinching in the small of his back. His left hand strayed to his scabbard, his right toward his sword hilt.

Something's missing! he thought suddenly, then realized that the accompanying footsteps of the sallow gentlemen had paused momentarily, and now their rhythm was changed.

He spun around to the left on the ball of his right foot, his right hand dropping his walking stick and drawing his French *colichemarde* as the other released the scabbard and slipped into his left pocket to pull a pistol. But the pistol snagged, so Edward, his hand still in his pocket, drew the skirt of his coat up to parry a backstabbing thrust.

He retired a step, parried another thrust with his sword almost vertically in prime, and broke measure again as his adversary recovered to his guard and retreated two steps. In the brief respite, Edward let go of the pistol, pulled his left hand from his pocket, and with it took his hat from his head to aid him in parrying.

Edward glanced quickly at Mohun. The rake had already unsheathed and skewered his opponent through the forearm and back.

The wounded man dropped his sword and ran, Mohun in drunken pursuit and shouting, "Sir Fowl! Sir Fowl! You have forgot your sword and I have yet to truss your other wing!"

Edward's adversary stood warily before him, on guard with most of his weight resting on his rear leg, his sword held straight out before him. He glanced left and right, then narrowed his eyes at Edward, who knew what he was thinking: his companion was both injured and pursued, Edward's companion might be raising a hue and cry or returning soon, or both, and Edward had successfully parried two thrusts, one at his back and then its immediate reprise. He was deciding whether to fight or flee, knowing that if he ran he might be pursued and backstabbed, and if he stayed he might be killed. Edward watched him warily; the man was surely full of tricks. He might pull a pistol, hurl dirt or snuff in his eyes, or dart his sword at him.

"Behind you, sir! The watch!" the man shouted at Edward.

Edward turned his head just enough to draw the man's attack, then, as it was dark and difficult to follow a blade with the eyes, made a round parry, found the blade, and thrust swiftly. Sensing his adversary's counter-parry, he turned his sword hand up, allowing it angulate around his adversary's parry, and, covering with his left hand as he thrust, hit his adversary just below the right collarbone.

The sallow gentleman grasped the wound with his left hand, retreated backward several steps, then turned and ran. Edward did not follow, using his still recovering foot as an excuse. In fact, he did not want this exchange to come to the attention of the watch or magistrate, for it might be called a duel, no matter that it had become a backstabbing affray before they could strip and fight like gentlemen in the dark. Lord Mohun had reputation, wealth, and friends with which to free himself, as they had done in the past when he was accused of murder or manslaughter. Edward did not.

"You prick him like a dog, but don't chase him?" Lord Mohun gasped, out of breath as he ambled drunkenly up like a seaman just setting foot ashore after months at sea. "But you're a quick one, sir! Almost as quick as I am! Come, you must join us at the whores. We'll roust Lord Deigle and his whore, too, and make your fortune while we're at it."

"My thanks to you, Lord Mohun. I won't forget this," replied Edward, annoyed even more that he would be in the debt now of not one but two men he neither liked nor trusted.

"Come, then, the night is young and you can't leave before the morrow! Tell me, do you prefer this hollow blade you wear tonight? I've heard you usually carry a colichemarde with a Spanish blade, four or six sided. Mine is a diamond blade, which some say is too heavy at the foible, as they would say of your usual Spanish blade, though I don't find it so. Here, sir, my handkerchief, you must wipe your blade so it doesn't rust in the scabbard."

And off they went, retracing their steps, Mohun singing an obscene *chanson á boire*, Edward angry and feeling like a prisoner, yet suddenly and perversely, and due entirely to the excitement of the fight, almost enjoying the anticipation of the revelry and debauchery to come.

They staggered down the streets, or at least Mohun did. It amazed Edward how attentively on his guard the rakehell was. Variously Mohun used his walking stick to fence with posts, shrubs, and passersby, shouting "Tierce parade and riposte, so ho!" and "Carte, damn you, and a hole in your belly!" and "Here's a 'sacoon' for thee, sa ha!"

They were accosted only once, by two night constables just as they arrived at the door to the whorehouse.

"Gentlemen! Gentlemen! You're making a noise!" said the elder, known as such by his long gray hair. His coat was deep red, his breeches blue, and in his right hand he held his staff of office.

"So, damn you, we are," replied Mohun smugly.

Edward generally had no issue with constables, using the reasonable method of being polite while maintaining an air of sobriety, martial self-assuredness, and implied rank. It was best not to argue with them, as the worst of their sort, contradicted even once, would commit even the sober for drunkenness.

"Now I'm sure you're drunk," the constable said, shaking his head. "A night's lodging in the compter will do you all good, and spare the neighborhood your bawdy tunes. And we've reports of swordplay on the Ham—might that have been you?"

"Who the hell are you, damn you, sir?" Mohun replied, his brandy- and wine-laced breath clearly offending the constable. "Can't you tell by our dress and deportment who we are?"

"I'm Constable John Wood," the law officer said, stamping his staff of office sharply on the ground. "Who the hell are you?"

"Charles, Lord Mohun."

It was several moments before the constable spoke, and then only to quickly apologize and take his leave. Edward, hating to see a man simply doing his duty be intimidated out of it by mere nobility, and not wanting to seem associated with Mohun, called out to the constable.

"Thank you kindly, sir, for your civility. Your servant, sir, and a good night to you."

The constable, wondering if he were being mocked, glared at him, then at his companion constable, shrugged his shoulders, and went on his way. Edward was ashamed at the deliberate condescension of nobility over the constable, and wondered if he himself might at some point be able to do England, or at least some several of her subjects, good service and take Mohun's life in a duel. He doubted Mohun could stand against him, at least if Fortune stood aside.

But no, he thought: *in fair fight or affray I lose if I kill this man whom constables fear to arrest. A man who can be acquitted of a notorious murder on account of his renown, and not that of the facts or his lawyers, is too great a man to be killed in the street at the hand of a Scotch privateer who doesn't want to be hanged. Fortune will whelp her bitches and bastards as she pleases.*

"Come, you sullen Scotsman!" Mohun shouted.

To the whorehouse they returned, ringing a bell until the bawd lighted them up the dark stairs, a rope nailed to the wall in place of a rail. The stairwell opened into a small coffee room in which were served only its namesake Turkish brew, cock ale, and an *aqua mirabilis* guaranteed to get male patrons up and keep them up. Pasted on the wall were a few pornographic postures from Aretino's sonnets, along with broadsides variously advertising pills to cure gonorrhea, white wash for the face, and a surgeon's services. Most of the windows were pasted over with brown paper. Three of the five waiting patrons, by their short hair, modest dress, and lack of swords, appeared to be merchants' sons. The other two were older gentlemen, a merchant factor and a doctor, perhaps. Only a monkey and a parrot lent the coffee room anything resembling an exotic air.

"Not quite the sort of place I'd expect you to frequent, my lord," Edward noted.

"It's not the cover, sir, but what's inside," Mohun replied, nodding in the direction of the two doors on the far side. From a bawd he ordered two cock ales, but Edward overruled him and asked for coffee for himself instead. Mohun immediately poured brandy from a flask into Edward's coffee when it came.

Occasional yelps, a howl or two, and the words "More! More!"—all echoed loudly by the red-plumed parrot, with occasional vocal accompaniment by the capuchin monkey—escaped from one of the briefly open doors, revealing a flagellation in progress: a gentleman on all fours leaning over a chair laid on its back, with his breeches down and his wrinkled cheeks bright red, his broad-hipped, small-breasted mistress afoot, her petticoats drawn up to expose herself, with a busy riding crop in her hand.

Other sights were far more mundane and typical: a half-drunk merchant's son fondling a woman aloft and alow before she took him to one of the rooms, the doctor telling the sad but occasionally merry story of his dull life to a prostitute pretending to care, and a darkly-dressed and quite sober merchant factor smoking a pipe while he told invented tales to which his mistress pretended fascination as she rubbed his groin with a stockinged foot. It was, all in all, the common sort of middling bawdy house.

Mohun's friend, Sir Robert, joined them eventually. An attractive young woman, her face heavily painted, who made a few adjustments to hair and dress, took a merchant's son by the hand and disappeared. Lord Mohun ordered more cock ale and forced Edward to accept one, half of which he poured into a vase of dead flowers when his companions were not looking.

A few minutes later, the submissive gentleman of the rod—the 'flogging cully,' as his sort were known in the house—departed. Mohun and Sir Robert made jibes—"Spare the rod, spoil the Puritan!" was one—as he was escorted to the front door, the bawd gently chastising them for embarrassing her well-paying customer. The cully's mistress, riding crop still in hand but skirts dropped and breasts covered, paused by Edward and gently laid the crop on his left shoulder.

"Care for a ride?" she asked with a smirk.

"I'll ask you to keep that one-tailed kitty to yourself, if you don't mind," he said, his smile and tone taking any sting out of his refusal.

"Without the whip, then? A pussy of the usual sort?"

"Not tonight, if it pleases you."

"No, sir, if it pleases *you*," she replied. "If you don't want a mistress with whip or without, how 'bout a young and beautiful —swarthy too!—'buggeranto' we keep upstairs for gentlemen who prefer something more between the legs of their *mistresses*?"

"Again, no thank you, my dear darling-with-a-whip," Edward replied, refusing to rise, so to speak, to the bait and prove by paying for her services that he preferred women. "Lord Mohun," he said, directing his attention to his undesired comrades, "I *must* depart, it's late and I have a long ride tomorrow."

"You could have one tonight, Captain MacNaughton!" ejaculated Mohun. "Alas, I must be in my cups after all—I thought my quip wittier before I shot it forth."

"Are you Captain MacNaughton, then?" the darling-with-a-whip asked.

"I am. Why do you ask? Would your price be any less?"

"More, not less, for a famous man like you, sir," she replied, putting him in his place.

"You know me, then?"

"No, sir. But two dirty gentleman were here asking about you earlier, wanted to know where to find you. Said they were looking all over for you, that you owed them money."

Adrenaline hit the pit of Edward's stomach hard.

"One tall, one short?"

"Aye, that's them."

"They wanted to bugger us, but we buggered them!" Mohun interrupted.

"My lord, shut up, please," Edward said. Mohun was too drunk to take offense. "Lass, did they say anything else? Do they have any friends?"

"Friends? Them? No, sir, only they do follow that bully Jack Lynch when he's around."

"Lynch? He's been here?"

"No, sir, not lately—but he'll probably come around soon. Someone stuck a sword in his arse a few months ago in Bristol; it shamed him so much that he won't go there anymore and only comes around here sometimes."

"Nothing else?"

"No sir."

"What's your usual price?"

"Ah, sir, I knew you'd be wanting something! A guinea for you, sir."

"A guinea? Who do you think I am?"

"What matters is that I'm a first rate frigate, sir!"

"A fine frigate *or* a first rate ship of the line," Edward corrected with a smile. "And I prefer the former." He drew a guinea from a small purse in his pocket and gave it to her. She took his hand.

"No," he said, declining. "For information, in case you hear anything else. This should be more than enough to buy your loyal intelligence."

"You disappoint me, Captain," she said, playing with his fingers.

"I'm flattered, truly. Another time, perhaps."

"It'll cost you another guinea—this one's for intelligence, remember?"

"I'll remember."

"Damn you, sir!" Mohun interrupted. "If you won't drink with me or lie with her, then I'm not your friend, therefore you insult me, but rather than ask you to measure your sword with mine, I'll curse you! May you find yourself mounted on the worst jade, an ancient poxed whore seated behind you, in a storm, in the darkest lane, ten miles from nowhere, with not a shilling in your pocket. Sir," he said, his speech much punctuated by sudden burping.

"Didn't I read that in that bawdy nonsense, *The English Rogue*?"

"You accuse me of plagiarism? Well, damn you, I'm guilty. Not *all* my wit is original. And so what, damn you, it's still wit! And Richard Head is a genius! Not of Rochester's ilk, of course, but a damned genius, of the low sort—like you might be, if you'd only indulge yourself as we do."

Here the young rake suddenly looked perplexed, unable to follow his own logic and unsure if he had just insulted himself. Sir Robert excused himself, took the darling-with-a-whip by hand, and left Edward and Mohun once more to fend for themselves.

"Come sir, I said I'll reward you and so I shall. Let's leave this place. Sir Robert is so besotted that he'll gallop for hours before he's spent. I have secrets to tell while we walk."

Edward would have led the way out, but Mohun claimed his rank, pushed his way forward, opened the door, and fell down the stairs to land unhurt at the bottom.

Children, drunks, and fools, thought Edward.

He needed to be rid of Mohun immediately; he needed to return to his apartments to warn Jonathan; he needed to better arm himself against assassination and to get the hell out of Bath as soon as possible. It was impossible that Jacobites could be on to him so soon after his return from Ireland—how could spies in Bristol have already acted on messages from their counterparts in Ireland? Bristol Jacobites would doubtless know by now that he had returned, but how could they have already had the time to make and implement plans to waylay him, even had they been warned to take action?—And yet so it seemed they might have.

"You must beware of Deigle and his whelps," Mohun advised as they walked. "He can be fair and just if it's in his purse's interest, but he bears close watching. This advice is my reward to you. I know you've done good service for the Crown, Jacobite though you are. So have I, as you know—we are brothers tonight, greater brothers than we were when as reformados we scorned the French at Brest."

"I remember it well, my lord."

"Lord Deigle tells me you have doubly vital information for the King. I'll arrange for someone to speak to you in London; I'll send a letter. With my influence and Lord Deigle's, you will be heard."

"Thank you, my lord," Edward replied politely, not giving a damn for any letter from Mohun, given the man's reputation.

The young lord paused, not as if lost in thought but as if he had lost a thought. In a moment or two he recovered it.

"Yes, Deigle—be careful in your dealings with him, this is what I meant to tell you: there's not a woman in the world who can't cozen him, except his wife of course. Ah, here we are! One more reward for you for being my brother tonight!"

Mohun had stopped in front of a rich dwelling. He banged on the door until a servant opened it, then ordered him out of the way and dashed into the house.

"Harry! Your wife, she's come to Bath!" he shouted while Edward waited discreetly in the background.

"Damn you, Mohun, I've not even had my pleasure yet!" Edward heard Lord Deigle shout.

A moment later he saw someone escaping through a side door.

Lydia almost ran into him. She looked shocked at first, then recovered and smiled broadly.

"Edward! I'm off to London," she said breathlessly. "Lord Deigle is going to introduce me to the theater there; he has influence with the companies in London! He knows Barry and Bracegirdle, the actresses!" she giggled. "And he wants me, he really *wants* me, not like you who only sometimes pretended to, but it's a snake, not a rod, he's shown me so far, and he wears a sheepskin thing over it, tied with a ribbon to his stones. Can you believe it? And you know how I am, Edward, when someone *wants* me."

She stood within inches of him. He tried to ignore her, knew he should take the opportunity to abandon Mohun, but her the scent of her sex was escaping everywhere and he had drunk just enough to lower his inhibitions. In fact, the possibility that she may have hired a man to run him through excited him.

"Don't you think you'd best return to your new patron if you're going to use him to make your fortune?" he said, doing his best to suppress his lust.

"I will," she said, "but not yet!" She threw her arms, then her legs, around him. He staggered backward, his foot in pain, until he banged into Lord Deigle's handsomely appointed carriage. With a few fumbles of coach door and petticoat and button and jammed sword hilt, they wedged themselves both into the caroche and into each other, Edward's left hand occasionally over Lydia's mouth to keep her moans from reaching other ears, her hands everywhere.

The caroche made great pitches on its thoroughbraces and slight rolls on its wheels for more than several minutes.

"Be my Jehu, drive me!" Lydia cried once, then a few moments later, "From behind, mount my caroche, mount it so you can protect me from the highwaymen on the road! Now, at the gallop! Drive away! Now, become my highwayman!"

Caroche and woman squealed in harmony.

"Your sword!" Lydia cried, having first bitten his hand to get him to move it from over her mouth.

"I know!"

"No, your *sword*."

"Yes? Oh, sorry," he whispered back, and pulled the hilt of his sword from her ribs as she kissed his hand then bit deeply into the lace at his cuff to stifle her cries.

The caroche pitched even more. In the back of Edward's mind he sensed an absurd yet stimulating contrast: he was here, doing this, while matters of State and regicide awaited.

"Oh my God," Lydia whispered in a sudden moment of post-orgasmic sobriety blowing through the Malaga fog that had clouded her reason, "Lord Deigle! We must hurry—I'll help you." And a minute later she whispered, "Did I contain you? I did? Good. Oh, God, it was just a jest, his wife isn't here? Damn you, Edward! Christ, I must return to Lord Deigle!"

As quickly as she had leaped upon him, Lydia wriggled from beneath, adjusted her clothing, and slipped from the caroche, followed by Edward, just as Deigle, realizing his wife had not truly returned, began to shout for his mistress.

"You shouldn't have done this to me, Edward!" Lydia said, grinning fiendishly. With short strides, she ran delicately back to the house, her hands holding her skirts a few inches above the ground. She smiled back at him before she slipped through the door.

Edward, reeling from the substitutes for the adventure he was addicted to, tried to put the day in order. The connections were logically obvious, yet absurd, and he would admit to only one conclusion: Fortune had set out to prove his philosophy wrong.

He failed to see the weakness in his argument. He was far too willing to engage the fickle goddess, especially when her agent was an attractive woman. He refused to acknowledge that he lacked the resolve to keep his distance, and thereby demonstrate his philosophy in practice so as to reap its rewards.

"Fortune will damn us all," he muttered under his breath.

Chapter 21

Hark! I hear the sound of coaches!
The hour of attack approaches!
—John Gay, *The Beggar's Opera,* 1728

Due to the past night's revelries and a long war council with Jonathan the next morning, Edward made a late start and rode only twenty-five miles the first day. He spent the night at the Catherine Wheel in Calne and rode hard the next day, through several villages and the town of Marlborough, but the muddy roads delayed him. It was well past dark when he finally banged his fist at the door of the Swan on the outskirts of Newbury.

The half dozen Bath-to-London flying coach passengers grew quiet at the sight of Edward's dark presence framing the door. Some stared rudely, others timidly. Edward glared in return, then realized what he must look like to them: muddy riding clothes, a large hat putting his face in shadow, a backsword hanging from a baldric, and a brace of horse pistols in their holsters slung across his left forearm—a threatening image underscored by the flickering candles that dimly lit the room.

It was not a common sight on the road.

Except perhaps for a highwayman.

Edward doffed his hat and smiled. "Ladies, gentlemen," he

said.

More silence.

He smiled more broadly and nodded his head at a well-dressed woman at one end of the room, a wealthy merchant's wife perhaps, or a country squire's sister with a taste for fine clothing, or even a penniless woman pretending wealth in order to find a rich husband. Only she returned his polite gesture.

Seeing neither conversation nor much amity forthcoming, Edward took a room, washed his face and hands, wiped off his boots, and returned downstairs to eat the three pence ordinary. He sat at the end of the table with the flying coach passengers, and learned from their conversation that they had been delayed a day by muddy roads and a broken axle.

In a tone of cautious contempt, a portly but well-dressed merchant was the first to address him.

"And your business, sir?"

"My own, in London," Edward said civilly.

"A rather rude reply, I think, sir."

"To a rather rude introduction and inquisition," Edward replied.

The merchant fumed for a moment, wondering whether his sense of entitlement was sufficient to intimidate this arrogant Scotsman. He decided not to put the issue to the test. He harrumphed once to his wife but asked Edward no more questions.

"Will you be accompanying us to London, sir?" asked the woman whom Edward had saluted upon his arrival.

"I'm afraid I must decline, as I'm in great haste," he answered.

"I'm sorry to hear that, sir."

"And I likewise, madam. Perhaps we'll meet in London."

"One never knows, does one?"

Another bored woman in need of adventure, thought

Edward; *it's the company she keeps. Another time, another road, but not today.*

The mostly cold reception reminded him of how he often felt in England, Scotland, and Ireland: as an outsider. Too long had he lived in America, in Jamaica and Virginia in particular, at least when he was not upon the sea. Circumstances had compelled him more than once to the British Isles and parts of Europe, but as fond as he had grown of its several peoples, many towns, and beautiful countryside, he could not call these islands home.

The passengers soon finished their meal and excused themselves. Edward stood and bowed to the lady, whose eyes implied regret. He finished eating, checked on his horses, and went to bed.

He rose early the next morning, intending fifty or sixty miles before the night. Almost immediately he noticed that the innkeeper appeared nervous, and five of the travelers were clustered together and avoiding him. Only the lady who had spoken to him the evening before would bid him good morning, and even she seemed inclined to keep her distance.

"I would have a quick breakfast," he said to a serving girl. She looked nervously about, then disappeared, never to bring his breakfast. There was none of the usual "Do you call, sir?" from a drawer, nor any other sign that anyone intended to serve him. All present avoided his gaze.

"Damn!" Edward said loudly a few minutes later, banging his fist on a table. "Are you all touched in the head?"

He called for a boy to bring his baggage, then stormed outside, backsword at his side, pistols over his shoulder. Between him and the stable were several armed men, all clumped together. Two had swords and pistols drawn, and the rest were ready to follow suit. Two more stood at the stable, holding his unsaddled mounts. Immediately Edward drew his backsword, thinking *Ambuscade!*

Yet as quickly as he drew his weapon and the armed men leaped back and stumbled one into the other, so did he realize this made no sense. He lowered his blade and did not advance upon them.

"We are on the King's business," said one man, finally.

"As am I," replied Edward coldly.

"Put up your sword, sir."

"Put up yours, and tell me your business," Edward replied with a commanding air. "I am on the King's business, and will submit to none but those commissioned directly by the King, damn you, not some few hired men or bailiffs of the county and clod-hopping volunteers."

"We're at a standoff, then," said the man who had spoken.

"Nay. There are several of you and only one of me. You may have at me as you please," Edward taunted. He slipped a pistol from the holsters hanging over his shoulder, his irritation overruling his common sense.

Yet Edward knew they would not attack. They were unsure of him, these 'clodheads.' They surely did not want to get hurt, and he had warned them he was on the King's business.

"Your name, sir."

"Captain Edward MacNaughton."

"It's a familiar name, but I can't place it. Your profession?"

"Need a gentleman a profession?" Edward asked sarcastically, just to be difficult, then realized that his title and pretended lack of profession might further imply that he was a highwayman.

"Sir, we must know who you are."

Edward, annoyed at the ridiculous display of frightened officers called by frightened innkeeper and frightened travelers, knew he must break the stalemate. Nearby, the hostler hastily hitched six horses to the flying coach. The passengers boarded quickly and went upon their merry way, all peering from the coach windows and wondering if they were going to miss some excitement.

"I am Captain Edward MacNaughton, mariner, master of fence, and former holder of the King's commissions on sea and land, on business of State to King William. I carry letters under the hand and seal of Viscount Deigle, addressed to the Earl of Portland. I am not to be detained or delayed." Edward put his pistol away, then offered his pass from Lord Deigle to the officer. Edward did not, however, sheathe his sword, and the bare blade so intimidated the officer that he would not approach. Edward flung the letter in his direction. The officer cautiously picked it up and stepped back several feet, motioning to his hired men to keep an eye on Edward.

When he finished reading the pass, the officer looked up. "Highwaymen have been preying on this road of late, and we must know that you're not one of them. You're well-mounted and well-armed, sir, and dressed for the occasion. Perhaps you stole this letter from Captain MacNaughton. I'm going to take this pass before the magistrate and you will wait here. If you try to depart, we'll arrest you."

Edward rested the blade of his Highland backsword on his shoulder. "I'll give you two hours to come to your senses and let me pass. If you detain me beyond this, I'll see to it that Lords Deigle and Portland, and even the King himself, shit upon your heads and wipe their arses with your shirts—if I even bother to leave you with heads to be shit upon, you clod-headed fules. While you're detaining me, the highwaymen you're looking for are probably robbing the flying coach that just departed. Two hours, mark my words. Now if you'll excuse me, I'm going to have my breakfast."

Edward sheathed his backsword and went into the inn. With a smile he told the kitchen boy, who, like the rest of staff, had been listening to the exchange outside, "You look like you fear no man, lad. I'll have my breakfast from you. Hurry now."

"So...*are* you a highwayman, sir?" the lad asked bluntly when he brought Edward his breakfast.

"What was that, boy? Damnation, no," Edward replied, then laughed out loud. The boy seemed disappointed. "But I've done as much in the past in distant lands to warrant such a reputation perhaps." The boy's eyes twinkled. "Have you heard of a buccaneer named MacNaughton who was tried in London two years ago?"

The boy nodded. Probably he did not really recall the trial, but to have met any buccaneer was better than to have met none at all. He scampered away to fetch more ale. Edward smiled and ate. Soon the entire staff was at Edward's table, including the innkeeper and his wife, and before long they were chastising the hired officers for detaining him. Eventually, as the end of the two hours approached, came the magistrate, a pair of the hired officers, and a witness who swore that Edward bore no resemblance to either of the highwaymen who had robbed him recently.

With the farce at an end, Edward brushed the hostler aside and quickly tacked one of his two mounts himself, first making certain that none of the horse's teeth had been greased to prevent them from eating during the night. He packed his bags on the other, then mounted and cantered away on the road to London. He had already drawn too much attention, and although he still did not consider it likely that he would be set upon by French or Irish agents, he could not put the idea from his mind, not after the night in Bath.

Molly, Lydia, Lynch and his ilk, all possibly connected somehow. And Jane, too, somewhere along the way.

The large wallet pushing into his stomach beneath his waistcoat reminded him of his purpose. Deigle's secretary himself, John Bunion, had delivered the correspondence the morning Edward was to depart.

"Are you certain no one else has had access to these letters?" Edward had demanded.

With great professional dignity and more than a touch of injured pride, the secretary had replied with a resounding, "Absolutely, sir! Not even Lord Deigle has a key to the chest where I kept the letters locked."

The secretary's confidence reassured Edward, and he began to consider, as he rode through the beautiful countryside, that perhaps his fears were ungrounded. Lydia sought to feather her nest, and at the moment Deigle was her best chance, even if he kept her only as his mistress. On the night she and Edward had taken each other in the coach, she was working on two fronts: one of practicality, one of pure pleasure, he argued to himself. Edward's vanity let him take pride in the fact that she was attracted to him, and he felt certain he would know if she were faking her sexual passion. Via this line of reasoning he was able to somewhat settle his apprehensions.

He rode into the afternoon at a quick trot, unhappy that he could not now make fifty miles unless he kept on the road until late at night. He carefully watched the woods and fields around him. He often looked behind, and just as often sought far ahead. In a wood he would look through it, focusing beyond the trees, letting his eyes and mind scan for the image of horse and rider, or of man afoot. He found none.

By mid-afternoon, after passing without stopping through Reading, he was ready to rest, to walk the horses and stretch his legs before changing mounts and riding hard again. For a mile he cantered, then eased his horse back to a trot, then a walk a few miles past Twiford. Both animals had pleased him. Both had good wind, went well at the trot and canter, ponied well, and were generally quiet and calm, seldom shying at strange noises or sights.

Ahead, the road took a dog leg to the right into a small wood. As Edward prepared to dismount to rest by walking in the shade of the trees flanking the road ahead, he thought he heard a voice. A few seconds later he was in no doubt: there were two voices, one a man's, commanding; its cadence might match "Stand and deliver!" although he could not make out the actual words, and the other a woman's, sharp and brief, a scream or exclamation. The voices came from ahead or just to the right, perhaps from where the road would be as it tracked slightly south through the cover of the trees. He looked down and saw the fresh impressions of wheels in the mud, tracks he had been gaining on all day.

Fool! he thought as he prepared to ignore his better judgment.

A purely practical man, one of business and nothing more, a fortune hunter, would never rush into the unknown to defend the unknown from the unknown, especially not when the unknown prospect might ruin his future prospects.

He drew his sword and pistols anyway. He hung his backsword from his right wrist, cocked and carried one pistol in his right hand, and held the other with his left, in which were also his reins and the halter rope of the ponied horse.

He lightly spurred his mounts into a good canter, muttering under his breath as he did. If all were innocent ahead, they would take him for a highwayman. Yet onward he rode, into the wood, and soon he saw the flying coach, saw it stopped, saw its passengers debarked, saw one man, no, two: one mounted, one dismounted, both armed.

"Do not prate, you fool, but deliver your money or, damn you, we will shoot you immediately!" barked one of the highwaymen, a pistol in each hand.

Edward let go of the halter rope and leaned forward. When

his mount did not fly to the gallop, he spurred it hard and almost lost his reins as he did, so hard did his mount buck and bolt into a hand gallop.

The masked highwaymen heard the sound of hoof beats. They turned and stared briefly, stunned. The highwayman afoot leaped to his horse and fled at the gallop. His mounted companion spun his horse in a circle, as if unsure whether to flee or fight. He raised a pistol at Edward then lowered it, perhaps realizing that if he shot and killed anyone the hue and cry to find and hang both highwaymen would be remorseless, then he raised it again and fired anyway, as passengers dropped to their knees or ran.

Edward raced through the scattering passengers and fired a pistol at the highwayman before him. At the sound of the shot, his own mount leaped sideways and nearly threw him from the saddle. Edward flung the empty pistol away, regained control of his horse, passed the other pistol to his empty hand, and saw the highwayman's other pistol coming to bear, but he fired accidentally before it was well-aimed. The thief wheeled about and fled at the gallop a second before Edward fired his second pistol. The retreating horse bucked and squealed as swan shot struck him in the crupper, and perhaps hit his rider as well.

Edward reined up, passing the empty pistol back to his left hand and grasping his backsword as he did.

"You!" he called to two men, one slight, in his forties, a well-off tradesman perhaps, the other the merchant he had exchanged words with the past night. "Fetch my other mount if you please, and my pistol as well." Then, "Ladies," he said, touching his hat with his sword hilt as a manner of salute. He passed his gaze over the other men. "Who here is armed or was armed? Coachman! The blunderbuss in the mud, fetch it, check that its barrel is clear and the priming still good. Who else? Fetch your arms from where you cast them or from where they're hidden, make sure they're loaded and primed. I'll escort you to the next town where you can raise the hue and cry. I'll want someone up with the driver; who will volunteer? You, good man! Hurry now!"

His heart beat with the rush of violence, of fight or flight. It would be a few minutes before it settled, although to the passengers he appeared entirely in cold-blooded control. Edward sheathed his sword and reloaded his pistols under the gaze of the woman who had spoken to him back at the inn, a gaze so warm and intense that he blushed and would not speak to her for fear he might say something stupid.

Two hours later they drew up at an ordinary in Maidenhead, the travelers shouting for a constable, raising the alarm, praising Edward profusely and embarrassingly, buying him food and drink from their own pockets and begging him to stay with them until they came safely into London. Edward, covered in mud from helping heave a coach wheel from a hole in the road, was too tired to argue. He would leave them in the morning after they were well on the road again, their courage bolstered and the edge taken off their excitement. He could be in London by tomorrow evening.

There was much talk at the inn, of highwaymen past and present, of how some were great gentlemen, or acted as such, never taking anything from a traveler, instead taking only what was carried in the mail, of how some never robbed the poor, only the wealthy, of how many were men of great wit and humor. They spoke of their horses, always dark and swift, of their women, always beautiful, maid or lady (often they had both, and more), and of their courage at the gallows, always a cheerful and generous final act. Most of this was mere folklore, but with enough truth to keep the myths alive. In reality, most people robbed by highwaymen were happy to see them hanged.

Given his notoriety, it occurred to Edward that he might better travel in company, if more slowly, but a safer prospect given the vital correspondence he carried.

He resigned himself to delay, but only of an extra half day. After a raucous meal with the passengers that evening, all of whom seemed enamored of his company and determined not to permit him to remain aloof, he finally relaxed by the fire.

"I would thank you again, from all of us, for what you did today," said the lady whose eye Edward had caught. "And please accept my apology for even thinking for a moment that you might have been a highwayman." She had an attractive forthright quality that likely derived from natural intelligence and insight matured by three or more decades of experience.

"It was foolish, what I did," he replied.

"Foolish? Why?"

"I imperiled us all."

"No more than we were already."

"They would only have robbed you. But in the exchange of arms some of you might have been hurt."

"But we were not. And our valuables were preserved."

"It was nothing but my pleasure."

"How gallantly you dismiss your courage, sir. But perhaps I should expect nothing less from a famous privateer captain."

"Do you know me, Madam?"

"Indeed, sir, I do. Word travels fast, and besides, I remember you now from Bath. One will hear of a famous former buccaneer—and a former pirate, some say—seeking a privateer commission. Doubtless you set all the ladies' hearts aflutter. I wish I had remembered you earlier, to spare you the indignity of false accusation. But then, if I had known you, you would have departed on time and been far ahead on the road, and not nearby to rescue us in our hour of need."

Edward blushed. "I assure you my business is not mere conquest or other trifles."

"A pity. I had hoped you might stay long enough to test my

own heart. It goes aflutter so seldom these days."

"You're fencing with me, madam, and not even seriously."

"Only to see what will pink your self-assurance. Are you sure you don't want to kill two birds with one stone? To keep company and protect your affairs, or privateering ventures or whatever they are, while you use the pretext to attempt to seduce me while I preserve my virtue, the goal being to enjoy the conversation and give-and-take?" she said impishly.

"It's quite tempting, but I've business and you've a reputation to protect, and probably a husband as well, no matter that your intent may be nothing more than to converse."

"How chivalrous! Come, then, if you won't make a subtle, gentlemanly assault on my virtue, at least let's talk for a little while, of all the great world and of all the small matters that make it so."

And so they talked by the fire until late into the night, the excellent conversation and imperfect wine leaving him as relaxed as he had been in Ireland while recovering from his wounds. He made no attempt on the woman's virtue, nor she on his, and he found himself briefly at peace. Afterward he fell easily asleep, and thoughts of assassinators, highwaymen, and swashbucklers on the road did not wake him that night. Brief dreams of the women in his life did.

At the woman's insistence, Edward remained with the flying coach the next day, making conversation as they went, he mounted, she speaking to him through a window. Periodically he rode ahead to survey the road, but there were no more rencontres or other adventures. That evening they arrived in London and said their brief goodbyes.

Edward found lodging at the Black Horse on Water Lane, an inn and neighborhood he knew well from the aftermath of his trials for piracy, then made a brief stop at John's Coffeehouse on Birchin Lane, a place of ship owners and mariners. A sea captain there advised him he would do better these days at Lloyd's coffeehouse if he were seeking maritime business. Edward took his advice, largely to get a better feel for the maritime circumstances of London in this time of war. Even at the late hour, Lloyd's was busy with Exchange brokers and the sound of their gavels.

Later, Edward headed afoot in the darkness toward his lodgings, alert to those who might follow him. He sensed, as he had in Ireland, that he was watched. Even so, his brief experience with the highwaymen reminded him that not all who had set upon him were assassins seeking secret letters. Lynch was probably just a jealous fool, Ingoldsby was a proven fool, and the sallow gentlemen in Bath were probably just amateur footpads.

Yet in spite of this reasoning, as he made his way west across Fleet Bridge the sensation of being followed was suddenly overwhelming. Moments later he put a name to the warning sense when he turned to look behind him.

He was certain he saw the bully ruffian John Lynch passing beneath a street lamp, and then he was gone.

Chapter 22

Have at you, Villain.
—Thomas Shadwell, *The Libertine,* 1676

Edward stepped away from a nearby lamppost and into the shadows, and waited. For several minutes he watched in all directions, but Lynch, or whoever resembled him, never reappeared. Edward walked quickly past St. Bridget's cathedral, hooked into an alley on the other side, jogged for one hundred feet, then slipped back to Fleet Street, hoping to slip behind his possible enemy.

This was the one area in London he knew well, not to mention the one that best served his purposes, past and present. For these reasons he had taken lodging here: Water Lane divided Whitefriars to the east from Salisbury Court to the west. The former had once been a criminal sanctuary and still retained a sense of its past, and the latter remained a sanctuary for debtors, a convenience Edward had twice found useful. In this area mingled the working, middle merchant, and criminal classes, and, near the Queen's Theater, the upper as well. It was Edward's favorite place in London, and his familiarity with it might save his life.

After ten minutes of observation, he found neither Lynch nor anyone like him, and he now assumed it likely that his former adversary was conjured in his imagination by a vague uneasiness combined with the figure of a man who somewhat resembled the sword-for-hire.

Edward headed west on Fleet Street toward the Black Horse. As he did, a woman chanced to bump into him, or more likely pretended it was by chance. Edward put his left hand to the wallet beneath his waistcoat and his right to the woman's shoulder in case she were trying to pick his pocket.

"Easy, my handsome man! We must agree first!" she said loudly.

Rather than replying immediately, he surveyed her as he might a ship in the offing. She wore too much paint and powder, he thought, not to mention one too many patches (one above her lip, another on a cheek, a third on her forehead). There was no kerchief above her breasts, pushed into sharp cleavage by her stomacher, and the skirt of her bright calico mantua gown was cut to valiantly show off her white dimity petticoats trimmed at the bottom in several bright colors. Over her mantua she wore a pin-up jacket of Scotch plaid, edged with cheap beaded lace, known as bugle, at the wrists and neckline. Her shoes had high stacked heels and narrow square toes, and were tied with large red bows. But it was her hair, neatly coifed with a medium-tall frontage cap, her winsome smile, and her bright, intelligent eyes that drew his attention.

"I beg your pardon, mistress," Edward replied as he stepped just out of reach.

"You're not afraid of me, a rum mort, are you?" she asked, shifting to the sweetly manipulative tone of suggestive emasculation that baits too many men, and which only some women, amateur or professional, can manage well.

"Tonight, of anyone, man or woman. Perhaps another time," he said, smiling wryly.

"Don't I know you?" she asked.

"I'll bet you say that to all the men you accost. Next you'll be telling me that I remind you of a great, strapping lover you once had, and am I sure I'm not him? Play your tricks on merchants' sons, not me, my darling. As I said, perhaps another time."

"Pity," she said. "I could tell you things if you don't want to clip and kiss."

"Again, thank you, no," Edward said, and turned away.

"Maybe about that ruffler following you?"

Edward stopped, turned back, and took the woman by the wrist.

"What ruffler?"

"I'm a tradeswoman, sir. Everything has a price."

"Half a crown if your intelligence is worthy."

"Two. And I'll forget you both."

"Half."

"One."

"Don't cross me. Half."

"All right then, half. Let go of me."

"Good," he said, releasing her. "Your half-crown—if your intelligence is useful," he said, withdrawing a coin and holding it up. "Tell me about the man you say is following me."

"He's down the street, on the right, pretending he's not watching."

"What does he look like?"

"A tall one, but not as tall as you," she said flirtingly, "with a fat, sweaty munns but not entirely unpleasing, a belly like he's a few months gone with a lullaby cheat, and a long, long rapier like the bully swordsmen wear, but it's not a rum or witcher tilter, not one a good thief would take the time to bite the bill from the cull. His beaver's white, but he's holding it by his side so you won't see it, and his coat is as black as a beadle's but trimmed with rusty white lace. The cul snilches."

"What?"

"He watches you."

"Stop your canting and speak English, I didn't understand half of that. How do I know he didn't hire you to lure me somewhere?"

"I've seen that bugger around here before; he talks a lot but won't pay for anything."

Edward gave the woman the coin. His reason suggested his was part of a trap, his instinct considered it unlikely. In either case, he was on his guard against two potential enemies.

"Come with me."

"Why?"

"You've just tipped me the wink, and I've paid haven't I? To Water Lane, then to a place we'll be safe from his eyes."

"If you want to dock, it'll cost you more," she said.

"Pardon me, mistress, but you're pricing your wares a bit high, aren't you?"

"I'm worth every penny and shilling of a guinea," she replied indignantly.

"I believe you," Edward said sincerely.

"The half-crown was for intelligence only. I think you're interested and I know you can pay. I'm not poxed or clapped, and not yet buttered tonight, you'd be the first. My ganns are soft and sweet, my pratts are as smooth as a gentlewoman's, or so I've been told, and my breasts as white as milk and sweet as any tit-bits. We can be quick about it if you like, I won't even un-rig."

Edward smiled. "Thank you again, but no, I just want that man to think I'm with you. Come, now, and you have my word I'll pay you another half-crown."

Edward grabbed her by the upper arm and drew her close, as if he had hired her. They walked quickly, from lamppost to lamppost in order to be seen, Edward holding the woman tight at his side. She in return played her part well, attempting to undo a few buttons on his waistcoat so she could reach into his breeches. Edward pulled her hand away, concerned about the safety of his letters, but to anyone watching, he appeared in haste to have his way with her, only not in public. At no point did she try to lure him in a different direction: either she was no part of a trap set by Lynch, if indeed it were Lynch he had seen, or by accident Edward's chosen destination was that of the ambush.

To make certain, Edward suddenly pulled her into an alley almost impossible to find by day, much less by night, and barely wide enough for a single person to walk. He drew the woman close behind him, made a sudden right turn to a very small courtyard, then a left down a few steps onto Hanging Sword Alley where they could barely walk two abreast, even as close as they were to each other. Here were backdoors to homes, brothels, gaming houses, and a canting gang or two. Formerly and appropriately, the alley had been home to fencing schools. Edward and his companion stopped in the darkness of an alcove roughly forty feet from a small lighted lantern at someone's back door.

"You know your way around here, sir!" the woman said admiringly.

"Whisht!" he whispered. "Keep your voice down. I've been here before, but not for some time."

"I really do remember you now! You were that pirate who lodged at the Black Horse!"

"And that man who follows might have told you this."

"No sir—I remember you pinking a bugger of a talley-man with your tilter!"

"Do you?"

"I saw you. He wasn't supposed to be here collecting a debt, you told him to bugger off, he drew his tilter and you pinked him in the stump. He was trying to put his hands on me without paying, I was happy you stuck him, everyone was."

"That was you, indeed? My apologies for not knowing you. Now, with further apologies, mistress, I have to search you, I need to know I won't be stabbed in the back."

"Not without paying!" she said angrily. "No one touches me without paying! You've no need not to trust me—I could have informed the thief-takers on you for a reward, or blackmailed you when you pinked that bugger who put his hands on me!"

Edward, casting an eye down the alley in the direction from which they had come, and an ear behind them, drew another half-crown from a pocket, felt for her hand, and put the coin in her palm.

"For your help, and with my apology," he said with a hint of sardonic condescension. "Now go!"

Edward gently shoved her down the alley behind him, then checked to make sure his sword was loose in its scabbard. He hoped he had done the right thing by not searching the woman. The last thing he needed right now was a knife at his back. He felt something brush against his leg: the woman had not departed. Both began to speak, but Edward's hand placed over her mouth cut her off.

"Go, *now*," he whispered sternly, this time pushing her firmly down the alley behind him.

"An enemy of yours, then?" she whispered back.

Edward grabbed her hard by the upper arm.

"This isn't your affair. For your own good, be gone, now, and forget me and him!" he hissed and shoved her away.

Yet instead of leaving at his order, she grasped him close and whispered, "There!"

Quickly Edward turned and saw the outline of a man walking quietly but very quickly in their direction, low candlelight glinting off the half-extended sword blade in his hand and off the high points of his face. His white hat was gone, surely to better hide himself in the dark.

"Lynch!" Edward cursed to himself. His hand flew to his sword. For safety he simultaneously opened his measure, bumping into the woman, then into a small corner where two houses came together. He heard footsteps behind him, the woman finally running away. Edward held a slight advantage in spite of having his back to the small corner, for the lantern vaguely silhouetted Lynch but left Edward entirely in the dark.

Lynch paused. Edward realized this was because he had lost sight of his adversary. It was one thing to sneak into an alley to murder a man as he felt up the skirts of a prostitute, but quite another to seek a forewarned, and thus forearmed, enemy in the darkness.

Lynch drew a dagger, not a pistol, with his left hand—clearly he wanted this business kept quiet, as did Edward, who for the same reason did not draw one of the turnoff pistols in his pockets. Lynch extended his sword arm and moved slowly forward, probing.

As he came into range, Edward, unable to retreat with his back to a wall, battered his enemy's blade up and immediately cut right to Lynch's bare left hand—no cheating gauntlets this time!—and cut it to the bones. Lynch dropped the knife, cursed "Bastard!" under his breath, and leaped back. Immediately the assassin recovered his wits and lunged furiously, breathing out with a sharp "Huah!" to fortify his courage.

In the blink of an eye Edward, having shifted to the high hanging guard, beat down his adversary's blade so sharply that sparks flew into the darkness, then thrust forcefully at Lynch's forearm, or where it should have been. But Lynch recovered swiftly; as he did Edward shifted quickly to the right, away from the corner, to give himself more room to fight, only to strike the opposite wall hard with his right shoulder—but now the way behind him was open. Lynch attacked again with a powerful straight lunge, hoping to force any parry Edward might make.

But Edward was no longer there, or at least not where Lynch expected. Completely covered by the inky darkness, Edward had lunged backward, his left hand dropping to the ground, his body bending inward, his blade shooting forward at Lynch's belly: the Italians called this *passato soto*, but some of Edward's English contemporaries called it the "night thrust" for its utility in the darkness.

The blade struck Lynch full in the belly, the best place to hit —no ribs, no cartilage. Yet Lynch only grunted, "Ha, fool!" as Edward swiftly beat his adversary's blade upward and recovered into the darkness.

Damn me for a fool! Edward thought. *I forgot his mail shirt!*

The assassin retreated three steps into the greater candlelight. Edward followed: his enemy must not get away. Lynch was now committed to open fight, for, reasoning as he believed others would in like circumstances, he was certain that if he turned his back and ran, Edward would stab him in the back.

Lynch lunged again as soon as he had recovered. Edward made a round parry, the best sort in the dark, at least when one's back was not to a wall, although some masters opposed it: but then, they had likely never been in a street fight at night. Edward found his enemy's blade and riposted but, sensing his enemy's counter-parry, disengaged and, using his left hand to prevent a double hit, thrust low, toward the lower belly and groin which might not be protected by the mail.

But again he struck metal links. Edward recovered quickly, his left hand ready to intercept a counter-thrust, but slipped on the muddy cobblestones.

He thrust high and dropped his left hand to the ground as he went down on one knee. Lynch bound his blade strongly as Edward pushed off hard with his front leg, trying to return to a good guard while subtly yielding to and parrying his enemy's attack.

Too slow! Edward realized. *A contre-temps! We'll both be hit!*

But neither blade landed, for a brick struck Lynch in the chest, surprising him more than hurting him, and forcing him back a step. Like lightning Edward re-engaged his enemy's blade powerfully and carried it wide to the right, and thrust to the face through the opening—and this time he felt the blade penetrate.

"Shithellfire!" Lynch hissed sharply as he felt the burning blade push through his cheek and into his mouth.

Quickly Edward stepped in and grasped his adversary's sword by the shell, ensuring that his enemy could not make a thrust in return, out of reflex or revenge. More than once Edward had almost been killed by an exchanged thrust, either having failed to secure his adversary's blade while recovering from a lunge, or simply failing to get the hell out of the away quickly enough.

But in spite of the deep wound just below the cheekbone, his enemy resisted, and Edward suddenly feared the man might wrest his blade free.

Having no choice, Edward powerfully jerked his blade a hand's breadth backward and jabbed again at the face. This time the blade passed through Lynch's right eye and into his brain.

Lynch fell. His face, illuminated for a moment by a faint ray from the lantern, contorted into a surprised grimace for a moment, then lost all emotion. The dead body almost pulled Edward over with it—one of the disadvantages of the thrust,— for Edward's sword was stuck in the back of Lynch's head. Heart beating strongly, Edward placed his foot on Lynch's jaw and wrenched sword from bone. The entire rencontre, from first blade contact to fatal wound, had lasted less than a minute.

Edward spun around. "Where the hell are you!" he whispered as loudly as he dared.

"Here!"

"Damn you and thank you!" he whispered sincerely. "And why aren't you gone?"

"I was afraid. I stopped and hid just back there. Please don't kill me," she said.

Edward sensed she was not nearly as afraid as she pretended, and had stayed behind to see if the incident could be turned to her advantage.

Or am I being too cynical? he wondered.

"Fool, why would I kill you? You helped me—you hit the bastard with a brick, for which I thank you again," Edward whispered sharply, then realized her fear might be entirely warranted under the circumstances. "Look, I'll not harm you, I think you know that already. You helped me, after all. And I wouldn't harm you anyway unless you attacked me. Lend me a hand, I want to search the body. This man is a Jacobite assassin."

"The twat-scouring pimp! But my crew are not Jacobites!" she whispered, then stepped backward. "Mayhap you are the Jacobite!" she hissed. "There's Scots in your tongue!"

"And Scots plaid in your clothing. If I were a Jacobite the crown would arrest me, not send an assassin after me, you little fool."

"I'm no fool!"

"And indeed you aren't. My apologies, mistress."

Edward worked quickly, even more so when he heard voices in the distance. Far away a watchman called the hour, his voice barely audible. Edward worried that the sound of sword on sword had drawn interest, for there is no sound like it in the world. But there was no sense of alarm in the voices, although this did not obviate the need to hurry. Quickly he checked to see if Lynch were really dead, using what little light there was in the alley. The man's unbloodied eye was open but stared vacantly into the darkness. He had no pulse at his throat; Edward could feel no breath from his mouth or nostrils.

Dead, Edward thought. *Warm, but dead, deservedly dead.*

For a brief moment he wondered if he should call for a watchman or bailiff, or present himself before a Justice of the Peace.

I can't. The only witness is a whore, and none will believe her; they'll think we worked together to murder and rob the bastard. I'll be damned before I'm jailed again in London, and again for a crime I didn't commit. Suppose someone says that it must be murder because he has two wounds?

Edward had no time to consider why Lynch had been following him, but he assumed the worst, that he was after the letters he carried. He searched the corpse quickly and found a small purse and silver watch, but no correspondence. He knew he'd probably missed some items, but had neither the time nor the light for a close search.

"Take the money for yourself," he said, "but leave the rest. Now go! I promise I won't know you if I see you again, and I ask the same of you."

"But the watch and cutlery—I know those who can sell them!"

"And the thief-takers can track you by them if anyone recognizes them. And if you're taken with them, you'll hang, but not before identifying me to try and save yourself. Only his coin will leave no trace. Now go, I'll nae tell you again!"

Yet still she did not. "You should be rid of the body," she whispered.

"Too dangerous," he replied.

"It can be done, you should dump it in the Ditch."

Fleet Ditch, actually the River Fleet leading to the Thames, which in three decades would begin to be bricked over and turned into a closed sewer rather than the open sewer which for all practical purposes it was at present, was flanked by wharves, warehouses, and oak palings. It was notoriously noxious, with excrement, dead animals, and other refuse floating in it. Some joked that more bodies were found here than at the undertaker. So filthy was it that barges and dung boats collected its "dirt" where it entered the Thames, and sold it for fertilizer. Even so, men and boys were known to bathe in the Ditch. Edward would be glad to see the body dumped there, but, "Too dangerous, I said!"

Growing angry, Edward ordered her to be gone for her own sake, and stepped toward her as if to force her if necessary.

"A guinea," she said.

"What?" he demanded coldly. "Are you trying to make me pay black-rent, you damned jade?"

"I'm a tradeswoman, not a black-renter," she whispered indignantly. "And I'm no friend of any Jacobite! A guinea and I'll see the body dumped in the Ditch, sir, and the rest too. It'll be better for you this way."

"A guinea! You *are* a damned black-renter!"

"It's what I charge for intimate services in private places, sir. I'm a tradeswoman, I must make a living."

"If that's the case, why then only a guinea when you might make much more by turning me in?"

"Why'd you pink that talley-man trying to feel me up when you could have walked away last time you were here?" she whispered back.

Touché! thought Edward, a small grin ranging itself on his face.

"I guess it's best not to have dead bodies at your door, either," he whispered. From his purse he pulled a gold coin.

"Get to your canting crew swiftly and have done with this. Good luck, mistress—and my thanks."

"And to you, sir, my Gentleman of Fortune."

She kissed him on the cheek, turned, and ran down the alley, south toward its more usual connection to Water Lane.

With one more glance around to see if anyone might have observed him, Edward walked as circuitous a route as he could back to his lodging, first ducking back onto Fleet Street by the almost secret entrance to the Alley, then along the filthy Ditch, past Bridewell Prison to the Thames River, then striding past the Queen's Theater and across Salisbury Court, and finally, near the Dorset Steps on the Thames, to the bottom of Water Lane clogged with wagons, carts, and sleeping drivers. His bed at the Black Horse beckoned.

He quashed the turmoil in his mind. As he passed the Water Lane entrance to Hanging Sword Alley, he thought that never had Fortune sent him a more appropriate omen.

Chapter 23

And two or three days afterward, all of a sudden, came down news from London of a bloody and horrid plot...
—Capt. Edw. Barlow, his Journal, writing of 1696

It was well past midnight before Edward fell asleep in his room at the Black Horse, and when he did he slept much too lightly, constantly starting at sounds and wondering who would next come for the letters, or who would come to arrest him for the murder or manslaughter of John Lynch. It was not that he was squeamish about the killing—he had taken life too often during his decade and a half of following violent trades— rather he was uneasy about the circumstances, no matter that it was self-defense.

Here he was, waiting for a privateering commission, a license to commit violence in the name of profit, yet he had drawn blood with sword or pistol ashore half a dozen times in recent months, and twice more at sea.

It was too much.

And too much subject to Fortune, too much ensnared in women and their secrets.

Too many damned coincidences, he realized, *yet too many rational arguments they're nothing more than coincidences.*

He must, however, assume the worst: the meeting was no

accident, and Lynch was after the letters.

He must disregard the possibility that Lynch had spotted him by accident and tried to have his revenge for his humiliation and new name. Still, who would not contemplate revenge for being named Double Bung? What bothered Edward was how Lynch could have followed him, given the pace he had ridden from Bath, or even how Lynch could have found him in London.

And yet, Edward had to accept that it was possible. Lydia could have learned his agenda, even his place of lodging, from Deigle, and sent a messenger the same day to Lynch, to arrive before Edward. The Scotsman's delay with the flying coach would have given a Jacobite messenger time to get to London a day before him. The connection between Lydia and Lynch was obvious—but Lynch was too stupid to have acted in any significant capacity as a Jacobite intriguer. Someone had to have given him orders.

Edward did not want to believe that Lydia could be so involved, or worse, go so far. He saw her as a more scheming version of Molly: a husband hunter who lived off of men, rich and not so rich, until one would provide her with the material security she sought as wife or mistress. And yet, just as Molly might well be more than she seemed, so might Lydia.

One hell of a damned mess all around.

And now, as he tried to sleep but could not stop thinking about the encounter in Hanging Sword Alley, Edward wished he had searched the body more thoroughly for papers or other evidence.

He awoke earlier than usual the next morning and got up immediately, realizing he would not fall back to sleep in the time that remained before dawn. He took the extra time to brush his hat, comb his wig, smooth his shirt with a smoothing iron, dust off his riding clothes, and polish his boots. Although the combination of wherry and walking was common, he would ride instead. He refused to consider hiring a sedan chair, a pretentious mode of carriage and one from which he could not defend himself.

Ruefully, he suddenly recalled that King William did not hold court at St. James, nor at Whitehall, which had burned, but at Kensington where the air was cleaner. Edward would need directions. The innkeeper happily provided them.

The Scotsman found himself lost among the crowd several times as he rode at a walking pace up Fleet Street. He had been to London only a few times, and during his longest visits he had been under arrest for much of his stay, and avoiding creditors most of the rest. Even so, he had come to know parts of the city, a great one in every respect, good and bad.

Half a million people, or more than that some say, he thought, *almost as big as Paris. The Thames with its merchant fleet. The Crown, Parliament, and merchants. Great, grand buildings.*

Here, he could find anything and everything. Wine, women, and whiskey of all sorts. Books and booksellers, arms and armorers. Plays and music. Coffeehouses and taverns of every sort. Prize fights. Bartholomew Fair in August every year.

Anything and everything was for sale. Here on the street were tattered children selling lengths of thread from sticks, and there a man and his wife selling sheet music, and over there a woman selling mops from a bundle atop her head. Down by the Thames were entire cargoes for sale.

The atmosphere was rich and cosmopolitan, yet there was a sense of anonymity too: here one could rise in renown or be lost forever to history.

At Kensington the wait was interminable. Edward was left to loiter among a throng of petitioners, most of whom had been waiting days for an audience. He had assumed his letter of introduction to King William's most trusted advisor, Lord Hans Willem Bentinck, Earl of Portland, would have admitted him immediately. He was wrong.

While he waited, he read one of the London news-letters, the *Gazette*, someone had left behind. He was surprised to read of his brief escapade on the road:

> "Capt. Edw. *MacNaught*, the once famous *Buckaneer*, charged upon two *Highwaymen* near Reading two Days past, believed to be Will Hollyday and Rich. Pollynton, and put the *Highwaymen* to Flight, for which he received a small Reward. Capt. *MacNaught* recently briefly commanded the *Virginia* Galley after her Master was killed by a Shot from a *French* Privateer. The Captain brought the Ship safely to *Bristol*, to the great Joy of her Investors."

And in the advertisements:

> "*Capt. MacNaught*, of Privateering Fame, is in London seeking Investors for a Privateering Venture. Inquiries should be directed to Him at *Lloyd's* Coffeehouse."

Edward knew nothing of reward or great joy in regard to Bristol merchants, was unsure if *once famous* was a good or bad thing, and was a bit surprised that the account and advertisement had been published in London, with details of where to find him and what his ultimate business was. But hacks and journalists had their many sources—the newspapers were all in competition with each other for the latest news—and perhaps someone thought it a favor to him to post his information in the advertisements, inviting inquiries from investors. Still, the fact of publication irritated him: if anyone else were seeking him, he would not be hard to find.

Four hours later Edward was admitted and escorted silently on a warren-like journey that seemed deliberately tortuous and designed to get him lost, as if in imitation of the Dutch gardens outside. At journey's end he was introduced into a room occupied by two men, one of whom he recognized as the Earl of Portland, the other an unknown gentleman.

Of them, only the Earl spoke. "Captain MacNaughton, I assume."

"Aye, your lordship."

"Do you know who I am?"

"Aye, my lord."

"I seem to recall that you served as a volunteer in a regiment of Inniskilling dragoons at the Boyne?" the Earl asked in his Dutch accent.

"Aye, my lord." Edward thought it better not to relate the fact that his service in the regiment was somewhat involuntary.

"I thought I knew you. It's not often that a *vryjbuiter* from the sea serves as a soldier."

"Circumstance only, my lord. I prefer the sea."

"Except, apparently, when there is a Spanish town on its shore," the Dutchman remarked dryly. "The Spaniards are now our allies, if you recall. You have the letters indicated by Lord Deigle's missive?"

Edward removed the several letters from the wallet beneath his shirt and passed them to the Earl, who shared them with the gentleman at his side. The pair spent half an hour reading and rereading the letters, often consulting with each other in whispers.

"My thanks to you, sir," the Earl said finally, standing and looking at Edward with a steady military gaze. "You have my leave to go."

Edward cocked his head slightly but said nothing. As he turned to leave, the earl addressed him again.

"Where may we find you?"

"At Lloyd's coffeehouse."

"And where do you lodge?"

Edward gave him a curious look. "At the Black Horse on Water Lane."

"You may go. And thank you."

Edward wandered London the rest of the day, assuming rightly that no action would be taken on the letters—if at all— for hours if not days. He inquired regarding plays at the theaters, ate a heavy meal of lobster with vinegar, fricassee of chicken, and cheesecake, all washed down with two large cups of sweet Malaga, and wondered how soon he should check at Lloyd's for a message from the palace, not to mention how many days he should wait for an answer. He worried that the Earl of Portland would see nothing in the letters from Ireland, or would find in them the mere imaginings of a man too strongly influenced by gossip and coffeehouse intelligence.

In his meandering he heard word of a duel or affray, of a man found floating, in spite of a mail shirt, dead in Fleet Ditch. The man had been thrust through the eye with a sword. No witnesses had come forward, no reward was offered, no one was accused or even speculated about. An old grudge, or an argument over a rich widow or common whore, or of cheating at cards or dice, the rumors suggested. There was no hint of Edward's involvement.

Edward remained nervous, though, wondering if another would come in Lynch's place, or if authority would come, seeking to charge him with murder.

He rose early the next morning, intending to stop first at Lloyd's, then to see more of the sights and sounds of London, this time by wherry and afoot.

As soon as he was dressed there came a knock on the door.

"Who's there?" he called.

"The maid, sir, with a message," came a high and slightly tremulous voice.

Edward, one hand on a turn-off pistol in his pocket, opened the door—but instead of a maid found a lobster-coated officer and four soldiers, all armed.

"Captain Edward MacNaughton?" the officer asked sternly. He did not wait for an answer. "Captain MacNaughton, I have a warrant for your arrest. I am under orders to take you peaceably, but take you I must, and take you I will whether you resist or not. Your sword, sir, and any other arms you may have."

That traitorous black-renting jade! Edward thought as he complied, and with angry resignation silently cursed Fortune, her minions, and his philosophy.

Two hours later he found himself locked away in a small room in the Tower of London, having passed through Traitor's Gate to get there.

Chapter 24

False witness at court, and fierce tempests at sea,
So Mat may yet chance to be hang'd or be drown'd.
—Matthew Prior, "For my own Monument," 1714

Ten days later came an older man alone and unarmed to escort Edward from his room in Beauchamp Tower on the west curtain of the Tower of London. The emissary was nondescript, except for his expensively tailored clothing: a Court functionary perhaps, or some nobleman's secretary, a man more accustomed to the duties of office than of field or sea, a man more accustomed to taking orders than giving them. His manner was friendly but professional.

Now for answers, Edward thought with great relief.

For an instant when soldiers had appeared at his door at the Black Horse, Edward was sure he had been betrayed by the woman who had helped him in Hanging Sword Alley, and that he was being arrested for Lynch's murder.

Quickly he had realized this could not be the case. A common murderer would not be confined in the Tower, nor would soldiers have come to arrest one. Nonetheless, for several hours after his arrest he considered that he would rather have been arrested for murder, because a crime worthy of the Tower must surely be treason. Yet incarceration here made no sense: even among traitors, usually only those of great rank were lodged here, although there were exceptions.

Further, Edward had been treated well since his arrest, although no one would name the charges against him. He had decent food and drink for which he was not expected to pay, an extraordinary curiosity. His personal effects, minus his arms and correspondence, were provided. No one harassed, harangued, interrogated, glared, or glowered. It was all quite unusual.

During the past two days he learned from his warders of an attempted assassination against the king, but the details were confounded with rumor and changed hour to hour. Among the tidbits he heard was that a large number of conspirators had been jailed at Newgate. This argued that he was not one of the accused, yet raised even more the question of why he was here.

"Am I still under arrest?" Edward asked the gentleman who had come for him.

"I can tell you nothing except that I'm here to escort you from the Tower. As you can see, I'm unarmed and alone, so you may make of this what you please. I trust in your sense of duty and honor, not to mention the embarrassment to you were you to flee and I to call the wardens."

"I am your servant, sir."

From Edward's stone-walled lodging they passed down a stairway to the open grounds. They walked across the green, onward through Bloody Tower to Water Lane—yet another coincidence in Edward's mind, that he would twice be lodged on a street with the same name — where a coach, its windows un-darkened this time, waited.

Edward glanced at the castle above and around him, took in its imposing construction and many great towers, the White Castle at the center, noted their evocative names, caught the sound of the waters at Traitor's Gate nearby, and almost shuddered. But he was too experienced, jaded perhaps, to feel anything more than a passing gratitude to Fortune. All he would leave behind was his name written in the book of prisoners, and also scratched on a wall: *EdwMacN—1696.*

The Tower: at least I've come up in the world, he thought wryly, regretting that Jonathan or some other cynical wit were not there to appreciate the sentiment.

He breathed an even greater sigh of relief when the coach departed through Byward and Middle Towers, and not via Traitor's Gate.

Two hours later, Edward found himself before an unnamed gentleman at an imposing desk, in fact the very gentleman who had been at the Earl of Portland's side when Edward presented his letters and warning. A recording secretary sat nearby at a smaller desk.

"Please, sit down," the gentleman said, directing him to a chair. "You've been well treated?"

"Surprisingly so."

"Indeed?"

"I remember the days of Titus Oates and his false claims of a Popish plot, when all men, no matter how likely innocent, were treated as guilty."

"Times change, sir."

"Indeed," Edward replied dryly.

"So you've heard by now of the attempted assassination of the King?" the gentleman asked, ignoring Edward's attempt to engage.

"From some of the warders at the Tower, yes. I don't know how much they really knew."

"Yes, rumors, there are so many. Briefly—"

"Pardon me, but why the Tower—and is it as my lord I should address you?"

"Mr. Secretary will do."

"Why the Tower, Mr. Secretary?"

"For you?"

"I'm no nobleman."

"Indeed you're not. We wanted you kept separate from the rest."

"There are other ways to do this."

"So there are. But you also have a reputation for escape from jails and prisons more secure than Newgate."

"I see."

"You should consider it a measure of your worth. It's expensive to keep a prisoner in the Tower; the King, unusually, and for which you must thank him, paid your way. But back to the matters at hand. There was in fact a plot to kill the king, forty men and forty horses to block his carriage and stab him to death. With God's grace it never came to pass. We've captured many of the conspirators and most are talking, telling a remarkable tale in the hope of saving their skins if not their souls. As for you, we know you came here to warn of a plot to kill the king, for which the King thanks you, of course." The gentleman poured himself a glass of wine. "Michael O'Neal," he said, before lifting the glass to his lips.

Edward was taken aback but said nothing. He collected his wits, then looked curiously at his interrogator, realizing this man very likely managed the king's network of intelligencers, or part of it.

"Wine?" continued the richly dressed gentleman. "It's an excellent claret, captured by an English privateer from a French merchantman. A trade I hear you intend to follow again, privateering, I mean."

"Thank you."

The gentleman passed Edward a glass of the red wine.

"Michael O'Neal. An Irishman. Do you know him?"

Edward raised his eyebrows, not expecting anything resembling this question. "I sailed with an Irishman of this name twice, many years ago. He came from near Kinsale, or maybe it was Cork, or so I think he said."

"You were friends?"

Edward shrugged. "After a fashion. We've since been enemies on the same battlefield."

"You owe him loyalty?"

"No more than any other comrade-in-arms. But he's dead."

"Indeed? You owe him nothing, then?"

"He saved my life once."

"A great debt."

"I saved his also."

"A great debt repaid. Is there animosity between you?"

"Was, you mean. As I said, he's dead. I marooned him once."

"We'll come to his life and death in a moment. Marooned, you say? Ah, the punishment of putting a man ashore in a desert place. Why?"

"For mutiny. He refused to abide by a vote of the company—we were privateers, but sailed under Jamaica Rule—and, rather than depart in the sloop we offered him, he led a mutiny. The ship's company wanted to hang him, but I persuaded them to maroon him. He blamed me because I championed the punishment, fearing that anything other than death or marooning might lead him to mutiny again."

"Pity he didn't die on his little island. This same O'Neal was here, in London, as an assassinator."

Edward raised his eyebrows. "The O'Neal I knew was killed at the Boyne, or so I was led to believe."

"He was not."

"Indeed?"

"Indeed."

"And you say he's alive, and an assassinator? And he's escaped?"

"Escaped? No, not to France or Ireland, not as far as we know. We believe he's in hiding somewhere in London. When did you last see him?"

"In the Caribbean, some years ago, when I marooned him. I never actually saw him on the battlefields of Ireland afterward, although I heard from irreproachable sources that he was there. Are you sure we're speaking of the same man?"

"They're one and the same, never doubt it. Don't you want to bring this pirate and assassinator to heel? Sympathy, sir, is subordinate to your duty to your King."

"He once swore to kill me, and now you say he's a Jacobite who might thereby thwart my ventures. Thus he's twice my enemy."

"You were yourself once a Jacobite."

"By circumstance. All were Jacobites, more or less, until King William and Queen Mary, God bless her soul, were proclaimed."

"James pardoned you, for which you must be grateful."

"For which I am grateful."

"And now?"

"King William reigns. James fled to France. I'm no papist and will never serve France. I've served King William honorably under several various commissions and circumstances these past few years."

"So you have. You're not English, are you, but a Scot, and much of the Highlands, even? His Majesty is well-acquainted with the Scots: Highlanders have served him well in Europe."

"I am a Creolian, to be precise."

"Ah, yes, an American, of Scots family, and not only that, Indian-bred—you were born and brought up there in your early years, were you not? In Jamaica, or someplace thereabout?"

"Jamaica, at Port Royal," Edward replied proudly.

"Indeed? Born in the famous buccaneer haven itself. And

you also lived in Virginia before you were sent to family and education in Scotland? The haughty hot temper of both a Scot and a Creole, yet I know both sorts are honorable. And your father, he was a buccaneer, I believe; like father like son? It must be difficult, these loyalties."

The man's habit of speaking in suddenly shifting questions posed as statements began to annoy Edward.

"My father was a warrant officer in the Usurper's navy under Admiral Penn, then served under Captain Myngs raiding the Spanish Main—in the Royal Navy under both the Usurper and King Charles. Call my father a buccaneer if it pleases you, but he served aboard ships of the English navy, at least at first. As for me, I serve King William."

"Yes, so you say. But you didn't come here just out of loyalty, you came, as you said, hoping to find a patron to assist in your search for a commission as a privateer as well."

"Whoever came to Court who didn't seek reward?"

The gentleman smiled but did not reply, and instead looked at a paper on the desk. Edward suspected this was merely an act, that he really looked at nothing. He did not fail to notice that the subject was no longer Michael O'Neal.

"You've been in Ireland recently," he said finally. "Your purpose, other than helping Lord Deigle?"

"I sought an investor, an old friend."

"Sir William Waller."

"You've read my personal correspondence."

"A matter of State. You shall have your letters back. Of course, it must occur to you that we have other sources as well. We are not as blind as you might think." He shifted in his chair and took a sip of wine. "What else did you do in Ireland?"

"Nothing except meet with Viscount Brennan and Sir James Allin on behalf of Lord Deigle."

"Yes, poor Lord Deigle. He hoped to receive secrets of some

use to us in order to improve his standing with the King. In particular he hoped to learn something from Lord Brennan, for until recently the viscount was a Jacobite with close ties to St. Germain, in particular to the Duke of Berwick, who has been trying raise rebellion in England, Scotland, and Ireland. But Brennan's too wise to tell too many secrets. All Brennan and Allin had for Deigle was a list of petty Irish conspirators, and these we knew already. Of course, the Irish Jacobites didn't know what was in the letters, so they attacked you. A wasted effort, in fact. Only what you found on them, and only by accident when they attacked, was of value. Handsome Harry will try to take credit for it, of course."

"And would leave me hanging if it were otherwise."

"I'm sure you knew his character before you agreed to do his bidding."

"If I had a better choice, I'd have made it."

"Of course." The gentleman nodded in agreement, sat down, and leaned back in his chair. "Are you sure you don't know if O'Neal knows anyone in London?"

Edward, tired of the verbal fencing in the form of changing subjects, smiled as he was wont to do before a fight. "I don't know who he knows. Indeed, I know nothing of his life outside of privateering a decade ago. Why are you asking me this?"

The gentleman ignored the question. "Not even in Ireland? Did he ever say who his family was or with whom he consorted?"

"No."

"O'Neal was to be married," the gentleman continued. "O'Meary is her name, or something like this, I'm never quite familiar with these Irish and Scottish names—your pardon, sir. She's a ward of sorts of Sir William? Or rather, he's her patron, she lives under his protection?"

Again Edward was taken aback, and to a far greater degree

this time. He did his best to dissemble again, although he was certain his face had begun to flush. He had forgotten that Sir William had named Molly's betrothed as a man named Neal or Nall. "Yes. You do have good sources."

"O'Neal was sloppy; in his haste he left letters behind, old ones, a lover's keepsakes."

"Clearly you have Irish sources, too."

"Naturally. You must forgive me when I tell you that my trade requires that I lie to you at times, although usually only by omission. She was not his mistress? Sir William's, I mean?"

"No," Edward said sternly. "But I know nothing more of what might lie between them. Some family history or kinship I believe," he lied.

"Sir William is loyal?"

"A Whig through and through, and of the Church of England forever, but fair in his dealings with the Irish. He fought for King William in Ireland."

"This O'Meary woman, how well do you know her?"

"Not well," he lied again. "She often acted as hostess on behalf of Sir William, but I usually had affairs elsewhere. I know nothing of consequence," he continued, skirting between fact and fiction. How well he knew Molly was no one's business, not to mention that he had given his word to Sir William to do all he might reasonably and in honor do to protect her.

"She might be a conspirator, then? No, not in the assassination attempt, but in the planned uprising?"

"I don't know how she could be," Edward lied, as he realized again, coldly, that she was well-placed to be involved.

"Perhaps you wish to protect Sir William? The woman is doubtless in a good position to be a traitor—as are others, of course." Edward said nothing. The interrogation continued. "The rapparee letters you brought to the Earl of Portland, you had them by accident when you were attacked on the road in

Ireland?"

"Yes."

"Who was in your company when you were attacked?"

Edward waited a moment before replying. "Mistress O'Meary."

"And one of the men who attacked you might well have been O'Neal. What do you think of this?"

"Is this proved?" he replied defiantly, yet unnerved.

"Proved? No, sir. It is intelligent speculation. Sympathy, my dear sir, sympathy: you show sympathy for O'Neal, you show sympathy for the O'Meary woman. How do you know that she didn't lead the rapparees to you and he didn't try to kill you for the Brennan and Allin letters? Sympathy, sir, can get you killed. Surely you learned this, if not as a soldier or honest privateer, then as a buccaneer?"

"I played no buccaneer tricks."

"Is that what you call putting men to the rack? Myself, I don't find torture very useful. But sympathy? A dangerous vice in my profession. Perhaps you're protecting the O'Meary woman for some reason? For Sir William's sake? No? I'm not so sure. Is there anyone else you might suspect of being spy or traitor in Kinsale? Anyone else who would know of your mission and movement?"

"I know only that someone had good intelligence of my affairs, but that could be any one or even several of many."

"Do you know a Dutch denizen named Janneke Hardy?"

"I do."

"Might she be a spy?"

"She's also well-placed, as are many," Edward said, then regretted it instantly. His interrogator noticed this immediately.

"As I said, sympathy, sir, beware sympathy."

"I've no knowledge that Jane Hardy is a spy, and would not believe it of her," Edward lied.

The interrogator smiled. "Nor would you believe it of Mistress O'Meary."

"Have you finished with me?" Edward demanded.

"Not yet, sir. Sit and drink some more wine please. O'Neal, O'Neal again—in his place what would you do now? How do you think he'll try to escape?"

"He's a seaman," Edward replied with resignation, "if he's the man I knew. He'll head to sea, alone I think, for that's the sort of man he was. He'll trust no one. The ports are closed, of course?" The gentleman nodded. "He'll move by night, then, perhaps to Romney Marsh or a to a small village by the sea. He'll steal a boat if he can, like Captain Sharp did, or hire one if not, something small. O'Neal is such as could row across the Channel alone if necessary. He's no true artist as a navigator, but is a good seaman and can navigate in waters he's familiar with."

The gentleman said nothing for a few moments, instead shuffling through the papers on his desk.

"Did you know he had a cousin, a Jesuit priest? The priest was a spy, but, alas, he gave us nothing before he was hanged. A man of great faith but poor politics and worse fortune. We had hoped he would identify a Jacobite spy among the English in Kinsale. In a curious turn of events, it was you who killed one of his escorts, an English officer. Do you make it habit of killing His Majesty's officers in duels?"

"Is twice a habit?"

The man smiled briefly. "You have a wry wit, sir. There were no consequences in Ireland?"

"It was a fair fight. Ingoldsby challenged me. There was an inquest."

"We're aware of the details. Your tracks are quite easy to follow, sir, for you leave dead men wherever you go, not to mention that you do it with a certain flair. A man who undertakes secret missions must have less notoriety. But then you already know this, don't you? Perhaps you have some theory of plain-dealing, like Captain Manly in the play? That you may dispense with all the world's cunning intrigues via a bold courageous front and a skillful sword? You are then a dreamer, sir, or at least more suited to sea than shore." Edward's interrogator smiled briefly. "You need not worry, sir, I mention the duel as a curiosity only, but will remark that Ingoldsby reputedly played some buccaneer tricks on the priest when they captured him. O'Neal would have preferred his company no more than you apparently did. But I hear you were on friendly terms with the other officers of the garrison."

"As I said, he challenged me, over nothing."

"As is ever the case. Usually." The gentleman paused yet again to peruse the papers before him, or pretend to do so. "Speaking of rencontres, there was, curiously, a man found dead in Fleet Ditch the day the Earl ordered you taken into custody. A passerby recognized him as one who frequented both Jonathan's coffeehouse and also Old King's Head and both are Jacobite rendezvous. He said the man lived in Bristol until recently, and now London, often travelled between here and Bath. A courier named John Lynch." Edward's manner disclosed nothing. "Do you know him?"

"Only that he's a bully and backstabber, although it appears he wasn't much of an assassinator," Edward replied.

"Who said he came to London to assassinate?"

"My idle speculation," Edward replied casually, his mind racing to recover from the near-error. "How else does a Jacobite courier come to rest in Fleet Ditch? A man with the business of rebellion at hand avoids duels and affrays. A courier might be attacked by those who work for you, but I think you would have told me this already. Ergo, knowing Lynch as I do, he probably died attempting murder in an alley."

"You're quick on your feet, sir, very quick," Edward's interrogator said with a curious smile. "As soon as Lynch was identified—we already knew of his Jacobite inclinations—one of my officers dispatched thief-takers with coin to bribe those who might have witnessed his death. A whore admitted to seeing a man thrown into the Ditch by some Egyptians or cheats, doubtless she lies and they were in fact her own rogues, and doubtless she robbed him—the thief-takers confiscated a guinea and a crown from her. But we're sure she didn't kill him, and she swore she had nothing to do with his death, nor did she know anything else about it. Certainly she wasn't capable of killing him, at least not in the way it was done. Lynch wore a mail shirt—whoever killed him was proficient enough to put a sword through an eye."

Silently Edward rebuked himself for having thought the woman had betrayed him. He had not even asked her name, not when he had first met her, nor when she helped him in the alley. It was an unacceptable transgression.

The gentleman paused, looked long and hard at Edward, and then continued. "It's a strange business I'm in, sir, in which everyone lies, yet I must distinguish between the lies that matter and the lies that don't. The dead man was not one of the assassinators, but a Jacobite agent nonetheless. Whoever killed him saved him a trial and hanging, but deprived us of a witness."

"Indeed?"

"Indeed. Odd that you fought a duel with him in Bristol before you departed for Ireland, or so I hear, over an accusation that you are a Jacobite. As you know by now, my intelligencers are very good." The gentleman picked up a paper from the desk. "We took this letter from the whore I mentioned; she said she found it near where she saw Lynch thrown into the Ditch. It came from Ireland. The signature is without doubt false, and the letter is phrased in fairly innocent terms, although there is no salutation. It is a request to recover certain letters that you—you yourself, sir—might have on your person. Let me it read to you:

> 'My dear Frend and Cusin Capt. MacNoten has Letters for me concerning our mutual Ventur. You may finde Him in Bristol Bath or London. Use all Intelligence as You requir. He will not expect you. Pls send Your Frend to ask Him for the Letters. Have a Care and Your Frend use all Care.'

"It seems intended to appear benign, yet it is poorly so. Frankly, to my mind it's an order to murder you for the letters, or at least to have them from you at any cost. Here, read it for yourself. Do you know the hand?"

Edward glanced at the writing, a round hand with attempts at flourishes in the French mode.

A woman's hand, he first thought, then his mind shifted to the existence of the letter itself. *Damn! I searched in haste and missed it. Yet had I discovered it, dare I have given it to this man? Of course I would have—the letter would have proved the man a Jacobite and I his target, it would have saved me from arrest.*

In spite of his anticipation that such correspondence existed, Edward was shocked, and tried to suppress his private concern that it very likely could have been Molly or Lydia who had given the order for his murder. A man may suspect much, and thus forearm himself, yet too often he reserves some hope that it might yet not be true—and thus the reality may still shock him to the core.

He shook his head. "I don't recognize it," he said as he tried to recover his wits. He refused to believe that Molly might have him murdered. Robbed, perhaps, if she were truly a rebel—or under O'Neal's thumb!—but not murdered. He had a difficult time believing it of Lydia as well. He had known many backstabbers, man and woman: neither Molly nor Lydia fit his experience of them.

"Unfortunately, there's no address. It appears to have had an outer folio for security. We have recovered some other correspondence from Lynch's lodging. Several letters were addressed to Lawrence Unwin 'for S. J. K.' at the Black Swan tavern in Bristol, with inscriptions added later for delivery to Lynch. We don't know who Mr. Unwin is, but S. J. K. is doubtless Sir John Knight, a Bristol Jacobite."

"I don't know these persons," Edward said.

"I didn't think you did. You are suddenly quite pale, sir, in spite of your saturnine tint."

"Are we nearly finished here?" Edward demanded as he passed the letter back.

"A moment, sir, a moment. Let us inspect this billet of assassination. It's not a well-educated hand, certainly not that of a secretary or scholar. Nor is the grammar exceptional, or perhaps it's that of a foreign speaker who knows English only well enough. A native Irishman is the natural suspect, but it might be any foreigner, or even an English person of middling education."

Edward was coldly silent for a few moments.

"In other words, it might be anyone," he said eventually, argumentatively.

"Indeed? Maybe. As for Lynch, an incidental affray is most likely, although a curiously coincidental one, given that you were his target and he died very near your lodging, not to mention that you assume him—rightfully it seems—an assassin." Edward's face remained impassive. The interrogator shrugged his shoulders. "I care not if you killed him, unless there were an understanding between you. I know you're a resourceful man, and not a fool either, except perhaps in the case of women. You've been busy since you returned aboard the *Virginia* Galley—a brave thing that, by the way, the chase you led from the French privateer. It put you once more in the news. I know what you must be thinking: what matter a spy in a place as small as Kinsale anyway?"

By now Edward was becoming less annoyed by the man's interrogation, and more impressed. He had a finely practiced habit of attacking as one was off-guard, of feinting in one direction and attacking in another in the distraction, although it was not working as well as he probably would have liked with his current subject. Edward, having been interrogated before, knew that in all cases it was imperative that one tell as much of the truth as one could, letting it provide cover to any necessary lies, white or black. He wondered fleetingly if the man might not also be as skillful with a sword.

"I knew well the likely consequences when I brought the letters here, as it was my duty to do."

"Yet I suspect you would have it both ways if you could—you would have your reward, and preserve the objects of your sympathy too. Is this why you didn't turn the letters over to the authorities in Ireland? Admirable yet foolish, your philosophy. And impossible too, but then, your sort have a reputation for the impossible. Unfortunately, people forget how often bold men like you also fail when trying to impress Fortune. Don't worry, Captain, we're almost finished, you've no reason to worry or fear. In fact, my country cousin tells me you're an honest man, and she's a fair judge of the sex," he said. "She's far more worldly than she might seem, and makes her way through many circles."

"Your cousin?"

"You escorted her flying coach into London, for which you have my thanks. An assassinator would have done nothing to draw so much attention, such as unnecessarily charge two highwaymen, I might add. I believe she's taken out notices to further your venture, so impressed was she."

One small mystery solved, Edward thought.

"I'm no longer a suspect then?"

"You never were. We committed you to the Tower to keep you safe for us, and for that matter, safe from Jacobites, and because you might have other information helpful to us. Sadly for you, your information came too late to us and was too vague. Three who knew of the conspiracy came to us with details of time, place, and traitor. Frankly, we've been too busy the past few days to deal with you."

"Then I'm free to go?"

"You have a curious relationship with Fortune, Captain MacNaughton. Akin to a cat's, I think. Particularly, you have a curious relationship, even if you do not recognize it, with parties involved in the attempted assassination and uprising, if only in a small way. As to your question, yes, you are free to go...."

"But?"

"But we prefer that you don't."

"I don't understand."

"Again, it has to do with your peculiar history and your relationship with Fortune. His Majesty would reward you, sir, and in such a way that you might use your fortunate affinity to help us find O'Neal and others like him. Money is scarce, but His Majesty strongly desires to reward you."

"How?"

"What does it matter how? We're in an emergency, sir: who wouldn't help his king in time of need?"

Edward stood, filled his glass, and drank more wine. "You have a point."

The gentleman picked up a large folio from his desk. "This is a naval commission for the duration of the emergency, for some few months perhaps, and longer if you please, assuming you please your superior officers. If you accept it, you'll command one of His Majesty's small vessels, a ketch I believe it is, the *King Fisher*, recently recaptured from the French."

"A commission as a naval officer?" Edward asked.

Commissions were rarely granted to former accused pirates.

"You seem surprised, Captain MacNaughton, that we would make this offer. Don't be. Yesterday, upon hearing of the loss of the vessel's commander and lieutenant, it was suggested to me —if you must know, by my cousin—to suggest to His Majesty that you be given the commander's place, to set a thief to catch a thief, so to speak. Please pardon the expression: I don't accuse you of being a thief, other than of the Spaniard's American property. And anyway, as the *King Fisher* is only a small vessel, you can't do much damage with her if you are actually a Jacobite, nor will the crew let you. There is precedent, of course, for choosing a man like you. First, you once briefly held the King's commission as a naval officer before your later notorious escapades, and there is further precedent: Captain Bartholomew Sharp, the pirate—you sailed with him once, didn't you, and helped put down a rebellion in the Bermudas?" Edward nodded. "I thought so. Sharp was appointed to command of the *Bonetta* Sloop, although he never took it up."

"That was a dozen years ago, but precedent is precedent, I suppose," Edward remarked, wishing to return to the subject at hand. "How did the *King Fisher* lose her officers?"

"Her commander died the day the emergency was declared. Drunk, he choked on his vomit after having escorted a small vessel loaded with French Huguenot refugees, and, I might add, some excellent French brandy, Nantes, I believe. Her lieutenant died of some accident of disease some days earlier, but I do not recall the details. A lingering illness made worse by the sea, and perhaps by an excess of French brandy as well."

Edward grunted.

"Just as I feel, Captain. If you accept this commission, you will take horse, escorted by a small troupe of His Majesty's dragoons, to Dover and there take command. You'll receive your formal orders there, but as far as I know they will be, for the present, to cruise close by the shore by day and night along the coast near Romney Marsh, to chase, board, and inspect all vessels, arresting or detaining anyone suspicious or who cannot properly account for himself. For that matter, you may arrest whom you please as you please. With luck—again, you have a peculiar relationship with Fortune and her hand in recent events—you may even find this O'Neal or some other of the few we have not yet captured. I place my trust in the skills you developed in your trade as a buccaneer, or, as you probably prefer to say, as a privateer. Men such as yourself can do good service for the Crown, in certain capacities."

Edward, unsure if he had just been insulted, briefly reviewed the proposal. His mind, which had taken the interrogation largely in stride, as it would have in any crisis or emergency, was now settling into confusion. O'Neal alive? And he Molly's betrothed? Was he then the man he had seen with her at the races, the man upon the hill when he arrived, the man upon the road when attacked? And Molly practically accused of being a spy, perhaps a murderer too? Even Lydia, too? And what of Jane, Deigle, and Lynch? And somehow Edward and the attempted assassination of the king were intertwined in all of this and them.

One thing I do know, he thought grimly: *Everyone's been playing me for a fool!*

Still, Edward realized, he had accomplished three critical things during the interrogation: he had given no useful evidence against anyone but O'Neal; he now knew much of what his allies and enemies knew; and, most importantly to his venture, he had done nothing to brand himself as a Jacobite, in fact quite the opposite.

The gentleman, perhaps sensing some of the reasons for Edward's hesitation, intruded on his thoughts.

"Captain MacNaughton, please accept my apology for the inconvenience of your brief confinement. And I apologize also for not having introduced myself: I am Matthew Prior, former secretary to the king, occasional poet, and, at present, interrogator of intelligencers. Here is your commission, you will accept it? It will surely lead to better things. I know you wish a privateering commission, but this naval commission is the King's wish for your recent service to Him, and I can tell you as a man who knows, it is never a good practice to spurn a king who would promote you. You will accept it then?"

"Of course."

"Good, sir, good. On your way then, and I'll tell my country cousin you intend more good deeds. A sergeant and his party wait outside to escort you, and they have the keeping of your arms and baggage as well. I'll forward your confiscated correspondence this afternoon. Good day to you, sir, God speed, and damnation to the Jacobites and the French."

A day later, Edward was aboard the *King Fisher*, and soon at sea. The all-consuming nature of command kept his mind from dwelling on his the painful paradox around him. The ketch was well-suited to Edward's mission, notwithstanding that she had seen a dozen years of hard service. One of a handful of ketches in the Royal Navy, the *King Fisher* was small, a mere sixty-one tons, seaworthy if not overly swift. Edward would have preferred she carried a few sweeps for rowing in calm airs, but he must make do with what he had. At least he had a stout crew, significantly better-disciplined than the buccaneer and privateer crews he had commanded in the past.

For several days and nights the ketch cruised near Romney Marsh, stopping and searching every vessel, and her captain applying a combination of liquor, interrogation, and elicitation to each captured vessel's captain. Ashore, Edward spread money and liquor around, dangling hints of great reward to be had for the capture of traitors, and for that matter, of smugglers and anyone who sought to leave England secretly, for after all, might they not be traitors in disguise? He noted ironically to himself that here at Romney Marsh, Captain Sharp had reportedly departed for the Caribbean after being acquitted of piracy: he had stopped here to steal sheep for provisions.

Early into the fifth night, the *King Fisher* anchored off Romney Marsh and made a signal. An hour later Edward was rewarded with a whisper in his ear as a sharp-eared seaman directed his attention to an area between the ketch and the shore.

Edward saw nothing. But if he listened carefully he could just make out the creak of muffled oars and their quiet bite in the water.

Chapter 25

At sea whose loud waves cannot sleep,
But deep still calleth upon deep...
—Henry Vaughan, "Abel's Blood," 17th Century

The Irishman heard the loud voices at the Mermaid tavern when he was but a few thrusts short of climax. He paused at the noise, almost bolted, but then the moment struck him—the maid beneath him and her erect nipples, pairs of moist lips, and wide-eyed fear, the sharp silence and sharper surge of adrenaline, himself hard, primed, loaded, waiting to discharge —and he thrust several times more until he spent himself within her body, his hand over her mouth as she struggled in fear to escape not his passion or seed, but the noose she realized might now await her only several yards away.

Finished, he leaped quickly from the bed and dressed, straining to hear the voices outside. Someone was searching the Mermaid, and now they had the tavern keeper.

Aye, and he'll not be silent for long, thought Michael O'Neal.

"But you'll be quiet now, my girl, won't you, until I'm gone?" he asked the half-naked woman on the bed. "Sure now, I don't want them to hang you for pleasuring a man you thought was only a free trader," he said.

It was more than a week since the aborted attempt on King William's life, and Michael had lain hidden most of the time in an alien capital in an alien land with treason upon his shoulders, a noose waiting to stretch his neck, and a thousand informers just waiting to tighten the hempen turns.

He had come ashore eighteen days before among the shoals and sands of the smuggler's haven at Romney Marsh after a journey aboard a French corsair. He'd stayed overnight at Hunt's isolated house, otherwise known as the Jacobite spy's gateway, lodging, and post office on the Marsh, then walked to Rye. At the Mermaid tavern he'd met a Romish monk who escorted him to a safe house in London, confirmed the assassination attempt, and dressed him as a middling merchant. It was a route already followed by other assassins-to-be, many of them members of King James's personal guard. Alone, Michael made his way to the Piazza at Covent Garden on a Monday evening, and there found his old Scottish commander, Sir George Barclay, a white handkerchief hanging from his pocket as a sign.

"I feared you'd never make it, lad," the old Scotsman said. "What brings you—loyalty, revenge, or money?"

"The last two. And I'll consider myself satisfied with little more than the latter of those."

"Ever the pragmatic hater you are, Michael."

"Do you have a warrant or commission from King James?"

"Right to the point—your scruples have improved I see. I do."

"To commit murder?"

"Have you come to fear the sight of blood, Michael?"

"Dutch Billy is a soldier, and I've spilled the blood of many. But I don't want to be left aground in London if it all goes to hell. You've a fine lodging to return to at St. Germain, and doubtless your own private escape route. I don't want my lodging to be a gibbet, nor my escape route the path to hell."

"We're all headed to hell," Barclay said with a smile, "it's just a matter of timing. Berwick is recruiting. James has promised a French army. England's Jacobites are armed and ready to rise."

"Is Berwick in London?"

"Not anymore."

"Where?"

"Come 'round to my quarters tomorrow night."

"Why isn't Berwick here?" Michael insisted.

"He's done his work, his plans are laid. *We* are the point of the sword."

"What you mean is that we must succeed. If we fail, there's no escape."

"It's a terrain you've been over before. And you're one who knows how to make an escape."

"As are you."

"Again, Michael, come to my lodging tomorrow night. A messenger will inform you of its location."

"You won't trust me with this information now?"

"It changes."

The two assassins parted company. Michael spent part of the next day hidden at his own lodging, then drinking at a Jacobite tavern in Maiden Lane with an Irish co-conspirator he knew from the war, an officer named Edward Lowick. With Lowick was a hothead named Chambers who, like Michael, harbored an anger of fierce proportion. Unlike Michael, however, his passions seemed ungovernable.

That evening, Michael met Barclay and his company of assassins. They were an odd lot, as are all men in all political conspiracies, made up of good men and bad, careful men and fools, sober men and drunkards, loyal men and greedy bastards, brave men and cowards, and even some of both courage and cowardice, depending on the moment.

Barclay showed Michael the warrant signed by King James. It said nothing about murdering King William, although it did authorize Barclay to make such acts of war as he saw fit, including acts of hostility against the Prince of Orange. It was truly a princely document of the finest Machiavellian sort, worthy even of a Cardinal Richelieu or Henry II. No matter the outcome, James's hands were clean. Importantly, it satisfied the conspirators. Michael doubted the document was a de facto order to kill King William, but he needed no such reassurances.

"And what were King James's personal instructions to you?" he asked out of curiosity.

"For my ears only, but you may be assured that the King wishes us to do what we do."

"I wish for many things I would never put word to, Sir George."

"The paper matters naught, Michael, you know this. No matter what the warrant says, if we fail, we are hanged and quartered. If we succeed, others are hanged and quartered. And you are here because I need steady hands at the killing."

Michael grunted. He knew that if this plot failed, it would likely not be at the final execution, but during the plotting or while they lay in wait. He grunted again, and looked at the company about him.

About half the men present were members of King James's personal guard, men of absolute loyalty. They had made their way to London by twos and threes. Their absence from St. Germain went unnoticed by English spies, for they had all given reasons for leaving James's service and had resigned one-at-a-time.

The rest were men recruited in London, not all of them by Barclay himself; and here, Michael felt, lay weakness. One was a petty, bullying patron of the gaming tables, another a hot-headed hater, yet another an arrant opportunist.

Barclay and Lowick he already knew, and Robert Charnock, one of the ringleaders and formerly dean of Magdalen College at Oxford. He had met Charnock on the Cornish shore last November, but until today had not known his name.

And the arrogant bastard pretends not to know me, thought Michael. *Best to be on guard against all of them.*

Barclay called Michael back to his side and reviewed the plan for him: they would ambush Prince William as he returned from hunting in Richmond Park. William's carriage would bog down, requiring that it be pulled through the mud, and he would thereby be vulnerable. Rookwood's company would attack one flank, Porter's the other, Charnock's the rear guard, and Barclay's, with Michael included, the carriage and the king. Parkyns had provided the horses and Cranburne the 'stabbing' swords and pistols.

Michael thought the plans as described were suitable enough, though he still worried that there were far too many men who knew of them. Forty and more men were enough to hide at least one traitor, probably more. Men were squeamish at actually murdering kings, though they might pretend to be brave enough during the planning, and plots provided ample fodder for political opportunists. It bothered him also that one man, Sir John Friend, had been informed of the plot but had refused to help, though Barclay was assured that the man would not inform on them. Maybe, thought Michael, maybe—but what about the others?

Two days later, Michael examined the killing ground, located between Turnham Green and the River Thames, and found it suitable. If the day came without betrayal, if the forty made it safely to the ambuscade, and if William came, then the plan would likely succeed. Or at least the assassination would succeed. Jacobite supporters must then rally to James and defeat the Whiggish army.

Damn! thought Michael suddenly, *what have I got myself into?*

To kill a king who was a soldier was nothing to him, but he had no intention of throwing his own life away. He enjoyed the waiting to kill, as he would enjoy the killing, but there was too much left to Fortune. He felt suddenly like a pawn, not an ancient Irish king. Time, he thought, to look again to his own avenue of escape should the plan fail. If it failed, the ports would be closed, city gates closed, all would be stopped on the highways.

Where to, then?

To the coast, probably, to steal a boat and sail to France. If he must, he might return to Romney Marsh and attempt to cross there. He made sure that concealed on his person were a dagger, a brace of pistols, a few biscuits, a pocket compass, and money enough for bribes, post horses, and passage.

Very well, he thought; *I'm prepared in case we fail.*

Finally had come the day and all lay in ambush to murder one king and restore another.

But Dutch Billy did not come.

Forty men waiting for the king's coach to mire in the muddy road, forty men waiting to drag him from the coach and stab him to a bloody Caesar's death. And now they were still forty men without blood on their hands, forty who must return to their lodgings and taverns to wait in anticipatory fear for seven more days.

Michael's suspicions surged—he had smelled betrayal since he had arrived.

"Nonsense!" said Barclay when they met the following Friday at the Sun Tavern in the Strand. The knight persuaded him to remain until the morrow, when the king would surely go hunting as planned. "Nothing to fear," Barclay said. "The king wasn't well last Saturday, but our informant tells us that he's recovered and will indeed hunt tomorrow."

But again King William did not hunt.

From Porter's lodgings the assassins had ridden to Blue Posts before departing on the final leg to murder. But at the last moment there came word that the Prince of Orange would not hunt this day either, that his coaches had returned, that something odd was up.

And now Michael knew for certain that something was wrong. It was time to run: treason, after all, would be a charge brought only against losers and other fools.

While others tried to fortify their courage and deny that they were discovered, Michael abandoned the enterprise and prepared to depart London that night.

He searched for Barclay that afternoon, but he was nowhere to be found. Barclay's sudden absence alone gave Michael enough reason to run. And that night, just as he headed back to his lodgings, the hue and cry were raised. By noon the next day every Jacobite contact Michael knew was gone to ground or arrested.

The bastard could have warned us! Michael cursed as he lay hidden. *And the rest, all fools!* he thought angrily. *They should've known better after the Dutchman had twice canceled his trip to Richmond! A fine plan it had been yesterday morning, but today? Ports closed, an invasion expected, the Habeus Corpus Act suspended, Fenwick and Charnock—and half of the others, it seemed—already taken, and soldiers and trainbands everywhere.*

King James would not bring salvation in the form of an army from Calais. The Irishman would have to make his escape from an alien land where everyone on the road would be questioned and everyone in every town knew everyone. He left his few possessions behind at his lodging, not daring to return there, fearing even friends and acquaintances, those few who might not already have been taken. Even the priest who had first hidden him had been taken. There was no longer any place to hide. He dare not visit Hunt's house on Romney Marsh, he dare not show his face anywhere—yet he must.

He rued his arrogance now, rued the fact that he had listened to someone else when making his final decision to join the rebellion. He swore at himself for being greedy, for indeed it had been greed more than loyalty that had brought him to this land, for surely those forty who would have a bloody hand in delivering England from the Dutchman would also have been well rewarded. Now only a gibbet would be his reward unless he could escape to Ireland or France: he was no nobleman to receive the headsman's ax.

And Molly? he thought. *No reward now for me, for you, for us.*

That his treason might be tied to her never occurred to him.

With no place to hide, there was but one thing to do. He stood and began running toward the sea.

Aye, beware the hue and cry!

To steal to eat, to steal to escape, to steal to live is to have the soldiers bring tight the halter around his neck. So for two days he did not eat, he did not sleep, he drank only water from puddles and troughs. He stole nothing and was cautious even of the air he breathed and of the dark and obscure corners in which he hid.

He found no succor or escape at the Downs the first night, nor the next morning. Fortune did him no favors. The tide worked against him, and he dared not try to enter as crew or passenger lest he be arrested. And not long after, shipping was embargoed; everyone was on the watch for those trying to leave, even the boats and wherries were watched. So onward he went by night and by rain.

By a miracle he made it back to Romney Marsh on the third day, and from there to Rye, to the Mermaid. He considered speaking to the tavern keeper, a noted smuggler and Jacobite, but changed his mind when the man appeared to recognize then shun him. Too late Michael realized he had violated his own rule: never go back the way you came.

Michael left the tavern and went instead to the back door of the young woman's nearby house, the woman he had—against the wishes of his priestly escort—bedded quickly and just as quickly abandoned when he had arrived here but two and a half weeks before. The look on her face was enough to tell him that her husband, himself a smuggler, was still away.

She took him in. Even more, she arranged his passage with a local smuggler, and heeded Michael's warning.

"I prefer it be a man who hasn't had your favors before, for I don't want a jealous man's knife in my back," he said.

"You think I'm a whore, then?"

"No, my lovely girl, but it's friendly and beautiful you are. Find a man who wants you but hasn't had you, and let him know he might yet."

Then came the searchers, but they found only the man they sought, a petty smuggler, and they never knocked at the door of O'Neal's temporary mistress. The Irishman had two more nights and days in her arms.

On the last night he would lay with her, Michael O'Neal met with the man who hoped to lie, as O'Neal was doing, with the smuggler's wife.

"Is it arranged, then?" asked Michael.

"A privateer out of St. Malo, tomorrow night. I'll row you out to her."

The Irishman was in place hours before his rendezvous, to make certain there was no ambush. From Rye he had traveled north across Scotch Flat, then across Craven's sluice and onto the Marsh the first night. He lay hidden all day in rain, mud, and mist, then slogged the next evening through the fens of the alien, surreal landscape of the Marsh itself, among its dikes and ditches and dramatically eerie damp grasses and twisted trees, among the small isolated churches built for secreting illicit cargos. Twice he skirted army patrols.

He met the smuggler by the shore at midnight, not far from the tiny village of Dymchurch, where a four-oared fishing boat was drawn up on the shore. He liked neither the size nor lines of the boat: it would not be a swift sailor. On the other hand, it would be easy to row, and its size would make it easy to miss in the troughs of the sea.

A signal came from the sea. The smuggler returned it, and the two men pushed the small boat into the sea and boarded it.

Michael was hyper-alert as the smuggler rowed and he steered. He had heard that an English man-of-war ketch had been seen in the area for the past few days, and it might surprise the French privateer. He searched keenly into the darkness and eventually found what he was looking for: a blackness blacker than the surrounding darkness, bobbing gently up and down.

"*Ho! Holà!*" Michael called.

No answer.

"*Holà!*" he called again.

Still no answer.

"Hold water!" he whispered sharply to the smuggler. "I don't like this!"

"*Nage à bord!*" came an answer finally.

"Give them the password," Michael demanded.

"*Vive le roi!*" shouted the smuggler.

"*Vive la France!*" came the response.

"Give way... Easy, though, easy," Michael ordered. "I don't like this, something's not right."

As they came closer a sense of near-panic settled on Michael. He could not point to a single thing out of place, but something about the vessel or circumstances was wrong.

"Backwater!" he ordered.

"What?" the smuggler replied nervously.

"Something's wrong! I want more distance between us! Give way, damn you!" he ordered quietly as he put the tiller to starboard. He shouted loudly, "*D'où êtes-vous?*"

"*Nage à bord vite!*" came the reply.

Hell, this isn't right, he thought. And then it came to him: *A French privateer here, when the fucking English navy is everywhere looking for traitors and assassinators? Possibly, but it's just too Goddamn convenient!*

"Christ, that's no French privateer!" Michael cursed.

"Ahoy the boat!" came a voice across the water.

In English!

"Quiet!" hissed the smuggler. "They surely can't see us yet!"

A splash followed at the stern of the fishing boat.

"What the hell was that?" Michael whispered severely.

"A packet of letters weighted with a rock. They can't be captured!" came the nervous whisper in reply.

"Fool!" Michael replied in a whisper. "Have *you* no sense to keep quiet?"

"Ahoy the boat! Come aboard or we'll fire on you!" came the cry.

Michael drew a small pistol from his pocket.

"Open your mouth and I'll kill you," he warned his companion as he pointed the pistol at him.

"Ahoy the boat! Come aboard or we fire!"

"Give way smartly, sharply now, and quiet about it, and do nothing to alter the course I steer, no matter what they do or say! And if you've betrayed me, you're a dead man! Give way, damn you!"

Michael steered under the stern of the vessel and into the English Channel.

"Fire!" he heard from the ketch, followed by a volley of musketry that stirred the surface of the water nearby like a small shoal of fish. But not a single ball struck the boat.

Almost by a miracle the challenging voice grew more and more distant. After half an hour, Michael put his pistol away and ordered the smuggler to step the mast and set the sail. The fishing boat picked up speed, but the smuggler was a lubberly sailor and Michael cursed him several times.

He glanced at his taciturn escort. The man had not spoken to Michael since they had escaped, and now would not even look at him. He appeared far more nervous than an experienced smuggler's caution should permit. Michael would not trust a man who by all accounts should have little to fear, given his years of smuggling goods and agents across the channel.

He's betrayed me.

He knew this in the same way he had instinctively known that the naval ketch was a trap.

He lashed the tiller, picked up a bucket, and began to bail. He tossed a half bucket of seawater over the side, waited for the smuggler to lean forward with the oars, and like a shillelagh he brought the bucket down upon the man's skull.

Crack!

The bucket staves sprung as the man's head split. Twice more Michael struck the man's head. Blood and fluid dribbled from nose and ears, yet still the man would not die. Michael heaved him onto the gunwale and let him lay there on his belly, breathing heavily, his limp feet resting on the bottom boards, his head hanging over the side and dipping now and then into the sea as the boat rolled back and forth.

"It's a mercy I now do for you, my backstabbing friend,"

Michael said to the dying man. "You chose your path, and now not even I can keep you from dying before your three score and ten, for no man will survive a skull broke in so many places. I should cast you into the sea and let you drown, for a backstabber deserves no better, but I know the reward on my head would have tempted even a saint."

With these words, Michael pulled his dagger from its sheath, jerked the man's head up, and shoved the blade into the dying man's neck. Pushing the sharp edge forward, from ear to ear he slit the man's throat, then released him.

Even over the wind he could hear the man's blood spilling into the channel waters. He heaved the body overboard, washed the blood from the thwart with the broken bucket, and then dipped the knife into the sea to clean the sated blade. He dried it well so that it would not rust.

He rested a moment, almost reveling in his work and the release it gave after the aborted assassination, but he was in many ways too proud and too impatient to gloat too much over any one killing.

Before long he would be in France, and from there he could return to Ireland. He set the mast and sail, stretched his arms, yawned, and, keeping an eye on his pocket compass— illuminated by a bit of slow match lit by flint and steel—and steered his course. The wind had veered, up the Channel now, and he would be unable to sail to Calais without hours of tacking, too dangerous under the circumstances. He would have to try for Dunkirk instead, or somewhere else up the coast. He kept a casual watch, fearing little in the night.

But the day was another matter, and at dawn he saw it, a sail astern and closing.

In his gut he was certain it was the ketch that had challenged him three or four hours before. Rather than flounder around in the darkness after him, frightening him into a different course, they had let him go, then set the course they anticipated he would take, knowing that wind and current gave him little choice, knowing at first light they might come up with him. And so they had.

It's but a damned poor sailor, this tool of a boat, Michael thought, *I've not even a fool's chance at outsailing them now.*

Struck by a sudden revelation, he reached over the transom and into the water, feeling around until he found a taut line. He hauled it up, and found at its end not a packet of letters, but a small grindstone hidden in a canvas sack.

No wonder we sailed so poorly! he thought, and silently cursed himself.

Michael cut the grindstone loose and stared at the swiftly closing naval ketch.

Chapter 26

What cursed chance is this?
—Aphra Behn, *The Rover,* 1677

For a moment at dawn's first clear light, Edward thought they might have lost their quarry, a four-oared fishing boat rigged with a small mast and sprit-sail—a seaworthy craft but a slow one, unable to outsail the ketch. It was a reasonable possibility that the boat might miss the rendezvous or fly from it, in which case Edward had told the smuggler to manage the boat in a lubberly fashion and, if possible, hang a grindstone from its stern to make it row and sail even more slowly.

But not all possibilities can be planned for—ill-Fortune being the most notorious—and it would be easy for the *King Fisher* to take the wrong course or sail past the fishing boat in the darkness in spite of all precautions.

Edward's master and mate had concurred with his estimate of the boat's course, although there was some debate over the effect of the Channel currents. There was little doubt the boat would head for France. A southeasterly wind, strong current, and choppy sea prevented the shortest passage.

"A sail! A small boat, sir!" came the lookout's cry.

"Where and how far?" Edward shouted to the maintop.

"Half a league, maybe two miles, two points on the

starboard bow!"

"What sail does she set?"

"A sprits'l!"

Good! Edward thought to himself. *We might have missed her in the trough of the sea if she were under oars alone.*

"What other sail do you see?"

"Nothing new, sir: two sail two leagues south, fisher-boats I think, and two sail of small ships four leagues north. More sail on the French coast, probably our fleets."

Edward, satisfied that this must be the boat they sought, ordered Scudamore, the ship's master, to set fighting sail—main-topsail and jib for the ketch—and bear toward the chase. Also at his orders the topmen rigged the remaining sails with rope yarns in order to set them quickly in case a potential prize or predator presented herself.

The wind had veered, and its southern breeze sped the *King Fisher* across the Channel after her prey. The chase would not last an hour.

"Make her clear for engaging?" Scudamore asked.

"Small arms and swivels only," Edward ordered. "I don't believe her carriage guns will be much of a threat," he said, joking.

For all practical purposes, the ketch was largely ready for action, given the dangers of the Channel.

Scudamore laughed. "We'll hull him with the swivels if he refuses to strike, or just run him over and send him to David Jones. Damned Jacobite bastard. Will there be a reward, Captain?"

"That will depend on who's in the boat," Edward replied.

"One of those assassinators, I hope. If we catch him alive, maybe we can have some sport with him."

"We'll see. The Admiralty and Crown want him alive and intact," Edward retorted, and thought, *And so do I. If it's you,*

O'Neal, you owe me answers.

He no longer cared whether his recent buffeting had been due to ill-Fortune, deliberate intrigue, or the simple failure of his new philosophy—or his inability to live by it. But the answer no longer mattered: it was open warfare now, he was in his element, and the first of his several prey was plausibly in sight.

"Colors, if you please, ancient, jack, and pendant. Aloft there! Keep a sharp eye out for Dunkirkers!" Edward ordered.

The proximity of Dunkirk's privateering fleet—corsairs ranging from small snows and *barque longues* of ten to thirty tons, to swift ships of two hundred tons or more—was Edward's only real concern. These famous Flemish privateers—now French corsairs—grew up in dual trades: fishermen or merchant seamen in time of peace, corsairs in time of war. They were notoriously successful and more than willing to engage enemy men-of-war. Edward had little interest in a rencontre with a stout privateer, not with his small crew and armament. A French merchantman, however, would be more than welcome for the prize money it would bring.

Minutes later the lookout reported that the two ships to the north appeared to be engaged. Edward was suddenly torn between two duties, that of chasing the prey who had slipped from Romney Marsh and might be an assassin, and assisting a vessel, prey or predator, which might be English or ally. He resigned himself to first pursing their quarry, then investigating the ships to the north.

Soon the lookout called again to the deck, confirming the flash and smoke of great guns. Given the wind's direction, there was so far no sound of gunfire great or small.

"Colors, can you see colors?" Edward shouted to him.

"Not to make out, sir! I see red and maybe white at the sterns. It could be our ancient, and the Monsoor's, but I can't tell at this distance!"

Edward aimed his spying glass at the two ships, now some two leagues distant and a point forward of the larboard quarter. Even with his spying glass he could in no way be sure of the colors they flew, but he suspected a French or Dunkirk corsair attacking an English merchantman.

"Are any of His Majesty's other ships in sight?" Edward shouted aloft, hoping there were. If so, the *King Fisher* could make a signal and perhaps bring assistance to the beleaguered merchantman, if she were English.

"Aye, sir, but leagues distant!"

"Damned bad Fortune for whoever she be," Edward muttered, "but our first duty is to capture the boat's passenger. Afterward we can turn our attention to the engagement."

But the *King Fisher* and her crew were too small to take on a three-masted privateer of any real size, at least if the privateer had a crew to match.

"Aloft there, keep your eye on the action and inform me immediately of every change!" he ordered.

"Aye, aye, Captain!"

The glass was turned. The fishing boat, now under sail and oar, was making better speed. As the fight between the two distant ships played out, the *King Fisher* closed to within musket shot of her prey.

"Wind's larging, Captain," the master noted.

"Southwest," Edward noted in confirmation.

"Even so, the bastard Jacobite can't get away now. He'll look like a bucket of spilled fuck by the time we get through with him."

"That's not what concerns me," Edward said, proffering him the spying glass and pointing.

The corsair had captured its prey and now stood southeast toward the *King Fisher*. She was small, perhaps one hundred twenty-five tons, but she was still twice the size of the ketch.

"France's white ensign, Captain, and Dunkirk's blue and white at the bow and masthead," Scudamore reported.

"We're going to have a fight on our hands," Edward said matter-of-factly. "She's a ship of force, and greater than we: we must be more clever than her captain and crew if we wish to sleep in a whole skin under English colors tonight. Make the *King Fisher* clear for a fight, but keep our course. We'll first have our quarry if we can, under the Dunkirker's nose if necessary."

The master returned Edward's spying glass and gave the necessary orders. Edward sent one of the two ship's boys below to fetch his sword and pistols, and gave orders for brandy and sugar for the crew. It felt good to command again, good to have a man-of-war of any size beneath his feet, ready for a fight.

And fighting a ship was something he knew well. He had learned the practical lessons first from his father, who passed on the lessons he had learned from Christopher Myngs and Henry Morgan. Later, more through accident than intent, Edward had twice sailed with Laurens de Graff, the Dutch filibuster who could command a ship in a fight better than any sea rover of the Caribbean, ever. Edward was even present during de Graff's successful engagement against the two greatest ships of the pirate-hunting Armada de Barlovento. Added to this was Edward's own extensive experience in command in action. To him, a rencontre at sea was nothing more than one with swords, only greater. The tactics and strategies were identical.

"Lads," he said boldly, after Scudamore had called all hands, "today we'll soon capture not only a likely traitor, an assassinator, a Jacobite enemy who would see the papist James put back on the throne, but we'll also capture a Dunkirker if she's so foolish as to try and take us! Remember that the *King Fisher* was once captured by the French after a glorious stand against an eighteen gun French privateer—but now the *King Fisher* is English again! We'll match that glorious English captain and crew for courage, and have their revenge! Remember for what you fight: your wives, your women, your children, your families, your King, your country—and prize money!"

"Huzzah! Huzzah! Huzzah!"

"Each man to his duty, and we'll give King William a traitor to hang and a white rag he can wipe his ass with!"

"Huzzah!" shouted the crew again, each man licking his lips, a few of them surreptitiously gripping rigging to wipe the sweat from their palms.

"You heard the captain!" Scudamore—a skinny, salty, tarry son-of-a-bitch—bellowed as he walked among the crew. "Fuck me and damn my eyes, we'll bugger all these Flemish bastards and the squinty-eyed, long-nosed French curs with them. Damn, I hate the French, even if their women are like long, low, snug frigates, and damn, that was a fine French woman who poxed me!"

A quarter hour later the fishing boat was within half-musket shot, one hundred yards or so, and the corsair, under topsails and foresail, bore down on both. Edward thought it curious that the Dunkirker had not set more sail, but perhaps her captain assumed the ketch intended to fight, or he was being careful to discover what she was before engaging. Or just as likely, she was still clearing up her decks and making repairs from her recent fight.

Less than a glass before she's on us, Edward realized. *We must work quickly.*

A few days ago, he might have regretted, if it actually were O'Neal in the boat, not what he was about to do, but that circumstances had come to this. But no more, not today, not now. He had no compunction about firing on the boat and on whomever was in it.

Edward picked up a speaking trumpet and walked to the bow.

"Ahoy the boat!"

No answer.

"Ahoy the boat!"

Again, no answer.

"Ahoy the boat! Strike amain, or we fire!"

Still there was no answer. Suddenly the boat changed course to starboard and came on a bowline close to the wind, a course that would almost immediately run her past the gauntlet of the *King Fisher's* broadside, but also one that would force the naval ketch to change course as well—and right into the arms of the Dunkirker.

"Damn, he's a bold one!" Edward cursed. "And a clever one too, knowing that if he escapes our broadside he'll probably escape us entirely. Mr. Scudamore, give him our broadside as he passes!"

And as the boat came under the starboard guns, Edward hailed once more, to no reply. The *King Fisher* opened fire. The partridge shot—bags of musket balls—on top of three-pound round shot tore into the fishing boat, punching holes in the hull, sending splinters across the water, and shivering the boat's mast, leaving its sail dragging overboard. No crew could be seen: anyone aboard had surely hidden in the bilge for protection.

"Mr. Scudamore, put the Dunkirker in our wake!"

"Aye, aye, Captain!"

The wind had veered again, to the west. Edward, the thrill of being able to fight surging through his body, wanted two broadsides in the corsair before he might be forced to run. Given the Dunkirker's speed, it looked as if there might not be much of a running fight at all, but a true rencontre.

Like most of his profession, the Scotsman loved a sea fight above almost all else. Today it was vital that the *King Fisher* fire the first broadside: it might disable the enemy, would doubtless diminish the effectiveness of the enemy's return broadside, and would definitely encourage his crew's fighting spirit.

The *King Fisher's* new course brought the Dunkirker directly astern.

"Mr. Scudamore, we can't outrun her. Send a few men aloft as if to set all sail, then be prepared to turn hard to starboard on my order and rake her fore and aft. Have the gun captains aim low!"

"Aye, sir!"

Using his spying glass, Edward examined the pursuing ship closely.

One hundred to one hundred-twenty tons, ports for twelve guns, six per side, all in the open on her main deck, no chase guns, looks like she carries ten or twelve three- or four-pound iron guns; we'll find out soon enough. At least twice our weight of broadside. Long, snug lines, small quarterdeck, no raised forecastle, a crew of fifty to seventy I'll bet, her decks are massed with men. Twice or thrice our crew. She just took a prize after a fight, perhaps has some wounded; if we're lucky maybe she has only forty or fifty men now, it's hard to tell; but we've a fighting chance, we might well take her if we can prolong the fight, and if not, we'll beat her bloody until she shows her heels.

By comparison, even with her increased armament and crew, the sixty-one ton *King Fisher* mounted only six small carriage guns, along with four swivels on the rails, and carried only thirty-five men. She set a tall course like that of a fishing buss, a topsail above it, a latteen and small topsail on a short mizzenmast, a small spritsail beneath her striking bowsprit, and a fore staysail and jib between mainmast and bowsprit. Her bow was bluff, her stern pinked. Although she sailed best quartering and might outsail most vessels right before the wind, her shrouds were set well back so that her yards could be braced up closer to the wind than most square-rigged vessels.

The corsair's captain did as Edward predicted: seeing his quarry send men aloft as if to set all sail for a running fight, he ordered some of his men aloft to do the same. The enemy captain expected the ketch to run, not fight.

"Now, Mr. Scudamore!" Edward ordered when the Dunkirk privateer approached within two hundred and fifty yards.

The *King Fisher* turned hard to larboard and fired her small broadside of three guns and two swivels, plus several muskets, low across the Dunkirker's decks, raking her almost fore and aft. Splinters flew when the shot from the three small guns hit their mark, although the curved bow deflected one of the light round shot. The weight of metal was small, but still killed and wounded men and cut up rigging and sails. The Dunkirker fell briefly off her course and was unable to bring her own broadside immediately to bear.

"Come about, Mr. Scudamore, and give her our starboard battery!"

Again round shot and musket balls flew, this time raking the lightly built Dunkirker truly bow to stern.

"Mr. Scudamore, ease the helm, put her back in our wake, set all sail!" he ordered. The seamen designated to handle the ship hauled on sheets, breaking the light rope yarns that held the sails to their yards. Almost instantly the ketch was under full sail on a southerly course. Edward would have preferred to run with the wind dead astern under only the main course and topsail, negating the frigate's advantage in canvas and putting the ketch on her only point of sail superior to her adversary's, but such a course would carry them to the enemy coastline.

"We'll sheer larboard and starboard while we run," Edward

ordered, "and give a broadside each way as long as we can. The Dunkirker has the legs of us, but we'll beat her bloody before she ranges alongside, then we'll seize our chance and board or destroy her! Point your guns as far aft as you can. Alternate chain and bar shot, elevate the muzzles, fire at will! Bugger her rigging! Musketeers and swivels! Load and fire as fast as you can, aim at her decks, kill her crew, swivels load with musket balls! I want to see blood from her scuppers! For England, King William, and our good Queen Mary who died too soon!"

"Huzzah! Huzzah! Huzzah!"

Most privateers preferred a boarding action to engaging broadsides, and this gave the *King Fisher* a fighting chance. She was nimble enough, if not faster than her enemy, and would fight large, before the wind. She was outnumbered, outgunned, and probably outsailed—exactly the kind of engagement that brought out the best in Edward and this crew of English tars. And it was a relief to the Creole Scotsman to be able to fight back after the chases between England and Ireland.

The English ketch sheered larboard and starboard once each, giving the Dunkirker two small broadsides. Thankfully, the enemy had no bow chase guns, nor ports for them, and bore the brunt of the *King Fisher's* chain and bar shot. It cut up the Dunkirker's fore course and some of her rigging, and flung splinters—jagged chunks and rapier-like slivers of them—across her deck to flay and pierce the flesh of men.

But it would not be long before the Dunkirker ranged from the *King Fisher's* wake. Edward had no idea of the damage to the Dunkirker's crew, but three of the English crew were wounded already from French musket-fire.

"He's furling his spritsail and bringing the yard along the bowsprit!" shouted the lookout aloft.

"Mr. Scudamore, do the same! We don't dare board him, but we can worry him a bit by making him think we might!"

Through his spying glass Edward inspected the enemy: several seamen were busy lashing her sprit-yard alongside the bowsprit, and boarders were massing on the forecastle.

"He intends to weather and board us, Mr. Scudamore," Edward said. "When he steers from our wake, put your helm to starboard and we'll clap on a wind and weather him. If we gain any distance on him, we'll tack again and again until we're back on the English coast."

As Edward anticipated, the Dunkirker began to bear windward from the *King Fisher's* wake, doubtless to shoot abreast of the ketch, fire a broadside, then bear in to board.

"Stand by your helm, wait for my order," Edward shouted to the helmsmen. Then, to Scudamore, "Keep the musketeers and gun crews below the rails; he might put a broadside in us when we change course. Wait, wait, here he goes... Now!"

The *King Fisher* turned hard to starboard to come on a bowline. But instead of following immediately, as Edward had hoped the Dunkirker would, the enemy kept to her course in spite of the ground she would lose. When her broadside came abreast of the ketch's stern, the Dunkirker fired across her larboard quarter: six four pounders, a small broadside by any standard, but almost thrice the *King Fisher's* weight of metal.

And by ill-Fortune it shot the ketch's mizzen-topmast by the board.

Edward cursed under his breath, then shouted, "Cut all clear away! Now, before she can board us!"

The Dunkirker came on a bowline and, with the *King Fisher's* sails aback and her mizzen topmast and sail in the water, was easily able to regain the ground she had lost, not to mention the weather gage. Soon the Dunkirker would present her starboard broadside again.

Shit-fire, piss, and damnation in general! Edward fumed. *Damned ill-Fortune!*

A second broadside came as the Dunkirker gained the weather gage, this one of partridge, *mitraille* the French called it, on top of round shot, a deadly vomit that struck the ketch's starboard quarter, killing one seaman and wounding two others.

The Dunkirker bore in toward the *King Fisher's* larboard beam, surely to board.

"We're clear, Captain!" shouted the bosun.

"I need steerage way, Mr. Scudamore!"

But even with the wreckage now cut away, there was no chance the *King Fisher* could avoid being boarded. Edward ordered the ketch brought as close to the wind as possible in order to bring her broadside to bear.

"Fire!" he ordered, and the ketch's tiny larboard broadside sent hot metal amidst the boarders massed at the enemy bow. "Reload! Double shot the larboard guns, quickly now, partridge on top! Fire only on my command! Cutlasses and pistols to the crew! I need three grenadiers with as many grenades as we have, amidships! Musketeers and swivels, keep up your fire, clear their decks!" Edward ordered, sword in hand, as he ran from stern to bow and back again, exhorting the crew. "At the helm! When I shout the order to port your helm, I want you to put it to *starboard*, as hard as you can, so we turn port, not starboard—do you understand? You must not hesitate! Mr. Scudamore, I need two seamen with grapplings and lashings amidships, we've little time!"

The Dunkirker edged in toward the *King Fisher*, musket and swivel fire now forcing nearly everyone below the rails.

Easy, easy, not yet, not yet... Edward thought.

Then, "Port your helm!" he shouted.

And as ordered, the helmsmen put the tiller to starboard, turning the ketch to port and ninety degrees to the Dunkirker's bow.

The vessels struck together, the Dunkirker's bowsprit piercing the ketch's main shrouds.

"Fire!" Edward shouted. "Grenades, clear their decks!"

The *King Fisher's* three small guns sent a pair of iron shot apiece, plus lead musket balls and burning wads, upon the sides and deck of the Dunkirker. Her musketeers fired into the open deck, and the grenadiers lobbed iron grenades. The two seamen flung their grappling hooks, hauled them taut, and belayed them, then, braving enemy fire, quickly lashed the bowsprit to the shrouds. Bullets and shrapnel flew about both decks, killing one of the lashers, as confusion, noise, smoke, fear, and violence reigned.

The Dunkirker was in a terrible position, the worst of any who wished to board. She was exposed to the *King Fisher's* guns but could fire none of hers in return. If she tried to enter her boarders, she had to do so over her bow and bowsprit, where only one or two could board at a time—near suicide.

But to survive, her commander had to do something, and boarding was now the only course. His crew had sought shelter behind gun carriages, the riding bitts and windlass in the bow, and behind the steerage bulkhead where some of his men fired from loopholes.

A fusillade of lead and a small hail of grenades flew about the *King's Fisher's* deck as the Flemmingsand French prepared to board. Ears rang and teeth jarred from the shattering detonations, and men fell dead and wounded. One grenade fired a cartridge box, which in turn fired a cannon cartridge, burning three nearby seamen and filling the air with even more smoke. Amidst this choking fog the enemy crew, all armed with pistol and cutlass, swarmed across their bowsprit.

"Shoot them down, lads!" Edward shouted, drawing a pistol and firing. He shoved it back under his sash and belt, drew another, and cocked it with the heel of his sword hand.

"Grenades! More grenades, hurl them upon their foc's'l!"

One his own grenadiers was shot down, his grenade landing at Edward's feet, its fuse burning. Edward, a small voice in his head shouting, *O Shit! O Shit! O Shit!*, dropped his backsword, grabbed the grenade, and hurled it among the Flemings and French massed at Dunkirker's bow. As he bent over to pick up his backsword, he found an enemy suddenly over him, a purple-faced obscenity with a sword, dripping sweat onto Edward's face and snapping a misfiring pistol at his head. From his low position, Edward thrust quickly into the man's belly, then with the pistol in his left hand shot another boarder in the face.

All around him was nearly the worst sort of fight, on open decks at sea. Only fighting below deck in the darkness could make it worse. Otherwise, there was nothing like it in the world, not even the worst of close battles against fortifications could compare with the ruthless savagery of such a battle. All around him men shot, cleaved, and clawed at each other, survival by violence now the driving instinct.

Several of Edward's crew were armed with half-pikes which did good service, keeping the Flemings at bay. With his backsword Edward cut powerfully at another of the enemy, already pierced by a pike and trying to pull himself up the shaft in order to bury his cutlass into the English seaman who had wounded him. Edward swung a hard, tight outside cut and buried his backsword in the enemy seaman's skull just above the ear. By the time the Scotsman had pulled his sword loose, he found himself grappling with another Fleming, but only briefly, as the corsair was stabbed in the back by an Englishman with a half-pike.

By now there was a pile of dead and wounded at the main shrouds, and the Flemings gave up their attempt at boarding. From cover they fired at their English enemy, and the English fire back in return. Edward unloaded his remaining pistols at the enemy, then quickly drew cartridges from his cartouche box and reloaded.

"The great guns!" Edward shouted, "Continue to load and fire, destroy their men! We must not let them board again!"

For an hour this battle from cover raged, Edward's crew now having the advantage. Twice the Dunkirk captain tried to rally his men to board again, and twice those who tried were shot down.

Several of the Dunkirker's guns were now dismounted, or their carriages so shattered that they were of no use. Her crew lay in bloody heaps on the deck, a score and a half by Edward's quick estimate. He felt certain that if he ordered the *King Fisher* to cut loose, she could batter the corsair at will and compel her enemy to strike. He would not risk his remaining men—only half were not yet dead or incapacitated by wounds—in boarding the Dunkirker, and if he remained here in a battle of attrition he might soon have too few men to repel another boarding attempt.

"Loose the grapplings and cut away the lashings!" Edward ordered, "And be ready to give a broadside as soon as we're free!"

Immediately the bosun and a seaman loosed the grapplings and with boarding axes cut the lashings away. The *King Fisher* began to drift clear.

"We're fouled!" shouted the bosun as the enemy's bowsprit caught in a backstay.

"Cut away the backstay if you must!" Edward shouted. The bosun had already anticipated him, but too late: the maintopmast suddenly went by the board, breaking the bosun's arm and knocking a seaman into the water.

"Cut all clear away! Fire your guns when clear!" Edward shouted.

We still have a chance, he thought, *we can force them to strike, we'll have their ship, and for now we still have sails and a rudder to work with. We might even take back that English merchantman if we can jury-rig a topmast.*

Once more clear of fallen mast and sail, the *King Fisher* put a broadside into the Dunkirker, and then two more, in return receiving only one badly aimed broadside of two guns.

Edward put the speaking trumpet to his mouth and raised his backsword. "Strike amain, *Monsieur le capitaine! Amène! Amain* for the King of England!" Edward repeated the request in mangled Dutch.

But the Dunkirker would not strike. Edward did not understand it: her rigging was in tatters and her crew so beaten that they could not prevail, even given the ketch's condition.

Edward glanced around him, and suddenly understood why her captain would not strike, an understanding punctuated by a shower of water and splinters from the Dunkirker's slightly better-aimed broadside this time.

Half a mile away was a black ship, Dutch-built but flying French colors, with as many as fifty guns. Edward immediately recognized her. With his own crew and rigging shattered, there was but one thing he could do.

"Mr. Scudamore, strike our ancient and lay us by."

The master, bloodied and battered, left scarlet footprints as he hauled down the colors at the staff at the stern, as the bosun, in spite of his broken arm, directed the management of the sails.

On the deck nearby was the lookout, shot from aloft, and if not shot quite dead, then killed by the fall. His jaw jutted at an odd angle. Edward wondered why it was that such things stood out in battle; he wondered that amidst fear and fight such details were noticed at all. Even had the lookout survived to warn them, even had Edward himself not been so preoccupied that he failed to espy an approaching enemy, there was still little they could have done to escape the ship under whose guns they now lay.

Edward cast his sword to the deck and looked at the shattered privateer. There was little cheering among the enemy crew. One lone seaman, a Frenchman by his accent, shouted, "*Bougres!*" and "*Fuckeurs!*"

Edward surveyed his crew, and over the business of the young man acting as surgeon's mate. The day was suddenly quiet but for the moans of the wounded, whose blood mixed with that of the dead and ran freely from the scuppers of both vessels.

Chapter 27

Women, wind, and Fortune, are given to change.
—Spanish proverb, 17th and 18th centuries

For much of the day, four vessels lay by in the trough of the sea.

Other sail were sighted, but no rescue in the form of English or Dutch cruiser appeared, although there should have been many such at sea. All of the wounded—English, and others of the British and Irish islands, Flemish, French, two or three Scandinavians and Africans, along with a solitary Venetian—were carried aboard the captured English merchantman, named *Carolina Merchant*, while the rigging of the two battered combatants was spliced and knotted enough to enable them to sail into Dunkirk.

The fourteen among Edward's crew who had not been killed or seriously wounded were stripped of most of their clothing and of all of their accouterments and other belongings, and divided between the corsair, called *La Fortune*, and the *King Fisher*.

The black ship was *La Tulipe Noir*, a Dutch prize of fifty guns, but pierced for fifty-six, now serving as a French privateer with a crew of equal parts Frenchmen and Flemings. Her captain was French, and Edward recognized her as the corsair from which he and the *Peregrinator* had narrowly escaped off

Kinsale. It was aboard this dark ship that Edward, after being stripped of most of his clothing, no matter that he was the captain, was carried and brought before the French commander on his quarterdeck. Up close, the dark ship did not seem supernatural, nor her commander a demon, as his dreams had once implied.

As Edward was brought aboard, he was startled to see Michael O'Neal, clearly plucked from the sea and little changed in the years since he had last seen him. He was uninjured, having miraculously escaped three guns' worth of round shot and musket balls. Michael surveyed Edward with an air of superiority. No words passed between then, and two armed seamen escorted Edward to the quarterdeck.

"A valiant action, Monsieur," said the French captain with a bow and in excellent but heavily-accented English. "I am *Capitaine* Roland Rimbaud, at your service." The French commander was as tall as Edward, maybe a bit taller, slightly heavier, and quite self-assured in the very French manner. "I welcome you aboard *La Tulipe Noir* of fifty guns, formerly the *Prins Friso* of the United Provinces, at present a commissioned *corsaire* of France. She was captured in '94 by the *comte de* Forbin and has proved, I think, more profitable to the French."

"Monsieur," Edward replied with a bow. Somehow it came across as a dignified act, in spite of his being barefoot and dressed only in shirt and breeches. "I am Captain Edward MacNaughton, commanding the *King Fisher* of His Majesty's Royal Navy. I ask that my crew be treated respectfully and according to the laws of war, that their wounds be cared for, that our surgeon's mate be permitted to assist in treating them, and that the dead be given a proper burial."

"This will be done, assuredly. *Capitaine* Sauret of *La Fortune* is an honorable man, but alas, sorely wounded. I have asked him to return your clothing to you, Monsieur, but I cannot compel him to do so, although I am certain he will not object. Given his valor, I will not accept that you surrendered to me, but to him. You will remain his prisoner, and your vessel his prize. May I send word to him that I have your parole of honor not to try to lead your men in an escape? Then you would have the freedom of the deck and the comforts you deserve after such a valiant effort."

"No, *Capitaine*, not while I'm at sea," Edward replied.

"I understand. Perhaps in *Dunkerque* you will consider ransom or parole?"

"In Dunkirk, assuredly."

"*Très bien.* I hear also that we have almost met before, off *Quinsael* of Ireland. Were not you the *capitaine* of the small *fregatte galère*?"

"Only a passenger."

"You had nothing to do with her escape?"

"I suggested a strategy, I commanded the guns."

"Then my compliments again, Monsieur," said the French captain, and bowed once more. Edward returned the bow, guessing that the information about the rencontre off Ireland had probably come from O'Neal. Edward had expected to meet his quarry here in the great cabin, and was disappointed he did not. The French captain poured him a cup of wine.

"To Fortune, Monsieur."

"To Fortune," Edward replied. He raised his cup to the French commander, then drank. "The man plucked from the water, O'Neal I believe his name is, he's aboard your ship," Edward said, after relishing the excellent wine. "And I believe you may know him already. I'm certain I know him."

The Frenchman drank, then smiled thinly before he spoke. "*Capitaine*, you know well I cannot discuss such matters with you, even if you claim to know the man who has been plucked from the fishes of the sea. You had reason to pursue him, therefore I have reason to protect him."

"Of course. Your reply is sufficient confirmation."

"As you please. Unfortunately, I must return you now to your captors. I and my crew have duty elsewhere. Even more unfortunately, unless I have your parole, I will strongly recommend to *Capitaine* Sauret that you be kept in irons until you arrive in *Dunkerque*, given the valor you and your crew have most recently demonstrated, not to mention your reputation as a *flibustier* in the New World."

"I understand," Edward said, setting the empty wine cup on the bittacle nearby.

"*Au revoir, Capitaine* MacNaughton."

"Indeed, Captain Rimbaud: until we meet again."

And so well shall, Edward thought, *for two famous meetings always imply a third.*

French seamen rowed the Scotsman back to the *King Fisher*, one of them keeping a wary eye on him, and a blunderbuss pointed at him.

Flibustier, they whispered. *Forban anglais! Gardez vous!*

Edward and five of his crew were shackled in pairs at the ankle in the after hold of the shattered ketch, and sat uncomfortably atop an old sail covering the vessel's stores, with only four and a half feet of headroom. The younger of the ship's boys—the other, of thirteen years, had been killed in the action, to Edward's great dismay—was aboard, and had been given the freedom of the vessel. The prize captain did not consider him a threat, and so put him to work doing menial labor.

As opportunity presented after the vessels got underway again, the ship's boy, with a confident look of stout resolve over hidden fear, came to the open main hatch above to keep the prisoners apprised in whispers. The prize crew was busy keeping watch and making repairs.

"Our consorts, where are they?" Edward demanded quietly.

"*La Fortune* is half a mile ahead and to windward, the *Carolina Merchant* is two or three cables leeward on our starboard quarter."

"How many are the prize crew?"

"Eight, sir."

"Arms?"

"The helmsman has three pistols at his girdle. There's a guard at his side, he's got a blunderbuss and a brace of pistols. A couple of the others also have arms, but they've laid them aside on the quarterdeck while they work. There's an arms chest and three or four cartouche boxes at the taffrail, too."

"Who has the keys to our irons?"

"That fat bastard of a prize captain, I think he's a bosun's mate."

"Are they on his person?"

"Aye, captain."

"Come back in an hour if you can, lad."

"Aye, sir!"

"Nightfall," Edward said to the men around him when the boy was gone. "I doubt they intend to make Dunkirk before tomorrow morning. We'll rise and take them in the dark."

"We're with you, Captain," Noble, the mate, said, "but we need arms as well as the keys. Two or three cutlasses would be enough: we can gut these Flemings and Monsoors. By God, sir, I'll be the first man up the ladder." He was a stout jack tar, a man with two decades before the mast.

"And if grasshoppers had muskets, blackbirds wouldn't eat them," Scudamore replied slyly.

"Damn, Mr. Scudamore, I do get tired of hearing you say that!" the mate expostulated.

Scudamore grinned.

"We do have arms," Edward said quietly. "Mr. Scudamore's just having a little joke at your expense."

"Sir?"

"Beneath the sail we're sitting on, among the stores. I had the master hide them just before we were boarded. What do we have, Mr. Scudamore?"

"Two loaded fuzees, two horns, a bag of swan shot, three loaded pistols, two cartouche boxes with twenty cartridges each, five cutlasses, two boarding axes, two grenades, plus match, flint, and steel."

"Christ! A bloody arms chest!" exclaimed the mate, too loudly.

"Whisht!" Edward ordered.

When the hour passed, the ship's boy came to the hatch again, a great fat Frenchman, one of two among the Flemish prize crew, shouting after him.

"Sir—they intend to make Dunkirk by nightfall!" he whispered loudly.

"Damn!" Edward muttered.

We'll have to take her in the light of day. The keys, we need the keys.

"Listen, lad, can you lure the fat man down here in half an hour? You must, for without the keys we may be lost, or at best in a stand-off until we reach Dunkirk, and there's no way out of there for us. Tell him I want to speak with him, tell him you don't know why. Half an hour!"

"Aye, sir, I'll do it!"

"Are you sure, lad? If he suspects you, he'll hang you from a yardarm if he doesn't first flog and bugger you to death."

"I'll bring him, Captain, by God I will!"

"Good lad!"

When the boy was gone, Edward ordered the arms distributed, and soon they lay ready beneath the prisoners' legs, well-enough hidden in the half-darkness of the platform in the hold. He gave each man his quarters.

"Cold steel only, unless you have no choice! I don't want our consorts to hear musket or pistol shot! I go up first and lead my party—Noble, Bonbonous, and Studdy—aft to attack the guards and secure the arms. Mr. Scudamore will lead the rest of you forward. Again, cold steel unless you have no choice!"

Half an hour later, the prize captain appeared as the boy had promised. The lad dropped through the hatch to join his captain. The prize captain cursed at him, then shouted down at Edward, who shouted back that one of his men was wounded, that he had not noticed it at first, that this was a common thing, not to notice some wounds when first received during battle, but now it was bleeding. Could the Monsieur please come below, if not to release and treat him, at least to examine him and give them something to stanch the bleeding? The ruse was feeble, Edward realized. The prize captain might ignore them, or just send the boy below with some rags.

Not surprisingly, he told them to go bugger themselves, and if they pleased, to use their breeches to plug the man's bleeding hole. What did women do in like circumstances? He laughed heartily at his wit.

At that moment, Edward would have killed the Frenchman if he could, then he recalled that no one was bleeding, that it was all a sham. Perhaps the man was a quite jovial fellow at home, or in time of peace.

From behind the prize captain came a few shouts. The fat man looked up, shouted something, then looked back down at the prisoners. Once more Edward pleaded with him for aid for his wounded comrade. Once more the Frenchman insulted them, telling them he would sooner piss on them than assist them.

"*Votre capitaine, Monsieur, je vous demande de voir votre capitaine,*" Edward replied, merely to keep the conversation, such as it was, going, in hopes of luring the man below.

"*Je suis le capitaine!*" the Frenchman said triumphantly, then turned around to present his ass to the prisoners, smacking his hands on it as he did. He turned back around and gestured for the boy to join him again on deck.

"Tell him to bugger himself," Edward whispered.

The boy did better. "I'll not fetch and be beat by you anymore, you French sow, you man-buggering garlic-eating son of a fat whore and some twig of a man with pea-sized stones and a yard not two inches long who didn't even know what hole to put it and his sour seed in. No doubt you were born shitted from your mother's ass and fell on your head and were fed pig snot and rat snot by your poxy mother from her shriveled poxed titties until you bloated up so big she couldn't get you out the door..."

The Frenchman, who understood English well enough, and even if he had not would still have understood the tone, dropped with surprising speed into the hold, falling foolishly for the trap—overconfidence can be fatal to the bearer—as Edward, with a big smile for the boy's impressive command of invective, drew his pistol and pointed it to the man's head. But for the fact that a firearm pointed at one's head is never funny, it would have made for an amusing scene: Edward, paired in irons at the ankles with another man, a large man towering above, and Edward speaking as if they were politely suggesting to an obnoxious guest at a dinner party that he pipe down or leave.

"*Les clefs, monsieur,*" Edward requested.

Cruel and obscene he might be, but the Frenchman was no coward. He raised his head to shout but squealed instead and collapsed to his knees, the ship's boy having kicked him in the groin.

Edward and his companion prisoner stood as much as they could, and Edward swung the barrel of his pistol sideways, striking the man in the head, an awkward but far more deadly blow than with the butt. The mate and his companion-in-irons reached out and grabbed him, one of them trying to strangle him with his thumbs shoved into the thick folds of the man's neck, the other, along with another pair of prisoners, holding him down.

All but the Frenchman and ship's boy were jumbled and restrained by their irons. The fat man half-stood, stumbled, and was brought to his knees again. He tried to cry out but could not, and to ensure his silence one of the seamen covered his mouth and pinched his nostrils shut. The Frenchman's throat was so fat and strong that he could not be choked completely.

It was more than a ridiculous scene: it was surreal. Men in shackles tried hold down a very large man who with one hand held his crushed stones, and with the other tried to shove his fingers into the eyes of the man trying to choke the life out of him, all as Edward hissed a whisper of, "The keys, get the fucking keys!" The mate pummeled the Frenchman, driving fists and elbows into his head until their captor began to collapse and fall slowly to his belly, giving the seaman the chance to finish choking him. A moment later the prize captain was unmoving but for a slight shifting with the sea. Amazingly, he still breathed.

"Lad, aloft with you now, lookout for anyone coming!"

Immediately the boy clambered up the ladder and stuck his head out. "Captain, half are aft or aloft, half are for'ard wolding the bowsprit."

"Good lad!" he whispered back. "Now stow yourself here! The rest of you, pull the Frenchman into the shadows, quickly now! Damn, where are the keys! Finally! Hurry now, off with our irons. Cheerily, lads, before someone looks in on us. All are ready? One... two... three!"

Edward, already up the ladder, his head just below the

hatch, leaped onto the deck and ran aft, screaming like a Highlander charging the English line.

One in front, engage him first, always attack first at the man directly in front! he thought, but already he had cut the man down, all else being afterthought.

Someone leapt onto his back and knocked him to the deck. The point of Edward's cutlass caught between two planks: the blade broke and the hilt flew from his hand. For some seconds he struggled with his enemy, not knowing how the rest of the battle went.

He stood, heaved, twisted, and fell to the deck again, his enemy beneath him and taking a hard fall. The man's grip loosened, Edward struck with his fists, knees, and elbows. His enemy grasped at him, tearing at his waistcoat, clawing at his eyes and testicles. The man got a knee up to his chest, then shoved, knocking Edward back. Quickly Edward pushed up from the deck and drove a knee into the man's chin, then grabbed him by the hair at the temple, flung him to the deck, and kicked him until the man spat blood from his mouth as he cried, "*Bon quartier!*"

Edward looked around to get his bearings, to find a weapon, anything to block the thrust of cutlass into his back. Instinctively he flinched, turned, and saw a man with a cloven skull fall to the deck.

A Fleming, one of them, not one of us, he realized after a moment.

Studdy, a stout able bodied seaman, had done this bloody service with a boarding ax.

"She's ours, Captain! Damn me, she's ours!" shouted Scudamore.

And so she was, and without a shot being fired. Three of the privateers were dead and four were wounded, including the prize captain below. The lookout had begged quarter and came off without a scratch. The English had lost none, nor had any wounds other than minor cuts and bruises and one broken nose. The surprise had been complete.

Edward rubbed his hands. They were bruised and sore, as were his elbows, forearms, and knees, but at least he hadn't broken any fingers. His back felt as if it had been kicked.

Must've been one of the falls, he thought.

Moments later Scudamore pointed out that Edward was bleeding. It was a small wound, the point of a cutlass having caught on his left shoulder blade.

It was the flinch; the bastard did get me after all.

Scudamore quickly stuffed a rag under his shirt and coat to stanch the light bleeding.

"We'll run, then, Captain?" asked the master after they had ensured control of the ketch, securely bound the prisoners, and tended to the wounded.

"Not before we take the privateer as a prize, and take back the merchantman too," Edward replied more casually than he felt. *La Fortune* was now abeam, about a mile to windward, and the *Carolina Merchant* some eight hundred yards away, ahead and to leeward.

And aboard La Fortune *is O'Neal,* Edward reminded himself.

Scudamore smiled at his captain. "You're not jesting, are you, sir? Captain, I've no doubt we could surprise the Flemings, but with the damage to our foremast and rigging there's no chance we can weather them. And we damn sure can't board them from the lee, sir, even if we do surprise 'em and kill half their crew. But damn me, sir, if it's the capture of the Dunkirker and the prize you want, then damn me, we'll do it. We'll need some of your buccaneer tricks—begging your pardon, sir."

"Indeed. And we'll show these Dunkirk privateers a few shortly."

"Aye, Captain?"

"Aye, Mr. Scudamore. See to it that the guns are loaded, and make sure the gun crews keep their heads below the gunwale. Don't open the ports. Load the swivels, too, and bring up and load every small arm we have on board, and I mean that, *every* one you can find, plus cartouche boxes and cutlasses. Bring four charges on deck for each great gun; I know it's dangerous but we haven't anyone to spare to fetch charges from below. Lay the grapplings on deck, and gag all the prisoners; we must have them quiet."

"And then, sir? We'll whistle and a wind will blow them alongside? No disrespect intended, Captain. I'm just wondering how this grasshopper is going to fuck with a blackbird that wants to eat him."

"This *grasshopper* will do it with the first of two buccaneer tricks we'll going to play, Mr. Scudamore."

The master cocked his head slightly, smiled, raised his eyebrows, shook his head, and departed to execute Edward's orders.

Edward removed his coat and waistcoat, to ensure he could not be recognized at a distance. The rag remained stuck to the wound in his back.

"All is as you ordered, Captain," Mr. Scudamore soon reported.

The small crew looked on curiously.

"You're wondering how we'll gain the weather gage, Mr. Scudamore?"

"Aye, Captain."

"Aye, Mr. Scudamore? Have you not other *eyes*? We already have the weather gage."

The master shook his head. "Captain?"

"Look there, Mr. Scudamore, what do you see?" Edward asked, pointing, but not at the Dunkirker.

"Damn me for a fool, Captain!"

"Make the French signal for the *Carolina Merchant* to lie by for us—the one the privateer was so good to provide us with when he signaled to the *Carolina Merchant* after we were captured—and bear down upon her."

The master, grinning from ear to ear, gave the orders.

Fifteen minutes later it was over. The *King Fisher* hoisted her signal, and, as the prize lay by to be hailed, the battered ketch ran alongside, hoisted her English colors, fired a broadside of partridge into her waist, put her tiller to port, and boarded. Four of the eight man prize crew were killed or wounded in the broadside, and the rest cried, more or less, "*Bon quartier! Moi, j'irai au Angleterre! Bon quartier, s'il vous plait!*"

Good quarter was granted. The English seamen very quickly trussed their prisoners, wounded and able alike, and put them in the hold. Just as quickly, they released and armed the dozen English merchant prisoners. Edward ordered the French colors left flying on the *Carolina Merchant*, and four men to carefully load and fire muskets from cover on her decks, repeatedly, over the *King Fisher* as she lay grappled alongside. He ordered grappling hooks and grenades readied, the pretense of a fight between the two vessels kept up, and the *Carolina Merchant's* ensign rigged so it could be hoisted quickly.

La Fortune's lookouts espied something wrong, and the privateer bore down on the grappled ships.

"She's bearing down fast, Captain, half a mile at best," Scudamore warned a quarter hour later. "We're ready to play your second trick."

The next five minutes passed tensely. With sails struck, the two grappled ships had turned up into the wind, leaving the *Carolina Merchant's* starboard broadside facing the oncoming privateer. Naval and merchant seamen squatted below the merchantman's gunwale, ready to run out her old sakers and fire a broadside of five and a quarter pound round shot topped by bags of musket balls. If all went well, *La Fortune* would assume the *Carolina Merchant* was still in French hands and, per good tactics, come alongside to reinforce her against the *King Fisher*.

But she would be greeted with a broadside.

"Captain, they're suspicious, they don't trust us, they won't bite," warned the master as *La Fortune* came into hailing distance.

"Wave at them as if we're in distress," Edward ordered, then, putting a speaking trumpet to his mouth, shouted, *"Aidez nous! Les Anglais preparent aborder ensuite!"* He wished he spoke Dutch, as if he were a Fleming, but French would do.

"Come, you French-Dutch HogenMogen hugger buggers, come alongside, board us...." muttered the master. "Damn, sir, I don't think they're going to board. They'll tuck their tails and run for Dunkirk. The sham won't take; they're not going to board us, damn them."

"They will, Mr. Scudamore, they will," Edward said calmly.

"Why are you so sure, Captain?"

"Greed, Mr. Scudamore. Greed will overwhelm their good sense, they don't want to lose their two prizes. See, here they come, they'll be alongside to board over our decks. Stand by, easy now..."

Close came the Dunkirker. It was the traditional tactic to support a consort who had been boarded, or who needed help boarding another ship, to board alongside and enter over the consort's decks. Although the Dunkirker's crew numbered no more than twenty, and perhaps less, they doubtless felt secure enough to board and render assistance against a small number of enemy who had retreated to closed quarters.

"Steady," Edward ordered. Within thirty feet came the

Dunkirker, then came shouts in French and Dutch. The plan was discovered, the Flemings were putting their tiller to port, intending to clap on a wind and escape!

"Hoist our colors and fire! Grapplings! Grapplings!" shouted Edward, "Grapplings! Heave away, and fire! Fire!"

Immediately part of Edward's crew fired a volley of small arms, while the gun crews raised the ports and fired four great guns into the Dunkirker's waist. Two seamen heaved the grapplings, each with a fathom of chain between hook and line, under cover of the heavy smoke. The hooks caught in the enemy's shrouds.

"Heave, heave!" shouted Edward, "You six there, lend a hand, heave, haul together now, pull, now, damn you, pull! Yo... hope! Yo... hope!"

An outrageously brave Fleming climbed his shrouds, reached beyond the grappling hook, and cut it free before being shot and falling into the sea to die.

"Heave another! Use the boat grappling!" Edward shouted. "And heave, heave, heave!"

Slowly the ships came closer together as English seamen heaved and fired, Edward exhorting one of the laggard merchant seamen with the back of a cutlass. The whitish smoke of gunpowder burned eyes, clouded vision, and, along with fear, parched mouths.

But the smell! It was to Edward glorious, something between acrid and sweet, a reminder of actions past.

The vessels closed on each other. The impulse to cower was overwhelmed by the nearness of death, by the urge to survive, by the need to stand by one's shipmates. Some of the Flemings were retreating to closed quarters, while a handful remained on deck to wield half-pikes and pistols against the English enemy.

At five feet, Edward shouted, "Grenades!" At three feet, "Board! Board!"

Cutlass in hand, Edward leapt from the cathead across the small chasm, slipped on the Dunkirker's gunwale, and just barely caught himself with his left arm before he fell between the ships.

He pulled hard to haul himself up, saw an enemy above him, bloodied but alive and ready to shove a boarding pike into his throat. Edward held onto the rail with his left hand and thrust with his cutlass, but could not reach this enemy, who lurched back out of instinct. His feet slipped on a wale as he tried again to haul himself up while defending himself. If he dropped into the sea he would probably drown or be pressed to a pulp of muscle, bone, and brain between the ships, and if he remained there he would certainly be crushed as the ships came together soon.

Others among his crew leaped aboard the privateer, but the Fleming with the half-pike was still there, poised to kill the Scotsman. Edward was going to die, he knew it; he had been here before, close to death, and each time as his mind recognized the nearness of the void, he found himself calmly noting that he was yet still alive, his heart pounded, his palms sweat, and his asshole puckered tight. Worst of all, perhaps, he worried that he might look the coward hiding at the rail. He had to haul himself up! He did not realize he had been hanging at the gunwale for only three seconds.

With a great effort he hove himself up and over, and rose to engage the man who faced him. But the Fleming was gone, dead, his head cloven asunder by a boarding ax, almost identical to another Fleming's head aboard the *King Fisher* earlier. Edward raced toward one of his seamen in peril, and saved him with a powerful back stroke to the neck of the enemy about to cut him down. A small geyser of scarlet sprayed from the dying man's wound. Edward turned to see if anyone were at his back, parried a cut but missed his riposte, redoubled, parried a counter-cut with his pistol, and, with the aid of an English seaman who had just come up, cut his adversary down.

The decks were soon cleared of living Flemings and Frenchmen, but for two who cried quarter. The rest had retreated to closed quarters at the quarterdeck bulkhead. Edward took cover with his boarders behind the deck guns and bitts.

"Grenades—do we have anymore?" Edward shouted.

His crew and the some of the merchant seamen fired at the bulkhead loopholes, and the Flemings fired back from them.

"None, Captain!"

"Then check the guns, find one that's loaded, or load one if necessary. We'll turn it on the bulkhead!"

And so they did, aiming a four pounder at the bulkhead and calling on the enemy crew to surrender. They wisely complied immediately.

It was over.

An hour later, having set the enemy crew who were not too seriously wounded adrift in a boat with bread, water, oar, compass, and sail, and after tending to the wounded, knotting and splicing the rigging, and then dividing the English seamen among the three vessels and seeing to their armament and defenses, Edward finally paused for a moment to look at the sky and sea around him.

Was it worth it? he wondered.

More than half of his crew were wounded or killed, but not one of them had abandoned his duty, none had surrendered, until they had no choice. Nor, for that matter, had any of the Flemings and Frenchmen.

The die was cast, I did what I must, the crew what they must, and this time we were victorious, thanks to courage, seamanship, and, damn her, Fortune. And after all, there will be prize money.

Edward was tired, too tired even to grow angry when he discovered that Michael O'Neal could not be found among the living or the dead; somewhere in the battle the Irishman had yet again escaped. One of two boats towed astern was missing. The man had the luck of the Irish and the devil's instinct for survival.

The Scotsman breathed deeply of the salt air and pondered on an infinity of nothing. At this moment he didn't give a damn about philosophies or persons, nor what part they had played to bring him to this place.

Here, amidst land, sea, and sky, halfway between England, Flanders, and hell, the three battered, bloodied vessels worked board and board against each other as Edward rubbed a gunpowder-blackened liniment of brandy and butter into his bruised and swollen hands.

Here, once more among the honest and faithful, away from the backstabbing intrigues of landsmen, his hands and soul felt clean again.

Chapter 28

That there were severall Reports in the Country, some saying she was a Privateer, others a Buckaneer,or that she had Landed some of the Assassinators...
—Farmer Glover, in his letter the 25th of June, 1696

The wind and sea were fair for France, and it was not long before Michael O'Neal sailed southeast into Calais, a letter of credit from Captain Rimbaud in his pocket.

He had considered remaining aboard *La Tulipe Noir*, but she had affairs elsewhere, and the Irishman's business would be better served in Dunkirk anyway, thus he had boarded *La Fortune*—and only narrowly escaped by boat as the ship's crew were beaten down and demanded good quarter.

That bastard MacNaughton! thought the Irishman, but he admitted that the Scotsman had a feline way of landing on his feet.

In Calais he slept for day, drank and whored for several, slept another, then decided it was time to seek a means of returning to Ireland, but not before considering at length whether he should remain in France and enter the service of Louis or James.

He took horse to Dunkirk where, after conferring with several privateer captains who had news of England and Ireland, he decided to wait a few weeks while the hue and cry of assassination died down.

While he rested, he bought a small Biscayan boat, extraordinarily seaworthy and serviceable, and found passage aboard a Dunkirk corsair with plans to cruise along the north coasts of Scotland and Ireland, the route of merchantmen trying to avoid privateers hovering to the south. He paid the captain to tow the Biscayan and put him off close to Irish shores in St. George's Channel, in the meantime serving as a gunner's mate, for which he was well-qualified.

Foul weather and an English frigate kept Michael from landing on the east coast. Two weeks later he was able to set sail in his Biscayan just off the northeast coast of Ireland, but storm once more spoiled his plans and left him a league off Dunfanaghy on the north of Ireland, his Biscayan dismasted and leaking. He cursed Fortune and wondered if she had finally abandoned him.

But no, he grinned in desperation, *the sea shall not have me. Manannan I am, the sea god who walks upon the waters.*

And there, but a mile in the offing and sailing toward him, was a sloop of about fifty tons, a coastal trader perhaps, or a privateer. The former was no threat, and the latter, of whatever nation, he could talk himself past, and besides, he had no cargo and little money to steal. He waved a shirt as the vessel came close. For a moment he thought the sloop might pass him by, but the small vessel lay by a half a cable's length away and hailed him in English.

"Ahoy the boat!" came a shout across the water, its accent English, of the West Country.

The sloop had been long at sea, and Michael counted some twenty seafaring men on her deck, far more than necessary for her fifty tons and four small guns. Her lines and rig looked American, of New England perhaps, and he thought the vessel too small to be a privateer in these waters, although she might have passed for one in the English Channel or the Caribbean.

"Michael O'Sullivan, sailing from Derry to Galway with a small cargo, now lost to the sea! Who are you and whence do you hail!" he replied with a shout.

"The *Sea Flower*, Captain Bridgeman, trading in brasiletta wood from Providence Island in the Caribbees!"

"Permission to come aboard?"

"Come aboard, aye!"

Michael rowed his small craft alongside, passed the bowline to a seaman leaning over the gunwale, and clambered agilely aboard. He smelled slow match, and noticed that a swivel gun on the gunwale had been prepared just in case.

A rough looking man armed with a brace of pistols, James Warren, he said his name was, began the interrogation. Nearby stood two other seamen with cutlass and pistol each.

"You're an Irishman, then?"

"I am, and proud of it."

"That's a Biscayer," Warren said, nodding aft at Michael's boat, now towed astern.

"It is."

"You're no fisherman."

"Not today."

"Nor a merchant trader, no matter what you say, nor even a smuggler unless you've coin hidden about you," said Warren.

"As I said, I lost my cargo at sea."

A man Michael took to be the captain by his mood of quiet authority stood silently behind Warren. With him was a woman, the only one aboard, or at least the only one on deck.

"You've a familiar look about you, though I don't know you," Warren continued.

"And you as well."

"You know these waters?"

Michael ignored Warren and addressed the man behind

him. "Not as well as I know the southeast, but I know them well enough. You're the captain, I think."

The man smiled. "I'm Captain Bridgeman. What port is that?" he asked, pointing.

"Sheephaven Bay. The great headland to the west is Horn Head. Dunfanaghy bay and town are about a league to the southwest inside the great bay."

"Dunfanaghy, you're certain?"

"Dunfanaghy."

"If *you* needed a small port on this coast, for wood, water, and few enough questions, where would you go?"

"Dunfanaghy is good enough," Michael said, and, gambling, continued: "It's small, so small you won't find it on many charts, but still large enough for your needs. It's a market town under the patronage of the Stewarts at Ards. You'll have at least two days to be rid of your sloop and be away before anyone can begin serious inquiries. You can buy horses and take the road for Dublin or to Donaghedy. I suggest the latter, for you can make an easy crossing, wind and sea permitting, to Scotland or England. Dublin is more dangerous, too many questions will be asked."

Bridgeman's eyes narrowed, then he turned away and spoke to several men whose demeanor Michael knew well. He returned shortly.

"Will you pilot us into Dunfanaghy? I don't want a local pilot, not if you can help us."

"For a price—some of the gold and silver you carry. You're surely some of Every's men," Michael speculated boldly. He raised a hand. "I bear you no ill will, understand, but a score of men aboard a sloop from an island that's nothing more than a haven for men of the roving trade leaves little room for doubt. In fact, Captain Bridgeman, I'll warrant you're Captain Every himself."

Word of the pirate's recent exploits—his capture of one of the Great Mogul's rich ships, his gang rape of the women aboard, his murder of prisoners and brutality toward those he did not kill—was spoken of in every seaport in Europe.

"I was once of your trade and have as much reason to come quietly ashore in Ireland as you," Michael added.

Every scowled, then grinned. He held up his hand to stop Warren as he stepped forward, pistol raised.

"You know us, then. You're a bold man, considering we could leave you here floating as fish bait. You're smart, too, maybe just a bit too smart."

"I've an Irishman's luck and will wash ashore soon enough with the wind still in me."

"If we leave it in you," Every said, unblinking.

Michael stared him down.

"Ha, you are damn bold one," Every guffawed. "How much, then?"

"Forty guineas."

"Call it pounds and that's the price on the head of a thief—if convicted. It's too much."

"It's my price to pilot you safely and then see you off safely. I can guide you—I'm Irish, you're not. They'll be more suspicious of you than me, no matter that some are Presbyters and I a son of the Holy Mother Church. I've traded here—"

"By stealth, I warrant."

"Which means I know my bearings here. I know where the hidden shoals lie."

Every shook his head. "It's too much; these men will never agree. If you and I agree to five shillings to a piece-of-eight, that's one hundred sixty of them—eight from each man, too much. The won't see the value in your services, they'll say we should pilot ourselves and make our own way without your help. We've made it this far, and we've an Irishman or two among us."

"Half, then, but no less. I doubt your Irishmen know the north as I do."

"It's still too much, but I think our situation will bear it. Pardon me for a moment, Mr.—what did you call yourself? Sullivan?"

"O'Sullivan."

"Aye, and I'm Bridgeman."

Every made the proposal to the crew. A few grumbled, but all agreed to pay four pieces-of-eight or its equivalent to Michael.

"I prefer Spanish coin, or English, Dutch, or French, no money not passible in this kingdom—none of your rupees or sequins," he told Every.

"You don't want to be taken for one of us, is that it?"

"I've my own tracks to cover."

"Well enough. Hungry?"

"Thirsty."

"We've rum. Come."

Michael piloted the *Sea Flower* to anchor at Dunfanaghy Bay in County Donegal near the end June, 1696, without incident. The local population, as he predicted, was suspicious of the sloop and looked askance as the crew unladed bags of coin, some twenty thousand pounds worth by Michael's estimate, without declaring it. He had no doubt that the town would soon be full of the King's officers. For two days he acted an agent or factor between the pirates and the locals. After he set many of the former on their way, he sold the Biscayer and set out to find or steal a good horse.

"Hold there, Irishman!" Every called.

"Aye?" Michael asked, his hand on a small pistol in his pocket, as Every, Warren, and the woman—Mrs. Adams, wife of Every's quartermaster, Henry Adams—approached. Warren was leading three local garrons.

"You'll be off, now?"

"Aye."

"Where?"

"It's my own business."

"We'll pay you to guide us to Donaghedy."

"I've given you directions, and didn't you say you've more business here?"

"I've already signed the sloop over to Joseph Faroe who sailed with us. He'll sail her back to America."

"You want me to guide all three of you?"

"All three."

"And Henry Adams, husband of the lady here?"

"Is traveling separately for security."

"Indeed."

"You don't like questions, we don't like questions either, Irishman."

"You're right, Captain, ah, Bridgeman, your affairs are none of my business. So, assuming we agree to terms, you must get rid of these nags," he said.

"We paid ten pound apiece!" Warren expostulated.

"They're not worth forty shillings, and you'll have the High Sheriff upon you for paying so much. Only a thief with the hue and cry just behind him would've agreed to such terms. We've not been in Dunfanaghy but two days and already the rumor's about that your crew are buccaneers, privateers, or even assassinators who tried to kill the king. I'll find more horses and not raise eyebrows about them. We need to get moving; I've no mind to be taken as a pirate or assassinator and hanged for crimes I haven't committed."

"I warrant you've committed your share, Irishman," said Every with a dark grin.

"Then let me be hanged for them, not yours."

"Your price?"

"Forty pounds to Donaghedy."

"Yet again, too much," Every said.

"You just paid thirty for nags hardly worth two pounds apiece, and some of you are losing more than that on their exchange of silver for gold, just because it's easier to carry. You can afford my price."

Warren snorted. "You're nothing more than a damned pirate like us."

"You'd rather pay the jailor to keep you well until the hangman turns you off and leaves you tarred and sun-drying in the breeze?"

Every laughed. "It'll be no hangman for me, Irishman: I'm Henry Bridgeman, honest seaman leaving the billows behind in order to keep a tavern. But we'll pay, we'll pay—and if you betray us, we'll kill you. I'm a man of my word, Irishman."

Michael led the way over the muddy Irish roads, soon procuring four good horses in trade for the garrons, plus three more pounds apiece, telling the horse jobber a tale of having bought the nags from some suspicious English seamen in a hurry to be rid of them.

The remainder of the journey to Dunfanaghy went with nary a suspect eye laid upon them, in spite of posted broadsides advertising a reward for the seizure and apprehension of Henry Every and other such "Nottorious Rogues." Michael won another forty pounds at dice from the two pirates en route, and upon arrival in Donaghedy advised them to make the crossing to Scotland as quickly as possible. After a brief scuffle and standoff between Michael and Warren on one side, and Captain Every-Bridgeman and Mrs. Adams on the other, caused by a lusty misunderstanding over the woman, the two parties separated.

Michael and Warren set off by sea aboard a hired fisherboat, first to Cork, where the latter landed, then to areas outlying Kinsale. Here Michael intended first to find his brother, who had been serving aboard a French privateer out of Saint Malo and to whom he had written to request he return to Ireland, then to gather his men and make sure Molly was still safe. Vitally, he must discover if he had been betrayed in Ireland as well.

He was too late: all had gone to wreck and ruin. His rapparee brethren were hanged or in hiding, his brother soon dead, and Molly months gone.

Chapter 29

The wanton troopers riding by
Have shot my fawn, and it will die.
—Marvell, "An Horatian Ode," 1650

The dark procession wended past the House, past the brew-house, dairy, and stable, then around to the front again and back down the hill, and finally to the small chapel and cemetery in the glen below, where Wallers had for a century buried their dead. It was an ugly, dirty day, shrouded in mist and darkened brows.

Lobster-coated soldiers from the garrison at Charles Fort lined the way, a guard of honor for a faithful old soldier, for a reluctant veteran of bloody Irish wars. Black-staved conductors and two trumpeters led the procession. A groom led a riderless horse, Finn, the old gentleman's favorite. Retired old soldiers mounted on aged chargers carried his armor piece by piece, brightly polished for the somber occasion. A local lord bore the brave gentleman's standard, the great banner, detailing his ancestry. Two more trumpeters followed, levets reverberating in the still air, and behind them marched the herald.

Six horses, black with black caparisons, drew a black funeral carriage, and a pair of wolfhounds followed. Four great gentlemen flanked the carriage, men whose respect for the old gentleman and for each other made up for their religious and political disagreements. Behind the carriage walked the chief mourner, then came sovereigns, judges, mayors, burgesses, chamberlains, marshals, provosts, and constables, men of importance from throughout the baronies of the county, old friends and old enemies, Irish and English, Protestant and Catholic, nobleman and merchant, all in their finest.

And last came those whom the old gentleman would have thought the most important of all: the people of the land whom he had known well, drunk with, and fought amongst throughout his life, their presence this day a greater tribute to him than were all the nobility and gentry who walked in his procession.

Sir William was dead, and she had killed him.

I did what I must, Molly thought, staving off her grief and guilt.

They had argued.

"When you're tried, the prosecution is not only going to claim that you waged war on the king simply by visiting France —a preposterous notion, but one that has succeeded before— but also that you're in league with a notorious rapparee, that bastard O'Hanlen! I know damn well he's that O'Neal you've been betrothed to for years!"

"Who's telling you this?" she demanded. "Parson Waters?"

"I'll hamstring that gossiping turd of a coward soon enough. Stick to the point, please! I've talked long with the magistrate, and he believes the only way you won't be convicted is if you deny O'Neal, or whatever the hell his real name is."

"Sir William," Molly said, voice trembling, "you've been good to me for many years. I know you've done this for the sake of my mother's memory. You've even been like a father to me, but I will not give Michael up. I truly believe that both Fortune and the hand of man, via God's will, will not let me be tried."

"Then you're a damned fool! They'll take your estate, they'll

hang your betrothed when they catch him on the roads one day
—and they will!—and they might even hang you if they're able
to tie you in any way to his robberies and murders, and
whatever Jacobite plotting he's been up to. Then what can I do
for you but grieve?"

"I will not be tried, Sir William, I'm sure of it."

"How can you believe this? The only way you won't be tried
is by fleeing Ireland, or…" Sir William's voice trailed off. His
face turned red, he gripped his cane so hard that his arm shook
as he stood from his chair. "By God, Molly, I won't believe it!
Not my own—"

But whatever he would not believe was never said. He was
struck speechless, his left side paralyzed. He fell and broke his
arm and jaw. A day later he was dead.

Molly was largely shunned after the funeral. It was a subtle
shunning, yet obvious to anyone with eyes open. Sir William's
brother already acted as if he were the great lord of the manor,
and Parson Waters lurked everywhere, gleefully obsequious.
Mourners gathered in the inner hall, but after half an hour
Molly could no longer stand the atmosphere and retreated to
her room.

"Agamemnon, Menelaus, will you protect me?" she asked as
she stroked the coats of the wolfhounds at her feet.

An hour later someone knocked on the door. Reluctantly
she opened it.

"You look like a woman with a great decision to make, one
she mustn't make lightly. Do you mind if I come in and help?"
Jane Hardy asked.

Molly's face flushed in anger, embarrassment, and
suspicion. "Must you?"

"I fear I must, my dear. And what I'm going to say mustn't
be heard by anyone else, so please stand aside, let me in, and
close the door," she replied, and pushed the door all the way

open.

"I hope this won't take long," Molly said sharply as Jane stepped boldly past her.

"That all depends. We do have some time, but not much, so close the door. Don't worry about the parson eavesdropping, he's too busy whistling "Lillibullero" and testifying below, swearing to things he's seen and more things he hasn't, including treasonable behavior between you and a local rapparee named O'Hanlen—and we both know who O'Hanlen really is. Sir William's brother is holding a small council of war at the moment, and much of the subject is you. It's my impression that he's decided he'll be the one to have your estate after it's confiscated. And it will be confiscated, my dear, there's nothing you can do about that now. Constable Rutson is with him: you might be arrested as early as tomorrow on new charges."

"Things might change soon," Molly said defiantly. "Fortune has a way—"

"Of buggering both men and women for sport. Haven't you heard the news?"

"What news?"

"Jacobites in London tried to murder the king, my dear. And they failed. There will be no rebellion, there will be no restoration of James to the English throne. Nothing will change in Ireland."

"My God!"

"I assume your despair is for the failure of the Jacobite cause, but we can both pretend your concern is for King William's safety. They're looking everywhere for plotters, and they'll be look here soon enough for the petty sort, after they've finished looking for those in London. Where's your betrothed, by the way?"

"I won't answer that!"

"As you please, my dear, but you probably wouldn't be telling me anything I don't already know. Listen closely: it's not just that they'll accuse you of consorting with O'Hanlen. They'll pin his treasons on you, too, whether or not there's evidence. You are Irish, Catholic, a woman, and you've consorted with a known outlaw who is assuredly a traitor too. Your betrothed is a noose around your neck and every tree a gibbet if you remain here."

"Why do you care what happens to me?"

"Molly, dear, I've always had my own sense of honor in my lines of work. I've made my own rules and lived by them as often as I could, which has been more often than not. I've done whatever I've done because I chose to, not because I had no say at all in the matters. I've made my own bargains and my honor has never been for sale. This is something unusual in a woman, and blasphemy in most men's eyes, and even in many women's. There are too few of us who can hold up their heads, even if men pretend not to recognize what we're doing.

Jane took a long pause before resuming. "I'd rather not see any of us hanged, and I certainly can't see what purpose hanging you would serve now." She waited for Molly to recognize the full import of her words, then continued. "Two of my servants, papists both, and two of Sir William's, also papists, are waiting at the stable with a saddled horse and a few supplies. I assume you've already planned where you'd run if it came to this?" Molly nodded. "Good. Now, let's get you dressed. I've clothing for you at the stable, we need only slip down the stairs."

"I've clothing here."

"A man's?"

"Yes."

"Clever girl! I guess it's safer to ride by night dressed as a man?" Jane asked rhetorically. Molly did not answer. "As you please, Mistress O'Meary. You're fairly tall for a woman, your breasts aren't large, I think you can get by as a man from a distance in daylight, and anyway it'll be dark soon."

From a chest Molly drew a man's clothing. Already she knew how to wear these clothes like a man would, she knew how to walk like a man in them, how not to move delicately or shyly. She knew how to be strong but silent, to move with a quiet assurance and purpose, to keep her hat down low, throwing a shadow across her eyes, to keep her cloak pulled about her shoulders. With Jane's help she wrapped her breasts and pulled on several shirts to give her body some size. She let her hair down and wore it loose about her shoulders. She tied her purse to her waist under her breeches and let it hang between her legs. She had a pistol, illegal though it was for papists without a license. She loaded and primed it, and around her neck and beneath the shirts she hung a small stiletto whose narrow triangular blade could inflict a fatal wound. She pulled on boots, coat, and hat, and packed a portmanteau with a woman's clothing and accoutrements.

"Here are a dozen guineas," Jane said as she passed her a small purse. "It won't get you far, but I'm sure you have other resources, such as those already between your legs? Good. If anyone sees you leaving the house, you're one of my servants, understand? Don't worry, Sir William's brother is in the library with his cabal, and the remaining guests are in the great hall."

Down the stairs they went, Molly a few steps behind, at a servant's distance.

"Here my help ends," Jane said at the kitchen door. "May Fortune have your back. If nothing else, it will be dark soon—and I'm sure you know well your way on the roads by night."

Through the kitchen and scullery Molly escaped the house unnoticed. At the stable she was met by four silent servants, one holding a horse, another who passed her a sword and belt to complete her costume. She mounted the horse, Finn, Sir William's favorite. He had given her permission to ride Finn as she pleased, and the animal was the most reliable in the stable. She rode at the trot from the manor.

The horse was not as fast as she might have liked, but he could go forever. Her clothes felt strange tonight, although she had worn them many times before. The money between her legs pressed her flesh in a way she might have found erotic were it not for the danger she was in. She rode as quickly as she thought was safe, pacing the horse, for the ride was nineteen miles or more, and she did not know if she might suddenly need to gallop away for her life.

She knew by instinct when to walk and rest her mount. She listened to him, and with her legs, hand, and low voice responded to him. But deep into the night she began to rest him less and less, for strange, evil shapes began to appear and disappear among the trees and bushes as she rode by; and fear, nay, terror, rode swiftly at her heels: she could hear him, his cloven feet echoing each clop-clop of her horse's hooves. She had no sense of time, only of distance, and even that was occluded by the darkness, as were the stars and moon that might have told her how many hours had passed. Soon, or much later, she could not tell, the sky began to brighten, but it was only the moon appearing from behind the clouds.

Onward she went.

Innishannon? Bandon Bridge? Ride around them, then back onto the road.

The river? Swim it, Finn loves the water—but be careful, hang on, these boots will drag you down if you let go of him! she thought as they plunged into the cold water and she held tightly to his mane. *Across and safe, now to the southwest, where's the road?*

Here it is, onward now... across the Argideen... past

Timoleague and Cloughnakilty... and now south along the bay, across from Inchydoney where the tide has risen and made the small peninsula into an island.

And there it was. She could smell first the marshes, then the salt air; she could hear the surge, and suddenly the hours and miles were behind her and forgotten.

She waited near the shore before the dawn in the cool, damp darkness, salty mists and sea sounds caressing her cheeks and ears. Strands of her hair clung to her temples. Finn snorted restlessly and looked back at her several times, questioning why she had stopped. He nipped once or twice at the toe of her boot. Gulls flew by; she could hear them, but could not see them. The ocean washing against the shore masked other sounds, and enfolded her, its strength and fortitude granting her a quiet courage, and she again lost any perception of time. She could see nothing in the darkness, neither ship nor boat. And then before her, gradually, was the first light of morning, revealing strange, blurred shapes and objects that soon altered their appearance. What at first seemed a crouching, imaginary beast became a plant, then finally a pitted, worn rock. A lump became first a sea beast thrown up on the shore, then a small boat. A hummock became a stone cottage.

She grew tense again. Finn tossed his head. Now Molly discerned the masts and spars of a small ship. She heard steps in the gritty sand, then she saw a short man—no, a boy— approaching. He spoke to her in Irish.

"Where do you come from, sir?"

Molly looked down at the innocent face.

"Then where then are you going?" he asked, when she did not answer.

"I seek the *Mary* Pink and Patrick Sarsfield," she said, using the name of the vessel expected and the password. She tossed him a brass shilling with the likeness of James II—useless 'gun money' that had briefly served as cash in Ireland among the Jacobites during the war.

The boy glanced at the coin. "Sarsfield's dead, sir. They say he was killed in the Spanish Netherlands in '93. And the shilling's worthless. But you can come with me if you like. You shouldn't be standing here like this; someone might think you were a spy trying to leave Ireland. Come, come!"

She followed the boy to a place near the shore where several hard-looking men drank around a small, smoky fire almost invisible in the dawn. They all stared at her.

"He's looking for Patrick Sarsfield, gave me brass shilling with the true king's likeness on it."

"What's your name?" asked one.

She did not answer.

"Well, you're not Michael O'Neal for I know him, and it's his password you use, nor are you any other we expect. So speak now or you'll feed the fish in the bay."

"I am Molly O'Meary," she said, pulling the scarf from around her face.

"That you are, that you are; you're too pretty to be a man. You're known among us."

"I've come for passage to France. I seek shelter and protection until I can get to sea."

"Are you sure?"

"I stand accused of treason."

"You're lucky then; the *Mary* Pink is anchored offshore, she arrived well before time," the man said. "You can leave your horse with the boy. Come, now, we must be going before we're caught ashore."

The men soon pushed a small boat through the ebb and flow while she sat in the stern. She was uncomfortable alone with them as they rowed to the pink, unsure even who they were. But they all behaved respectfully, at least in her presence. The crew of the small ship treated her much the same after she boarded. She paid the captain for her passage. After this they seldom exchanged a word.

She was violently seasick the first two days. The pumps squealed constantly and there were angry words exchanged about how badly the pink was leaking, and how they ought to get into a safe harbor, any harbor, before the vessel burst apart in the sea. By the afternoon of the second day, though, she felt as if she had grown her sea legs, and finally went up on deck when she heard the crew talking excitedly about something. She knew the swells were greater now than they had been when she had first grown seasick, yet they no longer bothered her much. She had put her masculine clothing away, wore her dress instead, and left her hair down and long to blow in the wind.

She saw three ships ranging from two hundred to four hundred yards away, one of which was a large black man-of-war. Then noticed what appeared to be a very large tourniquet, for she could think of no other words to describe it, right in front of her. It was a hawser wrapped several times around the hull and tightened with a spar, as one tightens a tourniquet, squeezing the hull together and keeping the pink afloat. This clumsy-looking jury rig—"wolded with her hawsers," a seaman would say—was not a reassuring sight, and four men still worked the pumps.

"They're all Dutch-built, but they're flying French colors. Could be French, could be Dutch. If they're Dutch, we'll be taken, for they'll never believe we're not trading with the French. Good afternoon, Mistress O'Meary," the captain said when he saw her, "Frenchmen, we think and hope. If they're anything else we're in trouble. They're hoisting out a boat; they'll want to search us. Jesus and Mary, I hope they're French."

A small boat came alongside from one of the two stores ships, called flutes. Six armed men clambered quickly aboard.

The boarding party's two officers surveyed the small vessel. They removed their hats and bowed when they saw Molly.

"*Bonjour, Mademoiselle,*" the first said, "*parlez-vous francais?*"

"*Oui, Monsieur,*" she said, sure now they were French by their manners and flawless accents. "I call myself Molly O'Meary, of Kinsale in Ireland."

"Is this an English ship?" the officer asked, ignoring the captain who came to join them.

"It is, but has French passes for safe conduct and it sails to France. I, however, am Irish, a fugitive from the English."

"A fugitive? You? *Mais non,* Mademoiselle, this I cannot believe." He turned to his petty officer. "Check their papers and passes, then their cargo," he said, then addressing Molly, "Pardon me, Mademoiselle, I wish to introduce to you my friend, Monsieur Alain de Baatz of the House of Montesquiou-Ferenza, a lieutenant in the *Compagnies detachées de la marine,* who travels with us to his new post. I am Lieutenant Timothée Kercue, an officer of *La Seine,* a flute in the service of our glorious monarch, King Louis. We are convoyed by *La Tulipe Noir,* a *corsaire* of France." The officers bowed again.

"Bonjour, Mademoiselle," said Lieutenant de Baatz.

"Montesquiou-Ferenza?" she asked him. "You are a d'Artagnan?"

"A lesser relation of that great house. May I ask how you know of my family, and also why you travel to France aboard this dirty little ship?"

"I lived in Gasgony in the early years of the war, and so am familiar with your famous house. As for this ship, it was my only means."

The petty officer interrupted them, and spoke for several minutes to the officers. Lieutenant Kercue turned to her.

"Mademoiselle, I must warn you now. My petty officer has

informed me this vessel is most unseaworthy, incapable of slipping through the English blockade along the coast of France. She will either sink or be captured. I have advised her captain to turn back until his vessel is in better condition."

"What then, Monsieur, do you suggest?"

"Why, that you travel with us, of course. We are three ships, very strong. You will be safe with us." He smiled at her. "You do not trust us. Please, there are two priests aboard our ship and our captain is a most perfect gentleman, as are we, his officers. Please, honor us with your presence. Come with us, if only for your safety."

Molly looked at the three ships, each of them several times the size of the pink. Surely they must be safer, and smoother, on the ocean.

"I'll go with you," she said.

She packed her few things quickly and returned topside. She was about to climb down the tumblehome into the boat herself, when Lieutenant de Baatz stopped her.

"No, no, Mademoiselle! You are a lady. We will hoist you over the side. You there, Captain..."

And up she went, then over, only a few feet, tied securely in the chair. Rough, yet oddly gentle hands helped her into the boat. She sat in the crowded stern with the officers and coxswain as sweating oarsmen rowed the boat back to one of the flutes. The oarsmen grinned behind their exertions.

"So, Lieutenant Kercue—"

"Timothée, Mademoiselle, Timothée."

"Timothée, then. So, Timothée, when will we reach France? How soon? Did you not say we were but days away?"

"France? Yes, Mademoiselle, we are but two or three days away in good weather. Alas, it will be, oh, six months at least, perhaps even a year, before you see France."

"What? Do you jest with me?"

"Mademoiselle, forgive our deception, but for your safety it was the only thing in honor we could do. Your little ship will never reach France. She will sink or be taken as a prize, perhaps even if she tries to make an English or Irish port. And you, admittedly, are a fugitive. To save you, I had no other choice but to get you off the ship, by any means." He paused, and smiled apologetically. "We sail, Mademoiselle, for the Antilles and Saint-Domingue."

Chapter 30

Fortune helps the Hardy ay, and Pultrons ay repels.
—Scottish proverb, published 1721

Nearly two months after setting sail aboard the *King Fisher*, Edward finally returned to London, no more to be an officer in the King's navy, no more an incidental player, or so he hoped, in the politics and practices of assassination, no more a pawn to kings, lords, and rapparees, all of whom had better information than he had.

Given the wind, tide, and the condition of the three vessels, Edward had sailed first to Ostend, an easier port to make in the circumstances. He'd spent more than a month there making the three vessels fit for sea again.

If, upon stepping ashore in London after anchoring the *King Fisher* Sloop, *Fortune* Prize, and *Carolina Merchant* at the Downs, he expected immediate reward for his efforts on behalf of England, he was disappointed. Two weeks he waited, indulging in the meantime the Admiralty's court martial regarding the brief loss of the *King Fisher*, for which he was acquitted of any negligence or dereliction of duty, before he was brought before King William. The Earl of Portland stood nearby.

"I am impressed by your courage and great Fortune, Captain," the king said quietly.

"Thank you, Your Majesty. But without the courage, skill, and wit of my men, and a bit of luck as well, we would never have prevailed," Edward replied, embarrassed for himself but proud for his crew.

"Spoken like a leader, not a man seeking a boon from his King, much less a courtier seeking to elevate himself at the expense of others. I applaud your sentiment and manner. I might even suggest you are given to wisdom, in that you understand the role Fortune plays in the affairs of men."

"I am still developing my philosophy on that subject, Your Highness."

"Indeed? May I advise you, then? Remember that every bullet has its billet."

"I will remember your words, Your Majesty."

"That is entirely up to you. But I was not only praising you for your adventure at sea; I would thank you for bringing us the secret Irish letters with evidence of a plot against me, and even for your past service as a volunteer in my army."

"Thank you, Your Majesty."

"Lord Mohun has even sent me a letter praising you," King William said flatly.

"Lord Mohun? I must thank him, Your Majesty, but I cannot explain his generosity. We are not well-acquainted."

"He writes that you are boon companions."

Edward said nothing, considering that anything he said would be worse even than silence.

King William continued. "You may tell me of the action you fought against the Dunkirker."

Edward described the adventure in detail, and noted especially the actions of the ship's boy whose courage had facilitated their escape, for whom he asked for a letter a preferment. The boy had some letters and arithmetic. Perhaps education at a Blue Coat school and then an appointment as a midshipmen, Edward suggested.

Near the end of audience, the king hung a small gold chain and medal around Edward's neck as a reward for his actions on land and sea.

"And what are your plans now, Captain?" King William asked.

"I seek a privateering commission, Your Highness."

"Indeed? I wish you well, and believe there is little you cannot accomplish."

Throughout the audience, there seemed a bit of hesitation on King William's part, but perhaps this was due to the natural aloofness of all kings. Edward had never been much impressed by nobility or royalty, and hoped this attitude had not been too obvious to His Majesty.

Damnation to them all, Edward thought, *to kings and princes and all their ilk.*

But he only said, "Thank you, Your Majesty," bowed deeply, and stepped away; the audience at an end.

In truth, Edward considered the king not all that bad, at least as royalty went, if a nation need even have a royal head of state. Perhaps the audience would be worth something one day, hopefully sooner rather than later.

That afternoon, Edward resigned his naval commission without too much regret. He had no good news in London regarding his privateering commission, although this should have been no surprise, his having been at sea and unable to pursue the matter, and having, as far as he knew, no ship. No investors, no ship: no ship, no commission. Letters Jonathan had sent to Lloyds in Edward's absence indicated only limited progress, some setbacks, and some reason for hope. Edward inquired at the Commissioners of the Lord High Admiral, but learned nothing except that inquiries had been made in his name, and a reply was mailed to his agent in Bristol.

From Lloyd's he posted letters to Bristol, and a week later Jonathan's reply urged him to return to the western seaport, as now it seemed he might have good news. Also at Lloyds he found a dozen letters of inquiry and interest in his venture, and he spent an entire day replying to them. More were to arrive over the next week. He would be surprised if London investors actually took their chances on what was in essence a Bristol venture, but who knew? Perhaps it would all work out after all.

On the brighter side, there would eventually be some reward from his recent adventure, in the form of prize money derived from *La Fortune* and the *Carolina Merchant*. It might be months before he had this silver in his hand, but sooner or later he would.

Immediate substantial reward may not have been forthcoming, but notoriety was. He now bordered again on fame or infamy. The *London Gazette* noted his recent adventure, and Randal Taylor published a single sheet front and back describing in detail and with fair accuracy his action at sea. Several young women flirted obviously with him, and a few prostitutes, from the most expensive to the least, even offering themselves for less than their usual charges; one, a Venetian, or so she said—and her Italian accent seemed real— even offered herself for free.

Admittedly, Edward was sorely tempted by these women, having been weeks at sea. It was not that he was necessarily averse to those of the trade—he had known a few in his time— but he had largely avoided them for more than a decade. He thought it wise to continue to do so, for he had little taste for the French or any other venereal pox; plus he despised taking advantage of women of any standing, for which many of his contemporaries thought him a fool, although only Jonathan said so to his face. Edward had sympathy for the poor to middling sort in this trade, and could not afford the most expensive.

Although he passed on these offers, believing them all ultimately intended to pick his pocket of the prize money he had not received, he did seek out the woman who had helped him in Hanging Sword Alley. He gave her a silver patch box made from a pair of English crowns, and also a guinea and crown to replace those confiscated by the thief-takers.

"So, you finally asked my name?" she asked, shaming him. "It's Lizzy—Elizabeth, I mean—Cates. That should make me easier to find if you ever need my services in Hanging Sword Alley again. I'm not always available at a moment's notice to rescue famous pirates."

Edward took off his hat to her, kissed her hand, and bowed as deeply to her as he had the king.

Lord Mohun, having finally returned to London, sought him out. They drank, Mohun three cups for Edward's one, they almost quarreled, they almost drew on each other, and they drank again. Edward was glad to be rid of the rakehell in the wee hours of the morning, and suspected the man would sooner or later get his deserved reward in the form of sharpened steel thrust repeatedly into his body.

Oddly, Handsome Harry was not to be found in London. After a few inquiries, Edward learned that the pompous lord had been there but had returned to Bristol or Bath with his latest mistress. He had not received the accolades he expected from his small role in Edward's London adventure, and after waiting a few weeks for the king to thank him personally, he'd departed unrewarded.

Edward saw a play while he was in London, *The Country Wake*, or perhaps it was the *Royal Mischief*, or maybe even the *Country Mischief* or the *Royal Wake*, he could never remember such titles, they all seemed much the same to him, this one with parts played by the great actresses Anne Bracegirdle and

Elizabeth Barry.

Edward thought he saw a former amour of his, poet and playwright Aphra Behn, in the audience; but knowing how she felt about those who had deserted the Jacobite cause, he chose not to discover if it really were she seated nearby.

Having some time on his hands, he sought out the competing publishers James Knapton, at the Crown in St. Paul's Church-Yard, and Randal Taylor, near Stationer's Hall. Both expressed great interest in a memoir of his travels and adventures among the buccaneers and beyond, and Edward agreed that he would write it as soon as his next adventure was over, and offer it to the highest bidder.

Matthew Prior's country cousin put herself in his way more than once. As ever, she had good intelligence.

"My cousin Mat, the poet, has great praise for you, sir," she told him.

"Indeed? Are you sure?" Edward replied, smiling warmly.

"He also told me I should stay away from you, that your luck may be even more dangerous than your reputation."

"Now I do believe you. Where may you and I share a bottle of good wine?"

"You're bold, sir: you assume I won't take my cousin's advice?"

"I assume you'll test his advice and send him a report. I assume that's why you're here."

She almost blushed. "Then, sir, let's drink some wine and see how much scrutiny your character will bear."

They conversed as they had on the road, of the great world and of all the small matters that make it so, and with much better wine this time. Yet they took their relationship no further; perhaps the woman took her cousin's advice, or if not, was herself wise enough not to venture her reputation on a tryst with a notorious sea rover. They parted ways amicably, although Edward did wonder if his luck with women were waning. Then he wondered if he had not been lucky at all in his consummations, but merely the object of pleasurable manipulation by spies and their ilk.

Finally, all matters of naval and royal duties done with, Edward was away. He took post horses to Bristol, making the trip in less than two days. Muddy and sweaty, with his Scottish backsword, recovered from the captain of the *Fortune*, at his side and a brace of pistols in their holsters laid over his left arm, he strode into the Black Swan to surprised looks, followed by smiles and "Huzzahs!"

After an hour of questions and answers, someone suggested the entire company retire to a tavern where they could better celebrate his escapades and hear the rest of his tale. Coffee, after all, was a business drink, liquid sobriety, it put the edge on the man who must come to terms, settle accounts, and sign agreements. Wine, brandy, rum, and punch were the drinks of comradeship and celebration. As the party slowly headed out the door, Edward was finally able to speak with Jonathan privately, after promising to meet everyone soon at the *Cup of Gold.*

Jonathan was all smiles, but with a hint of reservation, an odd combination, Edward thought.

And smug, the bastard looks smug!

"Well," Edward demanded, "the news? Damn you, have we a ship and investors? Will we get a commission after all?"

Jonathan smiled more broadly and tried to hold back his reply, but could not.

"It's all but done, Edward, it's all but done," he said in his lowland Scots accent. "The Commissioners intend to issue a warrant as soon as you sign. There's the bond to be posted and the usual details, but it all will shortly be."

"How? And the ship? We do have the ship, the *Virginia*?

The old letter from you, one you sent while I was at sea, said the owners would not sell, that you had to seek another ship. How then?"

"Edward, relax, we must get you to a tavern soon, or to a woman. You have the ship, the *Virginia* Galley, as you desired."

"They changed their minds, then? They realized the profit the ship would have as a privateer, they will retain an interest in the ship, then? Surely this is it. Damn, I knew it would all work out in the end."

"And how do you think it *did* all work out, Edward?"

Damn him, Edward thought, *the bastard's smug!*

"Your smile, Jonathan—damn you, sir, why that smile?" Edward asked, grinning just as broadly.

"It's knowing that you don't know how you came by this commission for a private man-of-war."

"I know damn well it was much due to my philosophy, although admittedly I might need to rethink it a bit. I kept my distance from Fortune and her minions until Fortune came to me on my terms. At sea I escaped my captors, I recaptured my ketch, I captured a French corsair and an English prize. And there's my experience in the West Indies and other places as a privateer—privateer, mind you, or perhaps a buccaneer, but a pirate only in the narrowest sense. Doubtless all of this together drew the other investors we needed. They saw profit in a captain who knows when to fight and when to run. And there's you: there's your losing often to Deigle at cards," Edward said, smirking a bit. "No one is better than you at selling the truth, no one can find and deal with investors better than you."

"Indeed? Well, that's surely one way it might have happened. Yes, you recovered the *King Fisher* entrusted to your care, and a captured merchantman too, and even captured a French privateer. But you also first lost the *King Fisher*, although outmatched. And you also lost your quarry—it's said you were in pursuit of an assassinator, but that he escaped. Some have said you could've done more to capture him.

"You also rescued the *Virginia* Galley, but what you don't know is that her owners wanted to sue you for damage to ship and cargo during the chase. They were desperate, having creditors at their door. This suit came to naught, by the way, as I'll soon relate. As for your other experience, once a pirate always a pirate in some minds, and there are many who think you would take their ship and go off pirating in the Red Sea, or run to Prince James to serve him as a privateer.

"And Deigle? Handsome Harry, it turns out, has less influence at Court than I thought; *mea culpa*, although he has had enough to move things along at the Admiralty. Further, I discovered that *my lord* Deigle considered setting up another as captain, some pimply bastard of his, I heard. However, for some reason—some influence upon him perhaps—in the end he decided you should command this venture after all, which to some of his few friends he now pretends is *his*. And it seems it may have had something to with your ability, after all."

"Indeed?"

"Indeed. Something about his recent mistress, that Upcott woman, believe it or not; he's become quite enamored of her, or at least of her flesh. A bit worried, though, that some Scottish privateer might be boarding her by night. He thinks this can't happen if the rover is seeking prizes elsewhere."

Edward shook his head and snorted ruefully, somewhere between a laugh and a sigh. "There are plenty of other privateers out there to board her; he'll discover this by and by. Something I haven't told you—you must keep this between us—is that that bastard Lynch came to London, apparently to kill me and rob me of the letters I carried. I left him dead in an alley and told no one, although the king's intelligencer suspects me. I wonder if Lydia weren't involved with Lynch, if she had a hand in my attempted murder, and whether or not we should warn Deigle."

"So ho!" Jonathan laughed out loud. "One begins to wonder at all these villains and their connections! Deigle, Upcott, Lynch —what a crew of fools and backstabbers!"

"Indeed," Edward said in a low voice.

He leaned back in his tall chair and drew deeply from his pipe. Jonathan said no more for now, knowing from experience that Edward was thinking it all through.

Had Deigle perhaps sent Lynch to kill him? Edward wondered. *Or had Lydia? Who was more likely to do so? Her father had been a Jacobite, after all. Had she cozened Deigle in order to learn Edward's Irish mission? Was she even sly and base enough for this work? Doubtless, though, the order had come from a spy in Ireland. Had Lydia simply passed it on?*

And now he recalled again that Jane knew of Lydia, had pretended at first that she did not know Edward, or of him, although in fact she did.

Is Jane then the spy?

Or is it Molly? She has access and, through her betrothed, connections.

Yet he had no proof of any of this, other than opportunity and circumstance. This was all too much to comprehend at the moment, not to mention that the emergency was over, so what did it matter anyway?

Lydia, if truly a Jacobite, will lie low out of fear of being taken as a traitor and hanged; she'll be satisfied with Deigle's money if not always his yard. Lynch is dead. Jane, if she's involved, will surely slip quietly into the background and do her best to preserve her son's estate. And Molly? Sir William will do his best to protect her.

Molly's treason bothered him most. Not that she might be a Jacobite, not that she might be involved in intrigue trying to restore James to the throne—neither of these likelihoods bothered him much. Such was to be expected. No, it was her personal betrayal, that from her hand may have come the order to kill him, if necessary, for the letters. Such betrayal was far too common ashore.

By comparison, he considered the sea to be pure, no matter the thieving, slaving, and bloodthirsty fighting that took place regularly upon its surface, no matter the winds and waves that daily drew ships and honest seamen eternally to its depths.

The sea, at least, is honest.

Yet this idea seemed somehow flawed, not matter how true on its face, and he suddenly thought that life at sea might be no more honest that life ashore, and Fortune no less fickle at sea than ashore. But no, neither did this seem quite right, either. He pondered some more, Jonathan eying him patiently as he tried to put it all together. And it came to him.

Aye, that's the difference: the sea is a common enemy, and therefore are men more willing to help each other, and thereby seamen have a greater sense of honor and duty. But how often do we find this ashore, where our most common enemy is our friend and neighbor?

And with this reasoning he excused Molly for her likely betrayal.

But the sea, at least, would have warned me.

And then he laughed out loud, and Jonathan eyed him knowingly, as if he could read his mind.

Damn! Edward realized, *Molly did warn me after all, twice she did, that I have enemies. She just didn't tell me she was one of them. And had I not kept so much distance from Fortune and her minions, I'd have recognized this much sooner, and not been so taken with doubts.*

"So, I'm not to command by virtue of my deeds sword-in-hand?" Edward asked, as he filled and lit his pipe again at the end of his reflection and revelation.

"Oh, I think it was by virtue of your deeds, but sword in something else!" Jonathan said rudely, but the jest was funny to ignore. Both men laughed, but Jonathan much more loudly.

"So, who are the investors? Sir William intended a third part, so who, then, the rest? From Bristol, I assume?" Edward asked, after both had stopped laughing. But now Jonathan's reserve came to the fore, the smugness gone.

"Sir William could give none, other than the goldsmith's note he gave us for expenses. I'm sorry, Edward, but Sir William is dead. His estate is in some legal entanglement; it's fouled, and damned if any can do anything about it for some time. Again, I'm sorry, I know you were good friends."

"How?" asked Edward, briefly stunned.

"How did he die? Apoplexy, the letter said."

"Damn," Edward swore quietly under his breath. Not for a moment did he think of the money Sir William intended, or of how it had been replaced, but only that the man was gone, forever. After a few moments: "What of his niece, or she he called his niece, Molly O'Meary?"

"I know nothing of her," Jonathan said, shaking his head and making no jibe about what Edward's relationship with her might have been.

Edward silently sipped at his coffee and puffed on his long churchwarden pipe for several minutes, remembering his promise to Sir William. With her father gone—and did she ever learn he was her father?—who would protect her? Certainly not O'Neal, an outlaw and a traitor who would not dare to return to Ireland.

"He was a good man, Sir William was. There are few enough anymore. These days, many think a good man is simply one who isn't bad," Edward said finally, after a long exhalation of Oroonoko.

"I'm sorry I never knew him, although I've done business with him. He was always true to his word."

Edward forced himself to ask who the part owners were, although the question seemed disrespectful at the moment.

"The owners?" replied Jonathan. "Quite a variety, many taking only a thirty-second. From Bristol, a pair of Quakers, seven merchants, and one ship owner have banded together to invest their small portions conservatively. These Bristol investors account for a third."

"Who else, then?"

"Lord Mohun, for one."

"Damn! And how? He has no money, his estate is indebted, he lives by gambling," Edward replied incredulously.

"Don't worry, his investment is a pittance, literally. He wrote that his real investment is in the letter he sent to the king on your behalf."

"Damn! And damn again!"

"A cold shoulder from the king?" Jonathan suggested. "He cares not for Mohun; he was present at his trial for murder and was furious that Mohun was acquitted. But I'm sure he's wise enough to know that you aren't of Mohun's ilk."

"He asked me about that little shit lord and gave me an odd look. One of several, actually."

Jonathan only laughed knowingly. Upon brief reflection, Edward realized the king had probably known of the commission's likely approval, and left its discovery to Edward. More and more he felt Fortune's influence on his affairs, and vice versa, in spite of his philosophy revised.

"Who else?" Edward asked.

"Deigle."

"I thought you said he has no money."

"He's borrowing it, I think from Lord Brennan and Sir James Allin. He wants a say in the voyage—*his voyage*, as I said he calls it now. He'll tie his small share, a thirty-second, maybe a sixteenth, to his 'influence' that helped procure your commission, and claim that his 'influence' also brought the Bristol investors aboard. Indeed, he already claims to speak for them."

"Damn him, too. Who else?"

"An anonymous investor, or group of investors, from London."

"From London?"

"From London."

"Anonymous?"

"Indeed. They account for but three thirty-seconds. I hear one is a woman."

"A woman?"

"A woman."

"I've never sought a shilling from a woman."

"Why not? Everyone else does. They just marry or cozen them to get it, often both," Jonathan said.

"I never wanted them thinking that what I was after, for I never have been."

Jonathan laughed, still smug. "You and your damned strange sense of honor. And who says it's a woman *you* know? This one is kin to someone at Court, a royal secretary I believe."

Edward shook his head. "I think I do know her, indeed. And the rest?"

Jonathan waved his hand. "There's your money, of course."

"And the rest, I said? Half of the money we need, less my small investment and prize money, when I have it, if I ever have it, for my investment will amount at most to a sixteenth part."

"You asked about the ship, about how suddenly the owners were willing to sell?"

"Yes, come to the point, damn you!" Edward demanded, trying to look serious, but he could not restrain his smile for long, and did not.

"The owners didn't sell, not to us. They had intended one more voyage, hoping one last time to stave off their creditors. However, one creditor, from whom the owners had borrowed and had in turn pledged the ship as security, refused them more time to pay. Instead of threatening to foreclose, she—*she*—offered to both take the ship from them and lend them more money to finance another. Then she proposed the ship for our venture, reserving a third interest in the voyage for herself, and offered to discuss terms if we were unable to find enough other investors."

"She?"

"She."

"Who?"

"You know, Edward, after all these years, you still don't know women, do you? You, who prate of Fortune all the time—and she a woman!"

"Who, damn you, Jonathan! Tell me who before I put your feet to the coals!"

Laughing, Jonathan pointed his pipe at Edward. "A Dutch woman, a widow, supposedly once a whore in the Netherlands; she acts on behalf of her son actually; name of Jane Hardy, not her Dutch name of course, but her married one; she wrote that she knew you on the crossing to Ireland, that you visited her there as well. You didn't board her too, did you?" Jonathan laughed harder than he had at his earlier jest. "What Fortune you have whelped, Edward—or perhaps it's Fortune has whelped you!" Jonathan laughed even harder.

Edward shook his head, smiling at Jonathan, wondering when his friend would split his belly.

"Actually," Edward eventually said, somewhat sheepishly, "I had thought she might be a Jacobite spy."

"A spy?" Jonathan, laughed. "I've heard it said she was a

spy, indeed, for King Charles and then King James. But I hear rumors of late that she now spies for King William. This matters naught to us. Why should we give a damn who the old widowed whore spied or spies for—her money has brought us a ship!"

Edward laughed quietly and ruefully, more to himself than to the world around him.

No matter the end—and here I am—the voyage is never as you expect. Nor must I forget that all ends but one are beginnings, and even the ultimate end is for others a beginning.

It still had not sunk in, his having finally succeeded in the first part of this voyage, that of the beginning, by whatever course of Fortune and her incarnations on land and sea. But for a passage to Ireland with a drunken fool of an English officer, followed by a foolish duel, a discovery of treasonous letters by accident, an plot carried by a variety of rebels, intriguers, and assassinators, all aided by the fortunes of war at sea and abetted by an Irishman bent on revenge, but especially by all the women in whose hand Fortune had played—but for all this complex web of circumstance and destiny, he would surely not now have his ship and her command.

But I have her now, I have a ship again, he thought, *I have a commission and a ship; I have money to outfit her; she's fast, and I will away to sea again!*

But it still did not yet seem real to him.

"*Virginia* Galley, a suitable enough name, don't you think, Edward? After all, it's in America you'll be seeking."

"No, a new name. She must have a new name."

"Isn't that unlucky?" Jonathan asked.

"Not at all. As buccaneers, we always gave a new name to our prizes, or even to a ship that passed from captain to another; and anyway the *Virginia's* been unlucky under her name and as *Sirène* in the past. She was never meant to be a merchantman or even a letter-of-mart ship, but a true seeker, a cruiser, a privateer—a rover, by God. Thus she must have a new name."

"What, then?"

"As you suggested, Jonathan."

"As I suggested?"

"Indeed. *Fortune's Whelp*, we'll christen her *Fortune's Whelp*."

"To *Fortune's Whelp*, then!" Jonathan shouted, then realized he had but coffee in his hand. "Damnation, this Mohammedan gruel won't serve! One can't even get a dish of laced coffee here! To the *Cup of Gold* tavern, now, before we're accursed for naming a ship in the absence of good spirits, not to mention being accused as Jacobites for staying late at a coffeehouse. You know how she is, Fortune—first among wenches! And no wench without wine, nor wine without wench, I always say!"

First among wenches? Edward thought. *No, indeed. First among women, she is, Fortune, and I her whelp. And across the sea we'll sail, she and I, across the sea we'll sail.*

Edward and Jonathan walked to the tavern, where, with wine and speech soon a bit slurred, Edward grudgingly regaled the company with tales of combats and riches upon sea and shore. Although inwardly he did briefly admit to enjoying some of the attention, his mind was truly only on the adventure ahead, provided, of course, that kings and princes saw fit to continue making war. He thought he had little to worry about in this regard, at least for another few years. As ever, he dared not guess what role Fortune would take, and he was content for now not to know.

He slept well that night, although he did wake once with a start, caused by a moment of absolute lucidity in a dream: of

Molly O'Meary first kissing him, then trying to stab him in the back, all while Jane Hardy looked on with an inscrutable smile; Michael O'Neal sharpened his cutlass; and Lydia Upcott ranged half nude in the shadows, one hand stretched out to him, the other hidden, Deigle and the ghost of Lynch hovering over her. The image seemed incontrovertible, an absolute truth. But before long, as is often the case with passing from dream to reality, he was unsure of what he had dreamed.

He slept and dreamed again, this time finding himself once more on the shores and seas of America, sword in hand, and a dark ship on the horizon.

The End

Historical Notes

The circumstances of Ireland in 1696 are accurately described and just as complex: political and social change are never simple in the details. The attempted assassination of William III did occur as depicted, except for the fictional addition of Edward MacNaughton, Michael O'Neal, and the Irish hints of assassination that led both on their respective paths. Similarly, the *guerre du course* or privateering war at sea is correctly depicted. Throughout *Fortune's Whelp*, original documents have been the principal resource in creating the historical setting.

There are numerous primary and secondary works available that describe the period. The best to begin with is Lord Macaulay's classic, *The History of England from the Accession of James the Second*. For a satirical yet largely accurate view of London circa 1700, see Edward (Ned) Ward's *The London Spy*, a period work which inspired several descriptions in the story. Readers interested in period cant or slang should read Richard Head's *The Canting Academy, Or, the Devil's Cabinet Opened* (1673), or one of the similar later editions—*A New Dictionary of the Terms Ancient and Modern of the Canting Crew* ("B. E.," 1690) or *A New Canting Dictionary* (Anon., 1725). A surprising number of these words remain in use today.

Throughout the novel, all city streets and country highways are correctly depicted from period maps, and many still exist today, including Hanging Sword Alley. Most of the taverns and coffeehouses mentioned were real, but I did name two as homages to piracy-themed literary works. There are two similar but less obvious piratical homages to be discovered in dialogue, and a handful of subtle others here and there.

Ballydereen—the estate of Sir William Waller—did not exist, but could have outside of Kinsale where similarly-named places were found. The baths in Bath are described per period documents and illustrations.

Several of the fictional characters were inspired by real persons of the era. Jane Hardy's existence as described is much due to the journal of seventeenth century seaman Edward Coxere. As a boy at sea he really did once stuff a bell with oakum so that the woman ringing it—"a Dutch woman... called [phonetically spelled, of course] Yuffrow Doctoers... counted to be a whore to the merchants in Spain"—would not keep him awake at night. Obviously the *Peregrinator's* boy, Jack, was inspired by young Coxere. Giles Cronow was inspired in part by mariner Edward Barlow, whose journal of his voyages, unpublished until 1934, is one of the most fascinating of this era, and even briefly notes the attempted assassination of William III. Almost certainly Cronow has a bit of Captain Nathanial Uring, another seafaring journalist, in him as well, not to mention of a number of old bosuns I have known.

Lydia Upcott's physical appearance is derived in part from that of historical actress Elizabeth Barry, and to some degree by Maria Louisa, French by birth but Queen of Spain by marriage.

A number of real persons are mentioned or have brief roles. Lord Mohun was a rake as described, and worse, and eventually met a deserving end. King William III's anger at Lord Mohun's acquittal for murder was well known. The Earl of Portland served in a capacity as described, and poet Matthew Prior served as both as a secretary to the king and as part of the king's intelligence network around this time, and might have interrogated Edward MacNaughton had he existed. Henry

Every, or Avery, alias Bridgeman, viciously attacked and plundered one of the Moguls' ship in the Red Sea. He and some of his crew escaped to Ireland, including Henry Adams's wife, as described with a bit of literary license in the person of Michael O'Neal.

Of those characters mentioned only in passing, Turlough O'Carolan was a famous Irish harpist, and the lawyer Cormac was the father of Anne Bonny, the pirate. The lords Thomas and Peregrine Osborne were real, as was Captain Seager. William Kidd was commissioned to hunt pirates in the Red Sea but failed miserably. He was arrested for piracy but was hanged for manslaughter. Thomas Wharton, later Marquess of Wharton, was a charming nobleman and rake of Puritan origin who invested in Kidd's voyage. He was also reportedly a swordsman of repute, and wrote the anti-Irish lyrics to "Lillibullero."

The several conspiring assassins named in the story—Barclay, Lowick, Chambers, Rookwood, Porter, Charnock, Parkyns, Cranburne, and Berwick—are historical figures. Berwick recruited English nobility and gentry to the Jacobite cause, in particular for the purpose of stockpiling arms and raising men to fight, but was not a member of the assassins. Most were tried, convicted, hanged, and quartered, along with most of their many co-conspirators. The new law permitting legal counsel during trial for treason, not to mention a copy of the indictment, may have made the trials more fair but was not enough to save the accused. Barclay escaped to France.

Will Hollyday and Richard Pollynton were highwaymen hanged on December 9, 1696. Bartholomew Sharp was a famous buccaneer whose escapades included those described; we will likely see him again. Laurens de Graff was similarly a famous sea rover we are also likely to see again. William Penn was the naval commander of the expedition that conquered Jamaica in 1655, not to mention the father of William Penn of Pennsylvania, and Christopher Myngs was a naval sea rover who led early buccaneers in attacks on Spanish shipping and towns. Henry Morgan needs no biography. Joseph Faroe, to whom Every's sloop was sold, and the wife of Henry Adams are also authentic.

Anne Bracegirdle was a well-known actress. One of her suitors, the jealous rake Richard Hill, ably assisted by his friend Charles Mohun, once tried to kidnap her. In 1693 Hill killed another of her suitors, the actor William Mountfort. Depending on eyewitness accounts, Mohun either looked on during the assault or assisted by putting a hand on the actor's shoulder so that Hill could run him through. Without doubt Mohun helped instigate the fatal, and according to some witnesses, premeditated assault: both he and Hill had been drinking and wandering the streets with swords drawn. Mohun was tried for murder before the House of Lords but he was acquitted; the verdict outraged King William. Some historians, however, consider the verdict to have been technically, if not morally, correct, and Hill's death to be the result of a duel or affray rather than outright murder.

Aphra Behn was a poet and novelist whose works seem fresh even today. Her service as a spy originally suggested this possible role to the characters of Jane Hardy, Lydia Upcott, and Molly O'Meary.

Timothée Kercue is based on a French officer of the same name described by Father Jean-Baptiste Labat, a chronicler of the late seventeenth and early eighteenth century Caribbean, among other locales. Lieutenant de Baatz of the Gascon d'Artagnans was obviously inspired by his very real kinsman Charles de Baatz, sieur d'Artagnan, of the king's musketeers and made famous by Alexandre Dumas. He was killed in action at Maastricht in 1673.

Of ships, the *Virginia* Galley, formerly the *Sirène* and re-christened *Fortune's Whelp*, is based on late seventeenth century *frégates legères* typical of those illustrated by seventeenth century artist Nicolas Poilly, and recently described in detail as *l'Aurore* of 1697 by Jean Claude Lemineur and Patrick Villiers. *La Tulipe Noir* is an homage to Alexandre Dumas's novel of the same name, and is based loosely on *Prins Friso*, a Dutch man-of-war captured by famous French commerce raider Claude de Forbin in 1694. Period illustrations by the Willem van de Velde father and son of similar Dutch ships dating two decades earlier may be viewed online at the Royal Museums Greenwich.

The *Peregrinator* and *Mary and Martha* are typical of the many small English merchant-galleys of the era. These ships were known as galleys only because they carried a few oars or sweeps for use in calms or light airs, primarily for maneuvering. Otherwise, except for their small sweep ports, they looked like any other merchant ship. Most merchantmen lacked crews large enough to row these ships for long at any appreciable speed.

The English men-of-war—the HMS *Pearl*, HMS *Dolphin*, and HMS *Shoreham*—plus the *Dolphin*'s convoy, the *Greenfish* store-ship, noted at or near Kinsale, were present there around the time depicted. The English hired ship *Betty* and the East Indiamen *Devonshire*, *Resolution*, and *Sussex* were actually captured at the time, as noted.

The *King Fisher* is typical of the handful of English naval ketches of the 1690s, and is based on the real *King Fisher* captured in 1690 by an eighteen-gun French privateer. The *King Fisher*, commanded valiantly by Robert Audley, repelled several bloody boarding attempts in spite of being severely out-gunned and out-manned. Captain Audley surrendered only after he had no one left to defend the ketch but himself, badly wounded, and five of his crew. An account of this action was published in April, 1690. There are several drawings in the Royal Museums Greenwich online that depict similar ketches.

The *King Fisher's* brief nemesis, *La Fortune*, was inspired by and updated from a small Danish frigate with Dutch lines, circa 1665, illustrated in Howard I. Chapelle's *The Search for Speed Under Sail 1700-1855.* Illustrations of similar Dutch ships may be found in the Royal Museums Greenwich online. The *Carolina Merchant* is typical of many small merchantmen of the period, for example the *Cadiz Merchant,* aboard which Edward Barlow once sailed and which was later made into a fireship. Both Barlow and the Royal Museums Greenwich online have illustrations of the *Cadiz Merchant.*

The chases and sea fights are based on a close study of the tactics of the period, especially with extensive reference to firsthand accounts, from which I have so far produced four non-fiction works. For more detail on the tactics of sea rovers of this era, I suggest starting with *The Sea Rover's Practice* by the author. Regarding swordplay, see the accompanying section, "Swordplay Notes."

Swordplay Notes

The descriptions of swordplay are based on extensive research into fencing of the day, especially via works written by men with practical experience with "sharps," and via detailed period descriptions of duels and affrays. All of this I have filtered through my own various experience, including nearly forty years fencing and twenty teaching it, both modern and historical. Edward MacNaughton's style of swordplay is already described in the story itself, but readers seeking further insight may start with the works of Scottish swordsmen Donald McBane and Sir William Hope.

Edward MacNaughton's book may also be consulted if a copy can be found, but I suspect that only one original exists anymore, and it is in a private collection and to date has not been reprinted or copied. Additionally, I have written a brief but comprehensive chapter on the swordplay of this period in a nonfiction work, *The Buccaneer's Realm*, and will also discuss pirate swordplay in a forthcoming work on pirate myths. The mounted duel in Ireland is based in part on Jonah Barrington's description of his own in 1759.

Describing swordplay in fiction is not an easy task, not if it is to be portrayed accurately yet without losing the narrative pace of the action. This is a subject I have discussed not only with the publisher of this novel and a variety of others interested in historical swordplay, both fencers and non-fencers, but also at length with Rafael Sabatini biographer Ruth

Heredia, who has consulted me on swordplay in Sabatini's novels. A balance must be struck between educating the non-fencer and creating a swiftly moving image. Too much exposition and the fight becomes a mere "after action" report, thus I have written this small appendix to augment what cannot reasonably be described in the narrative itself. It will aid the reader interested in learning more about the swordplay Edward knew.

Late seventeenth century European swordplay was composed of several schools covering several weapons. Broadly speaking, there were three forms of thrusting sword: the Spanish rapier, the Italian rapier, and the French smallsword. Of the Spanish we will learn more in sequels to come. Of the smallsword, a shorter, lighter thrusting sword which was descended from the rapier, and which at times was also still referred to as a rapier (meaning a thrusting sword), there were for all practical purposes two schools: "school play" or what today we would call sport fencing, although it was in theory also preparation for combat with sharps; and a practical form of swordplay intended for fighting with real weapons.

The former limited the target to the torso, had other artificialities introduced for appearance, safety, and matters of fencing theory, and fencers often engaged in actions unsuitable, or at least unwise, in a real duel or affray. The latter, practical swordplay, focused on actual combat, including thrusts to the entire body, although training for some actions was limited, given the lack of the fencing mask which had yet to be introduced. The unarmed hand was used to parry or oppose, and sometimes to hold a hat or scabbard to assist in parrying, and *in extremis* was even used to grab the blade itself. Most fencers practiced both forms of swordplay to some degree. Donald McBane, noted above, was primarily a practitioner of the latter; Sir William Hope of both. Edward also practiced both, but given his need for practical swordplay, emphasized the latter. Although the smallsword was of French origin, its many masters and practitioners added their own variations.

The swords described in the story are based on real weapons I have examined in person, in museum displays, in books, or online. Occasionally I have slightly modified a sword from its original, but still in keeping with the need for historical accuracy. Smallsword blades came in several various forms, which we will leave to Sir William Hope, via his *New, Short, and Easy Method of Fencing*, to describe: "*Rapier, Koningsberg* [colichemarde], and Narrow *Three-Cornered Blade*, which is the most proper Walking-Sword of all the Three, being by far the lightest," plus, in some smallswords, especially military, the "*Broad Three-Cornered* Blade." Rapier-style blades might be oval, four-sided, six-sided, or a combination thereof, with sharpened edges. Many smallsword blades at this time were thirty-three to thirty-four inches long. Some were shorter, and a few were as long as thirty-six or thirty-seven inches.

Karl Johann Königsmark, the younger of the two Counts Königsmark, is popularly credited with the invention of the colichemarde blade—colichemarde is in fact a corruption of his name—but he probably did no more than popularize it, quite possibly after being introduced to it in Spain. The younger Königsmark was a rake, and was tried for murder in London but acquitted. The older was assassinated for his romantic and probably sexual relationship with Sophia Dorothea, consort of the Hanoverian Prince George, later King George I of England &c.

Edward's grip on his Spanish-hilted smallsword or *espadin*, with a finger inserted through one of the rings of the hilt, was a practice not approved of in the French school, but nonetheless much in use, at least while the rings (arms of the hilt, *pas– d'âne*) remained large enough. This grip was usual in the Spanish and Italian schools. Edward otherwise grips his French-style smallswords in the conventional manner, that is, without a finger through one of the rings of the hilt.

There existed several schools of the various cutting swords, typically with national characteristics. Most associated with Edward MacNaughton are the Scottish broadsword (the true Scottish weapon), the English backsword (likewise the true English weapon), and the Hungarian Hussar saber (also a national weapon). There are no period texts, at least not in English or French, describing the use of the cutlass at this time, other than occasionally in general terms. It was likely wielded in similar fashion to the broadsword and backsword, with an emphasis on the very close actions natural to ship-boarding fights. It was often used in conjunction with a pistol in the other hand, and grappling was surely common. Many seamen doubtless wielded it, as many soldiers did their own swords, in whatever ad hoc fashion they had informally acquired.

A glossary is provided below for reference and further study. Note that the terminology could vary significantly among fencing masters of MacNaughton's day. Also be advised that this glossary is incomplete, and for the most part covers only the swordplay in the story. A much more in-depth study, preferably hands-on, must be made in order to gain an understanding of swordplay, past or present.

Angulation: not a period term. In modern fencing language, a thrust delivered at an angle in order to slip around a parry or the shell of the sword hilt. The most common angulations in MacNaughton's day were the *carte over the arm* in which the hand was turned from tierce to carte in order to angulate around the adversary's tierce parry, with the unarmed hand used to oppose the adversary's blade; a corresponding thrust in carte made against a carte parry by turning the hand from carte to tierce; and a thrust to the hand or arm from a low guard.

See *carte, tierce,* and *low guard.*

Attack: an offensive action made with a thrust or a thrust with a lunge. See *thrust.*

Battery: a *beat* or sharp striking action against the foible of the adversary's blade, intended to open the target, loosen the adversary's grip on his sword, delay his counter-action, or all three. Sir William Hope defines battery in a more limited way, as a beat with one's *foible* upon the adversary's foible. His preferred definition of *beat* is one made with *forte* upon foible, and indeed this is the most effective beat. In general, a synonym for *beat.*

Beat: usually but not always a synonym for *battery.* See *battery.*

Bind: in MacNaughton's day, a broad term covering any strong controlling pressure on the adversary's sword with one's own, without changing the line. The term has a similar meaning in the modern Italian and Hungarian schools.

Carte: guard or parry covering the high inside line, also the thrust to the adversary's high inside line. The hand is typically half-supinated. An Anglicization of the French *quart.* Carte is known today as *quarte, fourth,* or *four.*

Commanding: seizing and controlling the adversary's sword with the unarmed hand, usually by grabbing the shell of the hilt or the immediately adjacent blade, or both, often in concert with a binding action on the adversary's blade. The adversary is not disarmed; his sword is simply secured while he is threatened with his opponent's point. Also known as *joining the sword* or *seizing the sword.*

Contre-Caveating Parry: Hope's term for a circular parry in any line; McBane referred to it as the *round parade.* It was considered a good parry to use when the line of the adversary's attack could not be predicted, and also at night when the adversary's blade was hard to see. A circular parry is slower than a direct (linear, diagonal, and semi-circular) parry, thus more dangerous to the user at closer distances. Many masters did not approve of it, although both McBane and Hope strongly advocated its use. Circular parries are common today.

Contre-Temps: a double hit, that is, a hit on both adversaries when one or both has thrust inopportunely, for example, one thrusting as the other attacks. See *Timing* and *Exchanged Thrust.*

Covered: to engage or thrust in such a manner as to prevent the adversary's thrust in the same line from hitting, in order to help prevent a *contre-temps.* In other words, to properly cover one's own target in the line of engagement or thrust. Often a covered thrust is made while "bearing on the adversary's sword." Can be a synonym for opposition. In any case, the fencer making a covered thrust is less likely to be hit. See opposition.

Cutting Over the Point: in the high lines, lifting one's point over the adversary's point, rather than disengaging beneath it. Known today as a *cut-over* or *coupé.*

Disarming: an action usually made by a combination of

commanding with the unarmed hand and levering with the sword in the other, although there are disarming techniques attempted with the sword alone. Not to be confused with *commanding*.

Disengage: to change lines by dropping one's point beneath the adversary's blade when swords are engaged with points up, and by slipping over when swords are engaged with points down. Changing sides, in other words. Often combined with a thrust into the new line. Also a noun. Sometimes referred to as *caveating*.

Engage: to press lightly to moderately against the adversary's blade with one's own, thus *engagement*.

En Garde: a position, physical and mental, in which the fencer is able to immediately attack or defend. Also *on guard*.

Exchanged Thrusts: a hit on both adversaries, the second hit immediately following the first when one adversary fails to protect himself adequately after hitting his adversary. Not to be confused with *contre-temps*.

Falloon: a guard position with the hand held at the height of the head, usually to the outside, the point low and inside. Particularly useful against multiple adversaries. The *hanging guard*. From Walloon.

Feint: a false thrust intended to draw an expected parry, which the attacker then avoids (*deceives*) and thrusts into an open line. Also known in MacNaughton's day as *falsifying*.

Flanconnade: strictly speaking, a thrust to the flank. In practice, it was made with a binding action on the adversary's blade from carte, with the point slipped over the adversary's blade to his outside line, the point lowered.

Foible: the weak part of the blade near the point, variously defined. In MacNaughton's day, usually the part of the blade from the middle to the point. This part of the blade lacks significant leverage and is thinner than the *forte.*

Forte: the strong part of the blade nearest the hilt, variously defined. In MacNaughton's day, the part of the blade from the hilt to the middle. This part of the blade has the greatest leverage and is thicker than the *foible.*

Guard: in general, the position of the hand and sword in the *en garde* position, although it can be taken to mean the all of the characteristics of hand, sword, and body in the *en garde* position. Typically *carte* or *tierce*, occasionally a *hanging guard* or a middle guard between *carte* and *tierce.* There were other guard positions, but most were seldom used and many were dangerous to the user.

Giving the Point: extending the sword arm without lunging, or recovering from a lunge with the point extended. Known today as *point in line.*

Half Circle: in MacNaughton's day, a term used by some masters for a parry covering the low inside line, corresponding to the modern *septime, seventh, seven.* This was not a recommended guard position at the time, nor is it now. See *low quarte.*

Hanging Guard: a guard position with the hand held at the height of the head, usually to the outside, the point low and inside. Particularly useful against multiple adversaries. Sometimes called the *falloon guard* (from Walloon).

Inquartata: a quarter turn to the right (if the fencer is right-handed) while pivoting on the front foot, in order to evade the adversary's attack and make a counter thrust. Strictly speaking, a tempo action with an evasion. Also known in MacNaughton's day as *quarting* and *dequarting*. *Quart* and *dequart* may be used as both noun and verb.

Line: classically-speaking, the target is composed of four areas or *lines*: high outside, high inside, low outside, and low inside, all determined by the location of the adversary's sword. For example, a thrust to the low outside line may still be a thrust to the upper target if the adversary holds his sword high.

Low Guard: in the French school, a non-traditional guard made by lowering one's point near the ground. Often the guard was used to induce the adversary to attack, which was then countered by simultaneously parrying with the unarmed hand and thrusting. This guard was also resorted to by fencers with tired arms, and was probably used more often than recommended. This was usually a poor guard to use against a skilled adversary. It was, however, one of the common guards in the Spanish rapier schools. McBane refers to it as the *Portuguese guard.*

Low Quarte: a thrust to the low inside line. Also known as *quart under the wrist* and as a *cut* [derived from the word quarte] *under the wrist*. Often used in conjunction with a *volt* against a quarte thrust. The corresponding parry is the *half circle*. Known today as a thrust in *septime, seventh,* or *seven.*

Lunge: an attack made by simultaneously or near-simultaneously extending the arm, stepping forward with the front leg, and pushing with the rear foot, which remains in place. Sometimes the actions of the legs only is referred to as a lunge. In MacNaughton's day, the lunge was usually initiated with the hand, followed immediately by the legs, or was executed simultaneously with arm and legs. The arm was *not* fully extended prior to the action of the legs, but finished its extension during the lunge, as in the modern fencing schools, but unlike the classical nineteenth and early twentieth century schools which usually demanded a fully extended arm prior to the action of the legs.

Measure: the distance between two fencing adversaries.

Opposition: usually a thrust made while "bearing on the adversary's sword," but occasionally a thrust in the line of the adversary's blade, or where it is anticipated it will be. Can be a synonym of *covered*. In any case, the fencer making a thrust in opposition is less likely to be hit. See *covered.*

Opposition of the Hand: to use the unarmed hand to prevent a renewed attack after parrying the adversary's initial thrust, or to prevent a *contre-temps* or *exchanged thrust* during one's attack. The hand presses against the adversary's blade, keeping it from one's body. In other words, the hand provides additional security.

Parry: a defensive action that, in the case of a thrusting sword, deflects the adversary's thrust, and in the case of a cutting sword, blocks the adversary's cut. Parries were usually made with the blade, but in the case of thrusting swords were also often made with the unarmed hand. Also a verb. Also *parade*, from the French.

Parade of the Hand: a parry with the unarmed hand. Typically there were three: high inside, low inside, and high outside.

Passata Soto: a ducking action, often made with the left leg thrust backward and the unarmed hand placed on the ground for support, made in tempo as the adversary attacks. This action drops one's head and torso below the adversary's attacking blade. Unless perfectly timed, this can be a dangerous action to the fencer who attempts it. Also known as a *night thrust* by some masters. In some texts, an attack with a long low lunge beneath the adversary's blade, with the hand placed on the ground for support, is also considered a *passata soto.*

Pink: period term for wounding an adversary with one's sword.

Push: period term for an attack, usually made with a lunge. From French *pousser*, to push.

Riposte: an attack (thrust) made immediately after parrying the adversary's attack.

Seconde: the parry covering the low outside line (although it may cover the low inside as well), also the thrust to the adversary's outside line beneath his blade. The hand is mostly pronated. Seconde was generally not a recommended guard in the French school, but see *low guard.* Known today as *seconde, second,* or *two.*

Sixte: a guard and thrust associated with the high outside line, not known by this name in MacNaughton's day. See *tierce.*

Tempo: in the simplest terms, the most favorable time to thrust. Also known as *time.* See *timing.*

Thrust: an attack, counter-attack, or riposte made by extending the arm to hit with the point. Also, any arm action, associated with any footwork, made with the intention of hitting with the point. Also a verb.

Tierce: the guard or parry covering the high outside line, also the thrust to the adversary's high outside line. The hand is mostly pronated. Known today as *tierce, third,* or *three.* Tierce is a strong position, both in strength of thrust and parry, is less likely to be disarmed by a strong downward beat, and corresponds to the natural outside guard of a cutting sword as well, but it does leave more "light" (opening) to the arm and torso than if the hand is semi-supinated. In general, the half-supinated position, known later as *sixte* (*sixth, six*), is preferred today. Known sometimes as *carte in tierce* in MacNaughton's day, sixte did have a few advocates, more often as a thrust than as a guard.

Timing: at its most basic, to thrust at an opportune moment when the adversary is for a moment (a fencing *tempo*) open and unable to defend. Typically the action most commonly known as *timing* is made upon the adversary's step forward as he moves his blade, especially in seeking his adversary's. In practice, timing is often dangerous because many fencers do not bother to secure the adversary's blade during the action or otherwise cover themselves, and rely only on an advantage in time. This often results in a *contre-temps*— that is, a double hit. To be safe, in MacNaughton's era the unarmed hand was usually used to parry or oppose when timing. Also known as *thrusting upon time.*

Traversing: a movement to the right or left away from the fencing line. Circling, more or less. One of its primary purposes was to gain better ground. Otherwise, it was more commonly associated with cutting swords than with thrusting.

Under Counter: a binding thrust in seconde. Known today in the French school as a bind (*liement*) from quarte to seconde.

Volt: a lunge or leap to the left to the outside line, assuming both fencers are right-handed. Typically this was a tempo action, often made with a thrust in *seconde* or with a low quart/*quart under the wrist*. Also *avolt*. Also used as a verb: *volting, avolting.*

Glossary

Backsword: a cutting sword with only the fore edge, and occasionally a few inches of the back edge, sharpened.

Beaver: a hat, usually an expensive one made from beaver.

Bite the Bill from the Cull: to "whip the sword from the gentleman's side." (Cant)

Brandy Barrel: a Dutch ship. (Slang)

Bravo: a killer for hire.

Bretteur: a bully or brawler with a sword. Someone who picks sword fights. See *spadassin.*

Bully Rock: a bravo, a Hector.

Butter Box: a Dutch ship. (Slang)

Caroche: a luxurious or well-appointed horse-drawn carriage.

Cartouche Box: period term for a cartridge box in which musket and pistol cartridges were carried.

Chase: a ship being chased, also the act of chasing.

Chase Guns: guns place fore and aft, to be used in a chase. Typically, there were a pair of chase ports each bow and stern, although some large ships carried more, usually astern. Guns were typically not mounted permanently here, but were moved into place from adjacent broadside ports as necessary.

Clew: the lower corner of a square sail (a square sail has two clews), and the aft corner of a fore-and-aft sail.

Clip and Kiss: to hug and kiss; to have sex. (Cant)

Colichemarde: a smallsword whose blade is broad at the forte for up to a third of the blade's length, and narrow for the rest of the length.

Commission, Privateering Commission: legal document authorizing a captain and vessel as a privateer.

Corsair: a privateer. The usual French term was *corsaire.* In English, *corsair* usually referred to the Barbary corsairs.

Cruiser: a naval man-of-war or privateer cruising for enemy shipping. The definition at times was extended to a pirate ship. Also *seeker.*

Cul, Cull, Cully: a man, a fellow, a rogue; someone easily cheated or stolen from. (Cant)

Cup-Shot: drunk. (Slang)

Dutch Billy: King William III. (Slang.)

Dutch Courage: liquor drunk to make men braver in action.

Flute: a flat-bottomed, beamy, pink-sterned merchant ship, originally Dutch but in use by all European nations.

Foul: a nautical term meaning entangled, unfavorable, dirty, contrary. In regard to a vessel's hull, it refers to grass, seaweed, barnacles and other shells growing on the hull over the course of a long voyage, causing the vessel to sail more slowly that it would with a "clean" hull. For example, the term "clean heels" refers to a hull devoid of marine growth, which makes for better speed.

Frigate: in the seventeenth and early eighteenth centuries, a ship with a frigate hull, in men-of-war up to the fourth rate. A ship built for speed.

Galley, Galley-Frigate, Merchant-Galley: a frigate-hulled man-of-war or merchantman with sweep ports cut in the side for the use of sweeps for maneuvering in light airs or calms. A naval galley-frigate, with its large crew and number of oars, might be able to make three knots for a short time. Not to be confused with the Mediterranean galley, a war vessel propelled primarily by oars.

Gans, Ganns: the lips. (Cant)

Gun: in maritime language, a cannon. Also *great gun.*

Hogen Mogen. a Dutchman or Dutch ship. (Slang.)

In His Cups: drunk. (Slang.)

Jacobite: a supporter of the exiled James II. More broadly, a supporter of the Stuart claim to the British throne.

Ketch: a small two-masted vessel, bluff-bowed and sharp-sterned. The mainmast was typically rigged with a long buss course or mainsail, and a topsail; the small mizzen with a lateen and small topsail; and the bowsprit with a small spritsail. A staysail and jib were set between the mainmast and bowsprit. Ancestrally, the foremast had been removed to make room for fishing nets.

Larboard: period nautical term for *port* (*left*), except in the case of conning the helm, in which case the term *port* was used.

Letter of Mart, a.k.a. *Letter of Marque:* a privateering commission for merchantmen. A legal document authorizing a merchant vessel, in the course of its trading, to conduct itself as a privateer. Previous to the late seventeenth century, the term was synonymous with a privateering commission.

Lillibullero: a musical march dating to the English Civil War. Thomas Wharton wrote lyrics in 1686, satirizing the Irish. The song was popular among those with anti-Irish sentiment during the period in which *Fortune's Whelp* is set.

Lullaby Cheat: a child. (Cant)

Munns or *Muns:* the face. (Cant)

Partridge: small shot fired from great guns or swivels. Partridge was usually composed of musket balls contained in tin or wood cases, or in canvas bags.

Picaroon: a privateer. From Spanish *picarón*: a rogue.

Pink: an English term for a small ship with a 'pinked' stern like a flute's. A small flute.

Pirate: a ship or person committing or attempting armed robbery on the sea, or on the shore from the sea, for personal gain. A hanging offense.

Prats, Pratts: the buttocks. (Cant)

Privateer: a ship commissioned—licensed, that is—to prey on enemy shipping, in return for which a percentage of the plunder was paid to the government. In the eyes of some, a licensed pirate.

Rapparee: an Irish irregular soldier, also an Irish highwayman. Occasionally both.

Reformado: a volunteer officer.

Rencontre: a duel, an engagement, an affray, a fight. In particular, a single combat between two individuals or two ships.

Round Shot: a cannonball.

Ruffler: a notorious rogue. (Cant)

Rum Mort: a pretty woman or pretty wench. (Cant)

Running Ship, Runner: a merchant ship built for speed, not cargo capacity.

Seeker: a naval man-of-war or privateer cruising for enemy shipping. The definition at times was extended to a pirate ship. Also *cruiser*.

Snilch: to eye or watch. (Cant)

Spadassin: an assassin armed with a sword. A bully duelist. See *bretteur*.

Swivel: a small gun (cannon) mounted on the rails. Usually muzzle-loaded. Breech-loading swivels were commonly known as *patereroes, pedreros, chambers,* &c.

Starboard: the nautical term for *right* (as opposed to *left*). Used both for designating the right side of a vessel, and also for navigation and direction.

Tack: to sail a zig-zag pattern against the wind. Also, the larboard or starboard tack the vessel is on when *tacking*.

Talley-Man: a money lender. (Slang)

Thoroughbraces: the springs or shocks of a horse-drawn carriage or stage coach.

Tilter: a sword.

Tip the Wink: to give the sign or signal. (Cant)

Tory: a Royalist supporter of James II. More generally, one who supports the primacy of the royal head of state over Parliament.

Trainband: militia.

Whig: an Exclusionist; one who supported excluding James II from the English throne. A member of the political party supporting King William. More generally, one who supports the primacy of Parliament over the royal head of state.

Witcher Tilter: a silver-hilted sword. (Cant)

Williamite: a supporter of King William III.

About The Author

Benerson Little

Born in Key West, Florida, Benerson Little grew up variously on all three US coasts. As long as he can remember he has wanted to follow the sea. Following his graduation from Tulane University, he entered the US Navy and served as an officer for eight years, most of them as a Navy SEAL. After leaving the Navy, he worked at first as a Naval Special Warfare analyst, and later for a private intelligence collection and analysis firm.

Benerson now works as a writer and consultant in several areas, with an emphasis on maritime and naval issues. He is considered a leading expert on piracy past and present, and is a recognized expert on pirate tactics and anti-piracy operations throughout history. His four nonfiction works on piracy include *Pirate Hunting: The Fight Against Pirates, Privateers, and Sea Raiders from Antiquity to the Present* and *The Sea Rover's Practice: Pirate Tactics and Techniques,*

1630–1730.

He has been featured in two full length television documentaries and several shorter film clips on piracy, has advised on others, and is the historical consultant for the STARZ *Black Sails* series. He often advises filmmakers, novelists, historians, biographers, genealogists, treasure hunters, journalists, and others.

In his spare time, Benerson devotes himself to his wife and daughters, teaches modern fencing at the Huntsville Fencing Club, researches historical fencing, writes contemporary and historical novels, and develops proposals for potential television documentaries and series.

If You Enjoyed This Book

Please write a review.

This is important to the author and helps to get the word out to others

Visit

PENMORE PRESS

www.penmorepress.com

All Penmore Press books are available directly through our website, amazon.com, Barnes and Noble and Nook, Sony Reader, Apple iTunes, Kobo books and via leading bookshops across the United States, Canada, the UK, Australia and Europe.

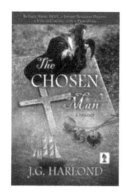

The Chosen Man

by

J. G. Harlond

From the bulb of a rare flower bloom ambition and scandal

Rome, 1635: As Flanders braces for another long year of war, a Spanish count presents the Vatican with a means of disrupting the Dutch rebels' booming economy. His plan is brilliant. They just need the right man to implement it.

They choose Ludovico da Portovenere, a charismatic spice and silk merchant. Intrigued by the Vatican's proposal—and hungry for profit—Ludo sets off for Amsterdam to sow greed and venture capitalism for a disastrous harvest, hampered by a timid English priest sent from Rome, accompanied by a quick-witted young admirer he will use as a spy, and bothered by the memory of the beautiful young lady he refused to take with him.

Set in a world of international politics and domestic intrigue, *The Chosen Man* spins an engrossing tale about the Dutch financial scandal known as tulip mania—and how decisions made in high places can have terrible repercussions on innocent lives.

PENMORE PRESS
www.penmorepress.com

Force 12 in
German Bight
by
James Boschert

Considering that oil and gas have been flowing from under the North Sea for the best part of half a century, it is perhaps surprising that more writers have not taken the uncompromising conditions that are experienced in this area – which extends from the north of Scotland to the coasts of Norway and Germany – for the setting of a novel. James Boschert's latest redresses the balance.

The book takes its title from the name of an area regularly referred to in the legendary BBC Shipping Forecast, one which experiences some of the worst weather conditions around the British Isles. It is a fast-paced story which smacks of authenticity in every line. A world of hard men, hard liquor, hard drugs and cold-blooded murder. The reality of the setting and the characters, ex-military men from both sides of the Atlantic, crooked wheeler-dealers, and Danish detectives, male and female, are all in on the action.

This is not story telling akin to a latter day Bulldog Drummond, nor a James Bond, but simply a snortingly good yarn which will jangle the nerve ends, fill your nose with the smell of salt and diesel oil, your ears with the deafening sound of machinery aboard a monster pipe-dredging ship and, above all, make you remember never to underestimate the power of the sea.

–Roger Paine, former Commander, Royal Navy .

PENMORE PRESS
www.penmorepress.com

The Lockwoods

of Clonakilty

by

Mark Bois

Highly entertaining, well researched and original in thought. Lieutenant James Lockwood of the Inniskilling Regiment returns to his family in Clonakilty, Ireland, after being badly wounded at Waterloo. After three years on active service his return is a joyous occasion, but home is not the perfect refuge he craves.

Twenty years before, he had married Brigid O'Brian, a beautiful Irish Catholic woman of willful intelligence, an act that estranged him from his wealthy family. Their five children, especially their second daughter, Cissy, are especially and irritant to the other branches of the family, as the children balance their native Irish heritage against the expectations of the Anglo-Irish Lockwoods.

PENMORE PRESS
www.penmorepress.com

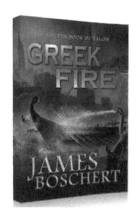

GREEK FIRE
BY
JAMES BOSCHERT

In the fourth book of Talon, James Boschert delivers fast-paced adventure, packed with violent confrontations and intrepid heroes up against hard odds.

Imprisoned for brawling in Acre, a coastal city in the Kingdom of Jerusalem, Talon and his longtime friend Max are freed by an old mentor from the Order of the Templars and offered a new mission in the fabled city of Constantinople. There Talon makes new friendships, but winning the Emperor's favor obligates him to follow Manuel to war in a willful expedition to free Byzantine lands from the Seljuk Turks. And beneath the pageantry of the great city, seditious plans are being fomented by disaffected aristocrats who have made a reckless deal to sell the one weapon the Byzantine Empire has to defend itself, *Greek fire*, to an implacable enemy bent upon the Empire's destruction.

Talon and Max find themselves sailing into perilous battles, and in the labyrinthine back streets of Constantinople Talon must outwit his own kind—assassins—in the pay of a treacherous alliance.

PENMORE PRESS
www.penmorepress.com

Penmore Press

Challenging, Intriguing, Adventurous, Historical and Imaginative

www.penmorepress.com

CPSIA information can be obtained
at www.ICGtesting.com
Printed in the USA
LVHW081440300321
682965LV00028B/207